THE
ENEMY
CLONE

I0588631

RANDY V. DANIELS

MENASCUS BOOKS

Randy V. Daniels

Cover design by Miblart exclusively for
Menascus Books, Simi Valley, California

Library of Congress, Reg. #
Cataloging-in Publishing Data, ISBN # 978-0-9855252-4-8
Printed in the United States of America

ISBN-10:
EAN-13: 9780985525248

For André, Devante, and Audriana,
Forever my inspiration!

For Deb,
The Foundation that keeps it all above ground!

Acknowledgments

Once again, I must extend thanks and gratitude to those who contributed selflessly to the arduous task of editing, proofreading, and researching.

Katherine Amoroso – for being that crucial set of eyes that every author needs.

Timothy Bednar and Family – for allowing me time with your family, and giving my research much needed insight.

Ashton D. Brown Jr. – for the partnership, the trust, the friendship. Let's keep moving it forward.

Jim Cole – for the continued encouragement and belief in my work. R.I.P., my friend. You are missed.

Deborah Daniels – for being by my side every step of the way. I love you.

Karen Hewitt – for offering another set of eagle eyes. Thank you.

Leyvan M. Jones – for three decades of friendship, and the willingness to always lend your eyes to my work.

Darlene Rideaux – for a straight and honest review. Believe me, no one shoots straighter than you.

Lacee Sherman – to my "Creative Consultant." Words cannot convey how much your input, time and support has helped me grow as an author.

Stone Media Consulting – for giving Menascus Books its first presence on the world-wide net.

Gary Tolin – I can't say enough about how you've always supported and believed in me. You're the best. Love you, G.T.

Randy V. Daniels

A person often meets his destiny on the road he took to avoid it.

-Jean de La Fontaine

Randy V. Daniels

Excerpt from The Harmony Project

The phone rang in Towers' ear. He looked around cautiously. 'For God's sake, pick up,' he thought to himself. His silent plea was answered instantly.

"It's Towers."

"I told you that *I'd* contact *you*," One scolded him.

"It couldn't be helped."

"Did you get the sample?"

"Yes. However, the situation--"

"The situation has become messy," One said. "Messy attracts attention."

"I know," Towers replied nervously. "But we have confirmation."

A slight pause. "Do we?"

"Yes. West saw it with his own eyes."

"That's good, but, unfortunate for Agent West."

Towers lowered his head in anger. He had not wanted it to come to this. He choked back his emotions and replied with a simple, "I know."

"Good," One replied. "Here's what I want you to do."

.

1

OUTSIDE OF ARLINGTON, VIRGINIA, USA
YESTERDAY

Special Agent Michael Rose finished making his rounds of the small Virginia cottage. He walked the perimeter of the front gate and stopped in the east corner. He tilted his head slightly and shook off a chill that ran up his spine; not unusual for mid-March. Still, Rose felt uneasy. He couldn't justify the apprehension that he felt until he heard the explosion coming from the back side of the house.

"Shit!" he yelled as he pulled out his weapon and took off at a full sprint towards the backyard. It took him a mere six seconds to traverse the length of the driveway and round the corner. Flames and debris shot out into the backyard from a gaping hole in the structure that wasn't there ten seconds prior. Rose took a deep breath. It wasn't like he wanted to rush into a burning building, but he had no choice. He had promised Dr. Patel that he would protect and deliver him to safety. Rose knew it was a promise he'd just broken.

Rose covered his eyes as he entered the cottage. The wave of heat that greeted him was so intense he felt as if, for one brief moment, that he might pass out. He coughed as he stepped into the long hallway. Rose had witnessed the devastation brought about by explosives on more than one occasion while serving with the Marines. Still, the sight never ceased to take his breath away.

The large, gaping hole in the wall revealed the den on the other side. Rose took notice that the majority of the debris was in the hallway. *Looks like the explosive detonated in the den. But how?* Rose wondered. *How did they find us so fast?*

Rose wondered where the other occupants of the cottage were. Special Agent Nichols was nowhere to be seen. Dr. Patel was in the den the last time Rose saw him. And the girl? *Oh, God. The girl.*

The smoke began to clear. Through the flames, Rose saw a body lying just outside where the doorway to the den used to be. He didn't have to get any closer to see that it was Nichols, or at least what was left of him. There was a hole the size of a baseball in his chest and his right arm was completely severed. If Rose had inspected Nichols more closely, he would have noticed a bullet wound in his neck, as well. Still, based on the more obvious injuries, Rose surmised that Nichols must have been standing awfully close to the explosive when it was detonated. Though he felt bad for his partner, Rose knew he had to press on. He had promised to protect Patel. *Where the hell is he?* As if in answer to his silent query, Rose heard an agonizing moan coming from down the hall. Rose raised his weapon to eye level and moved cautiously in the direction of the noise.

Rose reached the end of the hallway. When he rounded the corner, what he saw frightened him. He saw a body, but it wasn't that of Dr. Patel. The body was smaller, more petite. Closer inspection revealed that the body was female.

"Iris?" Rose questioned aloud. He wasn't even certain that Iris was her name. "Oh, God!" He moved in closer. It was then that Rose noticed something peculiar. Despite all of the debris from the explosion that littered the air, the young girl's clothing was dust free, clean, in fact. Rose heard a gasp coming from behind his position. He turned. There, lying under a pile of wood that used to be the wall to the den, was Dr. Patel.

Patel was covered up to his torso. The goatee on his chin was drenched in blood from the numerous lacerations across his face. His eyes bulged with desperation as he struggled to extend his right arm towards Rose.

Rose moved towards Patel. As he did, a look of fear crossed Patel's face. Rose felt pity for the man. He could only imagine the anxiety Patel felt as he breathed what were certain to be his last breaths. Suddenly, Rose stopped in his tracks. Considering the condition that Patel was in, Rose assumed the outstretched hand was a non-verbal cry for help. It was only after Rose looked again that he realized that Patel was pointing his index finger back towards the young girl. Rose made the connection, but it was too late. As he turned back to her, he realized that she already had the drop on him.

In her hand rested a Glock 23. Though it was a rather small handgun due to the shortened barrel length, it appeared much larger to Rose as it was being leveled at him. Without a moment's hesitation, the girl squeezed the trigger twice.

Even as the bullets impacted Rose's chest, sending a wave of pain and heat into his upper body, a split second passed where he took in the sight of the young girl. It was amazing how lovely and innocent she appeared; her beautiful, pecan-brown skin and thick, black hair. In that instant, he realized how truly young she appeared, even with a deadly weapon in her hand. Rose was thrown onto his back with a large thud. The impact from the first round had knocked the wind out of him; the second round penetrated his vest. He could feel the blood saturating his shirt and filling his chest cavity as he struggled for air. No chance.

Rose's right hand still had a firm grip on his weapon. He leveled it in the young girl's direction and squeezed off a shot. The girl dropped to the floor, allowing the bullet to sail over her head. She rolled to her left and onto her knees before springing forward towards Rose. The agent swung the pistol in the young girl's direction once again, but she had already moved within inches of him. She grabbed Rose's right wrist and began to squeeze and twist. Rose, though he was injured, believed he could out-muscle her. After all, she didn't appear to be strong at all. Rose realized within seconds that his assessment was undeniably false.

Rose felt his wrist begin to hyperextend downward as his female assailant continued to twist and apply pressure. He struggled against the pain, trying desperately not to relinquish his weapon. His struggle proved to be futile. With one final motion, the girl rotated her grip, snapping Rose's wrist. Rose howled in pain as his weapon fell from his grasp and landed on his right thigh.

The girl placed her left hand against Rose's neck and pinned him to the floor. He gasped even harder in an attempt to suck in air. Rose felt something cold, like metal, being forced underneath the lower covering of his Kevlar vest. A sudden feeling of despair enveloped as he realized a bitter truth. *She never dropped her weapon.* His realization was confirmed as the girl pumped two bullets into his gut.

Rose released a loud scream that was cut off by the unbearable, excruciating pain that ripped through his upper torso. His body stiffened momentarily in response.

Through it all, the girl never uttered a word. She stood and moved in the direction of Dr. Patel, leaving Rose to breathe his final breath. Rose gripped his chest. He felt himself descending into the abyss of unconsciousness. He fought against the impending darkness to no avail. He felt his body grow suddenly cold. In his last moment of awareness, Rose remembered reading that the sense of hearing was the last to go as death crept in. The sound of Dr. Patel screaming at the top his lungs filled the air.

"No!" Patel pleaded. A single gunshot followed. Then, silence!

DISTRICT PEDIATRIC CLINIC
WASHINGTON, D.C.

The doors on both sides of the long hallway seemed to rush by in a blur of wood and glass. Normally, while walking these halls, it seemed such a great distance from one end of the corridor to the other. Not so today.

Agent Maribel Molina passed the last door on the right before bursting through the set of double doors that led to the main waiting area. Despite her lack of makeup, and the glass eye that occupied her left eye socket, Agent Molina was a Puerto Rican beauty. Her dark hair was pulled back into a tight bun, revealing the natural luster of her light-brown skin and her one, real, chestnut-colored eye. Her smile, as she had been told many times in the past, was captivating. Throughout her lifetime, Molina had used that smile to her advantage whenever necessary. Unfortunately, when she entered the waiting room, she was not smiling. In fact, Agent Molina was livid.

There were three patients seated in the lobby. Kirsten, the twenty-six-year-old blonde receptionist looked up as Molina approached her. Kirsten opened her mouth to speak, but a raised finger from Molina was more than enough to silence her. Molina opened the door on the opposite side of the waiting room, and strode through.

She moved down a short corridor to the right before turning to the left into a small room that led her to the nurse's station. Gisela, a slightly heavy-set Latina nurse in her mid-thirties, acknowledged Molina with a smile.

"Hey, Mari. How are you?"

"Where's Dr. Patel?" Molina asked with a stoic expression.

The nurse read Molina's demeanor. "He's not in," she responded.

Molina's eyes narrowed. "Don't lie to me, Gisela. Please, not you."

"What are you talking about?"

Molina circled the nurse's station and began moving down the hallway to the left.

"Mari? What are you doing? He's not in."

Molina ignored her.

"Maribel!" Gisela called after her. It was no use. Molina was not listening. Under normal circumstances, Gisela would call security and have the intruder removed. However, she knew that Agent Molina was no ordinary intruder. Gisela knew that whatever it was that had Molina so incensed, she wanted no part of it.

Molina stopped at each of the patient rooms along the way towards the main Doctor's office. Of the seven rooms, two of them were occupied by a patient. Molina pushed open the last door on the left. There, standing behind the desk with a phone to his ear, stood a doctor. To Molina's disappointment, it wasn't Dr. Patel.

"Dr. Suri?" Molina said, surprised.

Dr. Arav Suri was a forty-five-year-old man of Indian descent. His towering, 6'5" frame was lean and strong. His jet-black hair displayed not a sliver of gray, and his brown skin's only blemishes were the small crow's feet that were only beginning to show on either side of his deep, brown eyes. Suri had been caring for both Molina and her daughter since the beginning. Though he always endeavored to maintain a professional distance from them, his concern for them had longed spilled over into the personal arena. His feelings were not of a romantic nature, rather, more paternal and protective. He'd known Molina long enough to be mutually surprised by her unannounced, emotionally charged visit. Suri gestured to the phone as he addressed Molina.

"Agent Molina, what's the problem? Kirsten just called and said you barged-"

"Where's Dr. Patel?" she interrupted.

"He hasn't come in yet," he answered.

"You're lying," she retorted quickly. "He has to be here."

Lying? Suri questioned silently to himself. *She should know me better than that.* He shook his head to hide the fact that his feelings were bruised by her accusation. The doctor crossed the room and closed the door. He turned to Molina. "Slow down. What are you talking about?"

"I'm talking about Dr. Patel taking my daughter out of school without my permission."

"What?" Suri was genuinely surprised.

"Luckily, I have a friend at the school. He called and told me that Dr. Patel came to the school and signed her out."

"Given her condition, Dr. Patel does have the authority-"

"He didn't inform me!" she screamed. "I want to know where my daughter is, and I want to know now!" She took a step back and began pacing back and forth nervously. As she did, she began mumbling to herself. "I knew something was going on. She's been acting so strange lately."

"Did you call Dr. Patel?" Suri asked.

"Of course," she answered in a tone that suggested Suri's question was unnecessary. Molina continued to pace. "I called him, I tried to call her. Neither of them answered. I even called Dr. Chen. Nothing." She stopped in her tracks and turned to Suri. "Maybe I should call Mr. Five, then he can call Mr. One and we can find out why none of the doctors here are on the same page."

"No!" Suri responded immediately. He tried to hide the fear in his eyes at the mention of Mr. One, but it was too late. Molina saw it. Suri conceded, "I'll make a few calls."

She took a step towards Suri. "I don't care who you call, Doctor. Just find my daughter. Find Iris."

2

BOSTON, MASSACHUSETTS

Kelli opened her eyes slowly. The sight of the female flight attendant leaning over her caused her to jump in her seat. Kelli looked at her hands. It was only then, after realizing that she was still in her male form, that she began to relax.

"I'm sorry, sir," the flight attendant apologized. "I didn't mean to startle you."

Kelli forced a smile. "It's okay." Her attention was drawn to the movements of the other passengers onboard. She looked back at the flight attendant. "Have we landed?" she asked through an unsuccessfully stifled yawn.

The flight attendant nodded. "Just a few moments ago. I didn't want you to miss your connecting flight."

Kelli glanced out of her window. Logan International Airport loomed beyond the terminal in front of her. Her male image was reflected back at her amidst the flashing lights that peeked out against the distant, evening Boston skyline. Kelli cursed silently to herself. She hated this city. To her, Boston represented an exile from which she wasn't supposed to stray too far for fear of someone recognizing her in her female form, her true self, who, as far as the world knew, died just one month shy of seven years ago. Sure, she appreciated the educational opportunities that were afforded her as an accelerated law student at Boston University's School of Law. How could she not? B.U. is an excellent school. Still, being in Beantown was a constant reminder that she couldn't go home to the Bronx, she couldn't see her family and friends, and she couldn't resume her life as Kelli Freeman. There was no telling what the Agency would do if they found out that she was alive. The Agency went to great lengths to try and kill her after she had discovered her gender-shifting ability. Staying dead was the only way she knew to keep her family out of harm's way. Staying in Boston was the way to play it safe. And yet, here she was, returning from a trip to the Washington D.C. area; potentially risking it all.

Still, Kelli had grown accustomed to the risk, especially after she realized that Kelli Freeman was the one who was always in danger of being spotted and, therefore, restricted to Boston. Kyle Cuffee, however, was not.

Kelli took one last look at her male visage. Her fake smile fell away. She disliked being in her male form. However, the reflection of her alter ego, Kyle Cuffee, was a very welcome sight at the moment. Over the last seven years, Kelli had learned to sleep in her male form without fear of reverting to her female form in the process. This was especially imperative while she was living with the Farmers, the family who took *Kyle* into their home believing *he* was an exchange student. However, she had learned, on nights when she was overtired and fell into a deep sleep, that her body would relax enough and revert back to female on its own. Though this was a concern when in proximity of others, it also turned out, at times, to be a blessing in disguise. Early on in her life in Boston, Kelli had discovered a side-effect to her shifting ability; the longer she maintained her male form, the more 'masculine' she became while in it. When Kelli was in her female form, she felt feminine, and true to herself. Kelli didn't want to lose that. But due to her witness protection status, she spent more of her day as Kyle Cuffee than as Kelli Freeman; sixteen hours a day, five days a week, sometimes weekends, for seven years. Trying not to lose yourself can be difficult when you're living someone else's life.

Still, Kelli *had* spent an exhausting two days in the D.C. area, and she feared that she would fall asleep as Kyle, but wake up as Kelli. She fought sleep as hard as she could on the ninety-five-minute flight back to Boston. Alas, fatigue won out and Kelli, in *Kyle*-form, drifted into undisturbed slumber. She had only God to thank for the fact that she didn't shift in her sleep. She knew that shifting would be a little difficult to explain. Regardless, even though she looked like Kyle on the outside, she was determined to stay Kelli Freeman on the inside.

She turned back to the flight attendant. "Thanks. But this is where I get off."

Kelli stood and gathered her backpack from the overhead compartment. She peered inside quickly to confirm that her laptop was still intact. Once she was satisfied all of her carry-on items were present, she stepped into the aisle and proceeded to disembark.

It took fifteen minutes to retrieve her single suitcase from the baggage claim carousel. Another twenty minutes passed while she rode the shuttle to parking lot C to retrieve her car. Kelli smiled as she approached her black

Audi TT Coupe. After all she had been through, her car was the one of the few things that brought her any true feelings of happiness or joy. It had been her dream car ever since she first arrived in Boston after being placed in the Witness Protection Program. Vividly, she recalled that foggy October morning she walked down Commonwealth Avenue, how enamored she was as a black Audi broke through the mist like something out of a car commercial. Kelli was only fifteen at the time, but she promised herself she would find a way to own a car like that someday. She wasn't certain how she was going to pull it off at that moment, but she thought, *I'm a genius. I'll figure it out.* And she did. Close to seven years later, Kelli had the car of her dreams, a beautiful one-bedroom apartment, and the beginnings of a promising career practicing law. This existence seemed to be going well for Kelli Freeman. Too bad it was Kyle Cuffee's existence and not hers. She had no real desire to be a lawyer, but completing law school was a necessary mean to the end that Kelli desired so desperately; to reclaim her former life. Her smile melted away as the reality of her current life settled like a crushing weight on her shoulders. She sighed heavily and cursed under her breath.

Kelli tossed her two bags onto the back seat and slid behind the wheel. It felt so nice to be back in her own car instead of that Camry she had rented over the weekend. Once she felt certain that no one could see her behind the tinted windows of her vehicle, she inhaled deeply, held her breath for a moment and then exhaled slowly. As the air left her body, Kelli shifted into her female form. She glanced into her rear-view mirror as if to confirm that the transformation was complete. Once satisfied, she pressed the keyless ignition button. Within minutes she was cruising along the State Highway 1A South in the heart of the city. She couldn't wait to get to her apartment and relax. Even though she'd just arrived back in Boston, she had a road trip planned to New York in the morning. Her parents, Arthur and Diane Freeman, were throwing a weekend party for Wilma's eleventh birthday. Wilma was Kelli's younger sister. Regardless of the conditions of Kelli's placement in the Witness Protection Program to limit her contact with her family, she was determined to take part in the celebration somehow. She had missed so much time with her family over the last seven years, and Kelli decided that something had to change. In spite of the feelings of resentment and betrayal she felt towards her parents for harboring the secret of her true origins, she loved them deeply.

Her mind drifted briefly to her last few days in D.C. While there, Kelli had set some important wheels in motion, most importantly, an interview at the law offices of Adler, Royce, & Bellamy. One of the founding partners, Jacob Royce, was especially impressed with Kyle Cuffee's resume. That, along with several highly flattering recommendations from the faculty at Boston University, convinced Royce that hiring young Kyle, who had just passed the Massachusetts Bar Exam, was an absolute no-brainer. As Kelli expected, Royce had difficulty in hiding his reaction to Kyle's very youthful appearance, so much so that he felt he was left with no other choice but to say it.

"I get that a lot", Kelli had responded. And it was true. Due to her genetic engineering, Kelli aged much slower than other human beings. Though she was twenty-one years old, her appearance led one to believe she was no older than sixteen, seventeen at most. This was true regardless of the gender she was showing to the world.

"I'm sure," Royce replied with a smile. His large oak desk sat towards the back of a spacious office. He gestured for Kyle to have a seat in the chair that was placed in front of the desk. As Kelli crossed the distance, she took notice of the many academic achievements and family photos that decorated all four walls. As she sat, the back of a large, silver picture frame that rested on the front corner of the desk caught her eye. A moment later, Royce was sitting in the leather-cushioned chair behind the oak structure.

Jacob Royce was a tall, average-looking Caucasian man in his early fifties. His short, black hair had just begun to sprout streaks of gray that spread from his temples to the nape of his neck. His light brown eyes were large and round, and Kelli could see the outlines of the contact lenses he wore. Only his skin, which was slightly sun-damaged as a result of the hours he spent sun-bathing as a teen, revealed that Royce was no longer a young man. However, Kelli noticed something else about Jacob Royce; something about his eyes. Looking into them, Kelli thought she recognized a man who had seen much in his life, and had grown experienced and tired all at the same time. Kelli shifted her focus back to Royce's smile. It seemed warm and genuine, and it allowed Kelli to shake off the twinges of nervousness she had been feeling since she entered the room.

"I don't want to waste your time," the lawyer said, "so I'll get right to it." Royce opened a file that had been placed on his desk. He skimmed it briefly before looking up at his young interviewee. "So, it says here that you were working as a Legal Intern at Tzinberg & Beach in Boston before you passed the bar."

Kelli nodded.

"I'm curious," Royce said with a slight left tilt of his head. "Why not just work *there*? With your academic achievements, summa cum laude among them, surely they'd want you to work for them."

Kelli allowed a small smile to grace her lips, though, in an attempt to appear modest, she averted her gaze, breaking eye contact with Royce. Her eyes focused briefly on another silver-framed picture that hung on the left wall, but for only a mere second. She glanced back at the attorney.

"Yes," she responded. "They even made me an offer."

"And?"

"I'd rather work in the D.C. area," Kelli replied. "My long-term goals beyond practicing law involve politics, running for public office, maybe the Senate one day. I can't think of a better place to start my career." All lies.

Royce smiled again and began to nod his head. "You sound like my wife." He gestured towards the frame that sat on the forward corner of his desk off to his left. He reached out and turned the photo around, showing it to Kelli. Inside the beautiful sterling frame sat a picture of Royce and an attractive woman with cropped brown hair, bright blue eyes and a stunning smile. Kelli recognized the woman immediately.

"I'm familiar with your wife's work," Kelli admitted. "I wrote a paper on the legal pros and cons of her bill on health care reform. I'd tell you she was my hero, but I don't want to seem like I'm brown-nosing."

Royce chuckled. He was clearly amused by Kyle, and he had already decided that he liked the young man. "I understand. She's my hero, too. Betty's an amazing woman. She was one of the founding partners here before she became a Senator and, subsequently, joined Congress."

"I hear she's running for re-election," Kelli stated.

"She is," Royce confirmed, surprised by Kyle's apparent depth of pre-interview research.

"Well, I'd love to see that first-hand."

"All the more reason to relocate," Royce added.

Kelli nodded. "All the more reason."

The rest of the interview had gone well. Royce indicated that he had several other applicants to see, still, he hinted more than once that Kyle should be prepared to pack his bags. There was also discussion about Kyle passing the Bar Exam to practice law in the D.C. area. Kelli assured him that it wouldn't be a problem. Although she could not reveal her true motivations to Royce, Kelli felt trapped in Boston, and a job offer in another state would give her a legitimate reason to leave the city where she was placed under witness protection. Perhaps then, she could release the constant anger that pressed against her chest every minute of every day. Maybe, she could finally live a somewhat normal life. *Normal*. She almost laughed at the thought. There was nothing normal about a girl who could switch sexes at will. Further, there was nothing remotely normal about allegedly having the cure for all diseases coursing through your veins. No. Kelli knew that, regardless of her activities in the D.C. area, there was nothing that could erase the extraordinary reality of who and what she was. For her, normal wasn't in the cards.

She shook her head in an attempt not to think about it. *A girl can hope*, she thought to herself.

Kelli snapped back to the present. She pressed the accelerator and pushed her black Audi into the fast lane. She cruised by a dark-colored Honda and disappeared into the darkness ahead.

Thirty minutes elapsed before Kelli rode the elevator to her second floor, Beacon Street apartment in Brookline. In her left hand, she held a small pile of mail that she had retrieved from her mailbox. Her backpack hung from her right shoulder as she held a firm grip on her suitcase handle with her right hand. She had donned a hooded sweatshirt which hid her face within the opening of the large covering. If by chance anyone approached her, she could shift back into her Kyle-form without arousing any suspicions. After all, the apartment, the car and everything she owned was in the name of Kyle Cuffee. No one in the apartment complex knew her as Kelli. None of them knew Kelli Freeman even existed. She asked herself often, *why take the chance of being seen in female form?* The answer was simple. She hated every minute that she spent as Kyle.

She slipped the key into the lock of her apartment door and gave it a quick turn. A second later, she crossed the threshold into her living room and tossed her bags aside. She placed the mail on her coffee table with no regard as to who had sent any of it. She shed her sweatshirt and hung it on the coat rack by the door. She tugged lightly at the bandana that wrapped her neat strands of dreadlocks into a pony tail and released her hair, allowing it to bob just above her shoulders. She kicked off her shoes and headed straight for her couch. She fell onto the soft cushions and allowed all the tension in her body to melt away into the sofa. After a few moments of lying completely still, Kelli lifted her head and glanced at her answering machine which sat adjacent to her sofa. The number 2 flashed at her incessantly. Kelli reached out and tapped the play button.

"Hey, Kyle. Monica here." Special Agent Monica Davies, the FBI agent assigned to Kelli's Witness Protection case, had made her routine monthly call. In the beginning, Monica called weekly. Kelli used to look forward to those calls. Monica was the only link Kelli still had to the world she had to leave behind. Then, over the last few years, something changed. Kelli would like to lie to herself and suggest it was Monica who had changed. But Kelli knew that she was, in fact, the culprit. The longer she stayed in Boston, the more bitter she became. After reaching her eighteenth birthday, Kelli wanted some slack on the FBI's leash. She began avoiding Monica's phone calls, cancelling and rescheduling their meetings and forgetting to check-in at the pre-planned intervals. It didn't take long for Special Agent Davies to notice the change in Kelli's behavior. She made it a point to speak to Kelli about it, and for some time, Kelli appeared to shape up and go along with the protocols of being in witness protection. Now, Kelli was twenty-one. Over the last seven months, Kelli had gradually slipped back into her recalcitrant behavior. She had plans of her own now and she didn't want Special Agent Davies or anyone else, for that matter, getting in her way.

Kelli breathed slowly as she listened to the rest of Davies' message.

"I was hoping we could get together soon," the message began. As usual, Davies made the messages sound nonchalant and casual, as if she were calling an old friend. She didn't want to risk saying anything business related if, perhaps, Kelli had a visitor. "We missed our last appointment and I wanted to see when we could catch up. I hope everything is okay. You know how to reach me." With that, the message ended.

Kelli lay still on the couch. Her mind went over all of the justifications she had for not returning Agent Davies' call. She had none. All she had were excuses. The truth of matter was, she didn't want to *catch up* with Davies. Kelli knew that if she spoke to her, the only thing she could tell her were lies. Kelli had told enough of them lately. She cursed aloud. Lies are what started this whole ordeal. Kelli never wanted to become a liar. She didn't want to become one of *them*. Through the hiding and the duplicity regarding her identity, Kelli wanted to maintain a bit of integrity, some semblance of hope that she wouldn't lose herself in the sea of deception that had brought her to this point. Unfortunately, she realized she had to tell lies to keep her cover intact. The real problem was, amidst all of the lying, Kelli had become good at it. So good, in fact, that she began telling lies that she didn't have to tell; not only to the Farmers, her co-workers, classmates, and her therapist, but to Special Agents Davies and West, as well. Of all the people in her new life, West was the one person to whom she really wished she could open up. She wanted to tell him about the anger that had built up inside of her over the past seven years, about the frustration of being trapped in the life of someone else, and most of all, the identity of Mr. One, the head of the Agency. Unfortunately, she knew West was the last person in whom she could confide. One reason for keeping West in the dark was that telling West would undermine everything. The other reason was that Kelli was upset at West, and had been for quite some time. West had become increasingly more distant and harder to contact as the last seven years went by. It wasn't long before he stopped calling all together. Two years ago, Kelli called West and gave him an earful. They had not spoken to each other since. At times, Kelli wanted to call him and clear the air so she could tell him what she was up to. However, Kelli could not afford that. Not now. Not when her plans were finally getting underway.

As usual when Kelli began to dwell on the circumstances that landed her in Boston, her thoughts wandered to Francine. She tried to push the image of Francine's dead body out of her mind. She was much too exhausted to deal with the emotions associated with Francine's death; the despair, the sorrow and the guilt. Kelli carried that guilt because, were it not for Francine being in the wrong place at the wrong time, an Agency assassin's bullet, a bullet meant for Kelli, would not have claimed her life. Kelli had re-run the scenario thousands of times over the last seven years. If Kelli had not frightened Francine by revealing her gender-shifting ability, Francine would not have been out on the street when the Agency operatives arrived. Kelli would never forgive herself for that. Instead, she intended to make the Agency pay. Somehow. Some day. Soon.

The second message was from Patrice Bass. Patrice was one of Kelli's law school classmates and now her fellow coworker at Tzinberg & Beach. Patrice and *Kyle* met three and a half years prior on their first day of law school. Patrice, having done her undergrad years at Howard University, was new to the Boston area. Kelli could tell immediately that Patrice was anxious about her graduate studies and, as Kyle, reached out and expressed similar angst, initiating their friendship. Kelli missed having a *girl-bestie* with whom to spend time, and it wasn't long before *Kyle* and Patrice were almost inseparable. Although they had spent a lot of time together over the course of three years, it was only recently that Patrice began to drop not-so-subtle hints that she was interested in more than just friendship with Kelli's male alter ego. This wasn't exactly a surprise to Kelli. In fact, Patrice's suggestions at expanding the boundaries of their relationship presented an additional complication to an issue with which Kelli was previously struggling. Due to the side-effect of her shifting ability, Kelli, as Kyle, had already developed romantic feelings for Patrice. Kelli had never considered having an intimate relationship with a woman. So, when she first realized that, as Kyle, she was attracted to Patrice, she fought it. Not because she couldn't imagine herself being with a woman, rather she believed that she wouldn't be having romantic feelings if she remained in her true form. Even after Kelli accepted the fact that Kyle, *she*, was attracted to Patrice, she still resisted. Kelli didn't want to lead Patrice on and give her any hope of a life with Kyle. A committed, sexual relationship would require full disclosure of her abilities, and the last time Kelli revealed what she could do, Francine ended up dead. No, the stakes were too high, and Kelli couldn't handle losing another best friend. Since Patrice's revelation, Kelli could now detect those desires in almost every word Patrice spoke. Her voicemail message was no different. Patrice's voice was youthful, soft, and carried a faint, please-call-me tone.

"Hey, Kyle, it's Patrice. Just calling to see how your trip went. Thanks again for taking me to the shooting range last week. After that horrendous Bar Exam, letting off a few rounds was exactly what I needed. And you know I still owe you for scaring the crap out of me that day. Anyway, give me a call when you get in. Hope to talk to you soon. Bye."

Kelli was at a loss about how to deal with the Patrice situation. The on-going inner conflict between Kyle's testosterone driven tendencies and her own, left her confused about how to display her sexual preference during her daily life as Kyle. Up to this point, Kyle lived an asexual lifestyle. If Kelli chose to follow her true orientation, then Kyle would appear to be homosexual. However, if she decided to conform to a heterosexual lifestyle as Kyle, well, that option required more consideration than Kelli had been willing to give. Still, neither option came without its problems. Whatever type of relationship or lifestyle she decided to pursue, Kelli knew that no relationship would survive without coming clean about her abilities, and that, for most, would be a definite deal breaker. This, unfortunately, Kelli had already learned. Rejection felt absolutely horrible.

She managed to pull her weary body from the couch. She moved across the living room into the bedroom and headed straight for the master bathroom. A quick shower later, Kelli emerged ready for bed. She threw the lavender-colored comforter back and nestled between the familiarity and comfort of her own sheets. Within minutes, she was asleep. Still, her subconscious mind was occupied by the last few days she had spent in D.C. Kelli hoped it would all be worth it someday.

Outside of Kelli's apartment building, the dark-colored Honda she passed on the highway more than an hour earlier, came to a stop by the curb and parked.

CRAWFORDSVILLE, INDIANA

It was 5 a.m. A hint of sunlight peaked around the clouds in the calm, morning sky as dawn began to break. An early morning run was nothing unusual for Special Agent Donald West. In fact, for several years, it was a normal routine. He enjoyed the fresh air and the quiet. The stillness of the morning allowed him to be alone with his thoughts. This morning, however, West was not experiencing any of the pleasures that came along with his daily jog. This morning, West was in a foot pursuit, chasing a known felon by the name of Richard Navarro.

Thirty-six hours earlier, West had been relaxing in his D.C. apartment, reading an article in the *Post* about the growing homeless crisis when his boss, FBI Assistant Director Steven Marsh gave him a call.

"Ferry gave me another tip worth investigating," Marsh had said. "Turns out the Agency is moving some type of important merchandise across state lines."

"What type of merchandise?"

"He claimed it was some type of drug," Marsh answered. "Though he wasn't specific, Ferry believes that whatever the Agency is moving, it is vital to the longevity of their operations here and abroad."

West had shaken his head slightly. "Drugs? That doesn't sound like something the Agency would be into."

"Maybe so, but if we knew everything the Agency was into, we wouldn't always be two steps behind. Regardless, I need you to check it out. Pack your bags. You're taking a trip."

Within three hours, West, along with his new partner Special Agent Quentin Bonner, and longtime colleague, Special Agent Monica Davies, was on a plane enroute to the great Hoosier-state of Indiana. Davies, aside from West and A.D. Marsh, was the only other person at the D.C. Field Office who knew about the Agency. Davies was a good agent, and West trusted her. He was glad that she had come along.

West took advantage of the time in the air and examined the information supplied by Marsh. Although the report contained very little information, it answered some of the questions that Marsh did not have time to answer over the phone. Questions like, *what's being transported and why should the FBI care?* Ferry, Marsh's confidential informant, or CI, claimed that the Agency was involved in some type of genetic research and that the drugs they were transporting were actually biochemicals that had not received FDA approval. Genetic research matched up with what Marsh and West already knew about the Agency, and what made the CI's report seem legitimate. Yet, this piece of information brought up another question. *If we don't know what the chemical is, how does the FBI get a warrant to search for it?* The answer to that question made West smile. The transport vehicle was a medical transport van that was equipped with a GPS tracker. Ferry supplied the necessary frequency to get a confirmed, current location on the van in Crawfordsville, Indiana. Ferry went a step further by supplying the name of the van driver, a man named Richard Navarro. Navarro was a notorious bank robber and murderer who, after killing a security guard, a young female banking customer and her eleven-year-old daughter during a bank heist in Delaware, found himself on the FBI's Ten Most Wanted list. *Bingo.*

Marsh had arranged for Special Agent Redding, an agent from the Indianapolis field office, to rendezvous with West and the others once their plane touched down. After a lengthy briefing, Redding's team provided support for the pending raid on a small yellow house nestled in a cul-de-sac on E. College Street in Crawfordsville.

As the convergence on the house commenced, West had taken notice of the thick border of trees that began about sixty feet behind the dwelling. Little did he know that in fewer than ten minutes, after a small exchange of gunfire inside the house, he'd be chasing the man they came to retrieve, through those very woods.

Now, West could make out Navarro's white T-shirt in front of him as he pursued the felon through the row of trees behind the house. Though West had only been in Crawfordsville for a few short hours, he had familiarized himself with the immediate lay of the land just in case, as it often did, a chase ensued.

"He's on foot," West reported as he ran, "moving east. Coming your way, Rover."

"Copy that," a deep, male voice responded through the earpiece.

West picked up the pace. He could see that Navarro had already cleared the trees and had stepped into the open lot within the adjacent residential neighborhood on Knoll Circle. Though he couldn't see the gray van in which he and his fellow agents had arrived, he could hear the screeching of its tires as they spun rapidly several times before friction was achieved and the van lurched forward.

Navarro saw the van approaching him from the left. He raised his weapon and fired five rounds at the vehicle's right front tire. Three of the rounds found their mark, puncturing the tire, rendering it useless. Navarro turned and darted to the right. He raced south along the sidewalk of Knoll Circle, making certain to stay close to the cars parked along the street in the event that he had to jump behind one for cover or slow the progress of his pursuers.

West broke through the trees and sprinted through the lot onto Knoll. To his left, two FBI agents stumbled out of the gray van in an effort to join the chase. The male agent was Special Agent Jay Temple from the Indianapolis Field Office. The female agent was Special Agent Davies.

West sprinted along the sidewalk. Up ahead to his right, he spied Navarro and adjusted his direction accordingly. West's frame was a lean and muscular 185 lbs. His exercise regimen consisted of a 75-minute session, three to four times per week which included a 3-mile run at the onset. Navarro, conversely, was a stocky, 215 lb. brute who, despite his 'prison-workout' physique, smoked cigarettes and drank several beers daily. This West knew for certain. He had no doubt that Navarro would not, or more accurately, could not outrun him. His only real concern was whether or not he could overpower the man long enough to subdue him. West had brushed up on his martial arts training over the last few years, but superior training wasn't always a guarantee against superior strength. West knew there would only be a matter of seconds before he would have to figure it out. As it was, he was already gaining ground on Navarro with every step.

Navarro must have sensed that West was catching up. He pivoted sharply and darted off to his left. He crossed the street and ran in between two homes on the opposite side. West followed relentlessly, continuing to close the gap between them.

West saw Navarro turn and move to the right again, avoiding a small body of water that he assumed was a pond. West could tell by Navarro's body language that he was growing tired. Up ahead, Navarro turned his head briefly, risking a quick glimpse to gauge his chances of slipping away. That simple act told West that he and Navarro were coming to the same conclusion. *He wasn't going to escape. Not this way.* West knew also that, once a perp realized his chances of getting away were slim, the likelihood of the perp committing a desperate act usually increased.

Navarro slowed his pace. He turned around suddenly and pointed the .45 in West's direction, however, West was nowhere in sight. Navarro looked beyond the point where he expected to see West. In the distance, he could see several agents rushing towards him. He turned once again to continue fleeing. As he did, he heard footsteps approaching rapidly. Navarro glanced over his right shoulder to find West dogging his heels. West had redirected himself around the house that sat to the right, gambling that Navarro would be confused just enough to drop his guard and leave him susceptible to being flanked. Fortunately for West, the gamble paid off. West tackled the large man, causing them both to skid across the damp grass.

West recovered first. He took a quick inventory to confirm that Navarro had dropped his weapon. He scrambled to his feet and charged at Navarro from a crouching position.

Navarro saw West coming. Due to his heavier, less athletic build, it took Navarro a moment longer to maneuver himself onto his knees. He braced himself for the impact of West's imminent second tackle. West collided into him in an attempt to push Navarro onto his back. Navarro's sturdy constitution allowed him to absorb the brunt of the attack. He wrapped his arms around West, twisted, and then carried him as he fell back towards the ground. This move, unfortunately for West, caused Navarro's 215 lb. frame to land on top of the young FBI agent.

"Ughh!" West groaned as his body slammed onto the hard ground. A sharp pain shot through his right shoulder.

Navarro rose to one knee, drew back his fist, and slammed it into West's left cheek. Once, twice, three times Navarro battered West's face before he was tackled again and pushed onto the ground.

Navarro continued to roll in an attempt to put some distance between his own body and his latest, unseen attacker. He managed to complete three rolls before he stopped himself and turned to face his new assailant. Navarro was pleasantly surprised. He knew that, at least, two other agents had joined in his pursuit. Initially, he figured that the duo had finally caught up. Instead, Navarro could see those two agents still closing in from about forty yards out. In front of him, stumbling to his feet, was a black man with a face he did not recognize. It didn't matter. The faces were irrelevant. They were from the FBI and their mission was to apprehend him or kill him, and Navarro had an idea of how this was all going to end.

Special Agent Bonner had already regained his footing and was in the process of pulling his Glock from its holster when Navarro was suddenly upon him.

Navarro punched Bonner squarely in the face, landing a powerful blow against his left temple. Bonner's grip on his firearm held fast. Navarro threw a left upper cut into Bonner's stomach, causing the agent to double over slightly. Navarro turned to his left as he heard West's footsteps approaching rapidly from behind once again. He planted his right foot and lowered his center of gravity. Instead of attempting yet another NFL linebacker-style take down, West stopped short of Navarro and kicked at the large man's left knee. Navarro yelped in pain and his body buckled to his left in response.

Bonner, back on the offensive, jammed his left fist into Navarro's jaw. Navarro's head jerked violently in the opposite direction. West, now in a boxing stance, launched a jab-cross combination, each blow finding its mark on Navarro's nose.

Navarro fell to his knees. He felt the warm blood from his nostrils dripping over his mouth. He grunted and groaned as West and Bonner proceeded to kick him in an attempt to subdue him once and for all. Navarro tightened his beer-engorged gut as to absorb the brutal on-slaught. He felt his strength began to wane, and that's when he saw it. There, only a mere foot away from his own hand, lay his .45.

Navarro reached for the large weapon. As he did, he noticed the kicking ceased immediately and was followed by Bonner's voice.

"Don't!" Bonner ordered loudly.

Navarro could hear the unmistakable sound of metal rattling slightly. He did not have to look up to know that both of the agents were now leveling their service weapons at his head. He froze. Slowly, Navarro turned his head and looked up to find, not only West and Bonner pointing weapons at him, but Agents Temple and Davies, upon arriving finally, had him lined up in their sights as well. Navarro weighed his options: let himself be apprehended and face the death penalty in Delaware for killing three people, or, make a play for the .45 knowing, without a doubt, that he would be put down here and now. Navarro was not fond of sitting idle, waiting to die, but going out in a blaze of glory was a death sentence he could accept. For him, the decision was easy.

He glanced at West and Bonner and smirked smugly. West saw the twinkle in Navarro's eyes, and instantly he, too, knew what Navarro was going to do.

"Hell, no," West yelled as he lunged forward and struck Navarro at the nape of his neck with the butt of his weapon. Navarro crumbled to the ground, unconscious. Bonner kicked the .45 away from Navarro's still frame.

West and Bonner nodded to each other; both breathed a heavy sigh of relief.

Thirty-minutes later, they were back at the yellow house with the rest of the FBI detail. The yard and house were cordoned off with yellow tape, and the cul-de-sac was full of flashing lights, nosy neighbors and media vans.

West sat in the rear cabin of an ambulance as a paramedic tended to the bruises on his face and placed his shoulder in a sling. Bonner had just received similar treatment from another ambulance and was making his way over to his partner.

"Nice tackle back there," West complimented Bonner as he approached. "High School Football?"

Bonner nodded. "Defensive End. I have eleven older siblings, so it was a skill I practiced a lot."

"And you're not playing pro football because…?"

Bonner deflected, "Not my calling, I guess."

West's cell phone began to ring. He pulled the phone from his pocket and glanced at the caller I.D. He smirked. "Marsh must've heard we caught our man," he said to Bonner.

"Is that him already?" Bonner asked.

West swiped his finger across the touch-screen of his cell and opened the call. "News must travel fast, sir," he said into the phone.

"Agent West," Marsh said. His tone was grave. "I need you back here right away."

"Is there a problem, sir?" West asked. "We just wrapped-"

"It's Ferry," Marsh interrupted. "Get here as soon as you can. We'll swap reports after your flight lands. Don't tell your partner." With that, Marsh hung up.

West knew that he must have appeared as stunned as he felt because Bonner asked, "Everything okay, buddy?"

West hated lying to his partner. But he knew, this time, like every time before when Marsh mentioned Ferry, he had no choice. "Yeah, Q." He tried to sound nonchalant. He figured by calling Bonner by his nickname, the matter would seem less urgent. "Everything's fine. Marsh wants us back today."

"Did he say why?"

West forced a smile, "Something about handling our own caseload back home."

"I guess he forgot that Navarro was on our caseload," Bonner said with a chuckle. "Same old song, right?"

"Yeah," West said, feeling guilty. "Same old song."

"Agent West," Davies' voice called from the entrance to the garage. "Redding wants to have a word with you."

"Uh, okay," West responded, attempting to sound surprised in front of Bonner. "I'll be right there. He turned to his partner. "I'll catch up with you later, Q. Go grab a bite to eat."

"Will do," Bonner said before turning and walking away.

West hurried over to the garage entrance where Davies stood waiting. He noticed her gaze was still focused on Bonner who was walking in the opposite direction. She raised a curious eyebrow as West reached her.

"What?" West questioned.

"You tell him yet?"

"Still debating," West replied. "I know I should, but-."

"Marsh is not going to like it," Davies said, finishing West's sentence.

"No, he's not."

"Well, if you're going to tell your partner about the Agency, you know my motto, *the longer you wait, the longer it's going to hurt everybody involved.*"

"Yeah," West acknowledged with a hint of tension in his voice, "How could I forget?"

Davies placed a hand on West's non-injured shoulder. She squeezed it gently as she spoke with a softer tone. "You asked me once to *be straight* with you, to keep things honest. I did *then*, and I will now. Bonner may want the same respect."

West opened his mouth to reply, but decided against it. His mind was still dealing with Davies' reference to *then*, a time in which their lives had become markedly intertwined. Shortly after Kelli was placed in witness protection in Boston, West and Davies' professional relationship crossed romantic boundaries. Unfortunately for West, Davies ended it after two years, claiming that West didn't know how to leave his work at the office. His obsession with the Agency leaked into every facet of their personal lives. It wasn't long before Davies questioned whether or not she was even a priority. West's lack of attention caused Davies to grow apart and out of love with him. By the time West realized that she was no longer invested romantically, the damage had already been done.

"Just be straight with me," West had said. "Am I too late?"

Davies, without shedding a tear, didn't mince words. "Yes, you are. There's no point in hiding how I feel. The longer I wait, the longer it's going to hurt both of us. You're hardly ever here, and when you are, I feel like I'm the only one in this relationship. I'm sorry if this hurts you, but I need to save myself."

It had been five years since that conversation. Though West knew she was right, it did little to ease the pain. He knew he didn't deserve her, but it never changed the fact that for him, Davies would always be the fish that got away. Eventually, West accepted that he would forever remain in Davies' friend zone. The fact that they would be assigned to work together on cases that involved the Agency had left him little choice.

West and Davies entered the garage. Several agents were swarming the medical transport van that was parked within. The side door was ajar. Agent Redding stepped out of the van with a grave look on his face.

"What do we got?" West asked.

"See for yourself," Redding replied, gesturing to the open boxes that filled the back of the van.

West moved to the van's opening. His heart pumped anxiously. *Finally, we'll have some solid evidence of the Agency's existence.* He peered into the first box. Suddenly, he pushed it aside and looked into the adjacent box, then the next.

"Shit."

"What is it?" Davies asked.

"The boxes are empty."

"What?"

"They're empty," West repeated. "We got nothing."

3

BROOKLINE, MASSACHUSETTS

Sharp images flashed through Kelli's mind's eye as she slept; images of staring through the scope of a sniper rifle and locking a target in between the crosshairs. Her index finger resting gently outside the trigger well, Kelli anticipated the moment when she could squeeze that trigger ever so slowly and send a hollow-point into the skull of her unsuspecting prey. Kelli had experienced several variations of this dream. At times, it was a pistol she was holding at point-blank range in front of her target's skull. Other times, it was a ju-jitsu choke hold that cut off the oxygen supply that did the trick. In the beginning, the dreams frightened her. The mere thought of stalking someone and taking their life seemed such a foreign and heinous concept to her; so far removed from anything that she would ever conceive of doing. But now, the effects of those dreams had changed. Now, Kelli embraced the visions that danced through her dreams. She liked to think of them as practice, a subconscious review of things to come. Only, the particular version of the dream she was having this morning was no dream at all. It was a memory, one where the sole variable that set it apart from reality was the sniper rifle, not a camera with a telephoto lens.

Kelli awoke with a moan. The persistent beeping of her alarm clock jarred her from slumber, pulling her back into the here and now. She rolled over in her bed. The glowing blue numbers from her digital clock were the only things visible in the darkness of her bedroom. It was 6:30 a.m.

"Damn," Kelli swore aloud as she read the time. The fact that she had set her alarm for 5:45 told her that she must have been hitting the snooze button in her sleep. That wasn't good. Kelli had more travel plans for the day, and now she was behind schedule.

She reached over and tapped the center button on top of the clock. She'd had the clock in the same place on that same nightstand for years. She didn't need even a flicker of light to shut it off. She rubbed her eyes as she pushed herself up into a seated position. She looked at the clock once more and shook her head. *I did not get enough sleep*, she thought to herself. After the last few days in the D.C. area, coupled with the flight back to Boston, she felt as if she could lie back down and sleep away the entire day. In fact, she wanted to do just that. Unfortunately, Kelli wanted to get on the road to New York as soon as she could, so catching up on her much-needed rest would have to wait.

The warm shower that cascaded over her *Serena Williams-esque* physique stimulated her senses, waking her from her somnolent state. No more than fifteen minutes later she was in her kitchen scrambling eggs whites, toasting two slices of sourdough bread, and peeling an orange. Her laptop sat open on the kitchen table. The screensaver displayed a collage of New York Yankees greats, both past and present. The stack of mail that she'd tossed on the coffee table the night before caught her eye. She scooped up the small pile and leafed through it as she ate her breakfast. One of the envelopes was sent from The Mackenzie Financial Group. Kelli smirked.

Mackenzie was a very popular and well-trusted name in the world of investments. They handled stocks, bonds, financial portfolios, even IRA's and 401k's. According to their logo, if you had money to invest or a financial future to protect, The Mackenzie Financial Group were the people to call. Just short of seven months prior, after winning a large sum of money in an Atlantic City casino, Kelli contacted the Mackenzie Group. She was looking for a way to make her money work for *her* instead of the other way around. Mackenzie Financial did just that.

Seven months since Atlantic City, Kelli thought as her mind drifted back. *Yeah, that was about the same time I started dodging Monica's calls again.*

Kelli opened the envelope that was addressed to Kyle Cuffee. As she removed the paperwork and glanced through the quarterly report, she recalled her initial meeting with Todd Mackenzie, a stern looking man who commented several times on being 'thirty-something'. As Kyle, Kelli had asked a few leading questions which led Todd Mackenzie to believe that he had, in fact, helped Kelli come to the decision of buying shares in a company called Quinlan Pharmaceuticals. Kelli was certain that Todd was enjoying his little power play; helping this young, innocent-looking kid get his life together. In reality, Kelli knew exactly in which company she wanted to invest, and she had no problem allowing the sharply dressed investment rep to believe it was all due to his unmatched business savvy and know-how. Taking the credit didn't matter to Kelli. Besides, she could tell that Todd Mackenzie's heart skipped a beat when she revealed the amount of money with which she had to play. It was then that the balance of power, or control, in the conversation shifted into Kelli's favor. From that point on, Todd Mackenzie was putty in her hands.

Kelli looked over the report. Quinlan Pharmaceuticals continued to make a profit. *That figures*, she thought. Kelli sighed deeply and tossed the paperwork aside. She looked around her apartment, knowing full well that without her casino winnings and the subsequent, continuous profit margin at Quinlan, she would have to go back to work. Not that she was concerned about that. After all, she had just passed the Massachusetts Bar Exam, and there were several law firms who were eager to snatch up a young, brilliant legal prodigy like Kyle Cuffee. However, as Kelli had told Jacob Royce, she wasn't interested in working in Massachusetts. If she had been completely honest with Royce, she would have divulged that she had no real interest in practicing law at all. Ultimately, Kelli wanted to leave the Bay State and Kyle Cuffee's life behind for good; getting the job in D.C. would be a good first step.

The Skype app on her laptop emitted a cheery, electronic melody that alerted Kelli to an incoming video call. She glanced at the screen, and then smiled. She pulled the laptop in front of her and clicked the phone icon. Within seconds, the face of Joseph Woods filled the screen.

Joseph Woods was a young, good-looking adolescent just three months shy of his fifteenth birthday. Thick locks of long, brown hair draped his slender shoulders. His brown eyes were dark and round, and his smile was warm. Like many teens, Joseph found solace in the solitude that came with his particular hobbies; the same hobbies that led him to Kelli Freeman.

Joseph was the last of four children born to the late Dr. James Connelly, the geneticist who was one half of the medical team that created the super-soldier program known as the Harmony Project, and ultimately, Kelli Freeman herself. Joseph, along with his older sisters, Calliope and Clara, was also a product of the Harmony Project. Each of them possessed the same biological sex-shifting ability as Kelli. However, Joseph had no interest whatsoever in shifting into his female form. After the death of his father, Joseph and his sisters were whisked away to London by their eldest sibling, Nicholas Connelly. There, the Woods children were raised by their biological mother, Charlotte Woods, who, with the aid of Nicholas, endeavored to help them cope with their extraordinary abilities. Calliope and Clara remained fascinated by all facets of their genetic engineering; the heightened senses, the accelerated healing, the elevated intelligence, the enhanced physical strength, and, of course, the biological sex-shifting which offered the added ability to conquer any known disease. Joseph, on the other hand, embraced all of them except the shifting. Once he had learned to control it, due to the urgings of his mother and Nicholas, he vowed to never gender-shift again. To this day, he had yet to violate that promise. Instead, Joseph focused on computer programming. By the age of twelve, Joseph was building his own computers from scratch, writing complex code, and constructing algorithms to create whatever his brilliant mind came up with, including malicious software. Eventually, Joseph was introduced to computer hacking where, within that questionable pursuit, he found his passion. He immersed himself in codes and algorithms, purchased the best hardware and software to hone his hacking abilities, while also learning how to cover his tracks. It wasn't long before no computer system was safe from Joseph, and it was this bit of information that caught Kelli's attention during a routine conversation with the Woods children seven months ago. Kelli contacted Joseph again shortly after her trip to Atlantic City. She offered to pay him for his services, claiming she needed to dig up certain information on a few particular power players involved in U.S. government and politics. Joseph was immediately interested. Once a fee was agreed upon, and Joseph accepted his assignment on a 'need to know' versus 'right to know' basis, the young man went to work, diving into the lives and business dealings of his targets. Kelli was quite pleased with Joseph's skills.

Kelli greeted him cheerfully, "Hey, Joseph."

"Hey," he responded. Joseph was a young man of very few words. It took Kelli some time to become accustomed to his reticence.

Kelli noted that Joseph was sitting in his usual chair which was located in the converted attic of the home where Joseph resided in London with his mother. On the far wall behind him, Kelli could see rows of computer equipment and technological gadgets that had become the tools of both Joseph's work and pleasure.

"Just checking in. Everything went okay?" Joseph inquired. Although he wasn't privy to all of the details of Kelli's recent excursion to D.C., he knew that the information he had provided her was extremely important to her task.

"Your intel was spot on, as usual. You received the payment?"

"Yeah. Thanks. Any new assignments?"

"Not at the moment," Kelli replied. "I'm sure I'll come up with something by the time I get back from New York."

"New York?"

Kelli nodded. "Yeah, I need a few days off. Take a few for yourself. I'll contact you when I get back."

"Okay," he said. Then, he added with a nervous stammer, "Uh, be careful."

Kelli smiled warmly again. Though Joseph would never admit it, Kelli knew that he had a small crush on her. She regarded it as *cute*. "You, too."

With that, they ended the call. Joseph had once commented that he didn't like saying goodbye. So, they never did.

Kelli rose from the table. She tossed her dirty breakfast dishes into the dishwasher and set it to run the Heated/Dry cycle. She dressed in a loose-fitting pair of blue, men's sweatpants and a white, long sleeve T-shirt with the words *Boston University Terriers* written in scarlet across the front and along the left sleeve. After brushing her teeth quickly, she tied her shoulder-length dreadlocks behind her head with a blue bandana. She unzipped her backpack, removed her black camera bag and set it aside. She closed the backpack, grabbed it and her suitcase, which she hadn't bothered to unpack the night before, and headed for the door. Kelli never carried a purse. In fact, she didn't own one. Living life as Kyle, all she ever needed was a backpack. *It serves the same purpose*, she told herself. *And I can carry more*. She checked through her backpack once again to ensure she had her cell phones; both of them. Once she spied them in the pack's largest pocket, stashed next to a deck of playing cards, she secured the lock on her apartment door and headed for her car. She morphed into her male form as she moved through the parking garage towards her Audi. Once safely inside and away from any pair of eyes that might be interested, she resumed her female form and started the engine.

Despite the cool March air, the sun was just beginning to peak out from under the distant horizon and illuminate the orange, cloudless sky. Kelli made it to the turnpike in record time. She cut into the fast lane as she cruised onto the 90 traveling west.

Ever since Kelli was a young girl, she'd always loved road trips. She remembered traveling to Niagara Falls with her family when she was only seven years old. For Kelli, that trip brought about the realization that there was a world beyond the Bronx. She loved staring out the window of her father's SUV as the open road zoomed by, bringing along with it new destinations and new sights. The best part was that the whole family was together. Martin was eleven years of age at the time, and Cassius was a toddling three-year old. Thinking back, it seemed strange having a memory without Wilma, who hadn't been born for another three years. Still, it was a happy time. The fond memories were the only things Kelli had to keep her connected to her family. It was these recollections that, throughout her time in Boston, had kept her sane.

Thinking of her family caused her to glance at her two cell phones that she'd placed on the empty passenger seat along with the deck of cards. One cell phone was her normal use, every day phone. It was the cell she used in her life as Kyle Cuffee. The only people who had the number who knew she was, in fact, Kelli Freeman, were Special Agents West and Davies. It was for that reason that her phone had been turned off for the last few days. She had considered changing the number when she moved into her new apartment six months ago, but she knew that would alert them to the fact that she had intentions of breaking the witness protection protocols. She didn't want that. Instead, she kept her phone on for only a certain number of hours during the day. *It's easier that way,* she had told herself.

The second cell phone was slightly smaller than the other. It had a blue tint to it which was amplified by the translucent blue phone cover that encased it. This particular phone was a pre-paid cellular. In order to use this cell, one had to purchase minutes, usually represented by a phone card, and then apply the minutes to the phone. This phone allowed Kelli to communicate secretly with members of her old life; her parents, her siblings, Calliope and Joseph Woods, Nicholas Connelly, and of course, Bryan Ling, who, after all these years, still went by his street-moniker, Bling. In order to ensure complete privacy, without the threat of being traced, Kelli had sent each of these people a pre-paid phone as well. Per her instructions, she was the only person they called with these phones, and they were the only ones to whom she placed calls as well.

She averted her eyes from the phones back to the road in front of her. As she did, the pre-paid phone began to ring. Luckily, her prepaid phone was Bluetooth capable and already synced to her vehicle's phone system. Answering the phone was as simple as pressing a button on her steering wheel. She did so without even looking at the incoming number.

"Hello," she said.

"Hey, Kel," greeted a familiar female voice.

"Hey, Cali." It was Calliope Woods, Joseph's oldest sister. Calliope was eighteen years old. She attended Yale University's School of Medicine. When she wasn't away at school, she lived with her mother in London. Since their initial meeting in Pasadena seven years ago and the events that followed, Kelli and Calliope had developed a special friendship. Given the circumstances, and their similar origins, it had been easy to build the kinship and trust that they now had for one another. At times, Kelli felt that Calliope had become as good a friend to her as Francine had been. However, it was a feeling that did not come without a certain amount of guilt; the thought that someone could possibly replace Francine? *No. Francine was dead, and no one could ever take her place,* she would tell herself. Still, Calliope's friendship had become a comfort to her, and Kelli was always glad to hear her voice.

"You're up early," Kelli said to her, glancing at the clock embedded in her dashboard.

"What else is new? On your way to New York?" Calliope asked.

"Yep."

"How was your D.C. trip?"

"Interesting, to say the least," Kelli replied.

"Least isn't what I'm looking for," Calliope snapped with a friendly tone. "How did it go?"

Kelli's heart began to race slightly. She took a deep breath before responding. She knew she was about to commit a lie of omission, and she wanted it to sound good. Deep down, she wanted to tell Calliope every detail of her little excursion. In fact, she needed very badly to open up and say, "I had him in my sights again. I wish I could just pull the trigger and kill him, Cali, and this whole thing would be over." What a relief it would be to unburden herself from the secrecy of her activities in D.C., or anything else she was planning for that matter. Still, Kelli was smart enough to know that Calliope's response would've sounded something like, "You know that's not true, Kel. If it were, you would've done it a long time ago." Kelli knew that Calliope would be right. Putting a bullet through Mr. One's skull would only provoke a major investigation and manhunt. The fallout prompted by Mr. One's assassination wouldn't be due to his status as the head of the clandestine government organization known as the Agency, but rather his *public* standing. The response would be massive. Kelli wasn't prepared for that. However, that wasn't the only reason she hadn't killed Mr. One yet.

Though Kelli had thrown herself into firearms and combat training over the last few years, she had yet to discharge her weapon at anything with a heartbeat. Shooting targets at the firing range was one thing, but killing another human being, no matter how much she felt Mr. One deserved it, was something else entirely. Kelli knew she wasn't prepared for that either. So for now, the only thing she had actually pointed at Mr. One was a *Canon 5D Mark IV*. Unfortunately, Kelli was not ready to share that tidbit of information either. Despite the years of friendship and trust between them, Kelli couldn't bring herself to tell Calliope the truth. Even though Calliope couldn't see her, Kelli forced a smile and said, "It was great. I think I could live in D.C."

"How's Martin? Did you see him?"

"Yeah," Kelli said, smiling again. "I crashed at his apartment. He's doing really well; just got hired at Jameson, Cross & Rothberg."

"Whoever they are," Calliope responded, chuckling.

"A pretty big law firm in D.C. is who they are. Martin is handling civil suits."

"Good for him. I'll stick with Bio-genetics. Now tell me about your interview."

"It went really well. Mr. Royce seemed genuinely interested in having me join his law firm," Kelli reported.

"Of course he was," Calliope said flatly. "Kyle's academic resume speaks for itself."

Kelli pressed the accelerator. "Yeah, he tried to hide his excitement. He inquired when I was planning to move to the area, to which law firms I had applied, where I saw myself in five years, you know, the normal interrogation. He seemed nice enough."

"Good," Calliope said before a long, pregnant pause. "So . . . have you talked to Joseph lately?"

"Of course," Kelli answered innocently. "Haven't you?"

"He may be my brother, but he talks to you more than he talks to me."

"That's ridiculous."

"Come on, Kel. We both know what my brother is into, and I remember how interested you were when you found out about it. Next thing I know, you two are extremely tight-lipped about your conversations."

"It's nothing to worry about," Kelli assured her.

"It's *him* I'm worried about," Calliope replied. "He has no interest whatsoever in shifting, which is fine, but I'm concerned. He never dealt with Daddy's death, and he hardly ever speaks to Mom, or to Clara. He acts like he's okay, but he's not. If he's not out screwing some high school girl, he's stuck in front of his computer-"

"He's fine," Kelli interrupted in an attempt to move the subject away from Joseph. Not only did Kelli want to keep her dealings with Joseph a secret, but changing the topic meant that Kelli wouldn't have to keep telling Calliope lies. "As far as I can tell, Joseph is pretty normal, I mean, considering the circumstances. Trust me. If he ever says anything to me that's a red flag, I'll let you know. Okay?"

Calliope sighed heavily. "Okay." Kelli could tell from Calliope's tone that it was not, in fact, okay. Kelli couldn't blame her. After all, Calliope was a genius, as well, and it didn't take an elevated I.Q. to figure out that Joseph, her fourteen-year-old baby brother, was quite possibly an elite cyber-criminal. No. As far as Calliope was concerned, it was not okay at all.

"You going to be free in about three hours?" Kelli asked, effectively switching topics. "I'm thinking about stopping by."

"No, I'm tutoring some of my classmates at the library." Not true. Calliope was clearly bothered by Kelli's reluctance to discuss Joseph. A visit from Kelli was suddenly a very low priority. "I'll take a rain check until your return trip. Okay?"

Kelli got the message loud and clear. "Sure. That's a plan," Kelli said. "Talk to you Saturday?"

"Yep. Be careful." That was the second time she'd heard those words today.

"You, too." Kelli pushed the appropriate button on her steering wheel and disconnected the call. She was disappointed that she wasn't going to see Calliope on her way to New York. Still, she understood Calliope's sudden change of attitude.

Kelli released a calming breath and focused on the road. She glanced up as her car raced by a turnpike sign that indicated Springfield was 70 miles away. She pressed the accelerator once more and pushed the car's speed past 80 miles per hour. As she did, she peered into the rearview mirror and watched as Boston disappeared behind her.

❧❧

WASHINGTON, D.C.

Molina took one last drag on her cigarette as she crossed the parking lot to the front door of the medical plaza where Doctors Patel, Suri and Chen practiced medicine. She held the tobacco laced smoke in her lungs as she tugged at the door. It didn't budge. Molina looked at the watch strapped to her right wrist.

'Damn,' she thought to herself as she took note of the time. The medical plaza didn't open for patients until 8 a.m. Until then, the only access granted to the building was through the use of an access card keyed for the card reader alongside the door. She exhaled, releasing the hot, white smoke into the air as she reached into her back pocket and retrieved her card. This process annoyed Molina, especially now, when she was in such a rush to get inside. She'd received a call less than an hour ago. Iris was here, and Molina came to retrieve her and get some answers.

West slipped out from behind the steering wheel of his car. From within the parking structure, he could see the towering edifice before him that was Howard University Hospital. West moved quickly to the elevator in the far corner of the parking garage. He pressed the *down* button and waited. As he stood there, he pulled his cell phone from the leather case that was attached to his belt. He held it in his hand as he watched for the wall light to indicate the arrival of the elevator. Thirty seconds later, the light flashed to life with a corresponding 'ding' and the elevator doors parted in front of him. In an attempt to appear inconspicuous, West put the phone to his ear and peered inside. The car was empty. *Good*, he thought as he lowered his phone and stepped inside. He pressed the button labeled 'B' and exhaled anxiously as the doors closed.

West relaxed his shoulders and leaned against the wall. He took in a deep breath and released the air slowly in an attempt to calm his nerves. For close to seven years, West had been chasing one dead end after another in an effort to find some, or rather any, evidence that he could use to expose the Agency and put an end to their unchecked, vigilante justice. Unfortunately, West's primary problem had less to do with exposing the Agency than it was about getting someone to go on record and verify its existence. In the seven years that West had been working the assignment, he had found three people who hinted that they were aware of the Agency. He had attended two of their funerals, while the third person had disappeared completely. Still, Assistant Director Marsh insisted that West keep digging. So he did. Ironically, it was about two years ago when Marsh himself came to West with a possible lead. After everything that West had experienced at the hands of the Agency; the unnecessary deaths, the ordeal with Kelli, and of course, the betrayal by his late partner and mentor, Special Agent James Towers, West was all ears.

Assistant Director Marsh had arranged a clandestine meeting with West and told him, under no circumstances, was he to inform his partner, Special Agent Bonner. Reluctantly, West agreed and met Marsh in a bar on Bourbon Street in New Orleans.

Marsh's demeanor, as usual, was calm. "Two days ago, I received a phone call from Paul Ferry, an old friend of mine," Marsh had said as he sipped a 7-up through a straw. "He and I were at Quantico together." Marsh swallowed hard and chewed on a small piece of ice before he continued. "About eight years after we graduated, Paul caught this big case, accidentally mind you, something to do with international espionage and American mercenaries."

"The Bureau was dealing with that?" West had questioned, surprised.

"No," Marsh had replied. "Strictly CIA, military intelligence type stuff, but Paul happened to be in the right place at the right time. In order to ensure his discretion, the CIA took him along for the ride and let him work with them. Next thing I know, Paul is leaving for Beirut or someplace like that. Three months later we get word that Paul had been killed in a hotel bombing."

"Oh my God," West said. "His family must have been devastated."

"Paul didn't have any family," Marsh had explained. "In retrospect, he was an ideal candidate."

"I don't follow."

"When Paul called, revealing that he had been alive all this time, he said that he had been recruited by our government to work on a White List project within an organization called *Department 12*."

"Department 12? Never heard of it."

"Yes, you have," Marsh countered. "Department 12 is a ghost organization, one that has so much freedom to exercise power and impose their will that no one really believes they exist. Of course, those of us who are aware of their existence know them by their more common, unofficial name."

West knew instantly which organization Marsh was describing. "The Agency."

Marsh nodded. "They gave him a new identity and assigned him to a mercenary team that travelled the globe, whenever and wherever they were needed."

"What's his new identity?" West had asked with the eagerness of a school girl about to kiss her crush for the first time.

Marsh killed it instantly. "Can't tell you," he said. "The less you know, the better right now. You know how these things work."

Despite his disappointment, West did know. He dropped the question of Ferry's new identity.

Marsh continued. "Anyway, Paul was back in the States and he'd been watch-dogging a lot of their assignments over here. He told me that he could actually see the necessity for an entity such as the Agency. Even so, at times he saw the lines blurring and he wasn't sure where the lines of decency, if any, were being crossed. He needed someone to talk to but he didn't know who to trust."

"So he called *you*," West surmised.

"Yeah," Marsh had said, seemingly disappointed, "he called me."

The elevator came to a jerky stop on the basement level of the parking structure, snapping West back to the present. As he stood patiently, he thought of all the 'heads-up intel' that Ferry had provided over the last two years. When it came to anything that could be perceived as a threat to the safety and complacency of the United States, the Agency had a hand in making it right. Unfortunately, the Agency would always clean up their messes before West, the media, or even the local authorities could arrive. Even with Ferry feeding Marsh information about when and where things would occur, the Agency always managed to stay one step ahead. The raid in Indiana turned out to be no different. *Whatever biochemical Ferry thought we would find in that transport van, wasn't there.* That revelation left West with two possible explanations; either Ferry was wrong, or Ferry led them on a wild goose chase. Based on Ferry's past intel and his relationship with Marsh, West found it hard to believe that Ferry would knowingly mislead them. Unfortunately, that train of thought led to another grave possibility; the Agency was aware that Ferry was leaking information, and they used us to prove it. West shook off the chill that ran up his spine. He considered the bright side. *At least we got Navarro off the street.* Despite that outcome, West couldn't help but feel that something bigger was going on.

The elevator doors parted quietly. West stepped out of the elevator. The cool morning air swept across his face, awakened his senses, and drew the fatigue from his body. He took a deep breath and began the short walk towards the edge of the parking structure that led to the adjacent hospital.

As he passed through the double sliding doors that granted access to the first floor of the hospital, West couldn't help but think of the time he visited Towers in Brooklyn Hospital. Towers had been wounded during the pursuit of murder suspect Keith Waters. West, one day after putting a bullet through Waters' skull, went to the hospital to retrieve his injured partner. It was then that Towers sent West on a blind mission that put him on a collision course with the Agency. It was the day that changed his life and his world view forever.

West took another elevator up to the sixth floor. As the doors slid to one side, the first person he saw standing in the corridor was Assistant Director Marsh. Marsh came to meet him as he stepped off the elevator.

"Donald," Marsh greeted him with a grave expression.

"Sir," West responded.

"I appreciate you getting here so quickly," Marsh said.

"Not a problem." West stared anxiously down the corridor. When Marsh summoned him to the hospital four hours ago, the only details he had revealed to West were as follows: Howard University Hospital, sixth floor, and the name Paul Ferry. Marsh ended his brief message with the words, 'Drop everything. Come now.' West knew that if Marsh was calling him about Ferry, it was tied to the Agency. West complied without a second thought or an explanation to his partner. Needless to say, Bonner was not happy. West felt bad about it. He knew what it was like to discover that you've been left in the dark. It wasn't exactly a feeling that engendered trust in your partner. After the whole ordeal with Towers seven years ago, West didn't want to be in another partnership like that ever again. Unfortunately, it was happening with Bonner. This time, however, it was West who was keeping secrets. He hated it. In fact, he struggled daily with whether or not to bring Bonner into the fold. He was hoping that, whatever the situation was with Paul Ferry, it would lead to an end of the Agency and allow West to come clean. Fortunately, West was not naïve. He knew that any resolution to the Agency problem would not come easily. Still, he was here. Ever hopeful and ready to do whatever it took to get the job done.

West exhaled slowly as Marsh led him up the corridor. Since they were meeting secretly in a hospital, West surmised that the patient was Paul Ferry and the prognosis wasn't good. This part of the job never came easy to West, especially when dealing with the Agency. Whenever they encountered anyone involved with or who had knowledge of the Agency, the person was soon dead or dying. Again, West imagined that this situation was no different.

They stopped at the entrance to Room 623. The door opened up slightly and Dr. Jeffery Horowitz stepped into the hallway. Horowitz was a 61-year-old Caucasian man.

His white skin was pale, and covered with noticeable wrinkles. His bright blue eyes sat behind a pair of expensive, black framed Perry Ellis eyeglasses. His hair was silver-gray and he stood at 5'10" tall. He breathed a sigh of relief when he saw Assistant Director Marsh.

"Thank God," he said. He gestured towards West with a nod of his head. "Is this who we're waiting for?"

Marsh nodded. "Dr. Horowitz, this is Special Agent West. He's one of my most trusted and dedicated agents."

"That's good," Horowitz replied. "And you will be assuming responsibility, correct?"

Another nod from Marsh. "You're in the clear, Doctor."

West looked at Marsh, confused.

Marsh explained quickly. "As you know, all gunshot wounds need to be reported. When they brought Ferry in earlier, he begged the good doctor not to call the locals, only me."

"He swore to me that calling the DCPD would put him in further danger," the doctor stated. "Though I admit, I was inclined to call them anyway. Of course, once I saw his credentials, I decided otherwise."

"And we appreciate it," Marsh assured him. He looked past Horowitz into the room. "How is he?"

"Fighting to hang on, but . . ." the doctor paused. "He doesn't have very long. His injuries are too extensive."

"Then let's not waste time," Marsh said, though it sounded more like a plea.

"Of course," Horowitz agreed. He turned and walked back into the room. Marsh and West followed.

Marsh approached Ferry's bedside. As if he felt Marsh's presence, Ferry's eyes snapped open.

West saw the unmistakable look of fear in Ferry's eyes. It was only after Ferry focused on Marsh and realized who he was that he relaxed.

Ferry managed a pained smile. "Stevie," he said.

"Hey, Paul," Marsh replied.

"Looks like . . . I'm really checkin' out this time," Ferry said.

Marsh reached out and touched Ferry's shoulder. It pained him to see his longtime friend in such bad condition. It wasn't that Marsh hadn't lost friends and colleagues in the past. In fact, he had lost plenty, both in the line of duty and personal. But this was different. Marsh and Ferry suffered through Quantico together. They, like any other pair of friends who had gone through any type of law enforcement academy, developed a kinship, a bond, a lifetime connection. During their training, Marsh and Ferry had shared their dreams with one another; visions of changing the world, becoming the best of the best, and making a true impact in the field of law enforcement. Seeing Ferry lying on his deathbed reminded Marsh of how young and naïve they were, and of the reality that the world was not at all how they once perceived it.

Marsh squeezed Ferry's shoulder. "Nonsense. We're supposed to go out together. Remember?"

"Seems like I'm gonna beat you to it," he said, then coughed heavily.

"Agent Marsh," Dr. Horowitz spoke softly, "Please hurry."

Marsh nodded. He leaned in closer to Ferry. "Sorry, Paul. I need whatever information you have."

Ferry managed a nod. He glanced over at West. "That your boy?" Ferry asked Marsh.

"Yeah. That's Special Agent West."

Ferry shifted his gaze back to Marsh. He inhaled deeply, mustering up what little strength he had left. When he spoke, his breathing was noticeably labored. "I was transferred stateside about three months ago. I was. . ." his voice trailed off. He managed another deep breath, then, ". . . assigned to safeguard a group of doctors, uh, geneticists . . . Specialists they called them."

"They?" Marsh asked.

"They," Ferry answered. "The Agency . . . Department 12. They had these doctors working on eugenics, human cloning. . . I bet that's what they needed the biochemicals for."

West and Marsh glanced at each other. West had already given Marsh his full report about the raid in Indiana. Marsh was not pleased.

Ferry continued. "There was this young girl that Dr. Patel was treating."

"For what?"

Ferry shook his head. "Don't know. I'd only been there three months and I wasn't in the need-to-know circle. I would pick up bits and pieces here and there . . . but Patel, while treating the girl, claimed he found something in her blood that would change everything."

West took a step forward and spoke up. "This girl? Who is she?"

"Young, teenager . . . fair skinned black girl, maybe Hispanic. I'm not sure. Iris. I think her name is Iris. Whatever it was that Patel discovered about her, he ran it up the chain. Someone at the top told him to stop barking up that tree."

"But Patel didn't," Marsh surmised.

"No. Patel was scared all of a sudden. I didn't even know what was going on when he asked me to come with him this morning. I mean, that was my assignment, right?"

"Of course," Marsh agreed. "So, what happened?"

"Patel grabbed the girl this morning and decided to run with her."

"To where?" West questioned.

"I don't know his end destination, but we ran to one of our safe houses outside of D.C. He needed a place to regroup. He said he was protecting her. I was outside checking the perimeter when the house was blown apart."

"A bomb?"

Ferry nodded. "Don't know how and when she got it, or even how she knew what was going down."

"She?" Marsh asked.

"Yeah, the girl," Ferry assured him. "She blew up the house . . . and then she put four bullets in me."

"Are you sure?" Marsh asked.

"I'm sure, Stevie." Ferry struggled for air. He exhaled heavily, forcing out the words, "The girl killed me."

Dr. Horowitz raised his right hand. "That'll be all for now. The patient must rest."

Marsh and West complied. After a soft pat on Ferry's shoulder and a sincere expression of gratitude, Marsh turned to leave the room. Ferry called to him once more. Marsh turned back. Ferry gestured towards the dining tray. A large paper bag sat there next to a Styrofoam cup of untouched ice cream. Marsh grabbed the bag. He looked inside to find Ferry's weapon, a .40 caliber Sig Sauer. Next to the gun were Ferry's Agency credentials. Marsh looked at Ferry.

"I don't want to be buried with that name. You understand?"

Marsh understood. Ferry, being an operative of The Agency, had been given a new identity. Marsh knew that underneath that new identity was a good man; a man that he'd known for years, a man who deserved to be laid to rest under his birth given name. Marsh would see to it that it happened.

Marsh exited the room with West in tow. He reached into the bag and retrieved Ferry's Agency I.D. He opened it up and looked at the name. *Special Agent Michael Rose.* Marsh looked over at West who had fallen strangely silent.

Since Ferry's revelation about the young female shooter, West hadn't spoken a word. His brain was still trying to process the information in hopes of coming up with a suspect other than the one to whom the evidence was pointing. West shook his head. He didn't want to believe it. He returned Marsh's gaze. In that one instant, he knew that Marsh was coming to the same conclusions as he.

"When's the last time you saw the Freeman girl?"

West shrugged. The last seven years working with the Bureau had kept him busy, especially on cases that smelled like they had the Agency's stink on them. During that time, West's visits to Kelli in Boston became much fewer and further between. Though Special Agent Davies was the primary liaison, West had vowed to stay in contact with Kelli. He promised that their friendship would endure the test of time. It was a promise that West had failed to keep. The last contact he had with Kelli had been over the phone almost two years prior. It was then that she'd made her feelings about his *abandonment* crystal clear. West wasn't proud of it. In fact, it was a sentiment he had grown accustomed to hearing. He wasn't proud of that either.

"You know her better than I do," Marsh stated. "You think Ferry was talking about her?"

"I don't see how," West responded. "Kelli's no murderer, and she certainly wouldn't be working for the Agency. They tried to kill her. Remember?"

"They also genetically engineered her," Marsh reminded him. "And it wasn't so she could be socked away in witness protection."

"They think she's dead," West countered.

"Do they?" Marsh questioned. He stepped closer to West. "Look. It's highly improbable that the shooter is your girl, but you know as well as I do, that when it comes to the Agency, nothing is impossible. So, I suggest you contact her so we can rule her out as a suspect," he paused for a second before adding, "Or not."

4

WASHINGTON, D.C.

West savored the familiar, comforting sensation of warmth as he gulped down a hot swig of his Starbuck's venti White Chocolate Mocha. He placed the white and green cup into the cup holder in the center console of his government issued grey sedan and refocused his attention on the freeway ahead. The dashboard clock read 6:35 a.m. West cursed silently and shook his head in frustration. Despite his morning jog routine, he was not a morning person. The only thing he hated more than having to wake up at the crack of dawn was waking up at the crack of dawn in order to catch a flight. It was a flight he was going to most certainly miss if he didn't put his coffee down long enough to navigate safely through the morning rush on the George Washington Parkway. Unfortunately, as luck would often have it, there was always a distraction when one was in a rush. West grimaced as this morning's distraction presented itself in the form of his ringing cell phone.

West pulled the cell phone from his jacket pocket and pressed the button. He hadn't bothered to sync his phone to the sedan's Bluetooth system, so he had no choice but to forego the standard 'hands free' protocol. Even though he was an FBI Agent, it still bothered him to do so. West didn't like breaking the law.

"This is West," he announced into his cell phone.

"Where are you?" Marsh's voice asked.

"On my way to the airport," West replied wearily. "I couldn't reach *our girl* on her cell. It kept going straight to voicemail, so I've got to go to Boston myself."

"Turn around," Marsh ordered. "I've already got Davies on it."

"What? Why?"

The tone of Marsh's voice was grave. "I'm at the hospital. Paul Ferry died ten minutes ago."

West opened his mouth to offer his condolences but found himself at a loss for words. He knew that no sentiment could offer sufficient comfort to someone who had just experienced the loss of a friend. Even though Marsh and Ferry had only sporadic contact over the last two years, West knew that Marsh was affected by Ferry's passing.

West swallowed hard and managed to say, "Sorry, sir. I know he was a friend."

"We can mourn later. Ferry went out fighting. Before he died, he gave me the location of that safe house where he was shot."

West perked up. "Yeah?"

"It's just beyond Arlington's city limits."

West used his left hand and pushed up on the indicator lever. The resulting clicking sound told him that his right indicator light was flashing, signaling his intention to switch lanes in order to take the next off ramp. "I'm all ears."

West surmised that the Agency had already gotten to the site of the decimated safe house and extracted any pertinent evidence. Still, he wanted to get there and go over the scene himself. Even though the Agency seemed to always be one step ahead of him, West hoped that maybe he'd get lucky and find something they missed.

৵৽

Marsh paced slowly up the hospital corridor. He had just given West directions to the safe house where Ferry claimed a young girl detonated an explosive minutes before shooting him at point blank range.

Marsh stared at the doorway to Ferry's room. Several members of the hospital staff were still in the room with Ferry's corpse. "They already covered his body, for Christ's sake," he mumbled under his breath. "What the hell are they doing in there now?" Marsh didn't want to wait for an answer. Instead, he wanted to leave the hospital, get into his car and drive away. But he couldn't. Marsh knew that he had a responsibility to his deceased friend. He had made a promise, and he intended to keep it.

Marsh decided he needed some fresh air. He turned and headed for the elevator. His mind was lost in thought as he lamented over his friend's death. He reached the end of the corridor and waited patiently as the elevator approached.

At the other end of the hall, Brandon Kincaid, a lean Caucasian man in his late twenties stood and watched Marsh as the elevator arrived. Kincaid was dressed in a gray suit with a black button-down shirt underneath. He wore no tie. He watched as Marsh stepped in and disappeared behind the closing doors. Kincaid retrieved his cell phone from his suit jacket and placed a call. He stood silently until the line clicked open on the other end.

"It's me," Kincaid said. "I found him."

"And?"

"He was already dead when I got here," he said flatly. "But we may have another problem."

"What's that?"

"A.D. Marsh was here."

"You think Marsh got to him before he died?"

"No way of knowing, my friend. But we need to report this."

"We will. Come in and we'll handle it together. I have to call and report in anyway."

Kincaid was confused. "Why? What's up?"

The voice on the phone chuckled. "Not sure. Some woman, a senior agent, just showed up, and she's clearly pissed."

Kincaid grinned. "Interesting."

"Oh, and Brandon," the voice on the phone called out, his tone lighter. "French Vanilla flavored, okay?"

"Excuse me?"

"The Spurs lost last night," the man on the phone teased. "That means you're buying coffee for the next week. Black, three sugars. Go to Dunkin Donuts, there's one on Benning off 44th. You trackin'?"

"Yeah, yeah. Got it," he muttered as he hung up the phone. "Three sugars. Geez."

BRONX, NEW YORK

A cool, March morning breeze parted the curtains and washed across Bling's face. He opened his eyes, took in his surroundings, and then smiled. Waking up in this apartment was still new to him, and he had experienced feelings of contentment and fulfillment every morning since he and his girlfriend, Zenaida Rodriguez, moved in twelve days ago. Bling rolled over in bed only to come in contact with Zenaida's sleeping form. Another smile forced its way across his lips. As she did often, Zenaida was sleeping on her right side. Bling reached out and touched her hip, which was covered solely by a single sheet. Bling ran his hand along her curvy frame, and then down to the small of her back. *Her skin is so soft*, he thought to himself. He still couldn't believe that he was here, with her, like this.

He moved his hand underneath the sheet and began to massage lower. Only then, did Zenaida reveal that she was awake.

"Mr. Ling," she said playfully, "I've got a mid-term to take today, so don't start something you can't finish."

She rolled over and faced him. Her thick, black hair fell away from her face, unveiling a pair of sparkling brown eyes set against a backdrop of pecan-colored skin. She smiled, revealing a set of perfectly aligned, white teeth. Zenaida had four years of wearing braces to thank for the beautiful smile, an attribute Bling made a point of complimenting every day.

"That will make three mornings in a row," Bling said.

"You complaining?"

"No way, girl," he said with a lascivious grin. "I just don't want you gettin' tired of a brotha, you know?"

She reached up and wrapped her arms around his neck, pulling him closer. "Treat me right and we'll have no worries."

She began placing a series of small pecks on his lips.

"What about *you* treatin' *me* right?" he asked between kisses.

"I think I've got that covered," she responded before they fell into a deep kiss.

Bling took Zenaida into his arms and held her tight. As their bodies began to move in sync with one another, Bling became lost in the moment. Never before had things in his life felt so right, so natural, and so safe. He was happier than he had been in a long time, and he wanted nothing to mess up the good life he had built over the last few years. As far as Bling was concerned, nothing could.

However, across the room, hidden deep within an inner pocket of his backpack, Bling's secret pre-paid cellular phone, in silent mode, received an incoming call.

WASHINGTON, D.C.

The doctor's office was quiet. It was close to 7:30 in the morning and the morning nurse, Gisela, had yet to arrive. Dr. Suri looked through the appointments that Kirsten had set up for him today. His first patient wasn't set to arrive for another thirty minutes. Still, Suri came into the office early today for another reason. That reason entered the room in the form of Agent Molina.

Suri turned to her as she entered. "Agent Molina."

Molina was far beyond the pretense of being cordial. She was angry and she didn't care who knew it. "Where is she?"

"She's here," Suri told her. "She's resting."

"Bullshit," Molina snapped. "You've kept me waiting almost an hour."

"What? No." Suri understood Molina's anger. After all, this concerned her daughter. Still, Suri was wounded by Molina's lack of trust in him. Despite her current state of emotion, Molina took notice.

"It's true," said another male voice from behind Molina.

Agent Molina turned as a middle-aged Asian man, who was quite short in stature, entered the room. He wore a white lab coat over his suit and he carried a patient file in his hand. Molina failed in her attempt to appear more relaxed at the sight of him. "Dr. Chen. Where's Iris?"

Dr. Chen stopped short of her position just inside the room. He reached out and touched Molina's shoulder gently, as if to calm or comfort her. "She's a little tired, but she is fine. I promise you."

"I want to see her," Molina demanded, shrugging off Chen's hand.

"Of course," Chen responded cheerfully, and then cast a menacing glare at Suri. "I don't see what the problem is."

Chen directed Molina through the open door and into the hallway. Before Chen could exit the office, Suri took him by the arm.

"What the hell is going on?" he whispered.

Chen yanked his arm free of Suri's grasp. "I'll explain what I know later." With that, he turned and exited the room.

Suri shook his head. Doctors Chen and Patel had done something that involved the patient, Iris Molina. *But what?* Suri knew why Iris was being treated by two world-renowned specialists in their field. What he didn't know was why he'd been left out of the loop. *What happened yesterday?* he wondered. *And why didn't they inform her mother? Or me?* Suri was suspicious. He knew that when someone was left in the dark concerning Agency business, there was a reason. Suri didn't like it. He didn't like it one bit.

Dr. Chen guided Agent Molina to a patient room at the end of the left corridor. As they approached the door, Molina realized that she'd been to this room before. This was a room that civilian patients never saw. This room was set aside especially for Agency operatives, and now, Iris was in there. Molina didn't like the implication. This wasn't how things were supposed to happen. When the Agency moved her and Iris across the country, they told her that the program had been terminated and that they could live out their lives like normal civilians. They promised that this was where Iris would receive the best medical care. Molina had wanted to believe it. She had ignored her gut feeling and convinced herself it was the truth. It wasn't until Dr. Chen opened the door and she saw Iris lying peacefully on the bed that she accepted the fact that it was all a lie.

Iris was a brown, fair-skinned beauty. Her thick, curly black hair flowed loosely upon her shoulders. Her deep, brown eyes were concealed behind her closed eyelids as she slept. Molina approached the bed slowly. She smiled to herself at the sight of her daughter. Lying there, Iris appeared to be a normal seventeen-year-old girl, one free from the harsh realities of the real world. Molina liked to pretend that Iris didn't have it harder than any other girl her age, and she would have allowed herself to live in that fantasy if it were not for the catheter that connected Iris to the dialysis cycler next to the bed. Instantly, Molina's heart grew heavy with sadness. The truth was, Iris did have it harder than most teenage girls, and for more than one reason.

Though Molina loved and cared for Iris as any mother should, the fact was that Iris was not her biological daughter. Iris was no one's child due to the fact that she was not the product of sexual reproduction, at least not in the carnal sense. No. Iris was a genetically engineered and enhanced super-clone. Molina was never told from whom Iris was cloned, but she did know that Iris' true age was closer to seven years, rather than seventeen. As it was in the original cloning experiment involving Dolly the Lamb back in 1996, Iris was not cloned from an embryo. As far as Molina knew, Iris was cloned from the cells of a four-teen-year-old girl; a girl who died seven years prior. Molina was brought into Iris' life during the clone's infancy. It was then that Molina was tasked with her guardianship, her care, and her nurturing. Though Molina was initially reluctant to taking on such an *assignment*, she fell in love with the child and soon, as any mother would, declared that she would, if necessary, protect Iris with her own life. Unfortunately, as she stared at the catheter, Molina knew she could not protect Iris from the one enemy that had plagued her short life from the very beginning.

Months after Iris came into being, her growth rate was measured and labeled as abnormal. After an initial physical exam, it was determined that Iris' renal system, specifically her left kidney, was dysfunctional. Dr. William Chen, a well-known expert in the field of nephrology, was enlisted by the Agency and assigned to Iris' health care. After months of treating Iris, Dr. Chen made two determinations. The first determination was that removing the left kidney was Iris' best chance for survival. The second, that Iris' renal problems were not the cause of her unusually rapid growth, in fact, it was the other way around. The accelerated growth caused the kidney dysfunction, and the acceleration was a bi-product of the cloning process.

Dr. Arav Suri, the geneticist who engineered Iris' cloned existence, had been transferred to another assignment to work on future phases of the Harmony Project. However, once Iris' health problems were diagnosed, Suri was brought back onto the case and paired with Chen and another renowned genetics expert, Dr. Ramesh Patel. Together, the three specialists monitored Iris' condition. Soon, they discovered that not only was Iris growing rapidly, but she was aging prematurely as well. Within the first twelve months, Iris aged four and a half years. Not surprisingly, considering her genetic enhancements, her intelligence was on par with most nine-year-olds. Suri and Patel surmised that Iris' rapid aging was due to the fact that the donor cell was taken from a fourteen-year-old subject, and that her accelerated growth and maturity was her body's response to match that age, in essence, fully completing the cloning process.

Over the next two years, Iris aged nine. As her body neared the age of her donor, Iris' growth rate began to stabilize. During the four years that followed, Iris began to seemingly age and grow as any other teenage girl. Molina could not contain her joy. She took Iris out to dinner every night that week to celebrate. Unfortunately, the celebration did not last long. It was Dr. Suri who placed the call informing Molina that, despite the fact that Iris' unnatural growth and aging had subsided, the damage to her renal system had already been done. Iris still had her right kidney, but there were definite indications that, despite her enhanced immune system, it would eventually fail as well.

As Molina approached the bed, Iris' eyes snapped open. She turned her head slightly to the right and smiled at the sight of the only mother she had ever known.

"Hi, Mom," she said softly.

"Hey, Mija," Molina responded, extremely relieved that Iris was awake. "How are you feeling? Are you okay?"

Iris shifted her body on the bed slightly as if to gauge how she was feeling. "Yeah. I feel fine." The young girl sniffed the air. "You're smoking again."

"Nothing gets by that super-nose of yours."

"You wouldn't need a super-nose to smell that, Mom."

"I'll quit again." Iris shot her a sideways glance, to which Molina responded, "I promise. I was just so worried about you."

"I'm okay," Iris assured her.

"Are you sure?" Molina questioned. "When I got the call yesterday that Dr. Patel had removed you from school- "

"I'm fine, Mom," Iris interrupted. "This had nothing to do with my kidneys."

Molina exhaled a quick sigh of relief. *Thank God!* "Well, then, tell me what happened. Where'd you disappear to?"

Iris opened her mouth to respond but no sound came out. All at once, her face crinkled in anguish and she started to cry. "I'm sorry, Mom. I know I should have told you. I mean, I wanted to, but he told me not to."

Molina leaned in close. She brushed her thumb across Iris' cheek and pushed away a tear. "Who's he? Patel?"

"Not Dr. Patel." Iris raised her head off the pillow slightly and whispered, "Mr. Five. He told me not to say anything until I was debriefed."

Molina became incensed. She could not believe what she was hearing, but the words that Iris spoke only confirmed what she had hoped was not the case; specifically the word *debrief*, and the mention of Mr. Five. Up until now, Molina had feared that Patel removed Iris from school due to a health issue involving her kidneys. But the realization that the Agency had used her child, her teenage daughter, on an assignment made her Latin blood boil.

"Mr. Five spoke to you? In person?" That was not standard protocol.

Iris nodded. She could tell by Molina's outward reaction, the widening of her eyes, and the clenching of her lips that her mother was beyond furious. As a result, Iris began to cry harder.

"I'm sorry, Mom."

Molina sat on the edge of the bed and took her young daughter in her arms. She held Iris close and rocked slightly. "Shh, it's okay, Mija. No tienes la culpa. Escuche. It's not your fault."

Through her tears, Iris continued to explain. "He told me that it was important to keep it a secret."

"It's all right," Molina continued to reassure Iris as she squeezed her tight. "I'm here now. Everything's going to be okay." Despite her calming words, Molina knew it was not going to be okay. Never before had she seen her daughter so visibly shaken and rattled. Whatever happened to Iris, it was big, and Molina was determined to get to the bottom of it.

⚜

Kincaid entered the conference room located in the far back corner of the medical building. In his hand, he held a Dunkin Donuts French Vanilla Coffee, which, upon entering, he handed over to the other man in the room.

"As requested," Kincaid said to the man.

Special Agent Darren Peppers was in his late forties. Though his face still held a youthful appearance, his hair was completely gray. In his pre-Agency operative life, which ended fifteen years prior, Peppers was a Lieutenant on a Navy seal team. A botched mission, one which left him the sole survivor of his unit, ironically, allowed for a new start and purpose with the Agency. For the majority of the time, Peppers maintained a calm, cool demeanor that allowed him to keep a level head, even in the most tense and dangerous situations. It was a quality that he was hoping to instill in his much younger, more gung-ho partner, Special Agent Brandon Kincaid.

Kincaid enlisted in the U.S. Marines at the tender age of eighteen. It was discovered quite quickly by his superiors that Kincaid had a very particular skill set; he could shoot an apple off of an aluminum soda can from beyond 500 yards. The Agency wasted very little time arranging his apparent death so they could recruit him into their ranks. Kincaid was more than happy to join the clandestine organization and serve his country on a higher level. It was a decision he had yet to regret in the ten years since he agreed to come on board.

"Any word yet on why we're here?" Kincaid asked his partner.

"Nope," Peppers responded calmly. "But I'm willing to bet it has something to do with the girl they brought in earlier."

"What girl?"

Peppers took a sip of the coffee. "I don't know, some kid."

"Where's the two-man unit that was originally assigned here?"

"Don't know that either. But I'd bet one of them is that dead agent at the hospital."

"Aw, man. Don't tell me they have us here babysitting."

"That's what I thought, too, at first," Peppers said. "But that woman, the senior agent I mentioned . . . from what I overheard, I think the girl belongs to her."

Kincaid was frustrated. "Then why call us? We don't handle this little crap, Pepp. When we get the call, we go overseas and silence whichever tyrant is threatening our country's interests. That's what *we* do. This *den mother* crap here-"

"May be bigger than it currently appears," said Peppers. "While I was eavesdropping, I heard the female agent mention Mr. Five several times, and she wasn't using her inside voice." Peppers gestured to the white phone that sat in the center of the only table in the room. "I wouldn't be surprised if he called in any minute."

Kincaid pulled out a chair and sat with a loud thump. "Huh. I wonder what's going on."

"Well," Peppers began, "they called us in for something, and I'd be willing to bet it ain't babysitting."

❧❦

"What on Earth is going on?" Suri asked Chen once they were back in Suri's office behind closed doors.

"I don't know if I should say," Chen confessed.

"What do you mean?" Suri took a step towards his colleague. "I know this has something to do with Dr. Patel's discovery."

Chen nodded.

"He was told to leave it alone," Suri reminded Chen, who, in fact, needed no reminder.

"Well, he didn't," Chen stated bluntly. "Not for long, anyway."

"William! Talk to me."

"Okay," Chen said as he took a step forward and closed the gap between them. When he spoke, his voice was considerably lower in volume. "Patel thought that Iris' blood had additional rejuvenating properties, that her body was somehow healing itself. She continued to show improvement even during the times when we took her off the meds."

"This isn't news," Suri informed him. "She's engineered to heal quickly. Tell me something I don't know."

"Right. After Mr. Five brought word that Dr. Patel was to ignore his findings, Patel wouldn't accept it."

"Yes, I know," Suri said, exasperated.

"Yes, well, what you don't know is that Patel kept digging."

"Into what?"

"The HP-47 Vaccine."

"What?" Suri was confused. HP-47 was an experimental vaccine supplied by Quinlan Pharmaceuticals that Suri, Chen and Patel had been using to treat Iris' renal condition. The vaccine showed slow, yet promising results. Unfortunately, Quinlan informed them that the supply of HP-47 had become depleted and they would cease their distribution of the drug within a three-month period. That unhappy news came three months ago.

Chen continued. "After we found out that the vaccine was going to be cut off, Patel decided to create his own version of the drug by reverse engineering what was left of the HP-47."

Suri shrugged. "What's the big deal? That's an ingenious idea."

"The big deal is that, while he was reverse-engineering the vaccine, he discovered that the healing properties did not originate in Iris' blood, but from the vaccine itself."

Suri was unimpressed. "That's what vaccines are supposed to do, William. That's why people get vaccinations, to prevent and cure illness."

"Yes, but when Patel took the vaccine apart, he found human DNA at the base."

Suri's eyes widened in disbelief. "What? Whose DNA?"

"He never found out. But Patel suspected it may have come from Harmony June herself."

Suri nodded. "Makes sense. Go on."

"After he came across the DNA, he ran it back up the chain of command-"

"And they still told him to abandon it?"

"No," Chen replied. "In fact, they told him to keep working on it, to perfect it."

"That's wonderful news," said Suri excitedly. "Did it work?"

"Initially, no. I mean, it worked as long as Patel used the DNA from the HP-47 as a base."

"But our supply was cut off."

"Yes, so Patel came up with the brilliant idea to disassemble the remaining HP-47 and clone the DNA itself to create an endless supply."

Suri smiled. "That's fascinating."

"Yes, it was," Chen agreed. "Patel even came up with a batch that he wanted to test on Iris. Everything was going according to plan, but over the weekend, Quinlan Pharmaceuticals swooped in and confiscated the new vaccine; research and all. They assumed control of the entire project and took over production."

"So when does Iris get it?"

Chen's posture deflated slightly. "She doesn't. Per orders from Mr. One himself, Iris' treatments were to be terminated."

"That's insane. She'll die. Why would they do that?"

"I don't know, but Patel felt he had to do something," Chen said. "Patel had one last dose of the original HP-47, so he grabbed Iris and decided to run with her. He wanted to take her somewhere safe, somewhere he could continue her treatments."

"Only a fool would attempt that. And, apparently, it didn't work because Iris is back and Pa. . ." his voice trailed off. "Where's Dr. Patel now?"

Chen's gaze met Suri's eyes squarely. "We both know the answer to that."

Suri felt suddenly weak in the knees and his stomach threatened to turn over and eject the contents of his breakfast. Suri sat in the chair behind his large oak desk to collect himself. "Unbelievable," he said quietly after a few moments. He looked up at Chen. "How do you know all this? And why didn't either of you tell *me*?"

"Patel kept me advised about most of it as it happened. We decided not to tell you because you developed the closest bond with the girl and her mother. We knew that you wouldn't be able to resist telling them and getting their hopes up. If it all fell apart-"

"It *did* fall apart," Suri snapped. He was disappointed in his colleagues for not confiding in him, and he was angered by the implication that his personal connection with the Molinas would influence his ability to keep the secret. At the latter, he could not stay angry for he knew his colleagues were right. However, being left out of the loop was unacceptable. "You should have told me," he admonished Chen. "Maybe I could have helped. I could have done something. Any solution would have been better than running away with the girl."

"I had no idea Patel was going to take the girl until after he had already done it," Chen said. "He called and left a message on my cell saying he was at the school. Once I realized what he was doing, I didn't answer my cell phone for the rest of the day."

"Why not?" Suri asked.

"I was distancing myself. I advise you to do the same." Chen turned and moved towards the door. He twisted the knob and pulled it open. Before he left, he turned back to Dr. Suri and added, "Trust me, my friend. If Mr. Five walks through this door and starts asking questions about yesterday, the less you know, the better."

Mr. One's personal cell phone rang only a few times during any given day. Depending on the time of day, Mr. One knew exactly who was calling him without having to look at the caller I.D. Day in and day out, Mr. One received the same calls from the same people at, relatively, the same time every day. Mr. One liked it that way. He took comfort in the unchanging routine. It was only on days like today, when his personal cell phone rang *off-schedule*, that Mr. One felt uneasy. More so, because this unscheduled personal call was one he was expecting. The phone rang four times before his old, bumbling, arthritic fingers secured it from his jacket pocket and pressed the button to answer the call.

"Hello," he said in a low, even tone. A short pause. "Yes, this is he."

Across the room, the door was pushed ajar and Mr. Two entered quietly. He crossed the room almost as silently as he had entered it. He took each step slowly, taking care not to stumble and fall. In his left hand he carried three sheets of paper bound by a paperclip. A walking cane was hooked around his left wrist and dangled by his side. In his other hand, he held a stainless-steel thermos that contained a juice concoction that consisted of kale, cucumbers, spinach, beets, green apples, fresh strawberries, and pineapples. This drink, most commonly known as the *Green Drink* or the *Green Machine*, was the only thing that Mr. Two had for breakfast each and every day. His doctor, who happened to be his ex-wife, recommended the green beverage over the steak and eggs that had been Mr. Two's routine morning meal for over forty years. He sipped his breakfast as he neared Mr. One, and though he tried to block out the older gentleman's phone conversation, he heard enough of it to know that Mr. One was not having a good day.

"Yes, Doctor," One said into the phone. "Thank you. I appreciate the call." He pressed a button on the face of the phone, severing the connection. Though he was aware of Mr. Two's presence, he didn't turn to face him. Instead, Mr. One stared out the window that was embedded in the back wall.

After a moment, Mr. Two broke the silence. "Was that the oncologist?" he asked.

"Dr. Fillmore. Yes.

"Good news, I hope," Two said, knowing it was not.

Mr. One did not waste words. "It's confirmed. The treatments aren't working."

The words lingered in the air while each man digested the significance of the statement.

"Mr. One . . . Roger. I'm sorry."

"Yeah," One said as he turned to face his friend. "Me, too." He swallowed hard and choked back a wave of emotion. He turned and gazed out the window once again, taking in the morning sun as it hung effortlessly over the D.C sky. After a long moment of silence, he spoke again. His tone was solemn and his words were heavily laden with sadness. "I'm not ready. I mean . . . Lizanne . . . she's dealt with enough. What do I say to her?"

Mr. Two was at a loss for words.

One continued. "When I consider all of the resources we have at our disposal, all of the power that we wield, only to realize that I am powerless, helpless, in this situation. . ."

"If there's anything I can do," Two offered.

"I know. Thank you," replied One. He took a deep breath, trying to make sense of the news he had just received. "I had anticipated this, but it certainly doesn't make it any easier."

A thought occurred to Mr. Two. "That's why you confiscated the new HP-47 ahead of schedule."

One nodded. "Yes. But will we be able to manufacture enough in time?" He shook his head before answering his own question. "I don't know. And Patel's little stunt didn't help." He took a breath to choke back a rush of sadness. "It's too bad. He may have been of some use with this."

Two placed a hand on Mr. One's shoulder. "Why don't you take the rest of the day off? You don't need to be here. Go spend it with Lizanne."

"Maybe I will," One said as he considered his friend's advice. "But first," he gestured to the paperwork in Two's hand, "tell me what's going on."

"Agents Peppers and Kincaid called in their report. Agent Rose is dead. They found him at Howard University Hospital. Unfortunately, A.D. Marsh may have gotten to him before he died."

One seemed unfazed. "Marsh, huh? It appears as if the doubts regarding Rose's loyalty have been confirmed."

"God only knows what he told Marsh before he died."

"Makes no difference," One replied, shaking his head. "The safe house should be all cleaned up by now, and the vaccine will be back where it belongs. The final report should reveal that there's nothing left to find. Besides, we've managed to stay one step ahead of Marsh for this long. We've got nothing to worry about."

"Still, I'm going to activate one of our resources in Marsh's office," Two stated. "Just to keep eyes and ears on him for a while."

Mr. One nodded. "Good idea. What about the girl?"

"Iris? As expected, she's a little overwhelmed," Two reported. "But she did very well, left no survivors. It's a shame she's dying. I feel she would have made an excellent operative."

"No doubt," One concurred. "It's her genetic predisposition. And don't think for one minute that I'm not disappointed about her predicament. But cutting off her treatment was necessary. I know it sounds like a selfish choice, but that vaccine is the groundwork for a potential cure. If the HP-47 wasn't in limited supply, if there was some way to ensure that our efforts to make more will be successful, maybe I wouldn't have to choose."

"I'm truly sorry," Two said, expressing his condolences again. "Even in our old age we don't have the ability to foresee everything. Perhaps if we had done things differently seven years ago, the Freeman girl would still be alive and we'd have the DNA to manufacture more of the vaccine. But there was no way we could have known."

"Maybe not," One responded. "But that's spilled milk. Old age or not, I'm not giving up. I can't. Not yet."

"Good. Again, if you need anything-"

"I do need something, my friend," One said quickly. "I need a miracle."

5

MILFORD, CONNECTICUT

Hunger had gotten the better of Kelli so, despite her urgency to arrive in the Bronx by noon, she pulled off of the interstate at the I-95 South Milford Service Plaza in Milford, Connecticut. Before exiting her car, she reached into her backpack and found a large white envelope from which she extracted a thick stack of twenty-dollar bills bound by a red rubber band. Ever since Kelli decided to dodge Agent Davies' phone calls and scheduled check-ins, she curtailed the use of the credit card that was issued to her in the name of Kyle Cuffee. Whenever Kelli left the designated haven of the Boston area, she used cash for all of her purchases. Cash didn't leave the paper trail that followed in the wake of credit card use. Though Kelli was not certain that Agent Davies or the FBI even tracked her whereabouts through her credit card statement, she felt better taking the precaution nevertheless.

Kelli stripped off two of the bills and stuck them in her pocket. She tossed the white envelope back into her backpack before sealing it and exiting her vehicle. The tension that had built up in her strong, muscular legs was instantly released as she stood and began to walk across the parking lot towards the front door of the structure. Once inside, she realized immediately that she wasn't particularly fond of the restaurant choices available to her. Still, the emptiness in her stomach forced her to push beyond her pickiness and settle on a vegetable salad from *Subway*. While she sat, munching away at the spinach leaves she had requested in place of lettuce, she pulled her pre-paid cellular phone from the pocket of her sweats and dialed Bling's number. Kelli chewed slowly as she realized that, again, her call would go unanswered and the automated outgoing voice mail message would begin playing in her ear. Why wasn't he answering her calls today? *He knows I'm coming.*

Kelli placed the phone back into the pocket of her sweats and finished her meal. Within fifteen minutes, she had devoured the salad, chased it with a bottle of water and was, once again, cruising down the interstate towards the New York border.

She glanced at her watch as she sped past a red Mustang that was doing seventy-five in the center lane. 10:30 a.m. She knew Bling's daily schedule and surmised that he was at work. Bling was an armed security guard for Solid State Security. Currently, Solid State was working a contract that required them to monitor and patrol the newly constructed Bronxview Terrace Apartments in upper Manhattan. Bling worked the day shift so he could take college courses at night. Kelli knew Bling's work schedule so well because Solid State Security was founded and owned by retired New York Police Officer Arthur Freeman. Kelli's father.

Kelli cursed silently to herself. *Bling knows I'm coming today*, she told herself again. *What's he doing that's so important that he can't answer my calls?* Kelli sighed heavily. She knew precisely what had Bling so preoccupied as of late. It was not so much *what* had his attention, but rather *who*. Kelli knew about Bling's new girlfriend, Zenaida, and just the thought of her made Kelli jealous as hell.

Traffic on the southbound I-95 through Connecticut was particularly heavy today. Still, the dark, cherry-colored Honda managed to keep pace with the black Audi that it shadowed stealthily along the New England highway. Behind the wheel, FBI Investigative Specialist Naomi Swann took a sip of the lemonade she had purchased at the *Sbarro* back at the South Milford Service Plaza just moments before. She stole a quick glance at the small screen on the laptop that sat open on her passenger seat. The red light on the screen signified that the tracker she'd placed on the Audi was still transmitting a signal.

Swann was an auburn-haired, green-eyed, plain-Jane type. Her simple *girl next door* looks failed to convey her stern, relentlessly competitive nature. Swann was the only child of a single father who was closer to fifty years old than forty on her eighth birthday. Herman Swann was a former high school athlete. His love for sports extended into coaching, and to his daughter, whose athletic journey began when she was four years old. Swann played various sports from elementary school through college: softball, tennis, volleyball, lacrosse, rugby, and football. Like her father, Naomi Swann thrived on competition. It was this very nature that pushed her to the top of her class in high school and in college where, at Duke University, she earned undergraduate degrees in Psychology and Sociology. Her father couldn't fathom how proud of her he was.

He had planned an elaborate celebration for her back home in Philadelphia that weekend. Unfortunately, Herman was hit by a car while crossing the street two days after graduation.

After a year of grieving and wandering desultorily around the country, Naomi enlisted in the United States Marine Corp. Her college degrees afforded her the opportunity to enroll in the Officer Candidate Course, and as a result, she began her active duty with the rank of Second Lieutenant. As usual, she excelled. She took a liking to hand-to-hand combat and became an expert in the field. She was recruited onto a Special Task Force that specialized in rescue and reconnaissance. It was during her time with this task force that she became proficient in surveillance and tracking. One day, while on a rescue op in a foreign country during her seventh year of service, Swann took a bullet to the chest, a clean shot that punctured her right lung and left an exit wound in her back. Though five members of her eight-man unit didn't make it out alive, two members, while carrying Swann to safety, managed to elude the local forces until another extraction team arrived. The overall mission was a failure. Swann, having been incapacitated by the gunshot, viewed her inability to contribute as a personal failure. After a long recovery, Swann served the remainder of her time posted at Camp Pendleton as a Combat Specialist where she trained a group of five young military cadets, kids, in the art of hand-to-hand combat. When her term ended four months later, Swann did not reenlist. Instead, she joined the Federal Bureau of Investigation. Swann spent a year as a field agent before her private battle with PTSD got the better of her. Still, her competitive nature wouldn't allow her to quit. She requested and received a transfer to the Special Surveillance Group, or SSG, a classified unit within the FBI that specialized in the tracking and surveillance of persons of interest. It was no surprise that Naomi Swann was very good at her job. Her assignment today, as it had been for the last two weeks, was to track and record the movements of one person in particular. A young man by the name of Kyle Cuffee.

BOSTON, MASSACHUSETTS

Special Agent Monica Davies' plane taxied down the runway at Logan International Airport after a safe flight from Washington, D.C. Despite the early hour at which she had climbed out of bed to make her flight, Davies was alert and wide awake. This was nothing new. As far back as grade school, Davies had always been a morning person, greeting each day with an eager curiosity and optimism; never too tired or grumpy as she climbed onto the school bus, or strolled onto the softball field or volleyball court. No. Monica Davies was the early bird that caught the worm.

Davies was particularly excited about being sent to Boston. Oh, how she loved Beantown this time of year; the cool morning air, the sound of bustling traffic coming from every direction, and the distinct accent found on the tongue of every native Bostonian. It was a beautiful city with impressive architecture that told the tale of a rich history. Every single time Davies had come here, she never wanted to leave. She did not quite understand why

Boston was so appealing to her, perhaps it was because being born and raised in Weston, Idaho did not offer her the excitement of big city living. She had been to several other big cities in the United States, around the world even, but there was something about Boston that she loved. Davies understood why Kelli loathed it here. Exile, Davies remembered, was the word Kelli had used on more than one occasion to describe Boston. Considering the circumstances, Davies couldn't blame her. Still, Davies loved this city. She couldn't get enough.

Davies felt that, indirectly, she owed her love of Boston to Kelli. It was not until Kelli was sent here under witness protection that Davies was assigned to her, and consequently, had to make regular visits to the city. Prior to the events that landed Kelli in Boston, Davies had never even set foot in Massachusetts.

Davies hurried off the plane; the only thing in her possession was her small carry-on suitcase which was compact enough to fit in the overhead compartment. She took a shuttle to Alamo Rent a Car, and thanks to her Bureau affiliation, was pulling out of the lot onto Tomahawk Drive within fifteen minutes of arriving there. The GPS on her phone was already guiding her to Kelli's address, so Davies tuned in the first radio station that came in clearly, and then enjoyed the drive. During the short trip, Davies placed a quick call to her partner, Special Agent Garrett Lacee. Davies and Lacee had worked together for five years now. During that time, each of them had made it a habit to check in with the other if, for some reason, they would miss work. Being an FBI agent who had lost previous partners in the line of duty, Lacee had become somewhat of a worrier. The daily check-in put him at ease. Davies was careful not to divulge the covert assignment to which she was assigned, nor did she mention that she was out of town. A little white lie, "I'm not feeling well. I'm staying in bed," was all it took. Immediately after ending her call to Lacee, Davies dialed Kelli Freeman. In fact, she called Kelli's cell phone twice but received no answer either time. She phoned Kelli's job at Tzinberg & Beach only to be informed that Kelli was still on vacation. Since she had no luck contacting Kelli beforehand, Davies continued towards Kelli's South Boston address. Twenty-five minutes later, Davies was knocking on the door of Apartment 105.

There was no response to her taps on the door. She waited a moment and knocked again. She thought she heard a noise coming from inside, so she called out.

"Kyle?" she said, being sure to use Kelli's alias. Davies moved to the door to press her ear against it, but before she could, she heard the lock being released from the other side. Davies stood back as the door was pulled open. To her surprise, the person standing before her was not Kelli Freeman.

"Can I help you?" asked the woman who answered the door.

Davies made a quick note of the woman's description. *Caucasian female, approximately five feet, six inches tall, dark hair, but graying, brown eyes, seems to be in her late forties, early fifties, reeks of cigarettes.*

"Yes," Davies said, trying not to be too obvious as she attempted to catch a glimpse of the inside of the apartment. "I was looking for a friend of mine, I thought this was his apartment."

"Nope," the woman said flatly.

"This is apartment 105, correct?"

"It is," the woman replied.

Davies was confused. It had been over three and a half years since Kelli turned eighteen and moved out of the Farmers' home in search of her own apartment, *this* apartment. Davies had been here several times before her communications with Kelli became more and more infrequent. She knew this was Kelli's apartment, or, that it used to be.

Reflexively, Davies slipped into interrogation mode. "How long have you lived here?"

The question caused the woman in the doorway to recoil slightly. When she replied, it was clear to Davies that the woman's defenses had gone up. "Who's asking?"

Davies chose her next words carefully. Normally, at this point, she would brandish her FBI credentials, which, often spoke louder than her voice while introducing herself. Today, however, based on the woman's reaction, Davies decided that an unofficial approach might be the better strategy.

"Monica Davies," she answered. "Kyle and I are old friends," she leaned towards the doorway so the woman could hear her as she whispered, "if you know what I mean."

"Oh," the woman replied, her tone relaxing.

Davies pressed on. "He and I were supposed to move in together, but then I had to go away for a while, but not before the baby thing happened-"

"Whoa, whoa," the woman raised her hand in protest. "He got you pregnant?"

"Yeah. Twins." Davies had no idea from where her fabricated story was coming, but she knew that she had to wrap it up quickly before the woman asked any more questions. Davies decided to ask one of her own. "I'm sorry," she began, "do you really want to hear all of my drama?" The question came out as innocently as any question could have.

The woman had heard enough. "No. Listen, I don't know anything about the guy who used to live here. I've been here about six months, moved in the first of September."

September, Davies thought. *I haven't been here since July, and in that time, Kelli moved out of her apartment. No wonder she hasn't returned my calls. Damn it.*

The woman in apartment 105 began to ramble, letting out her thoughts and opinions on men and deadbeat fathers. Davies tuned the woman out almost instantly as she became preoccupied with thoughts of her own. Her mind raced as she began to reconstruct her last conversation with Kelli. It had been months since they had actually spoken to one another. However, Davies recalled that Kelli gave her several reassurances that things were going well for her in Boston. Kelli had graduated from law school, passed the Massachusetts Bar, and was fielding potential offers from numerous law firms. Davies had checked all of it out just to be certain. All true. All used as a cover to divert Davies' attention from the fact that Kelli was planning to give the Bureau the slip. But why? What was Kelli up to? When A.D Marsh contacted her this morning and explained what had happened in Virginia, Davies refused to believe that Kelli could, or would, be involved in any way. Despite the fact she and Kelli had not spoken in a while, Davies thought she knew Kelli bet-

ter than that. But now, she wasn't so sure. Now, Davies
had to track her down.

Davies was so lost in her train of thought, *check DMV
records, check job records, check anything that will point her in Kelli's direction*, that she almost didn't hear the question the
current tenant in apartment 105 was asking her.

"Pardon me. What?"

"Your friend," the woman said, "you said his name
was Kyle?"

"That's right," Davies affirmed. "Kyle Cuffee."

The woman nodded slightly. "Wait here." She closed
the door and disappeared behind it. Thirty seconds later,
the door opened again and the woman stepped through
into the open air. In her hand were three envelopes. She
handed them to Davies. "These letters arrived during my
first month here."

Davies scanned the envelopes quickly. One of them
was sent from a local politician. It was postmarked Au-
gust 31 from the previous year and had a stamp on it that
urged the recipient to vote for Terry Gilbert for city
council. The other envelope was sent from a company
called The Mackenzie Financial Group. Their slogan,
which was emblazoned across the bottom of the envelope, stated "We're the ones to call." Davies dismissed
them both as junk mail. The third envelope, however,
appeared to be a bill. Closer inspection revealed it to be
Kyle Cuffee's cell phone bill. Davies breathed out a silent,
"Yes." This could be helpful.

Davies looked up at the woman. "No more letters arrived after the first month?"

"Nope," she responded with the same flat tone as before.

Davies surmised that Kelli must have changed her forwarding address at the local post office, but not before these three letters were delivered. She considered going to the post office to see if she could get the new address from them, but Davies realized that she might be able to retrieve that information from a source much closer.

"Is the building manager here on site?" Davies asked the woman.

"Usually," she said. "The office is around the corner; apartment 100."

Davies did not want to waste any more time. "Thank you," she said to the woman. "You've been a big help."

Davies turned and walked away. Before she moved out of ear-shot of apartment 105, the woman shouted, "I hope you find that bastard."

"Don't worry," Davies shouted back. "I will."

Within sixty seconds, Davies was standing in front of apartment 100. The sign on the door read *Leasing office*. The blinds on the large window to her left were parted slightly, and Davies could see movement inside. She wrapped her hand around the door handle and gave it a turn. Three seconds later, Davies was inside.

As she scanned the area beyond the front door, she noticed that the space had been set up more like an office than an apartment, despite the obvious break in the floor plan that separated what was still being used as a kitchen. The charcoal gray carpet under her feet felt relatively new and Davies could feel the recoil as she took a step towards the young woman behind the large, black L-shaped desk that was positioned close to the apartment door.

The woman at the desk appeared to be in her early thirties. She had shiny, dark brown hair that complemented the pair of black and gold designer Prada eyeglasses that adorned her slightly pudgy face. She wore a plain white blouse with a neckline that hung a tad too low for the professional environment in which she worked. A small nameplate, gold with bold, black letters, that sat on the left corner of her desk revealed her name to be Brittany Bergeron.

Brittany had looked up as soon as Davies entered the office. She smiled as Davies drew closer and she greeted her with a very pleasant, "Good morning. How can I help you today?"

"I was wondering if I could have a word with the building manager," Davies stated, and then asked, "Is that you?"

Brittany's smile widened, displaying a set of beautiful, bleached white teeth. "No. Mr. Hopper is out at the moment but he should be back shortly. Is there something I can help you with?"

"Yes, Brittany," Davies responded as she reached into her jacket pocket, retrieved her federal credentials and brandished them openly. "You can call him," she said with a smile, and then added without a hint of request, "please."

BRONX, NEW YORK

Bling fastened the belt to his security guard uniform as he moved to the door of the apartment. His early morning activities with Zenaida kept him in bed far beyond the time at which he had planned to get up and ready himself for work. Zenaida had managed to get herself ready for her classes at Bronx Community College in record time, and had left one minute earlier. The knock at the door caused Bling to assume that Zenaida had forgotten something in the apartment. *Probably her keys,* he thought to himself. *Wouldn't be the first time.* To Bling's surprise, it wasn't Zenaida who was waiting on the other side of the door.

"Kelli?"

Kelli flashed an obviously fake smile. "Oh, you remember my name," she stated sarcastically.

Bling gasped as realization set in. "Oh, snap. Is today-?"

"Yes," she interrupted as she pushed past him and entered the apartment. "Today is the day. Thanks for remembering that I was coming."

"Yo, I'm sorry. I forgot."

"Clearly." Kelli looked around and took in the apartment that Bling shared with Zenaida. As she did, conflicting emotions swelled up within her, causing her to take a deep breath in an effort to appear unaffected. She knew that Bling and Zenaida had been together almost a year; plenty of time to have taken photos of themselves smiling together, holding hands, and looking happy. Despite the fact that she didn't want to see photos such as those, her curiosity compelled her to look. Her eyes brushed past a hand-drawn piece of artwork that was framed on the wall to her left. Kelli recognized it as Bling's creation as he had a talent for producing detailed drawings of comic book superheroes. In spite of herself, she allowed her gaze to continue scanning the room. Her heart sank. There, sitting on the shelf to the right of the flat screen TV that hung on the left wall, was just the type of photo she was hoping not to find. In the picture, Bling and Zenaida were both displaying ear to ear smiles, the kind that accompanied a young romance. Zenaida's hand rested upon Bling's, and her head was tilted towards him ever so slightly. Kelli could tell from the background that the photo was taken at Coney Island. Kelli surmised that the snapshot was taken a few months into their relationship because, in this particular photo, Zenaida was still wearing braces, and she recalled Bling telling her that Zenaida's braces came off sometime around Christmas of the previous year. It didn't matter, Zenaida was gorgeous either way, and Kelli hated it. She found the strength to look away, but before she could, the photo adjacent to that one grabbed Kelli's attention. It was an old photo, at least seven years old. It was one of a series taken during a Rodriguez family portrait, except this photo did not display the whole family. This photo displayed only the Rodriguez children; Zenaida, her sister Roselyn, and her late sister Francine.

Kelli's gaze locked on to Francine's image. *She took that picture only a few months before she died.*

"Hey." Bling's voice caused Kelli to disengage and turn to him. "I said I was sorry. Alright?"

Kelli forced herself not to look back at the photos on the shelf as she said dismissively, "Yeah. Fine. Why aren't you at work? I thought you were working the morning shift today."

"I switched with Laurence. I had a late class last night and I didn't want to have to get up so early."

"Oh."

"I hate the fact that your dad tells you my schedule," he said as he pulled on his blue jacket that had gold and red patches with the Solid State logo on each shoulder. He shook his head disapprovingly. "That's not cool, yo."

Kelli brandished a proud smile. "He doesn't come right out and tell me. I usually find a way to get him to spill the beans without even asking. This time it had something to do with Wilma's birthday, and you and I hanging out so we could pick out a present for her, and me not wanting to get into town until you were off-"

"Ah, I get it. You connive to get the info. He probably doesn't even realize you're doing it."

"Not a clue."

"Yeah, well, your plan backfired today. I don't get off until eight tonight." Bling grabbed his keys from the hook on the wall. He opened the apartment door and made a small gesture for Kelli to exit. "Come on. I'm gonna be late."

Kelli stole a final glance at Francine's photo before complying. Once they were out in the hallway, Bling secured the lock and strode towards the stairwell.

Kelli kept in step with him and walked by his side. "So, I guess I have to wait until tomorrow to hang out with you?"

"Pretty much," he responded. "Zenaida's off tonight so we were going to chill at home, you know, watch a flick or something."

"Damn, Bling," she cursed loudly. "What's the point of us making plans ahead of time if you're just going to break them?"

"Hey, I'm sorry, alright?"

"No," Kelli said, becoming slightly annoyed. "It's not alright. It's not like I can come to town on a regular basis."

They reached the top of the stairwell and began to descend.

"I told you. Zenaida is not working tonight-"

"So tell Zenaida you made previous plans. It's not like you're hanging out with a girl. To her I'm dead, remember? You're hanging out with Kyle, your friend from Boston."

"I remember the damn cover story, alright?"

"It's not a cover story," Kelli snapped. "It's the truth."

"No, Kelli," Bling said as he stepped off the bottom step and moved towards the door that led outside. "It's not."

Bling pushed the door open and they stepped out into the chilly March air. Kelli stepped in front of Bling, stopping him in his tracks.

"When did you become so honest?" she barked at him sarcastically.

"Oh, I guess around the same time you became so dishonest," he countered.

Kelli's feelings were suddenly hurt. Yes, she knew she had been telling lies to the people in her life; Davies, Patrice, West, her parents, her therapist, everyone. Everyone, that is, except Bling. During Kelli's witness protection exile, Bling was the one person who maintained regular contact with Kelli. Whenever Kelli couldn't make it to New York for one of her clandestine visits, Bling would hop on a train, a bus, or a plane and make the trip to see her. And despite her need to keep everyone in the dark, she never once kept anything from Bling. She had even informed him of her true intentions during her recent visit to D.C. Every other person in her life had been granted small glimpses into who Kelli truly was, but only Bling had been allowed access to the full picture. Bling, the young, one-time gangster who used to run with the wrong crowd, had trouble staying in school, and had more than one brush with the law. This was the same Bling that Kelli watched, over the course of the last seven years, transform into a young man who focused on his grades, changed his social affiliations, and established real goals for himself. This was also the same Bling that already knew about Kelli's shifting ability. There was no need to break the ice with Bling, because he knew all there was to know. It was no wonder why Kelli had developed feelings for him. Her feelings were no secret to Bling either. Kelli realized, by granting Bling a full view of herself, he was privy to the good as well as the bad. Still, she had never considered, based on Bling's imperfect past that he would pass judgment on her. That is, until now.

"How dare you," she said through gritted teeth.

"Really, Kelli? Really? What happened to the girl who just wanted to get her life back?"

"Nothing happened. What are you talking about?"

"I'm talking about how you went from sneaking to the city to see your family, to sneaking to the city so I can hook you up with a fake I.D., or set you up with an illegal card game so you could practice how to steal money from people."

"That's not fair," she shouted at him. "You wanted me to do it just as much as I did."

"At first, yes. I mean, I'd never actually witnessed someone *counting cards* before," he admitted. "But once you perfected it, none of those guys had a chance of keeping their money. I know that I left the gang life behind, but they were still the people that I grew up with, people I was cool with. And you were using me so you could steal from them."

Kelli opened her mouth to respond, to scream at him at the top of her lungs. Her lips parted, but not a sound came out. Kelli's mind raced back four years to a time when she was still living with the Farmers. Doris Farmer, the mother, was part of a group of women that played cards every Thursday night at a different member's home. For the first two years that Kelli lived with the Farmers, Doris Farmer's card club would hold a four-hour session at the Farmer's home on the second Thursday of every month without a hint of interest from Kelli. However, one Thursday night in particular, when Kelli had finished all of her homework from BU, she happened to be in the room during a heavy blackjack session. Coincidentally, Kelli was seated behind Doris Farmer and had full view of each hand Doris was dealt. At first, Kelli didn't realize that she was counting the cards, she only knew that she had a strong sense of what cards were already played, and which cards were probably coming next.

"Why did you fold during that last hand?" she had asked Doris after the other women had gone home. "All of the kings and tens were gone."

Doris' eyes had widened. "How did you know?" she asked.

Kelli dispensed with the full truth of her genetic engineering. However, she did reveal one facet of abilities; her eidetic memory. Doris Farmer squealed with ecstasy. During the three weeks that followed, Doris taught *Kyle* everything she knew about blackjack. Kelli, who was already developing ulterior motives for learning the game, went out and purchased several books on the subject, including Arnold Snyder's *Blackbelt in Blackjack: Playing 21 as a Martial Art.* On the following second Thursday, Doris put *Kyle* to the test.

Kelli sat behind Doris under the guise of an innocent bystander who wanted to learn the game. She sat close enough to Doris so she could touch her back and tap her lightly to indicate whether to take a hit, fold, or bluff. Doris cleaned everyone out. It was only her guilt over deceiving her friends that allowed her to resist the temptation to cheat again. Kelli, on the other hand, was hooked. She called Bling in New York and asked him to contact some of his old Triple Deuce buddies and find a card game to buy into. Bling had more than one friend with a gambling problem, so finding a game was not a dilemma. Once Kelli arrived, she didn't bother shifting into her male form. Why should she? The blackjack table was surrounded by virile, lustful, young men. By this time, Kelli had developed the body of a woman, one with all the right curves in all the right proportions and places. One look at her and every one of them was more than willing to let her buy a spot at the table. Kelli played conservatively at first. She waited until each of them had a significant amount of alcohol in their systems before she executed her plan and all but left them with enough gas money with which to get home. Bling was amazed, so much so that he found other games for Kelli to join. Once Kelli had practiced enough with the locals in New York, she turned her attention to Atlantic City. After a methodical fourteen-night gambling spree that allowed her to hit a number of casinos, Kelli cashed in to the tune of $717,000; more than enough to live unemployed temporarily if she chose, and definitely more than enough to begin her surveillance and eventual take-down of Mr. One, the man she held responsible for Francine's death, her isolation in Boston . . . everything. Yes, things were going according to Kelli's plan. Unfortunately, she had not foreseen Bling becoming an emotional casualty.

"I wasn't trying to use you, Bling," she said to him.

"That's not what it felt like," he replied.

"I swear. I wouldn't do that to you." Kelli took a step and closed the gap between them. Her face came within inches of his. "You know how I feel-"

"Hey," Bling interrupted her. He took a step back. "We've discussed this. Remember?"

A knot formed in Kelli's stomach as a wave of anger erupted within her. The sudden rage bubbled in her gut and began climbing towards her throat. Kelli swallowed hard to force it back down. She *did* remember. She remembered that night just over a year ago when Bling had visited her in Boston. They were celebrating Bling's birthday, as well as his decision to go back to school to earn a business degree. They sat on Kelli's balcony, drinking beer and looking into the star-less Boston sky. She remembered they were laughing, and she remembered the kiss. So soft, so intense. In that moment, Kelli knew that Bling was feeling exactly what she was feeling; desire, real desire. But the moment was short-lived. Bling pulled away.

"I can't do this, Kel," he had said.

"Why not?" she asked. "What's . . . what's wrong?"

Bling had taken a deep breath. For several moments he had sat in silence. Even in the darkness, Kelli could see his wheels turning.

"Bryan. . . Bling, talk to me," she pleaded. "What is it?"

"It's not you, Kelli. It's Kyle," Bling had said, finally. In that instant, Kelli knew that she would remember those words forever.

Bling had grabbed his things and left Kelli's apartment right then and there. Two weeks later, he told Kelli that he had run into Zenaida Rodriguez on the campus of Bronx Community College. A month later, he reported they were dating. Kelli was devastated.

Kelli pushed the memories from her mind as she focused on the present, and on Bling.

"Yeah, I remember," she said bitterly.

"So you know how I feel." It wasn't a question.

"Yeah." She locked her gaze onto Bling and stared into his eyes. "I know how you feel."

An uncomfortable chill raced up Bling's spine. He turned away. "Quit it. Alright?"

Kelli shook her head. *How can he stand there and act like he doesn't feel something for me?* she asked herself. Kelli was furious, nevertheless, she was not going to stand there and grovel in front of a man who, once again, had rejected her because of what she was.

"Fine, Bling," she said, placing emphasis on his gang-pseudonym. "I'll quit it." She stepped away from him, but not before asking, "Who's being dishonest now?" With that, Kelli stormed off.

Bling watched as she walked away. "Dammit," he cursed to himself. He hated to see her go. He and Kelli had been through so much together, even after the initial ordeal with the Agency that had brought them together seven years ago. He wanted to call out to her. He wanted to stop her from leaving and try to make things right between them. But what would he say? The truth was, Bling *did* have feelings for Kelli, strong feelings. Unfortunately, as genuine as his feelings were, he could not get over the fact that Kelli could turn into a man. *How does a straight guy deal with that? Hell, how would any guy deal with that?* To those questions, Bling did not have the answers, and he didn't know if he ever would.

WASHINGTON, D.C.

The cold air licked at Mr. One's neck as he stood on the corner of First Street NE and Maryland Ave. He adjusted his gray scarf, pulling it tighter in an effort to block out the biting wind. One knew the scarf would do no good. He knew the chill that was, somehow, frozen in the middle of his back was neither caused by the wind, nor held off by the scarf. This chill was one of sorrow, emptiness, helplessness. The prognosis was not promising. The breast cancer had returned. Lizanne, his daughter, his only child, was going to die. Mr. One was so overwhelmed by emotion, that he couldn't process it all. In fact, he refused to, as if allowing himself to feel the pain would somehow diminish what hope he had left. No, he didn't want to think about it. In answer to his unspoken prayer, a large black SUV with blacked-out windows pulled up and stopped in front of him.

As the tinted window on the rear-passenger side began to descend slowly, the face of the woman seated inside came into view. Her name was Rebecca Thorn.

Rebecca's hair was silver. It was shoulder-length, brushed into a beautiful mane that caressed the youthful face that contradicted the 71 years that Rebecca had graced the Earth. Her style of dress, though conservative and gray, complemented her silver tresses perfectly. Her well-manicured nails were adorned with a clear polish, and her perfume smelled of lilacs. In her left hand rested the latest iPhone. In her right, she held a small blue stress-ball. One shook his head at the mere sight of her.

"You look disappointed," Rebecca said sarcastically.

One didn't protest. He was, in fact, disappointed. Despite their long-standing history and working relationship, it was no secret that she was not on One's list of favorite people. "Whenever they send you, it's never good news."

Rebecca's eyes narrowed and her voice soured. "First of all, no one sent me. You forget that I'm overseeing your department again. Now, are you going to stand out there all day or are you going to get your ass in this car?"

Without a word in response, Mr. One opened the rear-passenger door. Awkwardly, he climbed into the back seat, almost dropping his cane in the process. As soon as the door closed, the tinted window began its ascent, and the dark vehicle pulled away from the curb.

Inside, One took a moment to catch his breath. He placed his cane by his side and turned to Rebecca.

"I could have come to your office, you know."

"I'm on my way there now," Rebecca replied. "Besides, I like *this* office much better." She gestured to her vehicle using only a small tilt of her head. "It keeps me on the move."

"Some things never change. Thank you for the support, by the way," One said, changing the subject. "I'm sure you went to bat for me when I requested to remove the HP-47 vaccine."

"No worries," Rebecca assured him. "Phase two is done. We were playing with house money at this point. The Harmony Project has progressed nicely, and we have you to thank for that."

"Well, my request was personal, so, thank you all the same."

Rebecca nodded. She squeezed her stress-ball. "How *is* Lizanne?"

"Ready to fight, as always," One replied.

"Not surprising. She gets that from you."

"She gets it from her mother," One snapped.

A heavy silence filled the space between them. Rebecca squeezed the stress-ball even tighter before responding. "Well, if there's anything-"

"Just help me keep my daughter alive," he interrupted. "Please."

Rebecca nodded again.

Another wave of uncomfortable quiet hung in the air. Finally, One asked, "How's Marna?" He didn't really care.

"Grumpy, intolerable. But I love her." Rebecca paused for a moment before asking, "Is your house back in order?"

"We're working on it. The cleaners should be reporting soon. It won't be long."

"Good. Things worked out on our end, as well."

"Did they?" One questioned curiously.

"Yes. The false intel that we planted for Agent Rose led to the FBI showing up in Indiana. It confirmed that he was the leak."

"No longer a problem. Rose is dead."

"Unfortunate, but necessary, and it only cost us the use of a convicted felon. I call that a win. Anything else?"

"Not really. We still need to inform Agent Molina about recalling the vaccine. She's not going to take it well."

"She'll get over it. It's not as if she actually gave birth to. . ." Rebecca's voice trailed off.

One glared at her sharply, then looked away before muttering, "Unbelievable."

Rebecca rotated the blue ball in her right hand as she reflected on her last comment. She glanced at One. He made no attempt to hide his disdain as he scoffed and shook his head disapprovingly. Rebecca wanted to tell One to go to Hell. She knew that their history of loathing for one another was not solely her fault, and she had grown quite tired of the quiet implication to the contrary, especially now, when she had, uncharacteristically, gone out of her way to help him. Rebecca swallowed deeply to stifle the vituperative rant that threatened to spill out of her mouth. This was business. And where there was business to be done, personal feelings were never welcome.

"We're here, Ma'am," the female driver of the SUV reported suddenly.

"Thank you, Barb," Rebecca replied, thankful for the distraction. "Pull over. I'll get out right here."

"I can bring you closer," Barb protested.

"No," Rebecca insisted. "I could use a good walk."

Barb directed the SUV towards the curb and brought the vehicle to a stop in front of the Marriner S. Eccles Federal Reserve Board building on Constitution Avenue NW.

"Are we done already?" One asked.

"We are," Rebecca responded flatly. "Keep me apprised of the situation with Agent Molina." She glared at One. When she spoke, her tone conveyed the implicit reminder that she was the one in charge. "Don't let it get out of hand."

One received the unspoken warning loud and clear. "Understood."

"Take him back to his office, Barb."

"Yes, Ma'am," the driver responded.

With that, Rebecca opened the door and exited the vehicle. Before closing the door, she tossed the stress-ball into One's lap. He watched as Rebecca walked towards the Federal Reserve Board building that housed her actual office. One sighed. He understood that Rebecca couldn't fathom the specific weight that he was soon going to have to bear. Still, he knew that she had suffered the loss of loved ones to incurable illnesses in her lifetime. In fact, he witnessed it. And yet, though the circumstances were different, the helplessness, despite all the power and resources at their disposal, was exactly the same.

Mr. One picked up the ball and stared at it briefly. He thought of his daughter, and a pang of emptiness began to swell in his gut. He swallowed hard to stifle the feeling, but he could not. One was, all at once, overcome by sorrow. He squeezed the ball. A torrent of tears burst uncontrollably from his eyes and raced quickly down his pasty cheeks. One tried not to sob, but again, he failed. Barb, the driver, took notice but said nothing.

Moments later, the SUV was cruising in the opposite direction, taking Mr. One back to his domain.

OUTSIDE OF ARLINGTON, VIRGINIA

West found himself in a secluded, wooded area at the end of a long dirt road in a small suburb of Arlington. As he arrived at the location provided by Paul Ferry, West noted that the last house he saw was more than a half a mile up the road. That made this the perfect location for a government safe house. West parked his vehicle at the edge of the driveway. As he approached what little was left of the cottage, West noted that, with the exception of the foundation, every trace of the house that stood there a little over one day ago, was gone.

Despite his dislike for the Agency's practices, he could not help being impressed by their efficiency. Although the scorching on the foundation showed evidence of a fire, it was obvious that the entire area had been sanitized.

"How do they do it?" West asked himself aloud. He surmised that it must have taken a very large, very thorough sanitation crew who came in shortly after the explosion.

West's peripheral vision picked up a slight movement in the woods off to his right. A large tree stump rested in the center of a collection of dry, leafless trees. West's initial inclination was to ignore it. *It's probably an animal or something.* However, West decided not to dismiss the fact that the Agency may still be watching this area just to see who might come along to investigate.

West removed his weapon from its holster. He moved beyond the foundation of the house and stepped into the woods. Dried twigs and leaves snapped and crunched beneath his feet. Normally, this would not be a good thing as it would alert whoever, or whatever, was behind the stump that West was approaching. In this instance, however, as West moved closer, the rustling from behind the stump became more pronounced in response. This told West that it was not a whatever, but a whoever.

West was not certain if he should call out to the person hiding behind the stump. *Could it possibly be an Agency operative?* he asked himself. West considered it briefly, but then decided that an Agency operative would be much stealthier, and would probably not be skulking around in the woods. It only took a second for West to come to a decision.

"Whoever is there, I am armed. Put your hands up and come out slowly."

The rustling behind the stump ceased for a moment. West assumed that whoever was there was considering their options. The cracking of leaves began again. Slowly and cautiously, a figure emerged from behind the stump.

Based on his unkempt appearance, West determined that the man who now stood before him was homeless. His long, greasy black hair was partially covered by a filthy, red Washington Redskins cap. While an oversized brown sweater covered up several other t-shirts, and a pair of baggy jeans covered his lower extremities, West was surprised to see a fairly new looking pair of black Converse on his feet. His scruffy, bearded face was heavily wrinkled, displaying years of detriment and hardship. His hands were raised high in the air.

"Please don't shoot me," he begged.

West breathed a sigh of relief. Still, he kept his weapon trained on the homeless man.

"What are you doing out here?" West questioned for lack of a better inquiry.

"I live here," the man answered quickly.

"Where? Here?" he gestured back towards the decimated safe house.

"No, over there," he responded, pointing in the opposite direction. "About half a *klick*. I was just coming to see what was left."

West lowered his weapon slowly. "Did you see what happened here?"

The man nodded. "Yes, sir. I saw it all."

BOSTON, MASSACHUSETTS

Patrice Bass exited the law offices of Tzinberg & Beach amidst a sea of lawyers and clients. Her black hair was pulled into a tight bun, revealing the full beauty of her glowing, almond-colored skin. Her classy attire consisted of a fitted, navy, two-piece jacket-skirt set which was complemented by a lavender button-down blouse. Her lavender heels clicked against the pavement as she strode towards the parking lot.

She checked her watch. 12:08 p.m. Not much time to grab lunch and get back to the office. Patrice had recently been hired as a first-year attorney for the high-powered law firm that was located in downtown Boston. Patrice, along with Kyle Cuffee, served as a legal-intern for Tzinberg & Beach while she completed her law degree at Boston University. Needless to say, the partners at the firm were very satisfied with Patrice's knowledge and work ethic, and did not hesitate to offer her a place among their stable of lawyers. Patrice loved her work, even though, as it was with most first-year lawyers, it consisted of chasing scraps and low-profile cases. Patrice did not mind. She knew that she had to prove herself before she would be allowed to work the heavier, more *important* cases.

Patrice reviewed the remainder of her day as she stepped into the parking lot and reached her car. As she pulled out her keys, she noticed that someone had walked up and stopped next to her. Patrice looked up. Special Agent Davies returned her gaze with a wide smile.

"Patrice Bass?" Davies asked, although she knew full-well to whom she was speaking. During Kelli's time in Boston, it was Davies' job to vet anyone that Kelli befriended. Though it always turned out to be unnecessary, it was a required precautionary measure to keep Kelli safe.

Patrice's defenses went up. "Can I help you?"

Davies flashed her FBI credentials. "I'm Special Agent Monica Davies. I was wondering if I could ask you a few questions."

Patrice was confused. The last thing she expected today was to be approached by a federal agent. *And what did she say her name was? Monica Davies? Why does that name sound familiar?* Patrice quelled the rush of internal questions and decided to voice a few out loud. "Me? What's this about?"

"Kyle Cuffee. I'm hoping you can help me find him."

The mention of Kyle's name caused something to fall into place for Patrice. She had been at Kyle's apartment once when Monica called to *check in*. Kyle had explained that Monica was a family friend who happened to live in the Boston area. Kyle had let the call go to voicemail, and due to the innocent-sounding content of the message, Patrice accepted Kyle's explanation of Monica and dismissed it promptly. Now, Patrice was forced to accept that Kyle neglected to mention a few very important details.

"Find him?" Patrice was at a loss. She wasn't aware that Kyle was missing. As far as she knew, Kyle was on vacation. Fear touched her throat. "Did something happen to him? Is he okay?" she asked.

"I have no reason to think otherwise."

"Um, okay." Patrice relaxed slightly. Still, she was a little unnerved that an FBI agent had approached her. "I'm on a lunch break. I don't really have much time."

"Don't worry," Davies said warmly. "This shouldn't take long at all."

Patrice thought she sensed an air of sincerity in Davies' voice. Reluctantly, she agreed to talk, and led Davies across the street to a small park. They found a picnic table, and they each took a seat on opposite sides.

Davies did not waste time. "I know that you and Kyle are friends. Do you happen to know where he is?"

Patrice raised a hand in protest. "Wait. You're an FBI agent?"

Davies nodded. "Yes."

"Kyle never mentioned that."

"He mentioned me?" Davies was truly surprised.

"Yeah. He said you were a family friend. I just assumed you were some old lady who knew his parents or something. Not an FBI agent, and definitely not, um, pretty."

Davies could tell that Patrice was more bothered by the fact that she was young and pretty than by the fact that she was a federal agent. *Is that jealousy I'm detecting?*

"Thank you," Davies responded dismissively. "When's the last time you saw Kyle?" she asked.

"Is he in trouble?" Patrice countered with another question of her own.

Davies reached across the table and placed her hand over Patrice's hand. Davies could already tell that Patrice cared for Kyle. She was hoping she could use that to her advantage.

"I don't know," Davies answered honestly. "But I promise you that I'm trying to find out. I really want to help Kyle, but I need to find him first. He's not answering his cell phone or returning my calls."

"Join the club," Patrice said under her breath.

Davies squeezed Patrice's hand. Their eyes met. "Will you help me?" Davies pleaded.

Again, Patrice sensed that Davies' concern was genuine. She nodded. "He took some personal time from work, said he was going to D.C. for the weekend."

"D.C.?" Davies knew that was not good. If Kelli was in D.C. over the weekend, then she couldn't be ruled out as the shooter for whom Marsh was searching.

"Yeah," Patrice continued. "He said he went to visit his brother and check out a few law firms."

"He didn't get an offer here?" asked Davies.

"He did, but Kyle hates it here. He's always talking about how he can't wait to get out of Boston."

Davies nodded. *Sounds like Kelli alright.* "When is he coming back?"

"From D.C.? He supposedly flew in last night, but I haven't heard from him."

"And you don't know when he's expected to return to work?"

Patrice shook her head. "I wish I did."

Davies sat back. Based on what Patrice had told her, it appeared that Kelli told Patrice just enough to satisfy any curiosity but still keep her in the dark. As much as Davies hated to admit it, Kelli had done the same thing to her. She looked at Patrice once more.

"One more question. Do you happen to know where he lives? The building manager at his old place didn't have a forwarding address, only this work address."

"Yeah, I know where he lives," admitted Patrice. "It's a really nice place. I don't know how he affords that *and* a new car."

"New car? What kind of car?"

"Audi. Really nice."

Davies couldn't believe what she was hearing. Not only had Kelli given the bureau the slip, but she was somehow paying for a new apartment and a new car without having accepted a position at any law firm. Could she really be working for the Agency? Is it possible that Kelli, in the midst of everything, had switched sides? Davies searched her mind for another plausible explanation, something, anything else that would actually make sense and divert her train of thought from its present course. Unfortunately, she came up empty.

Davies reached into her pocket and pulled out a small notepad. She pushed it across the table to Patrice, and then handed her a pen. "If you don't mind, I'll take that address."

FBI FIELD OFFICE
WASHINGTON, D.C.

Bonner sat at his desk quietly. His fingers danced gracefully across the keyboard as he typed the official report documenting the events that led to the apprehension of the fugitive Richard Navarro in Indiana. Bonner did not mind the yards of paperwork that came with doing his job, nor did he ever complain. Growing up with eleven older siblings, he was privileged to learn about the benefits of a strong work ethic and to appreciate all that life gives you. Still, he was a little upset that his partner, Special Agent Donald West, wasn't there to fulfill his portion of this administrative duty. In fact, Bonner was annoyed because, as had been the case several times before, his partner had, once again, disappeared without warning, without explanation, and without a trace.

The phone on Bonner's desk began to vibrate. Without looking, Bonner picked up the phone and looked at the screen. A large number one appeared over the icon that resembled a talk bubble. It was an invitation to an active chat. He pressed icon and the chat window opened. The sender was listed as "423-911". It was a code that Bonner recognized. His eyes dropped to the message below.

"Good morning, Agent Bonner," the message read.

Bonner straightened his seated posture and pulled his other hand away from his keyboard. He knew exactly to whom he was speaking.

"Good morning," Bonner typed back. *"I didn't expect to hear from you today."*

"It's been quiet lately. However, I may be in need of a Hail Mary."

"Really?" Bonner typed. He paused a moment, and then added, *"I'm all ears."*

"Good, but for this, I'll need your eyes, too."

"Understood," replied Bonner quickly. *"What do you want me to do?"*

❧

Marsh stepped into his office and closed the door. His cell phone was ringing and the number on the caller I.D. belonged to Special Agent Davies. Her call was the first of two that Marsh was impatiently expecting.

He pulled his cell from the cell phone case on his belt and opened the line with the tap of a button. "A.D. Marsh."

"It's Davies," she announced through the phone. "No success on making contact with our girl in Boston. However, I do have a new address for her and I'm on my way to check it out now."

Marsh did not hide his disappointment. "You've been in Boston all morning and all you have is an address?"

"Actually, sir, no. I've got confirmation that our girl did, in fact, spend this past weekend in the D.C. area."

"I was afraid of that," Marsh said through gritted teeth.

"I would suggest running a check on her credit card activity, all airline passenger lists between Boston and D.C., maybe we can track her movements. Also, a coworker mentioned that she was looking at law firms, and may have visited her brother."

"I'll have West pay the brother a visit," Marsh said. "I can run the credit card check from here. Anything else?"

"Yes. Apparently, Kelli purchased a new car recently, a black Audi. I'll text you her address. A DMV check might be a good idea to get the specific year and model."

"I'll get someone on it. Good work, Monica. Keep me informed."

"I will." Before ending the call, Davies asked, "Sir, could it be possible that she did this? I mean, this is someone that we both know."

"Apparently we don't know her well enough," Marsh said in a grave tone. "And if it turns out she killed my friend, witness protection or not, I'll make sure that she burns."

6

BRONX, NEW YORK

Kelli didn't know why she bothered drinking alcohol. Due to her genetically enhanced metabolism, the intoxicating effects of alcohol lasted only for a short time, usually just long enough for her to begin to enjoy the feeling, and then, nothing. Nevertheless, she sat at the bar and sucked down half a draft of Sam Adams, her third, before setting the chilled glass down in front of her.

Kelli caught her reflection in the mirror behind the bar. She knew it was risky to be in her female form while she was in the Bronx. The likelihood of being recognized increased tenfold as soon as she had crossed the New York border. Kelli didn't care, at least not at the moment. She hated her male form, and her argument with Bling only served to provoke her careless tendencies; drinking in the middle of the day, or walking around in her hometown as Kelli instead of Kyle. She scoffed silently. Then, she turned and stole a few quick glances at the other patrons of the bar. Luckily, she recognized no one. This included Agent Swann who sat at the other end of the bar, watching.

The bartender, a middle-aged Caucasian man who had introduced himself as Michael, stopped in front of Kelli as he made his rounds while serving the other customers.

"You sure you don't want anything to eat, love?" Michael asked. "Buffalo wings or something?"

Kelli waved him away politely. "No, thanks. I need this feeling to last."

"Okay. Let me know if you change your mind," he said. With that, he strolled to attend to the rest of those who had decided they needed a mid-day pick-me-up at the local bar.

Kelli, though she appeared relaxed and pleasantly inebriated, was still fuming inside. But Kelli had to be honest. Although she was, indeed, angry at Bling, she was, by far, angrier at herself. Even before she had made the decision to come to New York for Wilma's birthday, she promised herself that she was not going to express her feelings for Bling, not again. And yet, she had done it. She broke her promise and told Bling how she felt once more. And what did he do? He rejected her. Again.

As she took another swig of her beer, her emotions got the better of her, leaving her conflicted. She didn't know if she wanted to scream bloody murder or break down and burst into tears.

She gulped down the last drop of her beer and raised her glass to signal to Michael that she wanted another.

"I'll pay for that one, Mikey," an unfamiliar male voice said next to her. Kelli turned. A tall, young man with cocoa brown skin and a shiny bald head stood beside her. He smiled at her, and added, "If that's alright with you."

Kelli stared at him and took in his full image. He was very attractive. He had a square chin and was clean shaven, which Kelli liked a lot. The roundness of his shoulders and the bulging, chiseled arms told Kelli that he was a young man who took care of himself. The buzz that she was still feeling from the first three beers made her brave enough to dispense with discretion and check him out, brazenly, from head to toe. She noted the tightness of his jeans, another thing that she liked. With her enhanced senses, she could smell his body odor underneath his light, musky cologne from where he stood. It was pleasant; another check in the plus column.

Kelli shrugged. "Fine by me. Thank you."

He extended his right hand. "I'm Terell."

Kelli hesitated. Not because she was afraid or had never been in this situation before. In fact, Kelli had found herself sitting at her favorite bar in Boston on many lonely nights. Being approached by men was something to which she had grown accustomed. And why not? Despite her youthful appearance, Kelli was stunning, even in a pair of sweat pants. Any man would find her striking. Why wouldn't any man want to be with her? No, Kelli hesitated because she thought of Bling. Oh, how she wished Bling was here to see this. She wanted him to see that other men are interested in her, that other men don't see a freak who can shift genders. All they see is a woman. All they see is her.

Kelli smiled and shook his hand. "Kelli," she said softly, and gestured for him to sit next to her.

Terell complied immediately. "Thanks. I've been sitting over there for fifteen minutes trying to figure out a way to approach you. I wasn't sure what to say."

Kelli leaned towards him slightly. "You did fine."

He brandished a wide smile. "You from Boston?" he asked, nodding towards her *Terriers* t-shirt.

"I went to school there," Kelli said. "But I was born and raised right here."

"No kidding? I'm a native, too. Grew up in Brooklyn." He chuckled. Kelli liked his laugh, although she wasn't sure if it was because she'd been drinking or if he really had a nice laugh.

"It appears we have something in common already," Kelli said with a hint of flirtation.

Michael placed another beer in front of Kelli. She took a quick sip and savored the flavor as it splashed onto her tongue.

"So are you living here now?" Terell asked.

"No. Just in town to have a little fun." She paused a moment, hoping her words would sink in. After a short breath, she shifted her gaze and caught Terell's eye. She could tell by his expression that her message was received.

Terell smiled. He chuckled again, speechlessly.

Kelli glanced at her watch. It was 12:30. She had three hours before she had to meet her parents and younger siblings at the mall. Plenty of time. *Screw Bling.*

She signaled the bartender. "I'll take the check."

Michael pointed to a thin slip of paper that protruded from a short rocks glass in front of her. "Right there, love."

Kelli reached into her pocket and pulled out some cash.

Terell protested, "I said I would pay for the last one."

"Next time, Terell." Kelli grabbed the check from the rocks glass and peered at the total. She realized that she had enough cash to pay the bill, but not enough for the tip. In her anger, she'd forgotten to grab another twenty from her envelope when she got out of the car. She glanced up at Terell and smiled. Since she had just decided to pay her own bill, she wouldn't feel right asking him to cover her tip. *No worries*, she thought, as she pulled out her credit card and then placed it in the glass with the check.

Terell was embarrassed. He wanted to pay for her drink, and didn't want to seem like the type of guy who didn't keep his word. He reached into his back pocket and retrieved his wallet.

"Really, Kelli. I can pay for that."

"Don't worry, Terell," she said with a lascivious grin. "You will."

Moments earlier, across the bar, Agent Swann made several notations on a small notepad which she kept in her left hip pocket. Her notepad contained all types of remarks regarding her surveillance of Kyle Cuffee; his movements, his eating habits, people to whom he spoke. Today, however, Swann noted a rather stunning realization.

Up until this moment, Swann had never gotten too close to Kyle as it was her own policy to always keep a safe distance between herself and those whom she followed. During the last two weeks of surveillance, she had adhered to that policy. In that time, Kyle had always worn baggy clothing, and the length of his dreadlocks often obscured any clear, extensive view of his face. But now, despite the fact that Swann's file on Kyle Cuffee listed his gender as male, Swann could undoubtedly see that Kyle was, in fact, female.

"Interesting," Swann whispered to herself. *I received a photocopy of Kyle's Massachusetts driver's license in my file; it clearly designates the gender as male.* She looked back through her notes and came across what she had written the day that Kyle entered the law firm of Adler, Royce, & Bellamy; most notable, Kyle's attire. Dark business suit, white button-down shirt, gold colored necktie, hair tied back; Swann had no reason to question Kyle's gender that day. *So why didn't I notice that Kyle was a female then?* A second passed before she answered her own question. *Because at a distance, based on how she was dressed, she appeared to be a male. Still, after two weeks, how did I miss that?*

Swann surmised that the initial mistake could have just been human error, that whoever created the file checked the wrong box in terms of gender. But then, that begged the question, *why does it seem like Kyle's style of dress lends itself to this particular mistake? Is there a reason why she'd be hiding her gender? If so, why? And why doesn't she seem to be concerned about it right now?*

Swann wished she had more time to think about it, but she realized that her time had run out. Across the bar, Kyle was paying her bill, and she seemed to be leaving with the young man to whom she was talking in tow.

This assignment just got more interesting, Swann thought to herself. She wondered if her superiors were aware that Kyle was a girl when they gave her this job. And if they did know, why wouldn't they mention it? Swann shook her head. It bothered her that this assignment was producing more questions than answers, and when that happened, it could only mean one thing; there was more to this case than meets the eye.

ॐ৵

WASHINGTON, D.C.

Molina entered the conference room. As soon as she did, she stopped suddenly in her tracks. Molina had no idea that the room was already occupied.

"Good afternoon," Peppers greeted her politely.

Molina looked at both men quickly before asking, "Who are you?"

"I'm Special Agent Peppers. This is my partner, Special Agent Brandon Kincaid."

Kincaid offered her a two-finger salute, but said nothing.

"Clearance level?" Molina asked.

Peppers raised an eyebrow, surprised that she would ask such a thing. "Level Four," he replied.

"Oh," Molina said, realizing that their clearance level matched her own. "Then can I ask you both to give me the room? I'm expecting a *call-in*."

Peppers and Kincaid exchanged a quick glance. Molina noticed.

"Is there a problem, gentlemen?" she asked impatiently.

Peppers moved towards the door. "Not at all." He gestured to Kincaid, who, in response, stood up and headed for the door as well. "It's all yours," said Peppers courteously.

The two men exited the room. Molina closed the door behind them and then took a seat at the table. She sat in silence for several minutes, stewing over the things she wanted to say, the things she wanted to know. As if in response, the phone rang.

Molina swallowed and took a second to compose herself. Though she was incensed, she was no fool. She knew who was on the other end of the phone line. And she knew, though she intended to speak her mind, she had to be tactful and respectful while doing so.

She picked up the phone and turned it over. She tapped the call button and opened the line. Then she tapped the speaker button, and the call began.

"This is Special Agent Molina. First name Maribel, division service number Alpha 5191969."

"Are you alone?" the voice asked.

"Yes, Sir."

"Good. This is Mr. Five. You requested a conference," he stated.

"Yes," Molina confirmed, "although I was hoping to speak with you in person."

"Agent Molina," Five began, "you know that face-to-face meetings are not standard protocol."

"Yes, I am aware of that, however . . ." she paused, making certain to choose her next words carefully, "I was hoping you would make an exception and extend me the same courtesy that you gave my daughter."

"Your daughter is a new operative who had very specific orders. We felt that the delicate nature of the assignment demanded a one-on-one."

"But she's only a teenager," she replied.

Five's voice was noticeably firmer when next he spoke. "You and I both know that isn't exactly true. We are both aware that your daughter was created and raised to be an operative. We gave her an assignment. That should have come as no surprise to you."

"Maybe it wouldn't have been a surprise if I had been debriefed, as well," Molina said sharply, and then added pointedly, "Sir."

"It was necessary," responded Five. "In this business, one must be able to maintain strict confidentiality. What better way for her to prove that she could be discreet than to keep a secret from you? Nothing personal."

"But I thought the program was over. That was the whole reason for moving us across the country."

"It *was* over, Agent Molina. Over, as in completed, not abandoned."

Molina's temperature began to rise. When she and Iris were relocated to the D.C. area five months ago, Molina was led to believe that the training program was being halted due to insufficient funding. But now, the gut feeling that had told her that something wasn't right had finally been confirmed. She cursed silently to herself in Spanish. She should have known. In fact, she did know. Nevertheless, Molina wanted to believe that things were going to be different for Iris, that her daughter was not going to be immersed beneath a tidal wave of espionage, international politics, and warfare. Now, Molina had to accept the fact that she and Iris were merely pawns whom the Agency had simply moved into a strategic position.

Molina choked back her anger. The last thing she wanted to do was upset Mr. Five. Despite her current emotional state, Molina knew better. Instead, she asked more questions.

"What about the other students in the program? Parker, Amelia, Lars, Ruben? Have they been assigned missions as well? And what about their mothers, er . . . *care-takers*?"

"None of that is your concern," Five answered firmly. "You have a more important matter to attend to, which, unfortunately, brings me to the next order of business."

"Unfortunately?" Molina did not like the sound of that.

"Yes. As it turns out, our supply of HP-47 has been recalled."

"What?" Molina questioned aloud. She stood, unable to contain herself. "But that's the vaccine that's been keeping Iris stable. Without it . . ." Molina's voice trailed off as her mind struggled with the implication of Mr. Five's announcement.

"I do apologize, Agent Molina. I know you've grown very fond of Iris, but the remainder of the HP-47 has to be used as a template to synthesize a new vaccine."

"How long will that take?" she asked desperately.

"We don't know. Months, maybe years."

"Years?" Molina's voice cracked as a cascade of emotion welled up inside of her. Despite her best effort, she could not contain it. Tears poured silently from her eyes. Though Molina was well aware that it was possible for Iris to live without kidneys, she also knew that it would mean Iris would be dependent on dialysis for the rest of her life. *No.* Molina knew that Iris wouldn't want that. *My daughter deserves better.* Molina's heart broke. When she spoke, her voice was uncharacteristically small, weak, and laden with sadness. "Iris doesn't have years."

"Yes, I know," Five acknowledged stoically. "And for that, Agent Molina, I am truly sorry."

It was several more minutes before Mr. Five could calm Agent Molina down long enough to end the call. Once he did, he pushed the phone slowly into the center of the table at which he and two other men sat.

"That went better than I thought it would," Two said to Five from across the table.

Five shook his head slowly. "It didn't feel good."

"I know it didn't," One said in an effort to console him. "But like you said. It was necessary."

Two glanced over at One. Their eyes met. Two nodded slowly. "Yes. Necessary."

"But why the half-truth?" questioned Five. "Why not tell her everything?"

One and Two exchanged another fleeting look. One inhaled deeply, for he knew that even Mr. Five himself didn't know everything. Mr. One and Two had informed Five that the HP-47 vaccine was recalled due to a flaw in the design, not that it was going to be used for One's personal interest. One exhaled slowly. "There's no point in telling her everything," One replied finally. "Besides, the half-truth she got is already bad enough."

The phone rang, startling Mr. Five. Reflexively, he looked at Mr. One who was already reaching for it.

"Yes," One said into the phone once he opened the line.

While One was occupied on the phone, Two took this moment to speak to Five.

"This job isn't always easy, Mr. Five, but what we do here in this building, in this office, is vital to the protection and survival of this nation."

"I'm fifty-three years old, Mr. Two. I've been sitting at this table for seven years now. Believe me, you're preaching to the choir, old man."

Mr. Two allowed himself a smile. "I know, but everyone needs a reminder every once in a while."

Mr. One pressed a button and severed the connection. He placed the phone down. A distant look clouded his face briefly before he turned and looked towards the two gentlemen seated at the table.

"The cleaners are done. All traces of the safe-house have been properly disposed of."

"All except Agent Rose's body," Five pointed out.

"He's dead," One reminded him. "I'm sure A.D. Marsh will handle that for us."

"Do the cleaners have Dr. Patel's briefcase?" asked Two.

One nodded. "They do, but there's a concern. The explosion may have damaged the chilled vial inside and compromised the live cultures at the base of the vaccine."

"How will we know for sure?" Two asked.

"I told them to bring it to the Med-clinic and give it to Dr. Chen. He'll analyze it and make sure it's still viable."

"I'll pick it up after hours," Five offered, and then added quickly, "if that's okay."

"That's fine," One said as he stood, his old bones crackling audibly in the process. "On that note, I need to go spend some time with Lizanne."

"Oh, I thought you saw her earlier," Two stated.

"No. *Duty* called."

"Well, give Lizanne my regards, will you?" Two asked.

"Certainly," One replied. He grabbed hold of the black cane that was dangling from the back of his chair. Within a minute, One crossed the threshold and disappeared behind the door into the hallway.

Once he was certain that One was gone, Five turned to Mr. Two. "Is he okay? He seemed a little distracted just then." Mr. Five was not aware of One's earlier phone conversation with the oncologist.

"I don't know," Two responded honestly. "He *does* have a lot on his mind right now. But don't you worry. I've known him for many years. If anyone knows how to handle their problems, it's Mr. One."

FBI FIELD OFFICE

Bonner entered Marsh's office. He noticed instantly that, in addition to Marsh's usual professional demeanor, there was an air of frustration that emanated from him as he looked up in response to the young agent's entrance. It made Bonner uncomfortable.

"You wanted to see me, Boss?" he asked Marsh.

"Yeah," Marsh replied as he handed him a sheet of paper. "I need you to find me a white rabbit."

Bonner looked at the sheet of paper. On it was written one name, followed by a set of numbers, and a picture of an American Express credit card. Bonner could easily see that the set of numbers was a social security number. The name on the Amex card matched the name that was scribbled on the paper. Kyle Cuffee.

"Who's this?" Bonner questioned.

"The white rabbit. I need you to track any recent usage of that card. If anything turns up, I want to know yesterday. Understand?"

"Uh, sure," answered Bonner, confused. "But, out of curiosity, why me? Shouldn't I be out handling my other cases?"

Marsh looked up at him. "Have you finished the report on the Navarro case yet?"

"No," Bonner replied, suddenly annoyed. "But it would be going a lot quicker if my partner hadn't disappeared on me again. You wouldn't want to clue me in as to where West is, would you?" he asked hopefully.

Marsh didn't miss a beat. "No. I wouldn't. And while you're waiting for the credit card info to come back, I need you to check passenger manifests for all the airlines that serve Dulles, BWI, or National. Cuffee flew in and out of the area within the last week. I need to know when and where."

"Are you serious?" Bonner asked with a small chuckle, although his inquiry was quite staid. "This could take all night. How about if I get Agent Lacee to help me? Apparently, his partner is out sick today."

"No," Marsh snapped. "*You* do this. Do it alone. Keep it quiet. And for God's sake, stop whining about your partner. West is out doing his job. Am I clear?"

Bonner was surprised. In all of the time he had been working in this field office, never once had Marsh snapped at him or made him feel like he needed to mind his own business. Frankly, it scared him a little. Bonner decided to back off.

"Absolutely, Boss," he managed to say. "I'll get right on this." With that, Bonner turned and exited Marsh's office.

Marsh exhaled long and hard. He reached under his desk and retrieved the brown bag given to him by Paul Ferry. Once again, he removed the billfold that held Ferry's Agency credentials. He opened it, and peered at Ferry's picture I.D.

"Don't worry, my friend. Justice is coming."

❧❦

Bonner slipped into the chair behind his desk. Immediately, he pulled his cell phone from his pocket and re-opened a chat window he had been using earlier. Quickly, he typed a message.

"Marsh just gave me an assignment. A goose chase targeted at a Kyle Cuffee. Anything to do with what you asked me to do?"

A few minutes passed before a response appeared in the chat window. *"Depends on what you find out. Keep me informed."*

Not exactly the answer I was looking for, Bonner thought to himself. Still, he typed in an immediate reply. *"Absolutely."*

❧❦

West was not very fond of lawyers. His dislike for those who practiced law did not stem from the notion that all lawyers were crooked liars or master manipulators of the legal system. In truth, West appreciated the hard work that lawyers did on a daily basis, and he knew that the legal system, a system in which he still wanted to believe, would not run as smoothly without them. No, West's issue with lawyers was much more personal.

West's mother was an attorney who had worked in the public defender's office for most of her legal career. Though his parents were still married to this day, the majority of West's childhood memories were ones that involved his father. His mother was present, but due to the demanding nature of her work, her profession took priority over all other things, including her husband and her two sons. West hated that he had grown to be just like her.

West fiddled with his cell phone as he sat patiently in the conference room of the law offices of Jameson, Cross & Rothberg. He watched as the lawyers walked hurriedly from one place to the next, each one lost in thought, probably focused on whatever case they were currently working. West shook his head as he remembered seeing those same focused looks on his mother's face almost every day of his childhood. He turned away, and decided to focus on something that had, once again, become a priority in his life; the Agency, and Kelli Freeman.

West recalled the conversation he had with the homeless man in Virginia only an hour prior to arriving at the law office.

"Sonny," the aging hobo had said when West asked him his name, "named after Sonny Jurgenson."

"Who's that?" West asked, not truly interested, but he figured it was a good way to break the ice with the homeless man, as well as to calm his nerves. After all, West had just pointed a loaded weapon at the man's head.

The man looked surprised, almost disgusted at West's naiveté. "Sonny Jurgenson, man; famous quarterback for the Redskins. Jesus, man, I swear, you youngsters."

"Sorry, Sonny," West had apologized quickly. "You were telling me about the people you saw at this house the other day."

"Oh, yeah," Sonny said eagerly. "One of those SUV's showed up here pretty early yesterday morning, say about 9:00."

"9:00? You sure?"

"Oh yeah," Sonny reassured him as he held up his right arm and showed West the watch that was strapped to his wrist. "I found this over by the school," he explained pointing off into the distance to his right.

West had no idea to which school Sonny was referring, and he didn't care in the slightest. He asked another question to keep the man on topic. "And you said there were four of them."

"That's right," he said proudly. "Three men and a young girl."

"Did you get a good look at any of them?"

"Not really," Sonny said. "I was hiding behind that stump over there so I was trying not be seen. I do remember, though, there was only one white guy."

West surmised that the white guy was Paul Ferry. "And the others?"

Sonny scratched his head. "They all had darker skin. One of them was definitely a black guy, and the girl may have been black, too."

West reached into the inside pocket of his suit jacket and retrieved a picture of Kelli Freeman. He showed the photo to Sonny.

"Is this the girl?"

Sonny stared at the picture for a moment. "Sure as hell could have been," he replied. "Like I said, I didn't get a good look."

West was disappointed. He was hoping that Sonny would confirm that the girl he saw at the safe-house was not the girl in the photo. Then, at least, West could put his suspicions and fears about Kelli working for the Agency to rest. Also, ruling Kelli out as a suspect in Ferry's murder would ease West's conscience. Deep down, he felt that if he'd kept in closer contact with Kelli, maybe he would have some idea of what she was up to. Maybe he could have done something to deter her from whatever path she might now be on. *Yeah. Maybe.*

"Then what happened?" West asked.

"What happened?" Sonny repeated. "The house exploded, man. Like an hour later, just, boom. I heard it clear from the spot where I'm squatting. The folks up the road must've heard it, too, 'cause they showed up not long after I did."

"What did you see?"

"Nothing at first. But another SUV showed up about five minutes after the explosion."

"Five minutes? You sure?"

Sonny held up his arm, displaying his watch once again. "Oh yeah. I'm sure."

"Then what?"

"Two men got out. A few minutes later, they came back to their vehicle."

"Did you get a good look at *them*, at least?"

"Heck, no. I was too busy hiding."

West's mind raced as he thought about the timetable between the explosion and the arrival of the SUV. The men driving it must have anticipated the blast, somehow knew it was going to happen. West turned back to Sonny. "What about the girl? Did they leave her behind?"

"Nope," he said confidently. "She came out and hopped in the SUV right behind them. Then they took off, just like that."

"Yeah?"

"Oh yeah, man. It was another minute or so before the ambulance showed up."

"Ambulance?" West wasn't expecting that. "So soon?" Considering how remote this location was, West had assumed it took quite some time for any first responders to arrive on scene.

"Oh yeah. Fire engines and police cars eventually showed up, too. I imagine the folks up the street called them. They were already hosing the place down when they pulled the white guy out of there."

Something that makes sense finally, West had thought to himself. *That explains how Ferry ended up at Howard University Hospital. Still, that's quite a distance. He must have requested to be taken there specifically. Of course, this also means that the Agency made a mistake. Whoever it was that came to retrieve the girl must have believed Ferry to be dead. And why wouldn't they? The guy had four bullets in him. That's the only explanation for why they left him alive. And the swift arrival of the ambulance ensured Ferry was gone before . . .*

"Wait," West raised a finger in the air. "The fire department didn't clean this area, did they?"

"Oh no," Sonny said. "A swarm of white vans showed up about half an hour into the job. They flashed some badges, barked some orders, and then everybody left. The fire department, *and* the PD, gone. Just like that."

"And the people in the white vans sanitized the area," West said as a statement of fact, not a question.

Sonny nodded. "They did a pretty good job of it, too." He looked around the area where the safe-house once stood. He was let down. "Didn't leave a thing."

West felt that Sonny had told him everything he knew, so he dismissed the old bum and sent him on his way with a twenty-dollar bill and a leftover scone from Starbucks. West hopped into his car and traveled back up the road a quarter-mile before arriving at the house he'd passed earlier. If the residents were, in fact, the ones who called the ambulance, perhaps they would have more to add to Sonny's story. Despite knocking loudly and ringing the doorbell several times, no one came to the door. West guessed that the residents of this house were probably at work. Upon further speculation, he decided that, even if they were home, they probably wouldn't be as forthcoming as Sonny had been. The Agency had probably intervened already and compensated these people very generously for their non-disclosure.

West had climbed back into his sedan once again. As he began the drive back to D.C., he received a phone call from A.D. Marsh informing him of Davies' discovery that Kelli had, in fact, been in the D.C. area over the weekend. During that call, Marsh tasked West with questioning Kelli's brother, Martin Freeman. One quick address verification and sixty-minutes later, West found himself at Martin's current location, surrounded by lawyers.

The sound of the faint hiss of air rushing out of the room alerted West to the fact that the glass door was being pushed open. The sound of footsteps confirmed that someone had entered the room. West looked up and stared at the person he came to see.

Martin Freeman was a handsome, young man who had recently turned twenty-five. His milk-chocolate brown skin was nicely complemented by the ivory-colored shirt, the brown and turquoise tie, and the taupe business suit. He strode towards West with confidence, like a young conqueror that had slain the dragon or defeated a long-rivaled enemy in battle. West had left his name with the secretary, so Martin already knew whom he was addressing when he extended his hand.

West stood and accepted Martin's handshake. "Martin. It's nice to finally meet you."

Martin knew of West's existence, of course, because of his connection to his sister, Kelli. He had heard West's name many times when speaking with his family back in the Bronx, and had even seen West's face on the news once or twice. However, this was the first time they had ever met face to face.

"Likewise," Martin said with a smile, shaking West's hand firmly. "What can I do for you? I assume this isn't a social call."

"No," West confirmed. He looked around the spacious conference room, particularly at the uppermost corners of the room where the walls met the ceiling; anywhere that a camera would most likely be mounted. "Is this room secure?"

Martin chuckled. He wasn't completely certain of the answer. "I hope so," he managed to say. "We discuss extremely confidential things in here, so . . ." his voice trailed off. He was hoping West would let it go and get right to the point of his visit.

West obliged him. "When's the last time you saw your sister, Martin?"

Martin, like every other member of his immediate family, knew that Kelli was alive and well and living in Boston under witness protection. His first inclination was to be misleading and ask if West was inquiring about his other sister, Wilma, but Martin figured that might simply annoy the Federal agent who stood before him. So instead, Martin answered the question.

"Kelli? Just this past weekend," Martin confessed. There was no point in lying about it. He assumed that West already knew the answer to the question, or why else would he be here at all? "Is there a problem, Agent West?"

"I hope not," West answered. "Does Kelli visit often?"

"Define often."

West cringed slightly. Martin's request for him to define often was reminiscent of the evasive response his mother would give to his father when she was being questioned about why she could not, yet again, participate in a family function that conflicted with her work.

West sighed. "Once a month, every two months, every six months."

"No," Martin replied. "Admittedly she's been down here a couple times in the last few months, but that's something new."

"Does she crash at your place when she's here?"

"Of course. She's my sister."

"Did she say why she was in town?" West asked.

"She said she needed a break. She just passed the Massachusetts Bar and she needed some time to unwind and get away from Boston. She hates it there."

West noted that Martin did not mention that Kelli may have been looking into prospective law firms. He wondered if Kelli had neglected to inform Martin of that fact, or if Martin, for some reason, elected not to mention it to him.

"Yeah, I remember," said West. His mind reflected on the fact that Kelli had just passed the Massachusetts Bar. He had no idea. It seemed like yesterday that she was only fifteen and he was visiting her in Boston for the first time outside of Fenway Park. Had that much time passed? Had he really been away for so long? West shook off the memory and continued his interrogation. "When did she leave D.C.?"

Martin took a step forward. "Agent West, what's with all the questions? Is Kelli alright? Did she do something wrong?"

"That's what I'm trying to figure out, Martin. Believe me."

"Well, you obviously know something, or you wouldn't be here."

West couldn't argue with that.

Martin continued. "Considering the fact that Kelli is in witness protection, you can't blame me for being alarmed when you show up here asking questions. So, Agent West, if my sister is in trouble, you have to tell me. Please."

West considered maintaining the position that he did not know what was going on with Kelli. Truth be told, it would not be far from the truth. But West did know something for certain, and was willing to gamble that Martin might be a little more cooperative if he was willing to share. Besides, Martin's argument was rather compelling. West was willing to bet that the young lawyer was a pretty good litigator.

"Look," West began, "I didn't mean to alarm you, but Kelli's off the grid."

"She's missing?"

West raised a hand in protest. "I don't want to declare her missing just yet. I have reason to believe that her disappearance might be self-imposed. I wish I could be more specific, but I can't. Right now, my top priority is to locate your sister. So, please, Martin. If you know anything, I'd really appreciate you helping me out. As far as I know, you're the last person who saw her."

A worried look had washed over Martin's face. "Sure. Okay. She took a late flight back to Boston on Monday night."

"Which airport? Which airline?"

Martin shook his head. "I didn't ask."

"You didn't drop her off?"

"No, she had a rental, Enterprise, I think. She flew in last Thursday while I was working. I met her afterwards. She didn't talk about her flight details at all."

"Did you work on Friday?"

"Of course," Martin answered.

"Any idea what Kelli did that day?"

Martin shook his head. "None. She was in my apartment when I left in the morning, and she was curled up on the couch, watching TV, when I got home."

"And what time was that?"

"Six. Six-thirty."

West pondered that information for a moment. Kelli had come into town and crashed with her brother. She rented her own vehicle so it wasn't necessary to inform him of any of the flight details. Then, on Friday, she had all day to do whatever she pleased; go on interviews, meet with Agency operatives, accept an assignment. Whatever. As long as she was back at Martin's place before he made it home, no one would be the wiser. West had to admit, if he were in her shoes, that's how he would have done it, too.

"So, let me guess," West said. "The two of you hung out all weekend, and she was hardly ever out of your sight."

"Well, yeah," Martin responded. "Except for Saturday morning. She went for a run. She might have been gone a few hours."

"And Monday was pretty much like Friday? She had the day to herself?"

Martin did not speak. Instead, he simply nodded his reply.

West exhaled heavily. He reached into his jacket pocket and retrieved his card. He handed it to Martin. "I appreciate your help," he said to the lawyer. "If you think of anything else-"

"Sure. Sure," Martin interrupted, clearly bothered by the thought of Kelli being off the grid. He took the card and stared at it absently.

West had no more words for Martin, nothing that would make him feel better anyway. He had the information for which he had come; unfortunately, it wasn't enough for West to figure out what Kelli was up to, or to where she may have disappeared.

He shook Martin's hand and dismissed himself. Within moments, West was back on the street walking towards his car. He felt awful for alarming Martin. He hated being the bearer of bad news. Nevertheless, maybe it was time to bring the news of Kelli's disappearance to her parents. If they couldn't provide information on her whereabouts, at least West could rule out New York as a place they needed to look. Wherever Kelli was, West hoped that she was okay. Still, there was a part of West that hoped he didn't find Kelli. Not because he didn't want to see her again, or because she was upset at him. No. West was afraid that his investigation would implicate her in the shooting of Paul Ferry. If that happened, West knew that the next time he saw Kelli, he might have to arrest her for murder.

❧

Martin walked calmly back to his office after his conversation with Agent West. Once inside, he closed the door, crossed the room, and took a seat behind his desk. His briefcase was leaning against his desk at his feet. Martin opened it, unzipped a side pocket, and pulled out a prepaid cellular TracFone. He dialed a number quickly. He listened as the phone rang in his ear. No answer. He disconnected the call and tried again. Like before, there was no answer.

Martin sighed heavily. He stayed on the line and allowed his call to go to voicemail. After listening to the outgoing message, Martin left a message of his own.

"Kelli. It's me. I don't know why you're not picking up your phone, but you were right. Apparently, you aren't just being paranoid. Agent West was here. I think they're on to you."

7

WASHINGTON, D.C.

Dr. Suri sat in his office with his face buried in his hands. Today had not been a good day. Based on his earlier conversation with Dr. Chen, Suri had been expecting a visit from Mr. Five. Instead, Mr. Five communicated with Suri via the *'white phone'* in the situation room and gave him a bit of news that was rather disturbing.

"Pardon me," Suri said, hoping he had heard Mr. Five wrong.

"I said you're being transferred out of the clinic. Your work there is done."

"But what about my other patients?" *Patients other than Iris Molina.*

"Your other patients will be attended to by a very capable physician," assured Five. "But now that the girl's treatments have been terminated, your talents are needed elsewhere."

"May I ask where?" Suri inquired, although he feared that he already knew the answer.

"Quinlan Pharmaceuticals," Five replied, verifying Suri's fears.

It wasn't that Suri did not want to go to Quinlan, but he knew that Quinlan had appropriated the HP-47 vaccine. Suri had spent the last six years keeping Iris Molina stable, healthy, and alive. Now, he was being asked to continue working on the vaccine, even though he knew that abandoning Iris would mean certain death for her. Suri hated being in this position, but what could he do? He knew that opting out of his Agency obligation would incur rather unpleasant consequences.

"It may take a day or so to clear out my office here," Suri said, conceding.

"Take two," Five said politely. "Report to Quinlan on Friday." With that, the call ended.

Suri marched back to his office and closed the door. He extracted a key from inside his wallet and used it to open a drawer in his desk. There, he found a thick file with the words Harmony Project printed on the outside.

For more than an hour, Suri poured through the documentation that detailed every aspect of the Harmony Project from its inception more than three decades ago to the present. Since Suri was the geneticist who engineered Iris' existence during the latest phase of the experiment, he was given full access to the notes of the late Doctors James Connelly and Marcus June. When Suri ran into any medical conundrums, he was afforded the opportunity to consult with Dr. Amanda Simons, the only doctor assigned to the initial Harmony Project that was still alive. Simons, due to her murder conviction of Dr. Connelly, was a permanent resident of Central California Womens Facility Prison in the city of Chowchilla. Simons did her best to fill in the gaps for Suri. However, when Suri mentioned a reference to something in the notes called the "June Gene" which was followed by an obvious redaction, Simons dismissed it as a path of trials and errors that elicited nothing worthwhile. Suri became immediately suspicious but, due to the circumstances, had no choice but to accept it. There was also a mention of a gender shift in the notes. Suri was uncertain as to what that reference was about. *Surely it couldn't mean what it implies*, he had thought to himself. Unfortunately, when he asked Dr. Simons to explain it, she became elusive, developed a sudden headache, and requested a guard to bring her back to her cell. Suri never saw her again. Not only because Iris, her mother, and all of the doctors responsible for her care were transferred from Camp Pendleton to Washington, D.C, but also because Dr. Simons refused, repeatedly, to see him. It wasn't long before the word came from Mr. Five to stop asking.

Suri turned the page. He scrutinized every word on every page, searching for something he may have overlooked, anything that would allow him to keep Iris alive without the HP-47 vaccine. To his disappointment, but not his surprise, he found nothing.

There was a soft knock on his office door. Suri ignored it. Considering the day he was having, the last thing he wanted was a visitor. He sat in silence, hoping that his unknown caller would go away.

"Dr. Suri?" a female voice called to him.

Suri recognized the voice. It belonged to Agent Molina. He stood and crossed the distance to the door. When he opened it, he saw Molina standing there, crying, desolate of hope, and defeated. In that moment, he knew that she had been given the news about Iris' treatment. Suri pulled her into his office, closed the door, and took the crying woman into his arms. He pulled her close and squeezed her tight. As he did, she began to cry harder. Her knees gave out, and Suri had to muster all of his strength to keep her from falling to the ground. It was almost a full five minutes before Molina collected herself enough to speak.

"I can't believe they're just going to let her die," she said through her tears. "They're just going to discard her as if her life means nothing."

Despite Suri's usual soothing bedside manner, he was at a loss for words. After all, Molina was right. They were simply casting her young life aside.

"Isn't there something you can do, some other treatment we can try?" she asked.

Suri did not want to lie to her. He felt that Molina had been lied to enough already. "Without the vaccine, I don't know."

Molina pulled away and began pacing the floor as she did before. "What about a kidney transplant? Wouldn't that work?"

Suri had considered the option of a kidney transplant at one point, but Iris' kidney function was showing so many significant signs of improvement as a result of the HP-47, that the medical team was optimistic that she would not need such an operation. Suri supposed a kidney transplant would still be successful, but he knew that it was far too late to be feasible.

"The transplant list is already extremely long," he explained. "Being placed on the bottom of that list would most likely mean years of waiting for a viable donor."

Molina did not relent. As she spoke, the volume of her voice began to rise. "What about the Agency? We work for this powerful organization that does all types of *unheard-of* things, that is capable of pulling all types of strings, and they can't get us on the top of a freakin' list?"

Suri made a quieting gesture with his hands. "Have you asked?"

Molina shook her head. "No. I've been so upset and so worried about Iris that I haven't been able to think straight."

"That's understandable," Suri said. "Listen, why don't you go home, get some rest, and I'll inquire about the transplant list for you."

Molina's expression brightened slightly. "Would you?" She asked.

"Of course," Suri responded honestly. "Don't you worry about it. Go home. Get some sleep."

Molina wiped tears from both of her eyes. "That's actually why I came to see you. Dr. Chen told me that Iris can go home but he's with another patient right now. I was wondering if you would sign her release papers."

Suri managed a smile. "Of course."

A few more minutes passed before Molina had fully composed herself. Once she had, Suri escorted her up the long hallway towards the nurse's station.

As they moved down the corridor, Nurse Gisela rounded the corner and walked towards them. She smiled at them as she approached, stepping to the right side of the hallway, allowing each of them enough space to pass. As the distance closed between them, Suri noticed that Gisela was carrying a black leather briefcase. Suri had seen that briefcase many times before in the office of Dr. Patel, and he recognized it instantly.

Suri returned Gisela's smile. "Nice briefcase," he chuckled. "It suits you."

"Oh, this? No," said Gisela, looking down at the briefcase as if she was surprised to be carrying it. "It's not mine. This just arrived for Dr. Chen."

"Isn't he with a patient?" Suri questioned innocently.

"Yeah, he's doing a biopsy; gonna be busy for a while. He told me to stick it in his office."

"Oh, okay," he said, then asked, "Who's at the nurse's station?" Not that he cared, but he didn't want to seem too preoccupied with the briefcase.

"Judy," Gisela said over her shoulder as she brushed past them and proceeded down the hallway.

Suri and Molina turned down the first hallway on the right and proceeded down the corridor until it opened up into a perpendicular, wider hallway. In the center was the nurse's station.

Suri greeted Judy as he entered the station. Judy, a ginger-haired Caucasian woman in her mid-fifties, barely gave Suri a nod as she remained focused on entering data into the computer in front of her.

"Do you have the release papers for Iris Molina?" he asked.

Judy did not bother to look away from her computer screen. "They're in the out-box next to the printer," she said.

Molina waited patiently as Suri retrieved and signed the paperwork. She had stopped crying long enough to place her sunglasses back on her face. Under normal circumstances, Molina kept the dark glasses on her face to hide the glass eye, about which she felt very self-conscience. Today, however, she needed them to hide the fact that she'd been crying. When she went to retrieve Iris, she didn't want to alarm her in any way. After all Iris had been through, Molina knew that was last thing her daughter needed to see.

Suri turned to her and offered a warm smile. "She's all yours."

"Thank you, Doctor," Molina replied. She took a deep breath before turning and re-entering the hallway that led back to her daughter's room. Within seconds, she had turned the corner and was on her way to retrieve Iris and take her home.

Suri filed the release papers in the proper folder and asked Judy to make note of it in the computer. He did not wait for her reply. Instead, he left the nurse's station en route to the corridor where the doctors' offices were located. However, Suri was not planning on going back to his office. Instead, Suri was going to the office of his colleague, Dr. Chen.

As he entered the hallway where Chen's office was located, he passed by Gisela as she headed back towards the nurse's station. He nodded at her, and then moved in front of the door to his own office. He watched Gisela, waiting for her to disappear around the distant corner. Once she had, Suri moved down the hall quickly and stopped in front of Chen's door. On the off-chance that Chen had already completed his biopsy, Suri knocked on the door. No one came. Suri tried the door handle but, as he had guessed, the door was locked. No matter. Suri was the head physician at this facility. He had keys to all the doors.

He reached into his pocket and pulled out his key chain which was jingling with an abundance of keys of different sizes and configurations. He located the master key and inserted it into the lock and gave it a quick turn.

He pushed at the door and, as expected, it opened. Suri entered the room.

The briefcase had been placed underneath Chen's desk. He placed it on top and flipped open the two latches that kept the contents secure. He opened the case and took note of the contents; a collection of black, fine point pens, several patient files, a small notebook, and a small stash of business cards in the name of the briefcase's rightful owner, Dr. Ramesh Patel.

Suri searched the smaller side pockets quickly. In many of them, he found several small notes, reminders of activities and appointments that Patel had written to himself. In one pocket, he came across a small tin thermos. Suri recognized it. Without hesitation, he unscrewed the lid, breaking the airtight seal. Contrary to what Suri expected, the gush of mist that brushed his fingertips as he opened it was several degrees warmer than usual. *That's not good.* Inside, Suri found a lone, semi-chilled vial with a crack in the glass that ran almost the full length of the container. The vial was partially filled with a chalky, pink liquid. Suri recognized the liquid, too. It was the vaccine known as HP-47.

"What the hell?" he questioned aloud. "This amount of the vaccine could treat Iris for several months." *With this much left, why would they end her treatments so soon? Perhaps this is why Patel made a break for it when he did.*

Suri surmised that Patel had run off with the vaccine so he could continue working on it. *Such a shame that he didn't get far.* Suri considered taking the vial and saving it so he could continue Iris' treatment secretly. Then, he dismissed the idea almost as quickly as it had come. He knew that the Agency would be collecting the briefcase and all of its contents. Suri was confident the Agency already knew what it contained. No. Suri knew if he took the vial, he'd be dead by morning. He returned the glass container to the small tin, and then placed the tin back in the pocket where he found it.

Suri cursed to himself as he prepared to close the case and leave Chen's office before he was discovered. Suddenly, something caught his eye. There was a patient file sticking out of another pocket in the lining of the briefcase. Suri had overlooked this pocket initially, but all of his fiddling about must have shifted the file's position to reveal the top of it. Suri pulled the file from the pocket. He looked at the cover. Iris Molina's name was written in black ink in the top right corner. Suri wasted no time and opened the folder. None of the preliminary information in the file was new to Suri, after all, he was the primary geneticist on this phase of the Harmony Project and was in charge of Iris' care. However, as Suri continued to read, he came across a reference to something called Project Rebirth. He paused. *No. That couldn't be what I think it is.* He hoped that a description of Project Rebirth would follow. Unfortunately, the next two lines were redacted. *No surprise there,* he scoffed silently. He began skimming through the pages with more haste in hopes of finding another reference to Rebirth. As he read further, he came to a particular piece of information that caught him completely off-guard. His jaw dropped as his eyes drank in every word on the page. Though it wasn't his intention, Suri turned page after page, and before he knew it, he'd lost track of time. It wasn't until the door handle turned and the door was pushed open that he realized he had overstayed his welcome.

Chen stood in the doorway, taking in the sight of Suri at his desk, reading Patel's notes.

"What do you think you're doing?" Chen demanded to know.

Suri did not answer Chen's question. Instead, he shook the file at Chen and raised his voice, as well. "You knew about this, didn't you, William? This is the real reason Patel took the girl, isn't it?"

Chen stepped into the room and closed the door. "You weren't supposed to see that," Chen confessed, his volume lower. "Not now, not ever."

"But we can save her," Suri said. "Hell, according to this, we could have already saved her with a kidney transplant."

Chen did not attempt to deny it. "I know," he said shamefully.

Suri's brow furled as realization set in. "It was you," Suri uttered. "Of course. You're the nephrologist. How long have you known?"

"I discovered it right before we left Camp Pendleton. I informed our superiors, but we were so close to having a perfected super soldier model, that I was instructed to run a few more tests just to be sure."

Suri was disgusted. "You used her as a guinea pig when we could have been looking for a kidney. You're a physician. How could you?"

"I was following orders, Arav. You know the consequences for disobedience."

"That's no excuse," countered Suri through gritted teeth.

"On the contrary, Doctor. It's *the* excuse. The sooner you get that through your head, the greater the chance you won't end up like Patel."

"Did Patel know?"

"Of course not," answered Chen. "He only discovered it recently."

"And that's why he ran with her," Suri deduced.

"Yes," Chen confirmed. "And that's why he's dead."

Suri tossed the file back onto Chen's desk. "How did I not see this? How did you keep this from me?"

"It wasn't easy," Chen said. "Constantly altering charts . . . believe me, this isn't the way I wanted this to play out. Like you, I wanted the best for Iris."

"No. Not like me," Suri protested angrily.

"Fine," Chen said. "Believe what you want. But I advise you to walk away. I know it won't be easy, but you need to do it, Arav. Walk away and forget you ever saw that file."

Tears began to flow from Suri's eyes as he thought of Iris. Though he didn't want to admit it, he knew Chen was right. His heart sank as he looked at his longtime colleague. "It seems I have no choice."

FBI FIELD OFFICE

Bonner walked quickly past the sea of desks on his way to Marsh's office. As he approached Marsh's door, Special Agent Garrett Lacee exited through that very door. Lacee was a thirteen-year veteran of the bureau. His youthful appearance belied the fact that he was a man only a few years shy of his fiftieth birthday. The contrast of his dark brown hair against his light blue eyes only enhanced his good looks, youthful charm, and winning smile. It was a smile he flashed at Bonner as soon as he saw him.

"You might not want to go in there," Lacee warned. "He's not in a good mood."

"Still?"

Lacee flashed a smile. "He's having a bad day, I guess"

"He's not the only one." Bonner gave Lacee a friendly slap on the right shoulder, and then brushed past him. A moment later, he was standing before A.D. Marsh once again.

"What you got?" Marsh asked.

"A hit on Cuffee's credit card," Bonner replied proudly. "Not here in D.C., though. It was used earlier today at the Lexa Bar and Garden in New York."

"New York?"

"Yep. In the boogie-down Bronx."

DULLES, VIRGINIA

West had pulled up all of the Enterprise car rental agencies that served the airports in the D.C. area. He knew it would be a waste of time to phone each one of them. Getting the information he was looking for would be next to impossible if he didn't show up in person and flash his FBI credentials.

West already knew that he had to contact Arthur and Diane Freeman, Kelli's parents, but he decided he would put that off until after he had confirmed that Kelli, in fact, had left the D.C. area. No need to get them all flustered about Kelli's whereabouts just yet, he told himself. Although Martin claimed that Kelli may have rented a car from Enterprise, he did not seem as if he was certain about it. West, doing his due diligence, needed to find from which car company Kelli rented a vehicle, and if she did, indeed, return said vehicle. According to Davies' report from Boston, Kelli was supposed to have arrived in Boston from D.C. last night, but no one had seen her to confirm that she had made it home. Martin's account of Kelli's time in D.C. corroborated the fact that she intended to take the flight back to Massachusetts on Monday night. The problem was, since Martin did not take Kelli back to the airport himself, there was no confirmation that Kelli actually left D.C. If West could track down the rental agency where the car was rented, he could, at the very least, confirm if Kelli did, in fact, return the vehicle. If she didn't, then West suspected that Kelli could still be in town, working for the Agency. He shuddered at the thought. But West needed to know whether or not Kelli left town. If she hadn't, then there was no reason to call her parents. Not yet. But if she had left D.C., and then disappeared, then and only then, would West reach out to her parents. *Damn it, Kelli. Why won't you answer your cell phone? If you did, we could verify your whereabouts and put our suspicions to rest.* Unfortunately, West knew he wasn't going to get that lucky.

West drove his sedan into the parking of the Enterprise rental agency on Autopilot Drive. This particular location served Washington Dulles International Airport. West chose this one because it was the closest Enterprise location to Martin's apartment, which was where Kelli stayed while in the area. He figured it was the most logical place to begin his search. He parked his car, and then entered the building. Ten minutes later, West exited the building with an answer. Kelli had, in fact, rented a car from that Enterprise location under the name of Kyle Cuffee. As soon as West had given the Enterprise employee Kyle's name, the young woman had no problem finding the corresponding reservation in the computer. West should have known that he could have gone to any Enterprise and retrieved that information. However, West wanted to find the exact location Kelli used so he could examine the car and look for anything at all that she might have left behind. The rental had been returned the day before at approximately 5:45 p.m. Unfortunately, the vehicle had already been cleaned and rented out to another customer. At this point, West knew it would be fruitless to have the car recalled. Any evidence that Kelli might have left behind had surely been washed away or contaminated by the current renter. He decided to leave. He had all the information he needed.

West had to assume that Kelli took a shuttle to the airport, and then hopped a flight. Unfortunately, he still couldn't confirm that she took a flight back to Boston. Wherever she went, West deduced that Kelli left D.C. approximately eighteen hours prior. That was quite a large chunk of time, and West knew that, at this point, Kelli could be just about anywhere.

West slid back behind the wheel of his car and reached for his cell phone. He had decided that now was the time to call Arthur and Diane. But first, he needed to call A.D. Marsh with this new information. Just as he picked up his phone, it began to ring in his hand. The caller ID identified the caller as Steven Marsh.

"Agent West," he said as he opened the line.

"You still have your bags packed from this morning?" Marsh asked.

"In the back seat."

"Good. We got a hit on her credit card."

"Really?" West said, surprised. Considering Kelli's level of intelligence, he figured Kelli would deliberately choose not to use her credit card to eliminate the possibility of creating a paper trail. If she's trying to remain elusive, why would she, all of a sudden, use it now? Despite the evidence so far, West began to wonder if he and Marsh had it all wrong. Maybe Kelli wasn't moving surreptitiously because she's working for the Agency. West knew already that Kelli hated it in Boston. She made no secret of that fact. Perhaps Kelli was traveling in secret because she was tired of being on the FBI's witness protection leash.

"Yeah," Marsh answered. "From a bar in the Bronx."

Kelli's hometown. West became even more confused. First Kelli came to D.C. to visit her brother, now she's possibly in New York where the rest of her family lives. West couldn't help but wonder if they were chasing Kelli for no reason. Still, West could neither explain away the fact that Kelli fit the description given by Ferry, nor the fact that Sonny could not say with certainty whether or not the girl he saw at the safe-house was, in fact, Kelli Freeman. But if Kelli wasn't the shooter in the incident that killed Paul Ferry, then who the hell was?

"Okay," West said. "I'm near the airport now. I'll catch the next flight out. I'll reach out to Kelli's parents, too. Maybe they've seen her."

"No," Marsh protest adamantly. "Don't call anyone. I don't want there to be any chance that she'll be alerted that you're coming."

"But, sir-"

"No calls. Are we clear?"

West sighed heavily. He did not like the idea of sneaking up on Kelli. But until he could find her and remove all suspicions of her involvement in Ferry's death, he was going to follow Marsh's orders, whether he liked it or not.

"Yes, sir. We're clear."

∂∽∾

BRONX, NEW YORK

Kelli sat directly beneath the flow of the rushing shower water for what seemed like hours. Curled up in a ball, she let the water inundate her as she cried uncontrollably. She couldn't believe it. She had done it again. She'd gone out and picked up a complete stranger, a man she didn't know from Adam. *Why do I keep doing this?* she questioned herself. *What the hell is wrong with me?*

She managed to pull herself up from the floor of the tub and climb out of the shower. She dried herself quickly, and then cursed as she looked around the bathroom. My clothes are in the bedroom, she thought. That's where I took them off. For him. Terell.

Kelli felt bad for the guy. *He must be freaking out,* she imagined. After Kelli had brought Terell back to her room at the Rodeway Inn, she wasted no time undressing and throwing herself at the young man. Terell tried to be respectful and demonstrate some restraint. He was successful for a while, that is until Kelli had removed all of her clothes. Once Terell was afforded an opportunity to look at Kelli's extremely fit and beautifully flawless physique, all of his defenses came crashing down. Kelli saw the look on his face as he stared at her naked form. Terrell was in awe, so much so that Kelli was certain Terell barely noticed, or didn't care about the old burn scars on her stomach and her right thigh. She had seen that look on the faces of several young men before him, and she knew, without a doubt, that she was in control.

Her attack was relentless and savage; practically ripping the young man out of his clothes. Terell managed to match her pace and stamina, and Kelli could tell the young man was enjoying himself. Unfortunately, within ten minutes, Kelli began to sob uncontrollably. Terell, worried and confused, tried to console Kelli as best he could. He even apologized for the act. Kelli assured him that he had done nothing wrong, but insisted that he leave immediately.

"Are you sure?" Terell asked. There was no doubt in his mind that he wanted to get out of there as fast as he could. He didn't want to deal with some crying woman and her issues. But he didn't want to seem like a total cad, either. Kelli relieved him of whatever guilt he may have been feeling.

"Yes. Go."

Fewer than five minutes later, Terell was dressed and, without so much as a backward glance, out the door. Kelli, feeling dirty and ashamed, headed straight for the shower. She scrubbed herself frantically for several minutes before collapsing into a ball under the shower's warm and soothing cascade. It took her twenty minutes to quell her emotions and get out of the tub.

Now that Kelli had calmed down, she opened the bathroom door and stepped into the bedroom. Though Terell was gone, the disheveled bed still displayed the evidence of their rendezvous. Her keen sense of smell confirmed it. Kelli took a deep breath to keep from losing control of her emotions once again.

She checked her watch. It was 2:30. She had an hour before she was supposed to be at the mall. She dressed quickly. She picked up the room phone and called the front desk. She requested maid service, asking explicitly for a change of bedding and new towels for the bathroom. Then, she reached into her backpack and stripped four twenties from the top of the stack within the envelope. Her hand brushed against her cell phone. She picked it up and turned it over. The device was still powered down so she tossed it aside. She reached for her prepaid Trac-phone and pulled it from the bag. The small, flashing red light told her that she had messages.

Maybe Bling had called, she thought, hopefully. She regretted her behavior with him today. She blamed herself for going back on her promise not to express her feelings for him, and for causing the resulting argument.

Kelli pressed a few buttons and activated the voicemail. She smiled to herself in anticipation of hearing his voice. After the events of the last hour, it would be nice to know that Bling did care enough to check up on her. Sadly, Kelli was disappointed. The message was not from Bling, but from her brother, Martin. Her breath caught in her throat as his message played in her ear.

She ended the call. She tapped in a series of numbers and listened as the phone rang on the other end in her ear. The phone line clicked open, and Martin's voice came back through the phone.

"Kelli," he said in a grave tone. "What the heck is going on?"

"You tell *me*," she countered. "What did Agent West say to you?"

"He said that you were off the grid," Martin answered. "I warned you, Kelli. I told you that if you kept sneaking off it would only be a matter of time before your friends at the Bureau caught on."

Kelli ignored her brother's *I told you so* rant. "Did he tell you how they figured it out?"

"No," Martin said, frustrated. "But it sure sounded like you're in trouble. Where are you anyway?"

"I came home for Wilma's birthday."

"You're in the Bronx?"

"I didn't want to miss her birthday, okay?" Kelli said. "And no, I'm not in trouble," she added, although she wasn't entirely certain if she was speaking the truth.

"So why don't you just call Agent West and tell him where you are?" Martin asked.

"I can't," she replied. "Not yet."

Martin exhaled heavily before he said, "Sounds like trouble to me. I hope you know what you're doing, Sis."

"Don't worry, Martin. I'm okay."

"If you say so." He didn't believe her. "Listen, I've got to get back to work. Call me if you need me."

"I will. Thank you."

"No problem. I love you."

Kelli smiled. Despite Martin's admonishments, it made her feel good to hear him express his love for her; his sister. "Love you, too."

"Be careful."

I've been hearing that a lot lately, she thought to herself. "That's the plan," she managed to say before she ended the call and tossed the phone back into her backpack.

She paced the room for a moment as she pondered Martin's recount of West's visit. "How did they know I left Boston?" she asked, thinking aloud. "And how did they know I was in D.C.?" She retraced her steps over the last week or so. She didn't think she had left any obvious trace of her movements while she was gone. Sure, she knew it would be easy enough to eventually determine that Kyle Cuffee booked flights to and from Washington D.C. Even though she paid cash for all of it, her male alter ego's name was still on the passenger list. The same thing applied to her rental car. According to the records, Kyle paid cash. Still, in order for the FBI to find any of that information, they would need a reason to look. "What did I do wrong? Could I have been spotted while taking care of my other business?"

Kelli remembered that Agent Davies had left a message on her apartment voicemail while she was away in D.C. Perhaps Davies had grown tired of her calls going unanswered, Kelli surmised. *Perhaps she came looking for me.*

Kelli reached into her backpack once again. She retrieved her cell phone, the one tied to her life as Kyle Cuffee. She hesitated. Now that she knew West, and perhaps Davies, were actively looking for her, turning on her cell phone could allow them to trace her cell signal to

New York. And what if they did? "What's the worst-case scenario?" she asked aloud again. For starters, Kelli thought, they would tighten their hold on me. They would make sure that I met with Davies on a regular basis and would probably try to put a stop to any quick escapes from Boston that I might have planned. And if they do grant me permission to leave, it wouldn't be without a federal chaperone. Kelli shuddered. She hated the very thought of that. Mostly because a chaperone would be watching her like a hawk, and Kelli had plans, plans that involved gaining leverage over Mr. One and getting her life back. There was no way she could continue her business in D.C. with a federal leash around her neck.

She stuffed her cell phone back into her backpack. Powering up Kyle's cell phone was too risky right now, even if it was just to listen to her voicemail. There was always the possibility of calling her voicemail from a completely different phone, but her paranoia about incoming calls to Kyle's phone being traced kept her from attempting it. Besides, now that she was aware that West was actively looking for her, Kelli needed to accelerate her plan to accomplish her goals. She couldn't let anything or anyone get in her way. Not West, not Davies, not anyone.

8

BROOKLINE, MASSACHUSETTS

Davies walked up the short concrete path that led to the front entrance of Kelli's apartment building on Beacon Street. Already she could tell that this apartment building was a step above the building where Kelli used to live. In her mind, she began to echo the question posed earlier by Patrice Bass. *How does Kelli afford this place?* Davies was hoping to find the answers inside Kelli's apartment.

Davies stopped short of the front entrance. She peered in through the glass double-doors and saw what appeared to be a small, enclosed reception area. The space was beautifully decorated. The floor was lined with modern, brown tiles that complemented the cream-colored walls. To the right, a flourishing aloe plant rested in a shiny black pot that sat atop a square, porcelain stand that rose approximately two feet from the floor. To the left, a brown podium rose up and housed a gold panel lined with an array of buttons, a speaker, and a display of the building's apartment numbers. The reception area extended approximately twenty feet before being blocked off by a second set of double doors. It was this set of doors that allowed access to the rest of the building. However, it was obvious to Davies that the doors were wired to the gold control panel on the podium.

"Damn," Davies said aloud. Gaining access to Kelli's apartment might hinge on Davies ability to get past the security doors. Though it was true Davies could go in there, dial up the on-site management, and then flash her federal badge, she didn't want to do anything that would draw the attention of too many people, specifically the onsite management. Davies had been informed by Marsh that Kelli's credit card activity pointed to New York. However, Davies couldn't be sure if Kelli had friends in this building that would alert her to Davies' presence. That was the last thing Davies wanted. Her intention was to get into Kelli's apartment without anyone knowing at all. Furthermore, Davies had no desire to deal with any legal issues that could arise from entering Kelli's apartment uninvited. It was not as if Davies was pursuing a confirmed felon or anything of that nature. In fact, there was still no confirmation that Kelli had done anything at all, and that alone was reason enough to necessitate gaining access to Kelli's apartment as quickly and as quietly as possible.

Davies turned as a young male walked casually in her direction. The man had long, sandy blonde hair and was clad in a pair of jeans, black Converse sneakers, and a maroon and gold Boston College sweatshirt. He carried a single book in his left hand and a cell phone in the other.

Davies could not be completely certain if he lived in the building or not, but she decided to roll the dice and find out.

"Excuse me," she said, stepping in front of the young man. "Do you live here?"

The young man stopped in his tracks. He looked at Davies confused. "Uh, yeah. Why?"

Davies pulled her FBI credentials from her jacket and introduced herself. "I'm Special Agent Davies with the FBI. I need access to the building but I'd really like to keep it quiet. Can you help me?"

The young man was dumbfounded. He struggled to find a response to Davies' query, but a mixture of embarrassment and confusion kept him speechless. After a brief moment, he managed to speak.

"Is this a joke? Did Zach put you up to this?"

"No," Davies replied. "No one put me up to this. I really need your help."

The young man was still skeptical. "So, that badge is real?"

"Very real," she assured him. She reached into her jacket once again and pulled out a money clip. She extracted a fifty-dollar bill from the clip and brandished it for the young man to see. "This is real, too. It's all yours if you help me."

The man's expression relaxed slightly. He eyed the money eagerly and asked, "What exactly do you want me to do?"

"Just get me through the security doors."

He pointed at the fifty in her hand. "Is this actually, um, legal?"

Davies smiled. "I won't tell if you won't."

WASHINGTON, D.C.

Molina stood in front of the open safe that she had built into the wall within the office of the home she shared with her daughter. As she thumbed a small key that hung from a short chain around her neck, she stared at the yellow manila envelope that rested just inside the door of the safe. The envelope was filled to capacity. Leaning against the envelope was a loaded .40 caliber Sig. Molina nodded to herself with a sense of reassurance before she released a breath and pushed the door closed. A large replica of the painting *Dia de los Reyes Magos* by Elizabeth Erazo Baez hung from a pair of gold hinges, securing it to the wall to the right of the safe. Molina pulled at the golden frame, causing the print to swing and close over the safe like a door, concealing it from view. Then, a noise caught her attention.

At first, Molina thought she had imagined the knock at her door. But after a few moments of silence, the ringing of the doorbell confirmed that she had an unexpected visitor.

She stepped to the door and looked through her peephole.

"What the -?" she questioned softly as she took in Dr. Suri's image.

She released the locks and opened the front door. Suri turned to her and released a strong gust of breath.

"Agent Molina, pardon the intrusion. But I must speak with you."

Molina sensed that Suri was nervous, almost uncomfortable standing outside her door. Upon further inspection, she also began to sense a touch of fear. "What's going on, Doctor?"

"Please," he implored her. "It's important. It's about Iris."

Molina opened the door and gestured for Suri to enter. As he crossed the threshold to her home, she noticed that he was carrying a rather thick, large yellow manila envelope, much like the one she had stored in her safe. She closed the door and re-engaged the locks. She gestured to the doctor to follow her through a large archway that opened up into her living room. She gestured again, this time towards the couch, and Dr. Suri sat down. Molina took a seat next to him and remained quiet. Whatever it was that the doctor came all the way to her house to say, she wanted to hear it.

"Do you remember the briefcase?" he asked her.

"What briefcase?"

"From earlier today. The one that Nurse Gisela was carrying in the hallway."

"Vaguely," she replied. "I was a little preoccupied at the ti-"

"It belonged to Dr. Patel," he interrupted. "I recognized it immediately."

"Are you sure?" she questioned. Molina knew from her earlier conversation with Iris that Dr. Patel had met an untimely end. She also knew that Iris was the shooter. Mr. Five confirmed both facts during her conference with him. However, she did not know that something of Patel's managed to survive the explosion.

Suri nodded. "I broke into Dr. Chen's office and opened it."

Molina's eyes widened.

"We can save her," Suri said. "We could've saved her all along."

"What are you talking about?" Molina asked in a grave tone.

"A kidney transplant. That's all she needs. That's all she has ever needed."

"But you said it was too late, the list is too long-"

"I know. I know," he said. Suri calmed himself before he continued with his news. "They've been using her. These last six months or so, they've just been using her as a test subject to work out the last few kinks in the Harmony Project. During that time, Dr. Chen already knew that the HP-47 vaccine had reinforced Iris' renal system to the point where it's strong and stable enough for a kidney transplant."

Molina began to fume. A knot formed in her stomach and a rush of anger raced up and became lodged in her throat. "What have they been doing to her?"

"Subjecting her to different hormones to test her resistance to different stresses, chemical agents, anything they could foresee trying before moving on to phase three."

Hot tears of anger gathered in Molina's eyes. She stood, unable to contain the cascade of fury that boiled within her. "They knew, and they didn't find her a kidney because . . . why?"

"Simple. If they had given her a kidney and cured her, they would have lost all justification to continue experimenting on her. They used these last few months to perfect the super soldier genetic design. In fact, creating the perfect soldier was the primary directive of the Harmony Project all along."

Molina erupted. "Those bastards. I am going to kill each and every . . ." her voice trailed off. She turned to Suri. "Wait. You said we could save her."

"Yes," Suri answered. He opened the yellow manila envelope and pulled out a large file. "The answer has been in here all along."

"What is that?"

"It's the original Harmony Project documentation. This was given to me when I was first brought on to the project, even before Iris was created."

"What does it say?"

"She has siblings," Suri stated. "The girl from whom Iris was cloned is identified in this file, and she has siblings. The odds of a successful kidney transplant increase when the donor is a blood relative." Suri opened the large file to a page bookmarked with a red paper clip. He placed the file in front of Molina.

Molina sat quietly as she read the highlighted notes in front of her. After a few minutes, she turned her gaze to Suri.

"How do we do this?" Molina asked. Though she was desperate to save her daughter's life, she was hesitant to agree to the plan she guessed that Suri already had in mind.

"I'm not sure," Suri said honestly. "But we have to try something. I've got a few days before I have to report in, so . . . we need to go there. You, me, and Iris. We need to go there now."

"What am I supposed to tell Iris?" Molina asked

"There's been enough dishonesty already, Agent Molina. Tell her the truth."

"The truth, Doctor? The truth is that we're talking about snatching some innocent child and stealing their kidney."

"It's Iris' only hope." He took a step towards Molina and took both of her hands in his. "I've sworn an oath to protect life, to do no harm, and normally, I would never, ever consider this. But these last few years have not been just a genetics project for me. I care about Iris, and if this is our only chance to save her life, then . . ."

Molina glanced at the open file on the sofa. "There's more than one sibling," she stated, quickly becoming resigned to the idea. "How do we decide which one to take?"

"If we're lucky enough to get a choice, we'll take the older one. But if an opportunity presents itself, then we'll take whichever one we can get."

∂∽∾

BRONX, NEW YORK

Wilma Freeman sprinted up the aisle in Target at the River Plaza Mall and landed in Kelli's embrace at full speed. Kelli picked her little sister up and squeezed her tightly. Beneath her dark sunglasses, joyful tears dripped from her eyes as she held Wilma's frame against her own.

"I've missed you so much," Kelli said finally. She placed her sister back on the floor and stared at her in awe. "Look how much you've grown."

"Mommy says I'm going to be as tall as she is pretty soon," Wilma announced happily.

"You sure will," Kelli agreed. She looked up as her parents, Arthur and Diane, closed the distance between them. Kelli's seventeen-year-old brother, Cassius, followed closely in tow. One by one, they each greeted Kelli with hugs and kisses, each one expressing how much they missed her.

"Target, huh?" Cassius asked jokingly. "Our meeting places get classier every time. This is quite a step up from Yankee Stadium."

"It's a public place with lots of people, and it has a wide variety of things for Wilma to choose from for her birthday this weekend," Kelli explained. Wilma beamed excitedly.

"Not to mention, baseball season hasn't started yet," added Arthur.

"Which is horrible," Wilma chimed in sarcastically, rolling her eyes.

"Are you sure these clandestine meetings are still necessary?" Diane asked.

Kelli thought about Martin's message. She couldn't say for sure if hiding from the Agency was still necessary, after all, as far as she knew, the Agency thought she was dead. The real reason why Marsh, West, and Davies only allowed her to travel in secrecy was to avoid the Agency's radar. The Agency believed she was dead, and the FBI wanted them to keep believing it. However, now it seemed as if Marsh, West, and Davies were the very people who were looking for her. And right now, Kelli didn't want to be found.

Kelli waved her hand dismissively. "Who knows, Mom? I'm just being careful like I was told."

"And we're glad you are," Arthur said. "I know all this hiding and separation is a pain, but we'll figure it out someday so you can come home. I promise you."

"Thank you for the pre-paid cell phones, by the way," Diane added. "It makes keeping in touch with you so much easier."

"No need to thank me, Mom. I did it for all of us."

"How did you pay for all of those phones anyway?" Arthur asked. "Wasn't that expensive?"

Kelli shrugged. "I saved my money," she lied, although in Kelli's mind, it was merely a small manipulation of the truth. She did, in fact, save her money to purchase the cell phones. But it was the money she won counting cards that she saved and placed into a very smart investment. Needless to say, Kelli had no intention of divulging any of that. "So," she began, changing the subject, and then turning to Wilma, "what are we going to get for the birthday girl?"

⁂

WASHINGTON, D.C.

Iris sat on the full-sized bed in her bedroom. The sleeve on her left arm was rolled up to reveal the tape and gauze bandage that covered the area where the IV had been inserted just hours ago. In her lap was an iPad Tablet which was running the Facetime application. On the screen was a young man of Korean heritage. His collar and the top of his shoulders revealed that he was dressed in military camouflage fatigues. A crisp and neatly cropped high and tight haircut added to the overall appearance. His name was Parker Yun.

Iris could recall, with vivid detail, the moment she first laid eyes on Parker, who, at the time, was an operative trainee just like her. It was close to four years ago when Iris was led by her mother into the classroom at the private Agency training facility hidden deep within the walls of Camp Pendleton. The facility, dubbed "Jarhead City", was, in fact, the size of a large town, with city limits and its own zip code. Jarhead appeared to be a self-contained municipality. In reality, the town was an enormous training facility geared towards one goal; raising and training promising young operatives from adolescence to adulthood. Due to Jarhead City's remote location, the Agency felt the town was a perfect place to train Iris and teach her how to use her genetically engineered abilities. Four other subjects, children, were being trained at Jarhead when Iris arrived. These subjects represented yet another facet of the entire super-soldier agenda dubbed the Harmony Project. Two of the children, Parker and Amelia, each of whom had already reached their fifteenth birthdays, had received post-natal genetic enhancements via gene splicing. These enhancements augmented their physical strength, stamina, and reflexes by a small degree. Regardless of the genetic enhancements they received while at Camp Pendleton, Parker and Amelia were not clones, nor were they anywhere close to being as strong, or intelligent, as Iris. Parker and Amelia were part of Experimental Group 1. Lars and Ruben, the other two students, were the control group. They were given no genetic enhancements. Finally, there was Iris; the clone whose enhancements were inbred. In addition to training future agents, the experiment was designed to observe how well each subject overcame adversity and obstacles given their special abilities, or lack thereof. Though Parker and Amelia had a definite advantage over Lars and Ruben, ultimately, none of them could compete, on any level, with Iris. Still, during the three and a half-year span that the students lived and trained at Jarhead, a sibling bond formed amongst all of them. The strongest bond, however, was the one between Iris and Parker. While it was quite obvious to the other trainees that Iris was growing at an accelerated rate, each of them accepted her as one of their own. The first to do so was Parker. As aspects of their training became more demanding and grueling, the kinship among the group grew stronger in kind. The five of them made a promise to always stand by one another. It seemed like an easy promise to keep until five months ago when the program was suddenly halted and each of the students was relocated to different parts of the country. Iris ended up in D.C. Amelia was sent to Groton, Connecticut, while Parker wound up in San Diego. Despite warnings against doing so, Amelia set up an encrypted video feed through her Facetime app where she and the other four students could always remain in contact. Once Iris had settled back into the comfort of her own bedroom, she used that feed to place a video call to Parker.

"They didn't give you a heads up or anything?" Parker asked.

"Well, they did," Iris said. "But it was a whole week before. I was totally surprised when Dr. Patel showed up at my school yesterday."

"Dr. Patel," Parker repeated the name solemnly. "I liked him."

"Me, too. But they said he had switched sides. They knew he was going to try and run off with me."

"Was it difficult?" Parker asked. "Shooting him?"

Iris nodded slowly. "Yeah. He was always so nice to me. But I was just following orders." Iris winced slightly. Somehow, the *following orders* justification did not sit right with her. She shrugged it off and continued to recount the events. "Once we arrived at the safe house, I was instructed to take out Dr. Patel and secure the briefcase he was carrying. As soon as the two agents took their eyes off of me, I went for it. I mean, that's what we were trained to do, right?"

"Yeah. We were." A slight pause. "Have you heard from the others lately?"

"I spoke to Amelia about two weeks ago, but since then, nothing."

"Well, you know I'll be on leave in three months. I'll come see you."

Iris smiled. "That would be great." Her gaze dropped to her lap. She remained quiet for a moment, and then she shook her head ever so slightly. Parker couldn't help but notice.

"Iris, what's wrong?"

She took a deep breath. "Something happened on my mission," she said. "Something I didn't exactly report."

Parker looked concerned. "What?"

"When I confronted Dr. Patel with the gun, he was talking to someone on the phone."

"Who?"

"I couldn't tell. He was speaking Hindi. I could hear the person on the line was speaking Hindi, as well."

"What happened?"

"Dr. Patel begged me not to shoot him. Despite our training, I started losing my nerve. I mean, I hadn't actually shot a real person before. Anyway, I ordered the doctor to hang up the phone."

"Did he?"

"Yes, but not before he screamed something into the phone. I don't speak Hindi, but I could tell that he was telling the person on the line what was happening. Next thing I knew, one of the agents, the black guy, came around the corner. He saw me pointing my weapon at Patel, so he reached for his."

"Let me guess," Parker interjected, "the training took over."

Iris nodded. "Before I knew it, I had shot the agent. Patel charged at me so I turned and shot him in the chest. Patel didn't die right away so I panicked."

"What did you do?"

Iris forced a small grin. "You know me. I was always fascinated with our chemistry class back in Jarhead. I went into the kitchen, found some household chemicals, and created an explosive."

Parker chuckled, "Firebug. But why'd you blow up the place?"

"Patel had managed to place a phone call so, in case the *cleaners* didn't show up before the cops, I needed to make it look like these men died in an explosion, at least initially."

"Not bad."

"Yeah," Iris said, "it looks a lot better than a triple homicide. The explosion blew out two walls, and a bunch of debris covered the briefcase. The other agent showed up when I was trying to retrieve it. Needless to say, I killed him, too."

"Three kills, huh?" Parker said, sounding impressed. "So, what was it that you didn't report?"

"The phone call. I was supposed to complete my assignment before Patel was able to make contact with anyone. Not only did he manage to call someone, but I couldn't tell who was on the other end of the call."

"So you omitted it from your debrief."

"Yeah. I was nervous. With any luck, they won't check his phone logs"

There was a slight pause, then Iris and Parker responded in sarcastic unison, "Yeah, right."

"Did you ever get the briefcase?"

"No, but I told the cleaners where it was located. I'm sure they pulled it free."

"Wow," Parker said, "that's one heck of a first mission."

There was a knock at the door, followed by Molina's voice, "You awake, Mija?"

Iris whispered into the microphone on the tablet. "I have to go. Talk to you this weekend." She closed the tablet and tossed it by her side on the bed. She cleared her throat before responding to the only mother she has ever known. "Yes."

"Are you decent?" Molina asked. "I have Dr. Suri with me."

"I'm dressed. Come in."

The door to her bedroom opened. Molina entered the room first, followed closely by Suri.

Iris was immediately on edge. It had been some time since Dr. Suri made a house call. Whatever the reason for his visit, Iris knew it had to be important.

"What's up?" Iris asked curiously.

Molina sat on the edge of Iris' bed. Suri stood to her right. Iris could sense that they had news for her, so she wasn't surprised to hear the words fall from her mother's lips.

"Dr. Suri has something to tell you," Molina confirmed, and managed a smile. Still, without the dark sunglasses to hide her mother's face, Iris could easily tell that she had been crying. And that terrified her.

"What's going on?" Iris asked, trying to sound brave.

Molina and Suri exchanged a glance. After a brief moment of speechlessness, Suri broke the silence and began to explain the situation to Iris. As he had advised Molina to do earlier, Suri was completely honest with Iris. By the end of the conversation, Iris was fully briefed and up to speed. Unfortunately, during the process, Iris could not hold back tears of her own.

"So what do we do?" Iris asked.

Molina embraced her daughter. "Iris, before we decide to do anything, I need to know that you understand what we want to do, and that you're okay with it."

Iris did not know what to say. She asked herself one question in silence. *Do I really want to live bad enough to do this?* In the midst of all the confusing thoughts sweeping through her mind, Iris reverted back to her training. In doing so, she asked herself another question? *Am I willing to take someone else's life to save my own?* If this were a combat situation, her training would demand that she answer 'yes'. Kill or be killed. Iris had no trouble rationalizing that this situation was no different. Take a kidney, or die. The answer became clear.

"Yes," she said. "I'm okay with it."

"Good," said Dr. Suri. "Both of you pack a bag. We're going to New York."

9

BRONX, NEW YORK

The hours seemed to pass by in a blur, and the times Kelli spent with her family were the highlights of the last seven years. It was nice to be home, surrounded by familiar faces. Kelli loved the fact that, here, with them, she could be herself, literally. Not Kyle Cuffee, not the clone of Harmony June, but Kelli Freeman. Of course, she had to be wary of running into family friends and acquaintances, especially those who believed that she died almost seven years ago. If they did happen upon such a person, Arthur or Diane would distract them long enough for Kelli to shift and appear as Kyle, their male cousin from out of town. They were lucky, though. In all of the times that Kelli had paid a secret visit to the family over the years, it had only happened twice, and Kelli hated it. She despised having her family time interrupted. Each moment to her was precious and fleeting, and since she knew it was only a matter of days before she had to retreat back to Boston, she intended to savor every minute of it.

The first hour with her family was spent allowing Wilma to choose birthday gifts from Kelli. Though Kelli planned on being at Wilma's birthday party on Saturday, she wanted Wilma to have some of her gifts now. With Agent West searching for her, Kelli knew she might have to pick up and run at a moment's notice. She had already missed so many family birthdays over the years, so many family events, that she didn't want to wait and risk missing another important moment.

The next hour and a half was spent dining at the Fresh Fast Asian Kitchen restaurant on W. 230th Street. It was a fast-food eatery that offered a mixture of Chinese, Japanese, and Thai fare. Kelli, who preferred a vegetarian diet, chose the Steamed Mixed Vegetables over brown rice. Arthur and Diane shared the Pu Pu Platter, while Cassius and Wilma opted for something a little more western and split a plate of the Barbeque Spare Rib Tips. The family laughed and joked, reminisced, and made plans and promises for the future. It was not long before each and every one of them had forgotten about the circumstances of Kelli's visit, and the situation that had affected all of their lives.

After dinner, as they strolled towards the subway entrance, Kelli and Arthur allowed Diane to walk ahead with the two younger kids. Kelli loved being around her dad. As a young girl, she had always admired him more than anyone else in her world. Not just because he was a police officer, but because he was a police officer who truly believed in doing what was right. He was a God-fearing man who was devoted to his wife and family. Arthur went to almost every track meet, every gymnastics or martial arts tournament, and anything else in which Kelli was involved. He showed undying support to each one of his children, and he never judged them. What more could a girl ask for in a father? Kelli wanted to walk in his footsteps and be just like him.

"What's your plan?" Arthur asked, referring to her future beyond law school.

"I haven't decided yet," Kelli lied. She was certain that her father was not ready to hear about her true career plans, so Kelli made an attempt to tell him something she assumed he wanted to hear. "I guess I'll find an open position at a law firm."

Arthur detected her lack of enthusiasm. "You don't sound too excited."

"I don't know, Dad. Have you ever wanted something, but then found that you weren't so sure about it once you had it?"

"I guess," her father answered. "But often, it was just my nerves and anxiety getting the better of me; the fear of the unknown and all."

Kelli shrugged. "Maybe."

"Hey, it's perfectly normal to be nervous about starting a new career, treading into unfamiliar territory. It can be scary. But I'm not worried about you. Know why?"

"Because I'm a genius?"

"No," he said with a smile, "because you're my daughter. Your mother and I have the utmost faith in you. I can't wait to see what your future holds."

Kelli did not respond to Arthur's comment. Instead, she turned and embraced him. In that moment, Kelli felt safe, protected, and confident. Being there, in the Bronx, in her father's arms, Kelli forgot about all the anger. Since arriving in New York just a few hours earlier, Kelli had already instigated an argument with Bling and given in to her drunken, primal impulses with a complete stranger, leaving her with a sense of shame and self-loathing. She had hoped that the time with her family would serve to alleviate those feelings and remind her of the life to which she wanted to return. Though the night had so far gone without so much as a disagreement, it was those words just spoken by her father that gave her hope that everything would turn out as she planned. Arthur tightened his embrace. In that moment, Kelli knew that this was why she was carrying out her plan; this embrace, and *this* life, with her family, was worth fighting for. She wondered, for an instant, if she should tell her father about her 'master plan'. Could she tell him? Would he understand? Would his faith in her extend to the dangerous prospect of taking down Mr. One, the man whom Kelli held responsible for her current isolation from her family? As much as she would have loved to say yes to all of those questions, the truth was that she just did not know. Not for sure. And that uncertainty dictated that she keep her plans to herself. For now.

Diane turned and called to them. "Ahem. You two want to pick up the pace a little?"

Arthur chuckled and spoke loud enough for Diane to hear. "Seems like someone is a little jealous."

"Seems like you might be right," Diane agreed.

Kelli and Arthur quickened their pace and rejoined the others. Wilma held tight to her Target bag which contained the gifts from her older sister. Kelli stepped in between Diane and Wilma and wrapped an arm around both of them.

"How about we all get a *mani-pedi* after you get out of school tomorrow?" Kelli proposed.

"I can't," Diane said. "I have two meetings after school that require my presence." Diane was the principal at Middle School 101.

"I don't have any meetings," declared Wilma.

"What about your homework?" Diane asked.

"Come on, Ma," Kelli intervened. "It's her birthday. Besides, it's not like we get to do this all the time."

"You know how I feel about her studies, Kelli."

"How could I forget?" Kelli countered. "Listen. After we get our nails done, I will help her with her homework. I promise. I'll even pick her up from school."

Wilma beamed. "Can I, Ma? Please."

"Are you sure that's a good idea?" Arthur asked. "I mean, you've gone through all this trouble to stay off the radar."

"And I *am* off the radar," she claimed. *Except for the fact that West is looking for me. But at least he's one of the good guys, and not the Agency.* "Don't worry. I've got a different car now. I'll take her into Manhattan or we'll go into Jersey or something. Everything will be fine."

Arthur and Diane exchanged a questioning gaze.

"Everything will be fine," Kelli repeated, attempting to reassure them.

"Hey, I want to hang, too," Cassius said. "Without the nail thing, of course."

"Of course," Kelli echoed.

Diane exhaled loudly. "As long as it's okay with your father."

All eyes landed on Arthur. He smiled and looked at Kelli. She batted her eyes one time, and that's all it took for Arthur to give in. Without a word, he nodded his approval.

"Yes!" Cassius and Wilma exclaimed in unison.

"Thank you both so much," Kelli said, hugging them both.

"I hope you know what you're doing, young lady," Arthur said playfully.

"You have faith in me, remember? Besides, what could possibly go wrong?"

๛๛

SOMEWHERE OVER THE NORTHEASTERN UNITED STATES

Doctor Suri sat in the aisle seat on the Boeing-737 airliner en route to New York's LaGuardia Airport from Reagan National in Washington, D.C. He marveled in silence as he watched Iris pour through page after page of the Harmony Project file, speed-reading at an amazing pace.

Molina, who was seated in the window seat on the other side of Iris, looked over at the doctor. When she spoke, it was almost a whisper. "So, once we get to New York, how do we proceed?"

Suri matched Molina's volume. "The Agency has several Specialists in place in the New York area. I reached out to a colleague, one who understands the importance of discretion. They're digging up any recent addresses that are on file for our target. Once we have eyes on our potential donor, we may have to tail them for a while and wait for an opportunity to act."

"This colleague of yours, do they know what our intentions are?" inquired Molina.

"They know that we'll be in need of a medical facility."

"An Agency facility? Won't that alert the Agency to what we're doing?"

Suri nodded. "But by that time, we will have already done it. Hopefully we can make them understand the desperation and importance of our actions."

"And what about the target?" Molina asked.

"My plan is to keep *my patient* sedated from the moment we acquire them to the moment we drop them off at a public hospital, after the transplant, of course." Suri shook his head as his eyes met Molina's. "I will have done enough harm by that point. I don't want there to be any more death."

"Agreed," Molina stated firmly. "I think the best time to acquire our target might be right after school lets out tomorrow. There will be lots of people; simple for someone to get lost, or go unnoticed, in a crowd. It could make the pick-up much easier."

"I'll leave the strategy and tactics to you," Suri said. "But whatever you do, it must be swift and precise."

"Don't worry, Doctor," Molina assured him. "I won't let anything, or anyone, get in our way."

FBI FIELD OFFICE
WASHINGTON, D.C.

Assistant Director Marsh moved the cursor down to the newest email in his mailbox. It was a correspondence sent from a man named Tito Perkins. Perkins was the head of the bureau's forensics department. As a favor to Marsh, Perkins sped up the process of running the bullets that killed Paul Ferry through ballistics and microstamping. The Agency had an amazing track record for covering their tracks, so he didn't truly expect much from the ballistics report. Still, based on Ferry's deathbed statements and West's report from the site of the safe-house, the Agency made a small error. The shooter, whoever she was, failed to confirm that Ferry was dead. Normally, the cleaners would arrive and clear out all of the dead bodies and evidence, leaving nary a trace. However, by the time the Agency's cleaners arrived, an ambulance had already shown up and carted Ferry off to Howard University Hospital. Though unlikely, Marsh was hoping that the Agency's oversight would pay off. Without hesitation, Marsh double-clicked his mouse and opened the email.

BROOKLINE, MASSACHUSETTS

Monica Davies had seen quite a few beautiful apartments in her day. In fact, her last apartment in Alexandria, Virginia, the one she had been renting before buying a home in the same city, had been a newly-renovated unit that garnered the envy of all of her friends. Since moving out of that apartment, Davies had not been in too many others that had been as nice as hers, until now.

Once Davies had been escorted past the security doors on the first floor, she utilized her SouthOrd Lock Pick set to gain easy access to Kelli's second floor apartment. A.D. Marsh had informed her that Kyle's card had been used in the Bronx, so Davies felt reassured that Kelli was not going to come home and surprise her as she spent the next few hours combing the apartment for anything that would aid in her investigation.

The first thing Davies did when she gained initial entry was to take a casual stroll through the apartment, get a feel for the space, and take notice of anything that Kelli may have just left lying around. After all, as far as Davies knew, Kelli wasn't expecting any unannounced visitors.

During her preliminary walk-through, Davies came across the beautiful glass table in Kelli's kitchen, upon which was Kelli's mail. Of all the letters on the table, only one had been opened. Davies picked up the letter and read the name of the sender. Mackenzie Financial Group.

Davies raised an eyebrow. This was the second time today that she'd seen that name. The first time was when she received old mail from the smoker who now occupied Kyle's previous apartment. At the time, Davies dismissed it as junk mail. But now, Davies had reason to scrutinize the letter much further. As she looked over the correspondence, Davies realized that she was reading a quarterly report.

Apparently, Kelli, as her alter-ego Kyle Cuffee, had purchased shares in a company called Quinlan Pharmaceuticals. According to the report, Mackenzie was managing Kelli's surprisingly sizable investment quite nicely, giving Kelli a nice, steadily increasing return.

Davies had never heard of Quinlan Pharmaceuticals before and couldn't imagine why Kelli would invest so much money there. *And about that money,* Davies thought. *Where is it coming from?*

Davies scanned the report quickly. She noted that Kelli opened her account with Mackenzie Financial approximately six months ago. *Around the same time she moved into this apartment,* Davies guessed. Davies was willing to bet it was also around the same time that Kelli purchased the new car that Patrice Bass had described. And not surprisingly, it all coincided with Kelli's latest bout of evasive behavior in regards to Davies and their routine meetings.

Davies pulled her notepad from her pocket and scribbled some notes. New apartment, new car, Mackenzie Financial, Quinlan Pharmaceuticals. Was Kelli working for the Agency? Davies couldn't answer that question just yet. But whatever Kelli was into, it paid very well.

Davies moved back into Kelli's living room, which Davies noticed, was furnished beautifully. On the coffee table by the couch rested Kelli's voice message machine. The red number zero was visible and was not flashing. Davies pressed the rewind button. Approximately fifteen seconds later, the messages began to play.

The first message was from Davies herself. Listening to her own voice annoyed Davies slightly, because it served to confirm that Kelli was, indeed, receiving her messages but was choosing to ignore them.

The second message was from Patrice Bass. Patrice's message confirmed Davies' suspicion that the young lawyer was interested in a romantic relationship with Kyle. Davies recognized the unmistakably soft and flirtatious tone. However, the most interesting portion of Patrice's message was the mention of the shooting range. It seemed as though, prior to leaving for D.C., Kelli, as Kyle, had taken Patrice to *let off a few rounds*. This suggested to Davies that Kelli had taken an interest in marksmanship. More damaging evidence. Davies shook her head. *What on Earth is Kelli up to?*

Against the wall next to the door, Davies found what looked like a camera bag. Upon inspection of its contents, Davies found a high-end digital camera, a pair of binoculars, and a small plastic case that held two SDHC memory cards. The camera and the memory cards were nothing unusual; however, a quick glance at the walls in the living room did not reveal to Davies that Kelli had any interest in photography. Most of the framed pictures that hung on the walls were of famous tourist sites or colorful sunrises, of which Davies recognized from Kelli's last apartment. Normally, one might assume that photography was a relatively new hobby to Kelli, and she'd only begun to take pictures. But it was the presence of the binoculars that caused Davies to think otherwise. She examined the binoculars more closely; definitely expensive. Davies wasn't a big camera enthusiast, so she didn't know if binoculars were a standard piece of photographer's equipment. Still, Davies made note of this on her pad.

Over the next few hours, Davies searched every room of Kelli's new apartment, careful to replace any object she moved so it wouldn't appear as if anyone had been there.

In the bedroom, nothing seemed to be out of the ordinary. The bed appeared as though it had been recently slept in. A maroon bath towel lay crumpled across the foot of the bed. Davies touched the ends of the towel. It was completely dry. Again, Davies scanned the walls quickly. Still, no evidence that Kelli had taken up photography as a hobby.

Davies inspected the space underneath the bed, where she found only a forgotten New York Yankees baseball cap, and then every inch of the closet. It was there that Davies found a small safe. She estimated the steel box measured approximately one-half cubic feet. Closer inspection revealed the safe to be of sturdy design, manufactured by Sentry Safe, with an electronic punch-key combination lock.

"Damn," Davies cursed. Her lock pick set would be of no use. Without the proper number sequence, or the override key that came standard with safes with electronic locks, there was no hope of getting the steel door open.

Davies owned a safe of similar design at home. The number combination to open her safe was her birthday. Davies figured this was as good a place as any to start. She knew Kelli's birthday was May 15. Once she scanned her memory for the correct year, she punched in the six-digit number. No luck. The door failed to open. Davies tried July 12, the birth date given to Kyle Cuffee. The door remained locked. Davies was unsure which number combination to try next. Perhaps she could try the birth dates of Kelli's siblings or parents, but she had those dates in neither her memory nor her notepad. She would have to call Marsh and have him dig up the information.

Davies' cell phone began to ring. She stood and walked back into the living room where she had left her jacket more than an hour before. She pulled the ringing device from the jacket pocket and glanced at the number. As luck would have it, the caller was A.D. Marsh.

"Sit-rep," Marsh demanded, once the Davies was on the line. Sit-rep was short for situation report.

"I'm in Kelli's apartment now, Sir. What do you know about a company called Quinlan Pharmaceuticals?"

"Quinlan," Marsh repeated the name. "Not much. It's based in Baltimore and is one of the largest manufacturers and suppliers of pharmaceuticals in the United States."

"We need to know more," said Davies. "Kelli has invested a large sum of money in Quinlan."

"How large?"

"Over one-hundred thousand dollars."

"Where does an unemployed law grad get that kind of money?"

"I don't know, Sir. But it doesn't look good."

"Well, here's something that may help us. I just got the ballistics from the bullets that killed Ferry. Micro stamping identified the weapon as a Glock 23 registered to an Oliver Tinsdale. Perkins took the liberty of running a check on the name. Turns out that Tinsdale was a Naval Intelligence Officer who was killed in action over fifteen years ago."

Davies released a weary sigh. "I'm not surprised. The Agency knows better than to use a gun that can be traced back to them."

"That's probably why they use weapons that have the microstamping technology; in the event something like this slips through the cracks, the weapon's trail leads to a dead end."

"Well, I'm almost done here . . ." Davies' voice trailed off as a thought occurred to her.

"Agent Davies?"

"You said the weapon was a Glock 23?" she questioned.

"I did."

"I need to call you back, Sir," Davies said. "It may be nothing, but I need to check something out."

Davies disconnected the call. She grabbed her jacket once again and reached into the inside pocket. She groped blindly for a moment before her fingers brushed against the business card for which she was searching. She pulled out the card and turned it over. Within seconds, she was punching numbers into her cell phone.

The phone rang three times before it was answered and a female voice announced, "This is Patrice Bass."

"Miss Bass, Agent Davies here. From this morning."

"Did you find Kyle?" she asked excitedly.

"I'm still working on it," Davies answered, "but I was hoping you could answer a question for me."

"I'll try."

"Great. Kyle took you to a shooting range recently. Did he rent a weapon from the range, or did he bring his own?" Davies knew this was a long shot, but Patrice had a crush on Kyle. Davies knew from experience that when a woman was interested in a man, it paid to know about the types of things in which that man was interested. Davies was hoping that Patrice had paid attention enough to remember the type of weapon Kelli used at the range.

"He had his own hand gun," Patrice responded.

"Do you remember the make of the weapon?"

"The make?" Patrice asked. "Uh, oh wait, I do. It was a Glock 23."

☙❧

LAGUARDIA AIRPORT
QUEENS, NEW YORK

West sat in the backseat of a taxi as it pulled away from the curb right outside of baggage claim. It had been at least three years since he had any reason to come to New York. He liked the city, unfortunately, he was rarely here for pleasure or vacation. No. Whenever West found himself in New York City, it was usually on bureau business. Today was no different.

"Alamo Rent A Car," West said to the driver as the cab moved into traffic. He looked out the window as other taxis, airport shuttles and personal vehicles packed the lanes on both sides of the road.

He leaned his head back and relaxed as he reflected upon a day that began in D.C. with a mad dash to the airport but was subsequently rerouted into a series of goose chases around the D.C. area. Ultimately, the day ended up with an unexpected flight to New York. He checked his watch. It was close to 9 p.m. He surmised, based on the time, that he could check into his hotel room, and then begin his search for Kelli in the morning without losing ground. West decided that, once he had his rental, he would drive into the area where the Lexa Bar and Garden was located, and then find a nearby hotel. He figured that if Kelli was drinking at that bar in the middle of the day, there was a good chance that she was staying someplace close. "At least, that's what I would do," he told himself.

As the cab moved onto the freeway away from the airport, West glanced out the taxi cab window at a distant plane that was beginning to make its final descent into LaGuardia. Little did West know, that onboard that plane, Doctor Suri, Special Agent Molina, and a teenage girl named Iris waited anxiously to begin a search of their own.

WASHINGTON, D.C.

Mr. Two entered the meeting room. Immediately, he could feel the tension that saturated every inch of open air. Mr. One and Mr. Five were the only other people in the room. As he approached Mr. One, he took note of a crumbled document in his right hand. Upon seeing him, Mr. One made no attempt to hide his agitation.

"What's wrong?" Two asked. "You left hours ago. Why have you returned?"

"This," he answered, holding up the document. "This is Patel's phone record from yesterday. Apparently, before he was silenced, he managed to make a phone call that lasted three minutes and fifteen seconds."

Two's gaze shifted to Mr. Five.

Five said simply, "Patel's phone was encrypted. We have to break the encryption before we can trace the call."

Two was confused. "But the Molina girl; she didn't report that Patel made any calls."

"No," One said flatly. "She did not."

"Have you contacted her?" Two asked.

"We tried," Five answered. "Her cell phone is off, goes straight to voicemail; Agent Molina's, too."

"Where the hell are they?" Two asked.

"Don't know," One answered. "We called the clinic. It turns out that Suri released the Molina girl hours ago. But now we can't find Suri either. His phone goes straight to voicemail, as well."

"We sent Agents Peppers and Kincaid to Molina's house," Five explained. "We should have a report any moment."

"Did you call Dr. Chen?"

One nodded. "He's the on-call physician tonight. He was with a patient. We're expecting his call, too."

Two swallowed hard. This was not good news. "What do you think is going on?"

"I have no idea, my friend," One responded. "But we need to find Iris so we can get some answers."

かめ

Peppers stood at the front door of the home that Agent Molina shared with her daughter. He had already rung the bell, and after waiting patiently, he decided to peer in through the small window to the left of the door. The curtains were parted slightly, hardly enough for Peppers to get a good look inside. It didn't matter. The room beyond the curtains was dark. In fact, the complete darkness that greeted him told him that none of the lights on the first floor were illuminated.

The sound of footsteps to his right caused Peppers to turn. Kincaid emerged from the shadows that enveloped the area on the right side of the house. A beam of light from his flashlight lit his path.

"Anything?" Peppers asked.

"Nada," Kincaid answered. "There are no lights on anywhere in the house. I don't think anyone's home."

"What about the garage?"

Kincaid gave a quick nod. "I could see a car through the window. It had one of those special physician designations on the license plate, though."

"Dr. Suri's car."

"Unless Molina is an agent with a medical specialist clearance, yeah."

Peppers pulled his cell phone from his pocket. "There's one way to find out. Go back and get the plate number."

Kincaid handed his partner a small slip of paper. "No need. I already got it."

DISTRICT PEDIATRIC CLINIC
WASHINGTON, D.C.

Doctor Chen's first inclination was to tell a lie, to cover up for his friend and colleague, Doctor Suri, by claiming he had no idea whatsoever about Suri's whereabouts. In truth, Chen could not say with complete certainty that he knew to where Suri and the missing Molinas had run off, but based on Suri's reaction to Patel's file, Chen had a pretty good idea.

He grimaced silently in response to the question, "Do you know where they are?" posed by Mr. Five. Chen wished that Suri had taken his advice and walked away, but Suri was a compassionate man who had grown a little too fond of the Molinas for Chen's taste. Chen was certain that Suri, wherever he happened to be, was accompanied by Agent Molina and her daughter. And although he did not relish the idea of disclosing his thoughts regarding Suri's whereabouts, he knew that telling a lie could, and most likely would, come back to haunt him.

"It's possible they went to New York, Sir?" Chen answered.

"New York? Why?"

"I believe they may be in search of a kidney," he replied once more.

"For the Molina girl?" Five questioned.

"I believe so. Somehow Suri gained access to my office earlier. He read the file that was in Dr. Patel's briefcase," Chen explained.

The tone in Mr. Five's voice changed immediately to one of deep concern. "You mean the one I just picked up?"

Chen swallowed hard before answering. "Yes, Sir. I would have told you in person but I was with a patient when you were here."

"That's not your fault, Doctor," Five said. "If I had wanted you to see me, you would have. How much did Suri see?"

"Only the section pertaining to the kidney transplant," Chen replied.

"What about the egg harvesting?"

"He didn't see that section," Chen answered confidently.

"How can you be certain?"

"I know Dr. Suri very well," Chen said. "If he'd seen that, he would have definitely mentioned it."

There was a brief silence on the line. Finally, Five replied, "Very well."

Chen breathed a small sigh of relief. The last thing he wanted Mr. Five to believe was that he was withholding information, or that he had any part in Suri's sudden disappearance.

"So, where does Dr. Suri intend to acquire this kidney?" Five asked.

"I assume from a sibling of the girl from whom Iris was cloned. According to the information we have on her in the file, she lived in the Bronx before she died," the doctor stated.

Mr. Five released a frustrated sigh. "Makes sense," he said sharply. "Thank you, Doctor. You've been a great help."

Chen opened his mouth to express his gratitude, but the connection was cut off before he had a chance to utter a sound.

He ran his fingers through his short, black hair. His heart began to race as he considered phoning Suri. Maybe he could convince Suri to come back and find a way out of the hole he was digging for himself. But no. Chen knew that was a bad idea. Any attempt to contact Suri now would be perceived as an act of collusion, and then he would suffer whatever fate that would soon be awaiting Suri. No. Despite his personal feelings, Chen decided to repeat the same action he took when he realized that Patel had run off with the Molina girl the first time, and that was to separate himself from the situation. As much as he disliked the idea, he had to face the fact that Dr. Suri was on his own.

❦

BROOKLINE, MASSACHUSETTS

Following her phone conversation with Patrice Bass, Davies considered going back into Kelli's bedroom to figure out how to access the safe, perhaps search for the override key. But Davies dismissed this idea. She knew that if

Kelli had gone through the trouble of purchasing the safe, she wouldn't leave the key where it could be easily found. It was very likely that wherever Kelli was, the key was with her.

Before giving up on the safe entirely, Davies did go back into the closet and lift the steel box from the floor. If she couldn't open it, maybe she could determine what was inside. She turned the safe upside down and listened as the contents succumbed to gravity. From the sound of it, and the shift in weight, there was definitely something inside. However, the absence of the sound of metal striking metal told her that a firearm was not among the contents. She turned the safe over a few more times to confirm her suspicions before she gave up and placed the box back into the closet. Satisfied, at least for the time being, Davies headed back into the living room and retrieved the camera bag she had found by the door.

She took out the camera and pressed the power button. Immediately, the camera came to life. Like most people, Davies had a fundamental knowledge of how to work the device, so she turned the camera around to inspect the screen on the back. She tapped a few buttons, hoping to bring up photos of whatever Kelli had been shooting. Nothing. The screen was blank. In the corner, however, was a blinking icon that resembled a memory card. Davies retrieved one of the SDHC cards from the plastic case and inserted it into the camera. Within seconds, an image filled the screen.

The first image was that of an elderly white man whom Davies did not recognize. The unknown man was dressed in a nice suit and was sitting at a table inside what appeared to be a cafe. Davies scrolled through the pictures which revealed more pictures of the same man. In some of the photos, the man was on the phone, in others, he sat alone drinking what appeared to be a cup of coffee.

"Who is this guy?" Davies wondered aloud.

She continued to scroll through the digital photos. She took note of the clarity in each of the photos. The angles and lighting in the photos suggested a professional eye. Still, Davies contemplated whether the quality of the pictures was due to Kelli's acumen, or the quality of the camera. Davies' limited knowledge of photography wasn't enough to answer that question. Still, she continued to gaze at photo after photo.

After about twenty frames, a woman was seen sitting opposite the man. The woman, who was much younger than the man, appeared to be in her forties, maybe even her fifties. Davies couldn't be too certain. She scrutinized the woman's face more closely. Although Davies did not know her name, the woman was vaguely familiar to her. She had definitely seen this woman before.

Davies continued to scroll. Eventually, the settings and the clothing changed, but the subjects of the photos remained the same; the elderly man and the woman. *Who were they?*

Davies grabbed her cell phone once again. She accessed the camera app on her phone and captured the images of the man and the woman from Kelli's camera. Davies didn't know who these people were, but she was an FBI agent who had access to those who could find out.

❧

MANHATTAN, NEW YORK

Bling reclined against the back of the bench on the sub-way platform as he waited for his train to arrive. The hip-hop classic, *Cream* by Wu-Tang Clan poured a gritty, pi-ano-laced beat into his ear buds as he outlined the begin-nings of a new superhero drawing onto his sketch pad. As always, it had been a rather quiet day at work. Bling couldn't imagine how guarding some buildings under re-furbishment could ever be more than boring. Still, it was a decent job with flexible hours, and he was thankful to have it. Now, all he wanted to do was get back to the apartment. Zenaida had the night off and they had planned to spend some quality time together. Bling en-joyed his relationship with Zenaida. With her, things were easy. Bling's relationship with Kelli was quite different.

Bling replayed his earlier confrontation with Kelli in his mind. He shook his head slightly. He didn't want to think about Kelli or her feelings for him. He knew that train of thought would only lead him to consider his feel-ings for her. As far as Bling was concerned, that conver-sation was off the table. He raised the volume of his mp-4 player in an attempt to drown out any thoughts of Kelli. Unfortunately, it didn't help. It never did.

Who's being dishonest now? That was the question Kelli asked before she stormed off earlier. Bling released a frus-trated sigh. The truth was, Bling was being honest, at least to himself. He knew that he had feelings for Kelli. How could he not? Kelli was brilliant, and beautiful. She was the first girl who looked beyond his shady past and ac-cepted him for the man he was, and she supported his efforts to become an even better man. Despite all of that,

Bling couldn't get past the thought of Kyle. Sure, looking at Kelli was easy, and it was hard not to imagine being with her. However, looking at Kyle was the polar opposite. There was no way he could look at Kyle and be comfortable with saying, 'Yeah, that's my girl.' As much as Bling tried to separate Kyle from Kelli, he couldn't. He spent hours questioning himself. *Am I wrong for feeling this way? If I feel something for Kelli, is it wrong to feel repulsed by Kyle? I mean, they're the same person, right? Is this a double-standard? I mean, I like women. What the hell am I supposed to do?* Bling had no answers. Still, the Kelli-Kyle conundrum was only the tip of the iceberg. Being with Kelli would bring another problem which Bling was determined to avoid. Danger.

Bling had spent years running the Bronx streets with the East 222's, a gang with whom the NYPD was very familiar. Bling craved the adrenaline rush of committing a petty crime, getting caught up in a skirmish with a rival gang, or running from the cops; or so he thought. Seven years ago, while running from the Agency, Bling came closer to losing his life with Kelli than he ever did running with the Deuces. Bling had no issues communicating his honesty about that; the experience frightened him. Bling wasn't a certified genius like Kelli, but he wasn't a fool either. Kelli had yet to resolve her issues, her vendetta, against the Agency. She told Bling about every aspect of her plan. Sure, he helped her out at first. The *counting cards* thing sparked his interest. It was after Kelli had come back from Atlantic City with all that money that Bling realized how intent Kelli had become in regards to making her revenge a reality. Kelli was once a girl who wanted to live a normal existence, be a normal girl. Now, Kelli was lying to her family, sneaking around, and deceiving everyone else in her life; the same lifestyle Bling had led as part of the 222's. Bling wanted no part of it. The moment he ran into Zenaida Rodriquez on campus was when he realized that he didn't have to be. He could still have a relationship with a girl who accepted his past and supported his future, except with Zenaida, there was no deception, no threats, no danger. Zenaida represented everything Bling wanted to obtain. On the other hand, Kelli represented everything Bling wanted to leave behind.

Bling felt bad about the way his conversation ended with Kelli today. Despite everything, he did love her. She was his friend, and he would honor that as long as he could. He decided he would sleep on it and give her a call in the morning. Perhaps by then, they would both be a little more level-headed. Bling wondered, *Is there a way I can keep Kelli as a friend without inviting all of her drama?* He could only hope. Still, Bling had already made up his mind about one thing. He loved Zenaida, and things with her were good. So if he had to choose between his life with Zenaida and his friendship with Kelli, Kelli was going to lose.

BRONX, NEW YORK

Agent Swann parked her car on a side street adjacent to the hotel at which Kyle Cuffee had rented a room. Cuffee, whom Swann had trailed the entire evening, had just returned from spending time with people whom

Swann guessed was his family, or more accurately, her family. Swann shook her head in disbelief as she updated her notes. She was still amazed at how she hadn't caught on to Kyle being a girl after two weeks of following her around.

Swann's initial surveillance began in Boston shortly after being assigned to the case. Within hours of arriving at Logan International Airport from D.C., Swann had found Cuffee's car and placed a tracker inside the rear bumper. A day later, Swann followed Cuffee back to D.C., where she shadowed Cuffee all weekend. *Strange,* she thought. *I watched this person stalk someone else, take photos of them as they ate in a diner, then go on an interview, and then return to Boston as if it was a normal routine. It all seemed a bit creepy. I mean, I get paid to do it. But her? Then, I follow her to New York and see a whole different side of her, literally. I'm not sure what to make of it. And once I report my most recent discovery, I'm not sure my superiors will know what to make of it either.*

WASHINGTON, D.C.

Mr. Five paced slowly around the table in the meeting room as the sound of a ringing phone filled the air. After two rings, the line opened, and Agent Peppers' voiced could be heard loud and clear.

"Agent Peppers," Mr. Five said, halting his movement around the room. He glanced quickly at Mr. One and Mr. Two, both of whom sat quietly at the table. Five turned towards the phone in the center of the table before he continued. "We have confirmation on that license plate number you provided us. It belongs to Dr. Suri."

"Any idea where he might be?" Peppers asked.

"Yes. We believe he and Agent Molina have gone to New York. In fact, you and Agent Kincaid are going to catch the next flight out."

"Our orders?"

"Bring the doctor and the girl back alive," Five said.

"What about Agent Molina, Sir? From what little I've heard about her, I doubt she's going to relinquish the girl without a fight."

"Make her see reason, Agent Peppers."

"And if I can't?"

"Then you do what you do best."

"Copy."

"Proceed to the airport, Agent Peppers. I will contact you with further orders." With that, he nodded at Mr. Two, who, in response, pressed a button on the phone and ended the call.

Mr. Five turned to Mr. One slowly.

One looked up from his seat and offered Mr. Five an affirming smile. "Well done, Mr. Five. I have no doubt that when I'm gone, you will the best man to take over the Northeast region."

"I'm sure you have quite a few years left in you, Sir."

"Yeah," One replied half-heartedly. "Perhaps."

"Are we certain that Peppers and Kincaid are up to this task?" Mr. Two asked. "They are accustomed to working abroad with fewer legal constraints."

Mr. One chuckled. "Yeah, I would've preferred to send Agents Burl and Jones, too. They're much more accustomed to working stateside. Unfortunately, Mr. Four pulled them to California to cover the Easy Street facility. For now, Peppers and Kincaid are on it. They'll be fine."

"I hope so," Two said. "After all these years, the Harmony Project can finally proceed to Phase Three. We can't afford to have something go wrong now."

10

BOSTON, MASSACHUSETTS

Davies glanced at the clock as she waited in the patient lobby of Dr. Verna Hughes. Hughes was a popular psychiatrist in the Boston area, who, according to Hughes' career history, had been in practice for twelve years. She was also Kelli Freeman's therapist.

When Kelli was first placed in witness protection almost seven years ago, she was assigned a psychiatrist to give her someone to whom she could talk, and to help her cope with her unique situation. It was for this reason that Kelli's therapist was not kept in the dark about her special ability. Within the first year, however, Kelli requested a change of therapist, claiming that she had no connection with the elderly Caucasian woman that was chosen for her.

"I'm sure she's a great doctor, but she doesn't get me at all," Kelli had said. Due to the fact that Kelli's history was being disclosed, A.D. Marsh had some initial reservations about allowing Kelli to switch therapists. In the end, however, he agreed to let Kelli research different psychiatrists in her area and choose one of her own. Kelli chose Verna Hughes.

Davies had yet to meet Dr. Hughes, but she was curious to see the type of person to whom Kelli felt most comfortable talking. *She obviously doesn't feel she can talk to me,* Davies thought to herself.

While Davies waited, she opened her notebook to examine the information that she and Marsh had been exchanging. Unfortunately, there was very little in the way of new information on Quinlan Pharmaceuticals other than a brief history of how long they had been in business, the company's net worth, the numerous locations around the country, and the names of their founders. Marsh had also sent her a list of the multitude of different medications that were manufactured and distributed by Quinlan. Aside from that, Marsh had not discovered anything too remarkable, and certainly nothing that would explain why Kelli would invest so much money there. The photos, on the other hand, exposed a rather interesting, yet puzzling, revelation.

It had not taken long for Marsh to contact Davies in regards to the images she had copied from Kelli's camera. She had been sitting in the middle of Kelli's living room as Marsh gave her the rundown.

"The man in the photo is Roger Tolin. He's a U.S. Supreme Court Justice, been serving for nearly forty years. The woman in the photos is his daughter, Betty."

Davies snapped her fingers. "Betty Royce, the congresswoman. I knew I recognized her."

"Any idea why Kelli would be following them?" Marsh had asked.

"Your guess is as good as mine," was Davies' response.

"I'm also guessing that there is a common thread; Quinlan, Tolin, Royce, and this new found wealth. Find the connection."

"I will, Sir. I'm going to see her therapist in the morning," Davies had said. "I'll need a disclosure order."

"I've already got a judge working on it. Any luck finding her Glock?"

"Not yet, Sir. I'll keep looking."

"Keep me posted," Marsh ordered firmly before he ended the call.

Davies had been sitting on the floor of Kelli's bedroom while she spoke to Marsh. She remained there for a few moments as she considered Kelli's Glock once more. She eyed the safe which she had retrieved from the closet once again. Though she knew Kelli was in New York, Davies did not want to waste time trying to figure out the combination. "Although," she said aloud as a thought occurred to her. "If I take the safe with me, I could work on it tonight, and then return it in the morning." Davies was still uncertain as to whether or not she would get the safe open, but the information provided by Marsh gave her a rush of optimism. Davies hoped that there would be some kind of paperwork, photo, or something in Kelli's safe that would link all of these newly found variables together.

Now, armed with this new knowledge of some of Kelli's activities, Davies was hoping that Hughes would be able to shed some light on Kelli's thought process, and maybe connect some of the dots.

Davies was so lost in thought that she didn't hear the door open. It was the sight of a pair of legs stepping into her peripheral vision that caused her look up and observe the woman who stood before her.

The woman stood at five feet, eight inches tall in heels. She had brown skin and straight black hair. She wore a tan suit jacket with a matching skirt. Her smile displayed teeth that were well taken care of. She extended her hand in greeting.

"Agent Davies," the woman said warmly. "I'm Verna Hughes. It's a pleasure to finally meet you."

BRONX, NEW YORK

Kelli rolled over in her hotel bed as vivid images of faces streamed into her sleep, unsettling her. In her mind, she saw herself sitting at a corner booth in a small cafe in D.C. A pair of binoculars rested in front of her next to a Glock 23. Seated at the table opposite her was Mr. One.

Mr. One was adorned in a black suit, complete with a black shirt and tie. He sat quietly as he surveyed the binoculars and handgun in front of him. His old, wrinkled face appeared calm and free of worry. He raised an eyebrow before averting his gaze and attention to Kelli.

"Is this all you've got?" he asked her.

"Of course not," she snapped angrily.

Mr. One raised his left hand to reveal Kelli's camera in his grasp. "How about this?" He placed it on the table and pushed it towards her. "You think this will be enough to compete with me, Miss Freeman? To compete with the Agency?"

"More than enough."

One leaned back against the booth. He shook his head as would a father who was disappointed in his child. "Miss Freeman, you have no idea with whom you're dealing. Oh, you think you do, but it's not in the realm of possibility that you're even close." He leaned forward. "How can you deal with me, when you haven't dealt with yourself?"

"I know who I am," Kelli said.

"You're a clone. You're no one," One countered.

"I'm Kelli Freeman," she retorted firmly.

"Try again."

"I'm Kyle Cuffee."

"Wrong."

"I'm . . . wait . . . I'm Harmony June."

"She's dead. As are you, my dear. Like I said. No one."

"Go to Hell," Kelli snapped. "I know who I am."

"Who are you?" he asked.

"I know who I am," she repeated sternly.

"Prove it," he demanded, challenging her.

"What?" she asked, surprised.

"You heard me."

Kelli picked up the Glock and pointed the muzzle directly between Mr. One's eyes. "I don't have to prove anything to anyone."

"Oh, really now?" he asked as he leaned forward enough to bring his forehead in contact with the short barrel of her weapon. "What about to yourself?"

"I will shoot you," she threatened.

"No, you won't. You know why? Because you don't have the guts; you need me so you have someone to blame for your mistake. You need a scapegoat, a patsy, someone, *anyone* other than yourself for having Francine out on the street that night-"

"No! You did this to me," Kelli screamed as she squeezed the trigger. The weapon did not fire. She tried again, but the result was the same.

A figure dressed in a long, black robe appeared next to the table. The sound of a ringing telephone emanated from within the robe. Kelli and Mr. One turned to the new arrival. It was Betty Royce.

In a raspy female voice, Betty asked, "What's going on here?"

Kelli's eyes opened. She stared blankly at the white ceiling for a few short moments before she realized that she had woken from a dream, and she was in her hotel room. She turned her head and her eyes landed on the Trac phone that vibrated in concert with every ring. Kelli reached out and picked up the phone. To her surprise, the screen on the phone identified the caller as Bling.

She pressed the button and answered the call.

"Sleeping in? Sounds like I woke you up," Bling whispered in response to her weary greeting.

"It's alright," she said, happy to hear his voice. "Why are you whispering?"

"Zee is in the shower, but these walls are real thin. I wanted to check on you; make sure you were okay, you know, after yesterday and all."

"I'm alright," she repeated. "Sorry about all that."

"Whatever, girl. Forget it. You gonna be around to-day?"

"Yeah," she said eagerly. "I'm picking up my brother and sister after school, but I can swing by before then."

"I'm actually going to spend a little time with my mom this morning," Bling said. "I'm working another early shift so I can get off in time for class tonight."

"I can come by the job," Kelli offered.

"That's cool. Just make it sometime after 4:00. Zee gets out of her class at 2:45, but has to be at work by 4. She likes to come through and see me along the way."

"No problem," Kelli said. "It's not like I couldn't shift if I ran into her. She knows Kyle."

"Yeah, but I don't want to have to explain why my friend Kyle from Boston is running around with my boss' kids."

"Got it. 4:00."

"Cool. See you later, girl."

Kelli ended the call and took a moment to allow a smile to grace her lips. It meant a lot to her that Bling reached out to reconnect. She only wished she felt as good about the other person who was apparently trying to reestablish contact with her. Agent West.

Though she had no intention of calling him, Kelli knew that she couldn't afford to ignore the fact that West went to Martin to inquire about her. Something must have happened that caused West to show up suddenly. What was it?

She retraced her steps over the last week. She paid cash for everything. Then, it hit her. Yesterday, she used her credit card to pay for her drinks at the bar. Still, according to Martin's phone call, West was looking for her before that transaction took place. No. There was something else going on.

For a brief instant, she considered calling West and asking him herself, but her pride got in the way of that train of thought. *Why should I call him? He's the one who stopped calling or visiting. He should be calling me.* Kelli thought about her other cell phone, the one tied to Kyle Cuffee, the one that had been turned off for the last week. She figured West had called her, along with Davies, several times. But due to her desire to move around covertly, she had cut off one of her only lines of communication to anyone in Kyle's world, including Davies and West.

Kelli was at a loss. Despite what she thought was a well-laid plan, she hadn't anticipated West and the FBI looking for her. And since they were looking for her, she knew it was only a matter of time before they did, in fact, trace Kyle Cuffee's credit card to the Bronx. *Then what?*

Kelli considered telling her father about the situation, but doing so would mean either divulging everything, or omitting details to keep him from learning the truth about her excursions to D.C. Either way, Arthur would worry. That was a given. But when it came right down to it, Kelli didn't want to lie to her father. Sure, telling lies was rather easy for her at this point, but she admired her father more than any other man on Earth. She wanted to be like him. The last thing she wanted to do was disappoint him. Instead, she chose to keep him in the dark, and hope, that one day, these problems, these lies, would all be resolved, and simply go away.

༚

Agent Molina opened the door to her hotel room at the Howard Johnson Inn Yankee Stadium. She and Iris had already devoured the breakfast they had ordered from room service, so Molina was startled to see Dr. Suri standing there, waiting patiently outside.

She stepped aside and gestured for him to enter. He complied and strode in. Iris, already dressed, was reading through the documents from the Harmony Project file.

"Good morning, Iris," he greeted her with a smile. "Still catching up, I see."

"She's read it twice already," Molina informed him. "Now she has questions. Lots of them."

"As I expected," Suri responded.

Iris did not waste any time. "This file goes pretty in-depth about how the Harmony Project began, the procedures, even the whole science of it all, but I want to know about the last super soldier that the project produced. The one before me. Kelli Freeman. Even though the file states that she was the project's greatest success, there is very little about her in the documentation. Nothing about her progress, no pictures, not much of anything."

"You shouldn't concern yourself with her right now," Suri suggested.

"Why not? Even though she was this great success, she was still eliminated. Why? Is that what they do with their test subjects when they are no longer of any use? Is that why they wouldn't give me a kidney transplant?"

Suri glanced at Agent Molina. He could tell that she, too, was interested in the answers to Iris' questions. Unfortunately, Suri did not have a clear picture of what happened to the previous super soldier subject. In fact, he was certain that only a few people, if any, did. He returned his gaze to Iris.

"I don't know why they terminated the previous subject, Iris. Really, I don't. As you can see, much of the information on her is either redacted or omitted all together. Believe me, when I was working to find a way to stabilize your condition, I asked these same questions, but received very little in the way of answers."

Iris sighed. She turned over a few pages, looking for one in particular. After a moment, she began reading a passage. "Though it is indisputably linked to Subject HP-3's remarkable abilities, we have been unable to confirm, locate or activate the aforementioned June Gene to which Dr. Marcus June laid claim and had accredited with the specific result." Iris looked up at Suri once again.

Suri shook his head. "Like I said. I asked these same questions. This June Gene, whatever it is, is only mentioned one other time in that entire document."

"In reference to something called a gender shift," Iris added.

"Yes," Suri said. "I can only assume that they found a way to select the gender of the subject before the experiment even began. It's the only thing that makes sense. I'm sorry."

"Hmph," Iris pouted slightly. Then, "What's Project Rebirth?" Iris held up a document. "This file mentions something called Project Rebirth."

Suri shook his head. "It's an entirely new program that hinged upon the success of the Harmony Project. But, considering the fact that we've strayed from protocol, it's safe to say that we needn't be worried about it. Let's stay focused."

Iris' jaw tightened but she said nothing. Instead, she returned her attention to the file that lay open before her. Within moments, she was completely enthralled.

"What about things on your end?" Molina asked the doctor.

"The specialist I spoke of is a lawyer. He used his connections to pull a number of addresses where our targets are likely to be. I've got home and school addresses. I've also managed to procure a van for the grab."

"The grab?" Molina repeated with a small laugh. "A little dramatic, don't you think?"

"What we're doing *is* dramatic, Agent Molina."

"I suppose," she conceded. "I'm going to take the rental out first so I can scout things out, get a feel for the area, map out our routes."

"I want to go," Iris spoke up.

"You don't have to come, Mija," Molina said. "You should get some more rest."

"I'm fine, Mom," Iris protested. "If I start to feel bad, Dr. Suri is here, right?"

Suri nodded.

"Besides," Iris continued, "I was activated two days ago for a mission, so that makes me an operative. I'm pretty sure that what we're doing could end up being dangerous, which means you're going to need me. And since this whole mission is about me anyway, I'm going."

Molina wanted to protest Iris' argument, but she couldn't. Iris was right. This mission was about her. In fact, it was more so about Iris than anyone else in the room. And in regards to her operative status, she had apparently proven herself to Mr. Five and the rest of the Agency. Lastly, she knew it would do her no good to argue with Iris. Iris had read the Harmony Project documents provided by Suri more than once. She was more than ready for this mission, and Molina knew that Iris deserved to go.

"Very well," Molina stated. "I guess it's settled. Let's get it done."

❧❧

"Oh yeah," Michael, the bartender at Lexa Bar & Garden, confirmed as he looked at a photo of Kelli, "she was here yesterday. Sat at the end of the bar over there. Such a beauty."

"Do you remember if she met with anyone?" West asked.

"No, she was drinking alone," Michael answered.

"Are you sure?"

Michael smiled. "Agent West, did you say?"

West nodded.

"Agent West, when a girl as pretty as that walks into the bar, I tend to notice, especially if they sit and drink alone most of the time. Not to mention, she looked so young, like a teenager, so you know I had to verify her age and all. Trust me, I'm sure."

The bartender's mention of verifying Kelli's age sparked West's curiosity. Although Kelli was of legal drinking age, she couldn't possibly have an I.D. with her real name on it, after all, Kelli Freeman was supposed to be dead.

"Do you remember her name?" West asked.

Michael nodded as he polished an empty pilsner glass. "In fact, I do. She had a boy's name. Kyle. Who's to say how she pronounces it, though? But it was a Massachusetts I.D. Like I said, when they're that pretty-"

"You tend to notice. Right." West allowed himself a small chuckle as he imagined that Michael was probably a closet pervert. Of course, he couldn't exactly blame him. Kelli was definitely a head turner. It was obvious to West that Kelli was using a fake I.D., and a damn good one, with Kyle's name, but her picture. That way, the name on the I.D. matched the name on the credit card. "You said most of the time," West said. "Did she engage anyone in conversation while she was here?"

"She did," Michael confirmed. "Terell, college kid, he's a regular here; always with his college buddies. She left with him."

"Left with him?" West asked, surprised. "Do you know where they went?"

Michael placed the polished glass on the bar next to another equally shiny pilsner. "I don't know where they went, Agent West. But based on the number of young ladies I've seen with Terell, and the amount of alcohol little Miss Kyle drank, I'm pretty sure I know what they did when they got there."

West was taken aback. That didn't sound like the Kelli Freeman he knew. Then again, he had lost touch with Kelli over the last two years, so it was quite possible that he no longer knew Kelli as well as he once did. Nevertheless, the idea was difficult for West to grasp.

"You said Terell is a regular," West said, more as a statement than a question.

"Every day around noon."

West offered a small grin. "Good to know."

❧

Agent Kincaid sat in the passenger seat of a dark blue Crown Victoria that was parked in front of the Dunkin Donuts on Southern Blvd. He scrolled through his texts, reviewing one of three recent messages from Mr. Five. The driver's door opened and Agent Peppers slid in behind the wheel. In his hand he carried a Vanilla flavored coffee. The pungent odor of the hot beverage filled the car immediately.

Kincaid glanced at the cup. "Got your morning fix?"

"Oh yeah," Peppers said with an air of satisfaction. "What's the word?"

Kincaid handed his cell phone to Peppers and delivered a short narrative as his partner looked at the screen.

"Looks like Dr. Suri has been active this morning. His cell phone's been in almost constant use for about an hour now. According to GPS triangulation, his cell signal is somewhere in this area." He reached over and tapped a button on his phone. In response, the view on the screen changed from text messages to a map of the Bronx. A blinking icon indicated the area from where Suri's signal was originating. Another press of the button caused the map to zoom in and display an area that covered a two-block radius. "How much you want to bet there's a hotel on that street?"

"I don't take bets that I know I can't win. You know that. Besides, I *like* my free morning coffee, and it certainly smells better than your cologne." He handed Kincaid a small slip of paper. "Here's your receipt, by the way. Cheers." He raised his cup before taking another swig of his hot, vanilla flavored beverage.

"What do you think of all this?" Kincaid asked.

Peppers shrugged. "I'm not sure what you mean."

"Our current assignment, in particular, our orders concerning Agent Molina. I mean, we don't know her personally but, come on, Pepp, she's an Agency operative just like us. She's serving her country just like we are, right? Doesn't it bother you that we're supposed to just scrub her if she puts up resistance? I mean, we're supposed to be the good guys."

"We *are* the good guys," Peppers assured him. "And our job is to eliminate threats to the safety of our country and its endeavors."

"A woman protecting her daughter is a threat? I don't get it."

"You know how this works," Peppers said flatly. "We get an assignment, we carry it out. We don't ask why. The less we know, the better. We just have to believe that the higher-ups know what they're doing."

Kincaid shook his head. "I don't like it."

"It's never bothered you before."

"We're usually in a foreign country, not here, and not stalking our own agents. It just seems wrong."

Peppers leaned back and knocked back another swallow of coffee. Deep down, he wished he could tell his young partner that he agreed with him, that the lines of morality were dangerously close to being crossed. However, Peppers refrained and remained silent. He knew, all too well, that developing a conscience on this job led to doubts, second-guessing, and eventually, hesitation; all of which could get an operative killed. That's what happened to his previous partner, and he knew it could happen to his current partner just as easily. Peppers surmised that the best thing he could do for Agent Kincaid was to keep him focused on the mission, and let the higher-ups worry about sleeping at night. Without turning to Kincaid, he managed to finally say, "We have our orders," and then he gulped down some more coffee.

Kincaid could tell that Peppers wasn't in the mood for a discussion on morality. He and Peppers had been partners for close to ten years now, so he was all too familiar with that disconnected look that came over Peppers' face. Kincaid knew that the conversation was over. Kincaid respected his partner. He valued his advice and the experience from which it stemmed, so he took Peppers' silence as a subtle hint to let the topic die. After a moment, Kincaid decided to lighten the mood.

"I can drive if you want to sit and nurse your drink," Kincaid joked.

Peppers tossed Kincaid the cell phone, and then started the car's engine. In his usual, calm demeanor, he replied. "Just tell me where to go."

Kincaid bit his tongue and refrained from making the obvious remark. Instead, he responded with only a sinister chuckle.

৯৵৶

BOSTON, MASSACHUSETTS

"I'll have you know, Agent Davies, that I have never been too fond of working with participants under witness protection," Hughes stated after she and Davies were safely behind the closed door of her office.

"No?"

From her seated position behind her desk, Hughes straightened her posture in her chair. She glanced down at the disclosure order that had been hand delivered shortly before Davies' arrival. Though Hughes was not pleased with the court-issued order, she succeeded in hiding her discontent. "Don't misunderstand. It has nothing to do with the patients themselves, rather the stipulations that obligate me to disclose things that would, under normal circumstances, remain confidential."

"But you knew Kelli was high profile before you took her on. If you had a problem with the protocol, why did you agree to treat her?"

Hughes smiled. "I didn't. But then one day, this beautiful, scared teenager showed up at my office door begging me to treat her. One conversation was all it took."

"When's the last time you saw Kelli?"

Hughes didn't have to think about the answer. "Last Wednesday. She usually comes in on Thursday afternoons, but she claimed that she was leaving town last Thursday, so I saw her a day earlier."

"Does she have an appointment for tomorrow?" A logical question, Davies thought, considering it was Wednesday.

"No. Not until next week," Hughes replied. She tilted her head to the right and her eyes narrowed slightly as the wheels in her head began to turn. "But you knew that, didn't you?"

"Only the fact that she probably wasn't going to be here tomorrow."

"Agent Davies, I assure you that I have no reason to mislead you. Just because I'm treating her, doesn't mean I'm going to lie to you. That would serve no purpose."

"And how is Kelli's treatment going?" Davies asked, steering the conversation back to a Q and A.

Hughes took notice. "Overall, Kelli has made some amazing breakthroughs. But sometimes, it really depends on the day, or the topic."

"Which topics give her the most difficulty?" Davies questioned.

Hughes paused. She knew that this day might come, when she had to look an FBI agent in the eye and divulge the very things that Kelli had confided in her. Of course, Kelli was aware that this day might come as well, but based on Agent Davies' sudden appearance coinciding with Kelli's absence, Hughes had to assume that Kelli was unaware of Davies' visit.

Hughes took a breath before she continued. "Her family, her life in Boston, her sexuality and her expression thereof, and of course, the loss of her best friend, Francine."

"Makes sense," Davies said. "I'd like to ask you questions about all of those things, but first, can you tell me if Kelli has developed any new hobbies over the last year or so."

"Specifically?"

"Photography, and marksmanship."

Hughes eyes widened. It was an outward expression she tried to stifle. But it was too late. Davies had seen her reaction at the mention of the two hobbies. She knew that Davies wouldn't relent until she revealed what she knew.

"I know that she had become quite interested in photography recently. She claimed to have read the camera's instruction manual from cover to cover, which, I must admit, is something I've never done."

Davies allowed a small grin to grace her lips. "Most people don't. They usually read just enough to gain a rudimentary understanding of whatever new item they've purchased."

"Not Kelli," Hughes stated. "She was very pleased with how proficient she had become with the camera."

"And what about gun training?" Davies asked.

"Same thing," Hughes said. "She took an interest in weapons and began learning how to use them. Although I challenged her on this point, Kelli wants to believe that her interests, and all of her training, do not go beyond casual."

"*All* of her training?"

"Yes. Marksmanship, martial arts, gymnastics, photography. Kelli's interests tend to border on the obsessive, which is understandable when you consider the circumstances. It's an issue that we have discussed at length."

"You said you challenged her?"

"Yes, to look closer at her own motivations," Hughes answered. "Kelli was confused about her training compulsions. She was afraid that she wasn't being driven by mere interest, but by genetic predisposition. As you know, Kelli was genetically engineered to be a super-soldier. She needs to be certain that her desires are truly her own, and not the result of her genetic programming."

"And is she certain?"

"We're still working on it. Kelli feels that her life is out of control. Her obsessive compulsions are the mechanisms that drive her attempts to regain that control."

"And what, in your opinion, drives her compulsions?"

"Guilt."

Davies leaned forward. "Not to sound antagonistic, Doctor, but why haven't you reported any of this?"

"My observations are documented in my transcripts. I only make specific recommendations when I feel my patients do not have the internal mechanisms to deal with their emotions and cope with situations safely."

"And you feel that Kelli can?"

"So far. Yes. Despite her training with guns, Kelli has stated repeatedly that she doesn't believe she could actually shoot another human being."

"Why else would she be training with guns?" Davies queried.

"Someone tried to kill Kelli when she was fourteen years old. Under those circumstances, it is not uncommon for a person to take measures to protect themselves should the situation arise again. Based on those reasons, I have yet to feel that Kelli is a danger to herself or anyone else."

Davies' upper lip tightened. "I hope you're right."

Hughes sensed the tension that clung to Davies' last statement. Unfortunately, her eyes shifted to the clock, and she knew she had to cut this conversation short. Again, Davies noticed.

"Are we out of time?" Davies asked.

Hughes nodded. "I have a patient coming in."

Davies stood. "Perhaps we can resume this conversation later?" Though Davies' inflection made it sound like a request, Hughes knew that it was not.

"Of course," Hughes said. "My last patient leaves at 5:00."

"Understood," Davies replied. "Before I go. . ."

Hughes raised an inquisitive eyebrow.

"You said Kelli's compulsions are driven by guilt. Guilt about what?"

"Francine's death. Kelli hasn't found a way to get over it." Hughes forced a smile. "I'm hoping we'll get there someday, if not, the consequences could be devastating for her."

"I agree," Davies said, and then extended her hand. "Thank you, Doctor."

Hughes stood and shook Davies' hand. As she did, Davies spoke again. This time, her voice was softer, friendlier, without the tone or demeanor of an interrogator.

"I want you to know that I'm in Kelli's corner."

Hughes smiled again. "I know that, Agent Davies. Kelli speaks highly of you."

Davies couldn't hide her surprise. "Does she?"

"Very much," Hughes said. "I'll see you at 5."

BRONX, NEW YORK

Kelli, who had shifted into Kyle mode, smiled as she maneuvered through the sea of screaming, young students that ran past her on the elementary school campus of PS 304, which occupied the same grounds as MS 101 where her mother, Diane, was principal.

Lunch time had just ended, and students from both schools were making their way back into the building in attempt to make it to their next class. In the distance, she could see a group of younger students being led by their teacher back into the school. The sight brought back vivid memories of her past-self amongst children, standing in a single file line, laughing and whispering to the other students, including Francine. She could still see Francine's long black hair, her smile, the space in her mouth that was left by a loose tooth that had finally fallen out. A feeling of emptiness pressed itself against the walls of her stomach. Although she was, in fact, hungry, Kelli knew the emptiness she felt stemmed from missing Francine. If she could just see Francine's face one more time, maybe then Kelli could talk to her and rid herself of the remorse she carried for the role she played in Francine's final moments. Once again, Kelli felt as if she was going to burst into tears. Fortunately, she did not have time to think on it further. Diane was approaching her from across the yard, and to Kelli, it was a welcome distraction.

"Hey, Ma," she said as they embraced.

"Hey, Baby," Diane said in return. She stepped back and stared at Kelli.

Kelli turned away, pulling up the hood on her sweatshirt to cover her face. "Ma, don't," she pleaded. As much as Kelli hated having to shift into her male form, she hated it even more when she had to do it in the presence of her family. When she did so, it made her feel like a stranger to the people she loved most in the world.

Diane reached up and stopped Kelli from covering her face, even though it was Kyle's image. Their eyes met.

"It's alright, Baby," Diane said softly. "I only see you."

Kelli choked back a wave of emotions. She didn't want to cry. If she let her guard down and allowed the flood gates to open, she feared she would not be able to close them.

Diane caressed her face gently. "Come on. I had lunch brought in for us. We can eat in my office."

Kelli followed Diane into her office where she shifted back into her female form immediately. Over the next hour, they feasted on linguine with pesto sauce, lightly buttered dinner rolls and a Cobb salad minus the meat. During lunch, they discussed plans for Wilma's weekend birthday party, and Kelli asked as many questions as she could about her family's daily activities during her long absences. Though the discussion weighed heavily on her emotions, Kelli loved hearing about her younger siblings' accomplishments, her father's business, and Diane's daily grind as a school principal. Diane paused several times during their conversation to comfort Kelli whenever she burst into tears. Still, Kelli urged her to continue, claiming that Dr. Hughes encourages her to cry whenever necessary to purge herself of pent-up emotions so she can deal with them openly and honestly. Despite the emotional roller coaster, her time spent with her mother allowed her to, once again, forget about her isolation in Boston, and her plan to bring her exile to an end. At the end of the hour, Kelli felt happy, and connected. She held her mother in a tight embrace before she morphed back into her alter ego, and then exited the office.

She strolled slowly across the yard before passing through the gate and making a bee-line for her car that was parked on the opposite side of Lafayette Ave. Once she was behind the wheel, she relaxed and allowed her true self to emerge. She checked her watch. She had ninety minutes to wait before school let out, at which time she would collect Wilma before going to the high school to pick up Cassius. She closed her eyes and enjoyed the peace and quiet around her, never once suspecting that the black sedan that was parked three cars behind her Audi had been following her for quite some time.

BOSTON, MASSACHUSETTS

Davies realized she had a few hours to kill while she waited to return to Dr. Hughes office and gather whatever information she could that would explain Kelli's recent disappearance. She decided to take advantage of her proximity to Faneuil Hall and find a restaurant where she could grab a bite to eat and compile her notes at the same time. Before long, she had made her way to the Union Oyster House where she enjoyed the best New England clam chowder that she had ever tasted.

She retrieved her notepad from her pocket and began to look over all of the information she had gathered. During her last call with A.D. Marsh, Marsh provided the confirmation that a brand-new Audi had, in fact, been registered under the name of Kyle Cuffee at the Beacon Street address where Kelli now lived. After Davies had spent time in Kelli's apartment, the confirmation about the car did not come as a surprise. Davies turned her attention to the notes she had taken while speaking with Dr. Hughes. A feeling of sadness overwhelmed Davies as she thought about all of the issues that burdened Kelli as a result of her engineered abilities. *No kid should have to endure what she's endured,* Davies thought to herself, *being separated from her family, hiding under the male guise of Kyle Cuffee, watching her best friend die in front of her.* Davies shook her head. *I don't think most adults could handle that type of stress.* Davies' mind lingered on Dr. Hughes' comments about Kelli's guilt, and Francine, when a thought occurred to her. *Next month will be the seventh anniversary of Francine's death, when all of this business began.* Her eyes widened. Softly, she said to herself, "The safe."

Davies pulled her phone from her pocket and dialed Marsh. When Marsh answered the phone, Davies couldn't get the words out fast enough.

"Slow down, Agent Davies," Marsh said to her. "Whose date of birth are you requesting?"

"Francine Rodriguez. She was Kelli's best friend."

"Yeah, I remember. Give me a few minutes." With that, Marsh was gone. However, true to his word, he called Davies back just short of five minutes later, which had given Davies plenty of time to return to her car where Kelli's safe was hidden in the trunk.

"April 21st," Marsh relayed to her.

"Got it," Davies said. "Stand by." She tapped the speaker icon on her phone and laid it on the dashboard. She turned to the safe and pressed the numbers on the front keypad, entering the date given to her by Marsh. As soon as she depressed the final digit of the year Francine was born, Davies heard the safeguards slide out of place. Davies pulled on the lever. The door to the safe swung open. "Bingo," she said aloud.

"Please tell me there's a Glock in there," Marsh voice said through the speaker.

Davies surveyed the inside of the safe. There was a folded stack of paperwork that was bound by a rubber band, and a sealed black bag containing gold-plated ammunition and two empty magazines. Davies surmised that the ammo and the magazines were for the Glock 23, but further inspection revealed no weapon in sight.

"Sorry, sir," Davies reported. "No gun."

"Damn," Marsh cursed loudly.

"What now?" the female agent asked.

"Now, I contact Agent West and put him on alert," Marsh answered. "He needs to approach Kelli Freeman as if she's armed and dangerous."

11

MANHATTAN, NEW YORK

Solid State Security, owned and operated by Arthur Freeman, had several accounts in the Bronx and Manhattan areas. The majority of the accounts consisted of newly constructed or refurbished buildings and properties that required a 24-hour presence to safeguard the investment. There were several connecting properties on Overlook Terrace, just across the Harlem River in Manhattan that constituted a broad residential renovation project. This particular property consisted of four buildings, three of which were residential buildings in the process of being renovated. The fourth building, designated Building Four, was an old office building that was being converted into residential apartments. Due to an ongoing rash of burglaries at construction sites across the Bronx and Queens, the holding company that contracted Solid State to guard their buildings did not want to take any chances, and as a result, required Arthur to have four guards on duty at all times.

Bling walked out to the street after completing his last patrol of the adjacent residential property. The sun was beginning to set and the air had grown slightly more frigid. He pulled the zipper of his thick bomber jacket up to his neck, all the while bobbing his head to the heavy Hip-

Hop beat that poured into his ears via his earbuds. Clipped to his left shoulder was the microphone that was attached to the two-way radio on his hip. He reached for the mic and opened the channel.

"Patrol 2 complete. All conditions normal."

"Copy that, Patrol 2. Conditions normal," came the response over the radio.

Up ahead, Bling spied Kelli as she approached with Cassius and Wilma in tow. He acknowledged the two younger kids in rapid succession before turning his attention to their big sister.

"Hey," Bling greeted her. "Seems like your whole family is here tonight. Your dad showed up about ten minutes ago."

"Yeah, he's here to pick up my brother and sister," Kelli said. "Is he up in the office?"

"Yep. And your timing couldn't be more perfect. I get off in a few minutes."

"And then off to class, right?"

Bling nodded. "Yeah. Seems we may not have much time to hang out this week," he said.

"Yeah. I figured that out," was her solemn response.

"Why are you so late? I expected you guys two hours ago."

"I took them out for an early dinner," Kelli explained. "Besides, I wanted to make sure I wasn't here when you-know-who was here."

"Zenaida blew me off, too," Bling said. "She left campus late so she went straight to work."

"Oh," Kelli managed to say before adding a sarcastic, "Too bad."

"That's funny," Cassius chimed in as he pointed in the direction from whence they just came, "isn't that Zenaida right there?"

They all turned. Zenaida moved steadily up the sidewalk. Kelli turned away from her and whispered to Cassius and Wilma, "Go to Dad's office."

Wilma began to protest. "What? Why?"

"Just go!" she ordered. She looked at Cassius, who, in response, took hold of Wilma's hand.

"It's cool. Come on," Cassius said to Wilma, and then walked away with her.

Kelli avoided making eye contact with Zenaida as she moved closer to where she and Bling stood. Quickly, Kelli pulled up her hood and shifted forms. She turned as Zenaida reached them. However, Zenaida had not yet turned her attention to Kelli, as she was still focused on the man whom she came to see.

Zenaida stepped in front of Bling and stood on the tips of her toes in order to plant a soft kiss on his lips. Kelli tried to ignore it. She wanted to look away so she didn't have to witness Zenaida's public display of affection. Regardless of the pit that formed in her stomach, Kelli was compelled to watch. She didn't really care to see Zenaida kiss Bling, but she was very interested in seeing Bling's level of investment, and reading his body language. *Was he truly into this girl, or did he just run to her to avoid his feelings for me?* Kelli hated that she was harboring these thoughts and feelings, especially in Zenaida's presence. But she had to know. She watched Bling closely.

As Bling's lips pressed against Zenaida's, his eyes remained opened and he stared forward into the distance.

Kelli smirked. *I knew it*, she thought. But then, as she stared closer at Bling, she realized he wasn't dismissing the kiss. In fact, his attention had been drawn to something else.

Kelli turned and looked down the street. There, standing silently on the sidewalk, stood Agent West.

Kelli's heart jumped into her throat. Her first inclination was to run, but she knew that would serve no purpose. Could she outrun him? Of course. But, what was she running from? A scolding for violating her witness protection protocol?

She released a heavy sigh and began walking towards West.

Zenaida turned. "Hey," she said to Bling, "isn't that your friend, Kyle?"

Bling opened his mouth to respond, but was interrupted by a call on his two-way radio.

"Patrol 2. Report to Zone 1 for shift change," a female voice ordered.

Bling's attention remained on the FBI Agent. *Why is Agent West here?* he wondered silently. Bling had not seen Agent West in over six years, so he couldn't imagine why he appeared so suddenly now.

"Bryan, are you okay?" Zenaida asked, noticing how distracted he was. She followed his gaze and focused on the unfamiliar Caucasian man that stood on the sidewalk. "Who is that?" she asked.

Another call came over the radio. "Patrol 2. Return to Zone 1. Do you copy?"

Bling snapped to attention. He grabbed the mic and called into it. "Copy. On my way." He turned to Zenaida. "Stay here. I'll be right back." He stepped away and began retracing his steps back to the security office which was designated as Zone 1. Though he moved in one direction, his attention remained fixed on Agent West and Kelli.

A half block away, Agent Swann sat in her dark-colored Honda, watching. Kyle had been on the move all morning, so Swann took advantage of the fact that, for the moment, Kyle was stationary. This allowed Swann to capture a few images on her digital camera and keep a visual record of people with whom Kyle came in contact and locations at which she met them. Though this was a standard practice, getting a picture of Kyle was especially important today.

Swann had contacted her superiors the night before and reported her discovery about Kyle's sex. Surprisingly, the only response she received was, "Interesting. Get me a clear photo of her." Luckily, Swann managed to zoom in and snap a picture of Kyle's face before she pulled up her hood suddenly.

Swann took note of the fact that Kyle, despite an attempt at subtlety, had concealed her face just as the other woman arrived on the scene. "Hmm," Swann muttered aloud, "I wonder what's going on?"

Agent Molina peered out of the passenger window of the van that was parked on Overlook Terrace. She gestured to Iris as their primary target arrived. Together they watched as a female, with the younger kids in tow, approached the security guard. Within moments, they observed as a fifth party, another female, approached and engaged the security guard, as well. Finally, a Caucasian male arrived on the scene. The man seemed to keep his distance, as if he was waiting for something. Molina noticed that the first girl pulled her hood up over her face. Then, within mere seconds, she watched as each member of the group began to separate.

Molina looked towards the lone girl left standing alone. The security guard had just left her side. The girl wearing the hood appeared to be having a heated discussion with the white male, causing them both to be distracted. The two younger black kids were farther up the path. Soon, they would turn the corner and move beyond everyone's field of vision. Now was the time.

She tapped Iris' shoulder. "I'm going in." A quick glance at her daughter. "Be ready."

Iris nodded. She pulled the hood from her sweatshirt over her head.

Without another word, Molina opened the passenger door and stepped onto the street. She crossed the distance and stepped up on the sidewalk. Silently, she maneuvered into position to grab her prey.

❧

"What are you doing here?" Kelli asked West as soon as he was in earshot.

"I could ask you the same thing," he countered.

Kelli took a moment to shift once again, transforming into her female self. "I'm visiting my family. I don't see what the problem is."

"The problem is that there are protocols that need to be followed. You know what would happen if the wrong person sees what you can do."

"I'm being careful," she said.

"Oh, really?" he asked sardonically. "I suppose getting drunk in a bar and using your credit card is what you consider careful."

"I don't get drunk," she snapped.

"Even worse," West retorted.

"Is that how you tracked me?"

"To New York, yes. After that, all it took was a conversation with a guy named Terell to find your hotel."

Kelli's breath caught in her throat at the mention of Terell's name. She averted her gaze away from West, hoping he didn't notice how ashamed she was of what she had done.

"That was a mistake-"

"A big one," West agreed. "Luckily, it's just me looking for you. Imagine if it was someone trying to hurt you. I went to your hotel and got there just as you were leaving. If you were being so damn careful, you would have noticed that I've been following you for hours." He gestured to the black sedan that was parked to his left.

She took a step and closed the distance between them. Though the volume in her voice dropped, her tone was stern and unmistakably bitter. "Oh, so now you care? I haven't heard from you in two years, and now you want to barge into my life because I left Boston without a phone call?"

A pang of guilt stabbed at West's stomach. He knew that Kelli harbored bitter feelings about his disappearance from her life. He wanted to tell her that he became so obsessed with his work and with hunting down the Agency that he forgot to call, forgot to write and forgot to visit. But that would only be half of the truth, because he did not forget to do those things. He chose not to. Not because he did not want to stay in touch with her and keep her apprised of the progress in his Agency investigation, but because he had not made good on his promise to find whatever information was necessary to take the Agency down. Instead, every lead that came West's way, quite simply, went up in smoke. Even now, after two years of *heads-up* intel from Paul Ferry, that lead threatened to dry up as well. West exhaled heavily. He fought the urge to settle his personal differences with Kelli right then and there due to a much more pressing matter. Just moments after West parked his sedan on Overlook Terrace, Marsh phoned him about the possibility that Kelli was carrying a Glock 23; the same type of weapon that had killed Paul Ferry. During that call, Marsh ordered West to detain Kelli Freeman on suspicion of first-degree murder.

"That's not why I'm here, Kelli," he blurted out.

"Why else would you be?"

West exhaled again. He looked away, pausing briefly to find the right words to tell her that he needed to take her into custody. Not because she violated her witness protection agreement, but because she had become the prime suspect in an Agency-related murder investigation. As he looked back at Kelli, a strange image in the distance behind her grabbed his attention. At first, he questioned what he was seeing, but it took a mere second for his brain to confirm the message.

West pulled his gun from his holster and pushed past Kelli. He leveled his weapon in front of him, and screamed. "FBI. Stop right there."

Startled, Kelli whirled around to see a hooded figure standing behind Zenaida, holding a white rag over her nose and mouth. To Kelli's keen eyes, the shape of the hooded figure was undeniably female. As Zenaida's body went limp, the woman began to drag her towards the curb.

West exploded into a full sprint. He yelled again, "I said stop."

Molina continued to drag Zenaida's seemingly lifeless body. A white van pulled up to the curb and stopped just short of Molina. A moment later, the back doors to the van were thrust open. Iris stood in the back of the van, beckoning Molina to hurry.

West realized he might not make it down the block in time to stop the kidnapping that was taking place right before his eyes. He slowed his pace and began to realign his weapon. Suddenly, Molina pushed the unconscious woman towards the open van doors and spun in West's direction. There was a black metallic object in her grip. West did not have to be told what it was.

Out of habit, West screamed, "Gun!" He dove to his right and hit the ground hard as two shots whizzed past him in the air. He turned and looked behind him. Thankfully, Kelli had heeded his warning and had dropped to the ground, as well. It then occurred to West that the woman, whoever she was, was not trying to kill him. She was merely trying to stall him.

Iris was having trouble pulling Zenaida's body into the back of the van, not due to a lack of strength, but because of the awkwardness, and dead weight that a comatose body presented. Iris readjusted her grip. With one motion, she lifted Zenaida into the air.

West jumped to his feet. Again, Molina raised her weapon. Suddenly, Molina heard heavy footfalls approaching rapidly from her left side. Her false eye offered her no peripheral vision on her left, and she knew a millisecond too late that she was being flanked.

Bling tackled Molina, forcing them both to fall into the street behind the van. The impact from the fall caused Molina to drop her weapon. Her hood fell back, revealing her face. Bling continued to roll, ending up on his knees. He turned and faced the woman. Unfortunately, his attention was drawn to the sound of Zenaida's body being dragged and laid into the back of the van. He refocused on the woman who had already regained her footing and had launched herself in his direction. Bling stood and threw a right hook. Molina stepped to her left, parried his blow, and followed through with a Muay Thai elbow strike that landed squarely upon his right temple. Bling folded immediately and fell to the ground.

"Mom," Iris yelled, warning Molina of another impending attack.

Molina dropped to the pavement and rolled forward. West, who had committed to a tackle of his own, sailed over her uncontrollably.

Molina sprang to her feet and lunged towards the open compartment in the back of the van. As she stepped up, someone grabbed her from behind and pulled her back onto the street. Molina rolled with the momentum of her new assailant's strength and spun to her right. As she did, her right hand lashed out in an attempt to deliver a back-hand strike. The blow sailed through the air but connected with nothing.

Molina turned to face Kelli, who, in her male form, had ducked the back-hand and was now moving forward to engage her. Molina extended a straight kick. Kelli caught Molina's leg, and then fell into a side roll. Molina lost her balance and began tumbling to the ground.

"Mom," Iris called as she jumped out of the van.

Kelli, being well-versed in the art of ju-jitsu, maneuvered herself on top of Molina and attempted to subdue her with an arm-bar technique. However, before she could secure the hold, a hard blow to her rib-cage knocked her over, forcing her to relinquish her grasp on the woman. Kelli couldn't help but notice how much force was behind the attack.

Iris helped her mother up from the ground. Iris hopped into the back of the van. She turned to assist Molina, only to find her mother being pulled back onto the street once again.

West wrapped his arms around Molina in an attempt to secure her arms. He lifted her off the ground, removing whatever leverage Molina had hoped to use to escape his grasp.

Molina launched a reverse elbow into West's gut. She could tell by the thud that the FBI agent was wearing a vest. She looked up and saw Iris coming to her aid once more. Before Iris could step out of the van, Molina called to her.

"Get out of here!"

"But, Mom-"

"Go!" she yelled.

Iris hesitated. She was caught between trying to save her mother, or leaving the scene to save herself, and by doing so, completing the mission.

"Go!" Molina ordered again as West spun her in the air wildly.

The sight of her mother being apprehended caused tears to burst from her eyes. Despite the love and dedication she felt for her mother, she knew that the mission came first. The training she had received since childhood told her that. She turned and began moving towards the driver's seat. As Iris stepped over Zenaida's unconscious form, she was attacked from behind. She fell to the floor of the van, landing hard on all fours.

Iris turned around and faced her assailant. Though it *appeared* to be a young man who had leapt into the van and attacked her, in truth, it was Kelli who stood before her, ready to fight.

The light from the overhead lamp in the van and the hood on Iris' face cast a shadow over her features as she advanced on Kelli. Kelli moved towards her as well. They jumped at each other and clashed hard in the middle of the van. There, they struggled to overpower one another. All the while, Iris could still hear her mother screaming for her to escape.

Kelli, in her female form, was already stronger than most men. But in her male form, her strength was augmented twelve-fold. She forced Iris back a few steps before tightening her grip on Iris' arms. She threw Iris to the left, slamming her against the wall of the van. Kelli threw a right jab which landed on Iris' jaw. Another jab connected at the same spot, setting up the left hook. Iris feigned to her left, raising her arm in time to block the left hook. She extended her leg and delivered a forward snap kick to Kelli's chest. Kelli's body flew back against the opposite van wall in response. Kelli was truly surprised by the amount of strength she felt behind that kick. She ducked immediately, avoiding the follow up kick by Iris that would have surely landed squarely between her eyes.

Kelli ducked under Iris' body. Iris, after missing with the kick, brought her foot down and, inadvertently, stepped on Zenaida's leg. She stumbled slightly. Kelli lunged forward. She reached for Iris, but due to Iris' attempt to recover her balance, only managed to grab hold of Iris' hood. She yanked at the hood, pulling it back until it caught Iris by the throat and forced her to fall backwards. Unfortunately, Kelli underestimated her own strength and fell backwards, as well.

Iris landed on the van floor. She rolled to her left and crouched on all fours once again. Kelli had fallen against the back of the driver's seat. The padding cushioned the impact and allowed Kelli to regain her footing in preparation to renew her attack. She looked up at Iris, and got her first clear look at Iris' face.

The coldest chill she had ever felt raced up her spine. She froze in place and her jaw dropped as she took in an image that was all too familiar. Kelli opened her mouth. One word, one name, came out. "Francine?"

12

Iris had been poised to engage her opponent once again, but she stopped when the young man she was fighting spoke the name of the girl from who she was cloned. Francine. The utterance of the name surprised Iris on many levels, especially since she had just learned the name herself. Countless questions began to inundate her brain simultaneously. Questions such as, who is this person? How did he know Francine? And why is he here right now?

Kelli was still in shock. So much so that, without realizing it, she let down her guard and shifted back into her female form. She took a step towards the girl with Francine's face. Kelli watched as a look of disbelief and fear washed over her. It was a look that Kelli had seen before. It was the same look she'd seen on Francine's face that night almost seven years. The night that Francine died.

Kelli managed another step towards Iris. "Francine?" she questioned aloud again. "How-"

Before Kelli could utter another word, Iris sprang forward and lashed out with a vicious right hook that caught Kelli on the left side of her face. Kelli tumbled to her right and fell to the floor in a daze.

Seeing that Kelli was disoriented, Iris pressed the advantage. She grabbed a handful of Kelli's dreadlocks and slammed her face into the van floor. Blood squirted from Kelli's nose and mouth as she collapsed into an unconscious heap next to Zenaida.

Iris turned and moved quickly towards the rear doors which still hung open. As she looked out, she saw that the white male, using his own weight, had pinned Molina to the ground beneath him. She felt the urge to jump out and go to her mother's aid. Movement from the path that led to the security office caught her eye. Iris looked up and saw a black male sprinting in her direction.

Bling, who had regained consciousness, was crawling on all fours near the rear of the van. His head still pounded from the elbow strike to his temple. Banging noises from inside the van had caught his attention, and now, as he moved into plain sight of the doors, he looked up and caught a glimpse of the young girl who was standing there. "What the-"

Iris pulled both of the doors shut. She made a dash for the driver's seat, jumped behind the wheel and threw the gear shift into drive. She pressed the accelerator and the van jerked forward violently. She turned the wheel, maneuvered the van into a wide U-turn which, momentarily, climbed the opposite curb, and then pushed the gas pedal to the floor. As the van raced by her mother, who was now completely subdued, tears flooded Iris' eyes and exploded onto her cheeks. She made a sharp left at the corner and pushed the van into the dark cover of the night.

Back at the corner, the headlights of a dark blue sedan came to life. Inside, Kincaid turned to his partner.

"What do you think? Should we help her?" Kincaid asked, gesturing to Molina.

Peppers' response came without hesitation. "She's not our mission. We're here for the girl and the doctor. Agent Molina is on her own." Peppers maneuvered the sedan away from the curb. He reminded himself to keep a safe distance as he began the stealthy pursuit of the white van up ahead.

Seated in her cherry-colored Honda, Agent Swann couldn't believe the turn of events she had just witnessed. As the melee unfolded in front of her, Swann's initial instinct was to jump out of her car and help. She'd heard the white male identify himself as an FBI agent, so naturally, she would have run to his aid. Unfortunately, the sound of the gunshots served as a painful reminder for Swann, transporting her back to the moment when she endured a bullet piercing her chest, barely escaping death, just a few years ago. Still, she couldn't deny that she felt drawn to the action. Swann fought against the instinct. She had to remind herself that she was no longer an FBI field agent, but a surveillance specialist who did not carry a firearm. Furthermore, running to assist the agent and, by extension, Kyle, would have definitely violated the 'keep your distance' directive in her orders. Though she felt compelled to help, Swann remained in her car. Within moments, the white van darted away from the curb with Kyle inside. Swann started her engine. She put the car in drive and made her way up the block. She made a left turn at the corner and cursed aloud as a dark blue sedan pulled in front of her. "Goddammit, move."

Swann began to sweat. The tracker she had been using to track Kyle was affixed to the black Audi that was still parked on the street. She knew that if she was going to track the van, she'd have to do it visually. Considering the overwhelming congestion of New York traffic, Swann knew that if she took her eyes off the van for one moment, she could lose track of Kyle for good.

Back on Overlook Terrace, Molina was being pulled to her feet by the FBI agent, who was involved in a brief exchange with an unfamiliar black gentleman who had, at some point, arrived on the scene. Molina heard none of their conversation due to the fact that her focus was elsewhere. She scanned the pavement quickly, hoping to catch sight of her weapon. Unfortunately, when she spied it, the weapon was in the grip of Arthur Freeman, and it was aimed directly at her head.

From the security office inside the residential complex, Arthur had heard the two gunshots that were fired by Agent Molina. Though the shots were faint, Arthur, a twenty-five-year veteran of the NYPD, had no problem recognizing them for what they were. He told Cassius and Wilma to stay put as he ran out in front of the adjacent building to investigate. As he approached, he saw two people struggling in the road. *Is that Kelli?* He increased his speed. His attention was diverted to Bling crawling aimlessly on the ground. It was only after the white van had completed a U-turn and made a hasty retreat that he realized Kelli was nowhere to be seen.

Arthur had noticed a handgun in the middle of the street. He retrieved it quickly and stepped in front of Bling protectively. He turned to the couple on the ground and ordered loudly, "Get up. Both of you. Right now."

West obliged quickly, bringing the woman up with him. He turned slowly to Arthur. It only took a brief second before recognition set in, followed immediately by confusion.

"Agent West?"

"Hey, Arthur," West replied.

"Where's my daughter?" Arthur asked, despite the fact that he'd already deduced Kelli's present whereabouts.

"Why don't you ask her?" West said as he nodded to his captive.

Arthur was still confused. He looked at the woman and knew instantly that he'd never seen her before. Fear crawled into his gut and began to churn away at him. What happened to his daughter? And who was this woman? So many questions, and according to Agent West, the woman standing before him had the answers. Arthur raised the weapon as Molina turned, facing him finally.

"I'm only going to ask you this once," Arthur said to her. "Where is that van going?"

❧❦

The rear entrance to the Urgent Care clinic was located on Netherland Avenue. Like the District Pediatric Clinic in D.C., the Bronx Netherland Clinic was a legitimate medical facility that treated many of the borough's residents with uncompromising dedication and unparalleled care. Unbeknownst to most, the clinic received supplemental funding to operate as an emergency medical outpost for Agency operatives in the field. Iris pulled the van to a stop just a few feet from the back entrance. She opened the driver's door and leapt from her seat. She circled the van quickly and pulled open the rear doors.

The entrance to the clinic swung open. Dr. Suri, followed by three nurses, exited the building and made his way to the back of the van. Two of the nurses were female, both Hispanic. Each of them pushed an empty wheelchair in front of them. The third nurse was a Caucasian male.

"Iris," Suri called to her. "You were so frantic on the phone; I barely understood what you were saying." He peered into the van and gasped at what he saw.

Iris was already dragging Zenaida to the van door. When she spoke, her words were rushed and laden with nervous energy. "Help me with her," she said to one of the nurses. She looked up at Suri. "She hasn't been out long. Mom used chloroform."

One nurse signaled to the other and the two of them proceeded to extract Zenaida from the back of the van.

"Where *is* your mother?" the doctor asked.

"They got her," she answered. She took a deep breath to force back the swell of emotion that pushed at the back of her throat. "They got her."

"Who got her? Iris, slow down."

"I don't know, okay?" she screamed. "Someone yelled FBI. I think it was the guy."

"FBI? The FBI has your mother?"

She nodded several times in a frenzied manner. "Yes."

Suri took a step back. His gaze travelled past Iris and into the van once more. "If they have Agent Molina, then who is that?" he asked, pointing to the other unconscious female.

Iris turned and looked at Kelli. Her mind replayed the encounter that had taken place just minutes before. Iris still had trouble believing what she had seen. Words and images from the Harmony Project file begin to appear in her mind, and Iris, began to connect the dots. She took a deep breath in an effort to calm her nerves and regain control of her emotions.

"Help me get her inside, and I'll tell you exactly who she is."

⌒⌒

Agent West entered the room that served as the security office at the Overlook Terrace location. He approached Arthur Freeman who had already paced close to one hundred laps back and forth across the room. Bling sat in a chair in the corner. He held an ice pack that he'd pulled from his small lunch cooler against the bruise on the side of his face.

West wasted no time apprising Arthur of the situation. "She's been secured in the other room. The rope you gave me will hold her."

"Did she tell you who she is?"

"No. And I don't expect her to, not willingly. If you have some clear masking tape and any kind of powder, I can pull her prints. We can, at least, get the ball rolling on her identity."

"Like you're going to find out who she really is," Bling said sarcastically. West and Arthur turned to him. Bling shook his head. "We need to get out of here. This is the Agency, dude. All over again."

Arthur shifted his attention back to West. Although he didn't want to admit it, he suspected that West's sudden reemergence was not a random coincidence. He searched West's face for a small glimmer of protest or denial of Bling's claim. West offered nothing. Arthur's heart sank. "And now they have my girl."

West placed a consoling hand on Arthur's shoulder. "Yes, but don't forget, we have one of theirs, too."

Arthur brushed West's hand away. "She works for the Agency. She's expendable." The volume of his voice began to rise. "You think they're going to trade that woman for my daughter? They chased Kelli across the whole damn country trying to kill her, or have you forgotten?"

"Of course not, Arthur. How could I?"

Arthur stared at West. He knew that West was with Kelli when the Agency tried to capture and kill her almost seven years ago. He knew that if it was not for West's interference and protection, his daughter would have been long dead. Arthur turned away. Over his shoulder, he managed a barely audible, "I'm sorry."

"Don't be," West said. "Besides, I don't think this woman is as expendable as you think."

"Why not?" Arthur questioned, turning to face West once again.

"Because the girl in the van called her mom; more than once, I might add."

Bling jumped to his feet suddenly, as if he had been burned by something in his chair. "Oh shit!" he exclaimed.

"Sounds crazy, right?" West said, convinced Bling was referring to his latest revelation. However, Bling had an astonishing revelation of his own.

He ignored West's question and said simply, "I saw her face. The girl in the van."

"Could you I.D. her?" Arthur asked.

"Oh yeah. It was Francine."

Dr. Suri and the male nurse wheeled Kelli into one of the exam rooms in the back of the Urgent Care clinic. In the corner, Zenaida remained unconscious, slumped over in a wheelchair. As one of the female nurses prepared a needle to extract a blood sample from Zenaida, the other nurse secured Zenaida to the wheelchair. The male nurse began to secure Kelli's arms as Iris entered the room.

"You might want to tie her up tight," Iris suggested. "She's pretty strong."

The male nurse chuckled. "How strong can she be?"

"You'd be surprised," Iris responded.

Suri looked over at Zenaida. "Prepare a dose of Lorazepam," he said to the nurse fiddling with Zenaida's restraints. "We need to keep her sedated." Suri breathed a small sigh of relief as he looked at the Rodriguez girl. He turned to Iris. "You grabbed the older sibling. That's good."

"It took us a while. There were too many people around her when she got out of class, so we followed her and had to wait until the right moment; which didn't turn out so well, after all."

"The important thing is that we have her," Suri stated. "I need to do some tests before I can begin the procedure; a physical exam, cross-matching. I'll need some blood from you, as well. It could take a few hours."

"Good. That will give me time to figure out how to get my mother back."

"What about her?" Suri asked, gesturing to Kelli. "Do you really believe she's the previous super-soldier?"

Iris nodded. "If you saw how she changed, you'd believe it, too."

Suri wasn't convinced. He couldn't believe the tale that Iris was telling. Despite the references to gender shifts in the Harmony Project documentation, he could not bring himself to believe that such an ability was possible. "Perhaps you were seeing things. Maybe the lighting made it seem as if-"

"I know what I saw," Iris interrupted sternly.

For reasons he could not explain, Suri could see that Iris needed to believe what she was saying. He exhaled heavily and decided not to press the issue any further.

"I'll get started on the cross-match." With that, Suri exited the room.

The male nurse stepped back and admired his work. "She's all secure," he announced proudly. "And just in time, too. She's coming around."

Kelli's breathing changed. Her head rolled forward.

Iris eyed Kelli closely, curiously. Though Kelli's head was angled downward, Iris could see the tops of Kelli's eyelids as they snapped open. Iris felt the need to say something, but despite her life-long Agency training, she felt ill-prepared for the current situation. Iris had come to grips with the fact that she was a clone long ago, but her belief system would have never allowed her to bridge the gap to include what she witnessed tonight if she had not done so with her own eyes. As incredible as it sounded, what she had read in the Harmony Project file began to make sense; the mention of abilities, the gender shift. It was real. All of it. Presented with all of this evidence, it wasn't much of a leap for Iris to deduce the identity of her unfamiliar captive. However, Iris came to the realization that confirming this girl's identity also unveiled another unwelcome truth. Throughout her upbringing, Iris had been led, or allowed to believe that *she* was a clone of Harmony June, but now, she had to confront the possibility that the true clone of Harmony June was sitting right in front of her.

It only took a mere second for Kelli to become completely coherent. Her heart rate increased as sheer terror enveloped her. Waking up to the realization that she had been tied up was unsettling enough, but Kelli couldn't shake the last image she saw before being rendered unconscious. Kelli lifted her head and, as she expected, took in the image of her childhood friend, Francine, once again.

Though she wanted to believe that the girl in front of her was, in fact, Francine, logic demanded that she believe otherwise. After all, Francine died right in front of her almost seven years ago.

Their eyes met. A barrage of questions filled Kelli's head, so many questions that she didn't know which one to ask first. Instead, because her heart was hanging on to one last ditch hope that her best friend was still alive, she spoke her name once again. "Francine?"

Iris wasted no time destroying Kelli's fantasy. "No," she stated flatly.

Kelli wasn't surprised. Still, the confirmation didn't pain her heart any less. "But how? Who are-?"

"*Who* I am can wait," Iris stated. "And if what I suspect about you is correct, then you already know the *how*."

A small pool of tears began to well up in Kelli's eyes. She knew exactly what Iris meant, and the thought of it saddened her to the core of her being. "You're a clone." Kelli went silent for a moment as her own words sank in. Another wave of emotion swept through her, this time overwhelming her, pushing a cascade of tears onto her brown cheeks. "They cloned Francine." Another pause, and then, "How? Why her?"

"I don't have answers to those questions," Iris responded honestly, "but I do need the answer to a question of my own."

Kelli's mind was too preoccupied with the thought that the Agency had cloned her dead friend to pay attention to her captor at the moment. She began to shake her head. "No. No."

"Hey. Listen to me," Iris ordered.

Kelli continued to ramble to herself. "How? I saw her die. When did they do this?"

Iris raised her voice. "Hey!"

No effect. Kelli continued to mumble to herself as she replayed Francine's death in her mind once again. She thought about the impact that Francine's death had on her life, how it dictated her actions, and left a vacant feeling in her soul. Kelli's sadness began to turn to anger. Francine took a bullet for Kelli. Francine saved Kelli's life. How dare they desecrate her memory by cloning her. How dare they. "How could they?" she asked aloud. Her mind produced an image of Mr. One. Her rage increased. "I should have killed him," she said.

Iris could tell that Kelli was beginning to spin out of control. She needed to halt Kelli's downward spiral if she was going to get the answers she needed. "Hey," she said again in an attempt to divert Kelli's attention. Nothing.

"I should have killed him," Kelli repeated under her breath. "I should have followed him home, I had so many chances-"

"Kelli!" Iris shouted.

The sound of her name caused Kelli to snap back to the present. She stared at the girl with Francine's face, wondering how she knew her name.

Iris smiled. "Well, that reaction answers my first question. You're Kelli Freeman. My next question is, how is it that you're alive?"

Kelli was confused slightly. The appearance of a clone with Francine's face confirmed the Agency's involvement in whatever was going on, but if the Agency still believed she was dead, then, why . . . her thought faded away as she replayed the incident that landed her in this predicament. Although the Agency was at the Solid State Security location, Kelli realized that she wasn't the target.

Kelli looked to her left. There, strapped to the chair next to her, was Zenaida Rodriquez. In the midst of her conversation with her unidentified captor, Kelli had not noticed that Zenaida had regained consciousness. Iris had not noticed either.

Zenaida stared at Francine in disbelief. Her jaw dropped as she focused on the face of her dead sister. "Francine? Is that really you?"

Iris turned to Zenaida but said nothing. She had not expected Zenaida to be awake so soon. Again, she was not prepared for this particular chain of events.

Zenaida repeated her question. "Is that you, Francy? You're alive?"

Iris was suddenly overwhelmed. Despite her espionage training, she felt more like the seventeen-year-old teenager that she was instead of the Agency operative she was raised to be. She panicked slightly and responded in the only way that seemed prudent in this moment. She called for help. "Doctor!" she shouted, hoping Suri would hear her from the next room. "Doctor!" she screamed louder.

"Go ahead," Kelli said to her. "Tell Zenaida who you are." It was only after Kelli spoke that she realized that she had made a terrible mistake.

Zenaida's attention was now focused on Kelli; another girl whom Zenaida had thought was long since dead. "Kelli? You're alive, too?" Zenaida's gaze travelled between the two supposedly dead girls in front of her. She shifted in her chair, becoming aware, just then, that she was securely tied to it. Fear sprang into her chest. She looked back at Iris. "Why am I tied up?"

"Doctor!" Iris called out again.

Zenaida noticed that Kelli was bound to her chair, as well. "What's going on?" Zenaida squirmed violently in her chair. "What the hell?" she screamed through a mixture of anger and fear. Then, as she looked at Kelli, an astonishing realization set in. Kelli's clothing, her hair; it all looked familiar. Her eyes widened as a look of complete and utter confusion emerged on her face. "Kyle?"

Iris raised an eyebrow. "Go ahead," she said to Kelli, throwing her words back at her. "Tell Zenaida who *you* are."

The door to the room was pushed open and Suri rushed in carrying a Lorazepem-loaded syringe. He stopped in his tracks as his brain registered the fact that both captives were awake. It was in that moment that he realized their abduction plan had just taken another turn for the worse. A look of surprise washed over his face as he uttered a barely audible, "Oh my."

❧◦❦

Arthur Freeman entered the office at Solid State Security and closed the door behind him. In his hand were two items; a small bottle of baby powder and a make-up brush. "One of my guards had these things in her purse. Not exactly standard issue, but they should do the trick." A slight shake of Arthur's head alerted West to the fact that something was wrong.

"What's going on?" West asked.

"My wife is freakin' out at home."

"You told her?" questioned West.

"Of course." Arthur answered in such a way as to suggest that lying to his wife was not an option. "She wants me to bring the kids home right away."

"Maybe you should," West suggested.

"It's not like I have a choice. Cassius has a driver's license but there's no way I'm letting them out of my sight right now."

West nodded. "Good call." West turned his attention to Bling who was fiddling around with a police scanner that Arthur kept in the office. Though Arthur was no longer on the job, he liked to know what was happening in the city. Having the scanner, somehow, made him feel as if he was still connected to life in the NYPD.

"Anything?" West inquired.

Bling shook his head. "Nothing. If anyone heard those gunshots, none of them reported it."

"Amazing," West said in disbelief.

"Welcome to New York," Arthur countered sarcastically. "Speaking of which, you haven't told me why you're even here."

"I was tracking Kelli," West responded.

"Um," Bling interrupted. "Are we not going to discuss the Francine thing?"

"In a minute," Arthur snapped, before turning his attention back to West. "Tracking her? I don't understand."

"I didn't know where she was, Arthur," West revealed. "She and I haven't spoken in quite some time."

Bling chuckled under his breath.

Arthur's brow furled. "Define quite some time."

"Two years," Bling answered aloud before West could reply.

Both West and Arthur looked at Bling in surprise. West fell silent. It was the kind of silence that brought Arthur to the sudden realization that he had been kept in the dark about a few things.

"Somebody start talking."

Bling opened his mouth but said nothing. He was still focused on the fact that he had just seen Francine, a girl who was shot dead before his very eyes almost seven years ago.

West, on the other hand, was asking himself silently, *Where do I start?* Arthur's next question gave West the beginning for which he was looking.

"You said you were tracking Kelli? Why? Did she do something wrong?"

"No, I mean, I don't know."

"Well, which is it, Agent West?" Arthur demanded, becoming more aggravated by the second.

"I was working a case involving the Agency and our primary person of interest matched Kelli's description. Our preliminary investigation places Kelli in the D.C. area at the time of the incident-"

"Investigation?" Arthur interrupted. "What type of investigation?"

"Homicide, arson. . . our C.I. died, but not before he described the young girl who shot him point blank . . ." West's voice trailed off as a sudden cascade of thoughts disrupted his words. His eyes widened and his mouth fell open as the wheels in his brain kicked into overdrive. "Holy crap. How did I miss that?"

"Miss what?" Arthur asked.

West turned and headed for the door.

Arthur dogged his heels. "Where are you going?"

"To talk to our prisoner. Francine matches Kelli's description, as well."

Excitedly, Bling jumped from his chair to follow Agent West. "Finally."

"What is that?" Zenaida yelled as she eyed the needle and syringe that were being carried in her direction. She began to squirm in her chair, hoping that somehow, she would overcome her restraints.

"Nothing to worry about," Suri tried to assure her. He could tell that Zenaida was terrified, and he could not blame her. She had been volunteered for an experiment without her knowledge, consent or consideration; kidnapped and brought to an unfamiliar location to endure God knows what. No, Suri could not blame the young woman for the hatred and fear she was experiencing, but he could surely blame himself. He, who had pledged to do no harm, who was now willing to do just that in order to save someone for whom he cared. "This is merely a sedative," he tried to console her, and himself, as he swabbed her arm with an antiseptic cloth.

"For what? Why?" Zenaida demanded to know.

"Leave her alone," Kelli screamed at Suri from her chair. She mustered all of her strength and tugged at the zip ties that bound her wrists together. To her surprise, she felt the restraints loosen ever so slightly. Due to her genetically augmented strength, Kelli knew that if she kept trying, it would only be a matter of time before she would free herself. Unfortunately, it would not be in time to spare Zenaida whatever fate to which the contents of that syringe might lead her.

"We have no intention of hurting you," Suri said to Zenaida as he brought the needle closer to her arm. *Half truth*, the doctor told himself.

Zenaida squirmed even harder, rocking the chair from side to side. "No. Get away," she screamed repeatedly.

Suri nodded at the two nurses who were in the room; the male and one of the females. Immediately, they grabbed hold of their frightened patient and attempted to restrain her movements. In response, Zenaida mustered as much strength as she could, twisting as far as her restraints would allow in order to avoid the impending injection.

Kelli screamed out again, "Stop it. Let her go. Let her go!"

Through all of the excitement, Iris watched quietly from her position by the door. She stared at Zenaida, an unsuspecting innocent being used for the advantage of another. It was a feeling that Iris had recently come to understand. Despite her own life being at stake, Iris couldn't help but feel sorry for her.

The nurses managed to secure Zenaida's arm. Zenaida released a blood curdling plea as the needle penetrated her skin and Suri pushed the drug into her veins.

Kelli continued to struggle against her bonds. Each tug loosened the zip ties a little more. Suddenly, the room became silent. Kelli stopped struggling. She strained her neck to get a glimpse of Zenaida within the circle of bodies that surrounded her. Slowly, the nurses and Suri stepped back. Kelli watched as a sedated Zenaida slipped reluctantly into a peaceful slumber.

"What did you give her?" Kelli demanded to know. "If you've killed her-"

"That would defeat the purpose," Suri said calmly. He turned to Kelli. "I promise to take good care of her."

Kelli wanted to scream at the unfamiliar doctor. Instead, she stared into his eyes and detected something that she did not intend to see. Sincerity.

Suri marched towards the door. He gestured for Iris to follow him out. Within seconds, Suri and Iris were out in the hallway on the other side of the closed door.

Kelli looked towards Zenaida's sleeping form once more. She had no clue what was going on, but if she'd had even the slightest idea about escaping with Zenaida, that plan would now have to be abandoned. Kelli knew that if she was going to escape, she would have to go it alone. She would also need the element of surprise.

The two nurses were still in the room. The male was disposing of the bio-hazard bag that contained all of the used syringes, needles and whatever other instruments that had come in contact with bodily fluids. The female had stepped behind Zenaida's wheelchair, preparing to wheel her out of the room. Kelli decided that the time to act was now.

She tugged at her restraints. Again, Kelli could feel them loosening. To her left, the female nurse began wheeling Zenaida towards the door. Kelli attempted to pull her wrists apart once more. Still, no release. Kelli surmised that if she shifted into her male form, it might be easier to free her wrists, however, she had already revealed her gender-shifting abilities to Francine's clone, she did not want to risk exposing her secret to anyone else.

Kelli took a deep breath. With all of her strength, she attempted to pull her wrists in opposite directions. The zip tie cut into her skin. She could feel the warm blood as it squirted onto each of her wrists. However, Kelli refused to relent. As the female nurse reached the door, Kelli's restraints succumbed to her augmented strength. She grunted slightly as the zip ties snapped. Both nurses turned in her direction, but for the female nurse, it was already too late.

In one motion, Kelli sprang towards the female nurse. She grabbed at the collar of the young woman's scrubs with her left hand and pulled the nurse directly into her right cross, which landed squarely on the woman's left temple. Before the nurse's unconscious frame could hit the floor, Kelli had already moved in the direction of the male nurse.

The young man, who was the nurse who had secured Kelli to her chair, threw a wide right hook. Kelli sidestepped the attack, and parried the blow, grabbing on to the man's wrist. She secured his fingers as she pressed her palm into his elbow. She applied a wrist-lock, which forced him to turn away in order to lessen the pain. With the back of his head in full view, Kelli launched a palm strike towards the base of his skull. The impact caused the male to drop to the floor in an unconscious heap.

Kelli moved towards the door. From the other side, she could hear the clone's voice, followed by footsteps that grew closer with each footfall. Based on the clone's display of strength during their fight in the van, Kelli had already deduced that the clone was a product of the Agency's super soldier program. If that was the case, then Kelli had to assume that the clone possessed heightened senses, as well. If so, there was no doubt in Kelli's mind that her brief melee with the nurses had been overheard.

Kelli stepped around Zenaida's wheelchair. Her own heightened sense of hearing warned her that whoever was coming into the room was standing directly in front of the door. The turn of the door knob confirmed it. Kelli took a step forward and planted her left foot. She raised her right leg and launched a forward kick directly into the door by the knob. The wooden door jerked violently as it sprang open, sending the metal pieces from the doorknob spraying through the air.

Doctor Suri and Iris stepped into the hallway. Suri was shaking his head in disbelief over the sudden turn of events. First, Iris had returned from the mission without Agent Molina, but with another young girl who Iris identified as Kelli Freeman, the previous Harmony Project creation who was presumed to be dead. Then, to make matters worse, both of their captives woke up before Suri could sedate them. The last thing Suri wanted or needed was to be identified should this whole ordeal go wrong. Instead, Suri wanted everything to go as planned with no loss of life. Unfortunately, it did not look as if that's how things were going. He strode slowly up the corridor with Iris at his side.

"This is not good," Suri said to Iris as soon as the door closed behind them.

"Why didn't you give her the injection sooner?" Iris asked. "We could've avoided all of this."

"I'm well aware of that," Suri snapped. "Pardon me for being slightly distracted. I did not expect any of this to happen." He took a breath. "Maybe we should contact Mr. Five-"

"No," Iris protested immediately. Her temper flared suddenly. "After the way they've used my mother and me, I would freakin' kill him."

Suri shuddered at the thought of it.

"Besides," Iris continued. "We can handle this."

"What do you propose we do?" Suri asked, completely in shock that he was seeking the guidance of a teenager.

"After the transplant, we're going to trade Zenaida for my mother."

"And what of Miss Freeman?"

Before Iris could answer, she stopped in her tracks. "What was that?" she asked, and then cocked her head to one side

"What was what?"

Iris turned and looked back at the door. Without warning, she rushed back towards the exam room. As she neared the door, she exclaimed, "Holy crap."

"What is it?" Suri inquired nervously.

Iris stepped in front of the exam room door. Unexpectedly, the door sprang open. Iris was caught off guard. The edge of the door slammed into her forehead and she fell backwards. As she landed hard on her buttocks, she looked up to see Kelli Freeman burst through the opening.

Kelli stopped. Her eyes locked onto Iris' glare. Then, Kelli turned and sprinted up the corridor.

Instinctively, Suri stepped into her path. He questioned the action as he took it, but he considered the circumstances, and then threw caution to the wind.

Kelli threw a stiff arm at Suri's chest as she reached him. Suri's body was launched backwards onto the floor. In a last-ditch effort, he grabbed on to Kelli's right leg as she attempted to step over him.

Kelli stumbled slightly before shaking herself free. Unfortunately, Suri's distraction allowed plenty of time for Iris to pull herself to her feet and tackle Kelli from behind. Both girls hit the floor hard. The impact caused them to separate. Kelli rolled away. She used her own momentum to push off the floor and land in a crouching position. As Kelli turned to face her attacker, she was not surprised to find Francine's clone poised and ready for action, as well.

13

The room in which Agent Molina sat was rather bare. Though it appeared to be designed for use as an office or a small bedroom, there were no furnishings, no rugs on the dusty, brown wooden floor, or no paintings on the dingy white walls. The only furniture in the room was the chair to which she was secured with a rope, and a small table that resembled a TV tray.

Molina did not flinch when the three men re-entered the small room where she was being kept. Their earlier attempts to ascertain her identity produced no results, and even if it had, Molina was not worried in the slightest. Her only concern was that her daughter escaped with the Rodriguez girl. As long as the kidney transplant was successful, Molina had no reason to be worried about anything else; least of all, these three men.

Arthur placed a bottle of powder and a small brush on the table next to Molina. A quick glance at the objects informed Molina of their intentions to procure a fingerprint in an effort to identify her. Still, Molina was unfazed. She could care less if they ran her prints. Every database in the world would reveal that Agent Maribel Molina was an intelligence operative working for the NSA. The mere inquiry would send a red flag to the Agency, and any further investigation into why an NSA operative was an accomplice to a kidnapping would be handled by them. In truth, Molina was fearful of what punishment the Agency might dole out to her once this matter was resolved; the Agency frightened her. 'But these men?' she thought confidently. 'They've got nothing.'

The white gentleman had previously identified himself as Special Agent West from the Bureau. Molina expected him to play the tough guy role, to act is if he was holding all the cards. Molina did not care. That was, of course, until West began speaking.

"We're tracking Iris," West said flatly. He remembered that Ferry identified his young female assassin by that name. Up until now, West had assumed that Iris was a pseudonym or code name that Kelli may have been using if, in fact, she had been working for the Agency. As far as West knew, all Agency operatives were given new identities. Though Ferry had not been certain that he'd heard the name correctly, West decided to gamble and say the name aloud. He was hoping that the woman's reaction to the name would betray her. West was not disappointed.

The sound of her daughter's name struck Molina sharply in the chest. Though she tried to suppress any body language that would give West a thread upon which to pull, Molina knew that her concern for her daughter was written all over her face.

West read the woman's facial expression. He was on to something, so he pressed further. "It won't be long before we have her in custody. Our intel has identified several Agency safe houses and facilities." West had no such intel.

Dozens of questions inundated Molina's brain. Who is this guy? How does he know Iris' name? How does he know so much about the Agency? How does he know of their existence at all?

West could see Molina's wheels turning. It did not matter how tall the tale. As long as Molina was buying it, West would continue to probe. Still, West knew that the girl, Iris, was the key to getting whatever information he needed. As long as he made it seem as if her daughter was in danger, West knew that the woman would eventually crack.

"We know about the incident in Virginia a few days ago." he said to her, "the safe house explosion, and the deaths."

Arthur stood back and listened. He glanced over at Bling whose facial expression revealed that he had no clue what West was talking about. Arthur resisted the urge to interrupt and ask questions about Kelli. The cop in him knew that it was a bad idea to step on the toes of an interrogator who was, clearly, on a roll.

West knelt down in front of the woman. He knew that he had her undivided attention; all he had to do now was close the deal. "Listen. I don't know what your end game is. But I do know how the Agency responds when things don't go their way. And I'm sure getting captured wasn't part of your plan. As far as I can tell, you're in a no-win situation."

Molina remained silent.

West played his final card. He gestured towards the powder and the brush. "We both know that as soon as I send your prints through the system, the Agency will know something is wrong. That's bad news for you, and bad news for Iris. Help me find your daughter before the Agency does."

Molina considered West's words. Was he bluffing? Molina had no way of knowing, but considering that West was on-scene when the Rodriguez girl was abducted, coupled with his obvious knowledge of the Agency and their protocols, how could this be a ruse? Also, she contemplated the consequences to herself and to Iris if, no, *when* the Agency got wind of this current debacle. Molina was not concerned about her own safety, but Iris' safety was the highest priority. Besides, Molina was already angry at the Agency for deciding to let Iris die. As far as she was concerned, they had already given up their right to her loyalty.

"I can't," Molina responded reluctantly. "Not yet."

Arthur could stay quiet no longer. "What do you mean, not yet? Lady, we're trying to help you."

"And I'm trying to protect my daughter," Molina retorted.

West could sense that Arthur wanted to scream at Molina. Arthur, too, was trying to protect his daughter. West raised a hand in front of Arthur in an effort to silence him before he said anything more. Despite his strongest temptations to do the contrary, Arthur bit his tongue.

"Let us help you," West responded.

Molina fell silent once again. West's assessment of her being in a no win situation was accurate. Also, she knew the kidney transplant would require several hours to complete. West's offer to help seemed genuine and, all things considered, was Iris' best chance of making it out of this alive. Still, Molina knew that she needed to stall. She had to give Suri the time he needed to perform the transplant. How could Molina do that and keep West from running her fingerprints, as well? Molina was cornered. She had to give West something.

"We're trying to save her life," Molina said finally.

"So are we," West countered.

Molina shook her head. "No, you don't understand. She needs more time. If you run my prints, they will come before she gets . . ." Molina stopped in mid-sentence as a single tear trickled from each eye.

"Before she gets what?" West questioned. "Listen, you're right. I don't understand, but you've got to help me here."

Bling chimed in, "Start by explaining why your daughter looks like Francine Rodriguez."

Molina looked over at the young security guard. She was not aware that anyone had seen Iris' face. Molina had seen Zenaida conversing with the young man right before the abduction, they even shared a kiss, so it made sense that, upon seeing Iris, he would recognize her as Francine. She opened her mouth to offer an explanation, but she knew how crazy the truth would sound, so instead she said, "You wouldn't believe me if I told you."

"Clones," the three men said in unison.

"Super soldiers," West added.

Molina was speechless. She could not comprehend how these men knew so much about a highly classified project, and how they were here, at this place, and this time. Again, she asked herself, *Who are these guys?*

West turned to her again. "I might be able to help you. But first, let's start with your name."

Arthur had heard enough. "Agent West?"

West looked back.

Arthur gestured for West to follow him to the far corner of the room. Bling, not wanting to be left out, tagged along.

Once all three men were standing in the corner, Arthur spoke in a whisper. His tone was stern. "You're not actually considering helping this woman, are you? If you don't run her prints, we can't confirm anything she tells us."

"Like we'd be able to confirm it anyway," West whispered in response. "This *is* the Agency we're dealing with."

"You don't think I get that? I just want my daughter back, and I'm not sure that working with an Agency operative is the best way to achieve that."

"Do you have a better idea?" West asked.

"Yes, Goddammit! For starters, we could move to an unknown location. Then, run her prints and let the Agency come and clean up her mess."

"Should we do that before or after we get Kelli and Zenaida back?" Bling asked.

Neither man responded. Instead, they simply exchanged glances.

West placed a hand on Arthur's shoulder. "Listen, Arthur. It's in all of our best interests to work together. Just follow my lead, please. Besides, I'm going to call in some reinforcement."

"Someone who can fix this?" Arthur asked.

"No, but we need more help. I mean, it's the Agency. It's clear that we're outgunned." West leaned closer to Arthur. "Are you with me?"

Arthur released an anxiety-laden sigh. Although he was not fond of West's current course of action, he was at a loss to produce a better, safer plan. Reluctantly, he nodded.

"Good." With that, West turned to Molina. He crossed the room and stopped in front of her. "I believe you were about to tell me your name."

Molina's eyes narrowed. "No prints?"

"No prints," West agreed.

Molina wasted no words. "My name is Special Agent Maribel Molina, and I work for an organization called Department 12; but those who are aware of its existence commonly refer to it as the Agency."

⁂

Iris closed the distance between Kelli and herself with one powerful lunge. The left jab she threw at Kelli missed by only a hair, and she followed quickly with a right cross that failed to find its mark, as well.

Kelli extended her right leg forward, keeping it low. She swept Iris' left ankle, causing Iris to lose her balance and tumble in Kelli's direction. Kelli launched a right elbow strike which caught Iris squarely on the left cheek. Iris, dazed, dropped to the floor at Kelli's feet.

Iris looked up at her adversary and prepared herself for the impending attack. Kelli returned her gaze, staring at the familiar face. Though she knew the girl who sat in front of her was not her best friend, when she looked at her, it was difficult not to see Francine. Kelli took a step backwards.

"I don't want to hurt you," Kelli said to her, gesturing for Iris to stay down.

Iris pushed herself from the floor and lunged at Kelli once again, wrapping her arms around Kelli's waist. "You won't," she snapped as she attempted to force Kelli off balance.

Kelli absorbed Iris' momentum and used it to pull the young girl towards her. Kelli fell into a roll, carrying Iris with her before flinging her to the floor on the other side of her body.

Kelli rolled onto her knees. "Francine. Stop!" she yelled.

"My name is not Francine." Iris made no attempt to get up. Instead, she spun around on the floor. She lifted her leg and delivered a spin kick to Kelli's temple. The blow launched Kelli into the wall. She extended her arms reflexively to keep her head from slamming into it. Before Kelli could regain her composure, Iris was on her, forcing Kelli onto her back. Though Iris' frame was slightly smaller than her own, Kelli could feel the sheer strength in Iris' arms as she pinned Kelli supine to the floor. Kelli attempted to overpower her by simply lifting her arms. In any other circumstance, if she were fighting a *normal* human, be it man or woman, Kelli would have no problem freeing herself. Even in her female form, Kelli was eight times stronger than any man. In her male form, the numerical comparison jumped to twelve. However, this was not any other circumstance, and her assailant was far from normal, rather a genetically-engineered super soldier with augmented strength that rivaled her own. In fact, as Kelli struggled beneath her attacker, unable to free herself, she decided that the clone's strength was superior. Kelli contemplated shifting. *No. Too many other people in the hallway.* Before she could piece together another thought,

Iris lifted her head slightly, then slammed the top of her head into Kelli's forehead, missing the bridge of her nose by a mere inch. Kelli saw stars.

Iris placed her opened left hand around Kelli's throat and begin to squeeze. She cocked her right arm back before connecting with a jab to Kelli's face. Another jab connected, then another. With each blow, Kelli became more disoriented. Instinctively, she reverted to years of ju-jitsu training. Kelli lifted her hips with all her strength. The unexpected thrust caused Iris to topple forward and relinquish her grip on Kelli's neck. Kelli seized the moment and rolled out from under Iris' small frame.

Kelli grabbed the handrail and pulled herself to her feet. Iris, still on her knees, turned to face Kelli once again. This time, Kelli did not wait for Iris to attack. She charged at Iris who, in defense, dropped to the floor and tried to sweep Kelli's ankles out from under her. Luckily, Kelli had anticipated a lower-body attack. She leapt into the air, and performed a no-handed somersault that, thanks to her gymnastics training, allowed her to sail over Iris' body untouched. Kelli landed the somersault perfectly, and then pushed herself into Iris' direction once more.

Iris sprang from her position on the floor. She performed a spinning round house kick in mid-air. Kelli blocked the kick and retaliated with a two-fisted attack to Iris' rib-cage. Iris fell to the floor once again.

"Stop it!" Suri yelled as he approached Kelli from behind. His eyes were fixed on Iris as she pulled herself slowly into a standing position. It wasn't difficult for Suri to see that Iris was fatigued. But was her fatigue a result of the fight, or from her condition? Suri wasn't sure. Sweat beaded on Iris' forehead, and Suri knew that he needed to stop this confrontation for fear that Iris might pass out from sheer exhaustion. Little did Suri know, Iris felt fine.

Kelli reached out with her left hand and grabbed Suri as he tried to brush past her to get to his patient.

Iris charged at Kelli yet again. "Don't touch him," she ordered Kelli, who pulled Suri into Iris' path.

Iris collided with Suri. She reached around the doctor's body in hopes of grabbing onto Kelli to no avail. Kelli sidestepped Iris' reach. She stepped forward and placed her right foot behind Iris' left ankle, and then pushed with all of her strength. Iris and the doctor toppled backwards. Iris released a shriek of pain as the full weight of Suri's body landed on top of her.

Suri cried out to her, "Iris!"

Kelli stepped over the two bodies on the floor, making a mental note of the girl's name. Iris. Kelli felt a hint of relief. She hoped that knowing the clone's name would make it easier to remember that the girl was not, in fact, her dead friend, Francine. She moved beyond Iris' reach on the floor and began to accelerate up the hallway. Unfortunately, the sight of a gun barrel being leveled at her head caused her stop on a dime. A sensation of cold fear raced up her spine.

Agent Kincaid kept his Ruger pointed directly at Kelli as he surveyed the situation. The unfamiliar young woman who stood before him had a large welt on her forehead, swelling around her left eye, and was bleeding from her wrists. Iris was sporting only a fresh bruise on her left cheek, though Kincaid did note that she was sweating slightly. After a moment, a smug grin crept across his face. "Well, you two don't ever stop fighting, do you?"

Kelli remained silent. She choked back tears as she stared at the gun that hovered within point blank range of her face. *Oh, God, don't let him shoot me*, she prayed silently.

Iris and Suri scrambled to their feet. The doctor turned his attention to the stranger holding the gun. "Young man, I don't know who you are, but you are about to make a grave mistake."

Kincaid's smile widened slightly. "No, Doctor Suri. I'm actually here to fix yours." Kincaid was clearly enjoying himself.

It didn't take a second for Suri, at the sound of his name, to put two and two together. The Agency realized he had gone AWOL and sent someone to retrieve him, or worse. His heart sank. Not because the Agency had found him, but because they would interfere with the kidney transplant that would save Iris' life.

The sound of footsteps drew everyone's attention to the arrival of another man, an older man. Agent Peppers stepped around the corner. A cell phone was in his left hand. He took in the sight of the scared faces before him, then turned to his younger partner.

"Everything under control?" he asked calmly.

Kincaid nodded. "I'd say so."

"Good," Peppers said. He raised the phone to his ear and spoke into it in his normal, calm tone. "Targets apprehended, sir."

LOGAN INTERNATIONAL AIRPORT
BOSTON, MASSACHUSETTS

Davies sat in the waiting area of Gate 10 as she listened for the boarding call for her flight back to the D.C. area. It had been a long day, one that had produced as many questions as answers. On her way back to the airport, Davies stopped at a local hardware store and purchased a small packing box. Into the box, she deposited the safe she had stolen from Kelli's apartment. Davies made sure that all of the contents, every document, every dollar, were in the safe before she sealed it, but not before she photographed it all. She wrote Kyle's name, address and apartment number on every side of the box before dropping it in the 24-hour lobby at the Post office down the street from Kelli's building. As she purchased the postage from the machine, Davies had a thought. Before she left, she pulled out her pen and signed the box: *Love, M. Davies.* She had several mixed feelings when she added her signature, however, she wasn't exactly sure which of those feelings, worry, confusion, or anger had motivated her to write it. Davies was worried because her investigation had revealed that Kelli was dealing with adult issues that no one should ever have to face. She was confused because she didn't understand why Kelli chose to shut her out. Granted, she and Kelli were not best friends, but Davies had thought they'd developed a rapport, maybe even somewhat of a friendship over the years. *Wishful thinking on my part*, she decided. Finally, Davies was angry at Kelli for abandoning the protocols that were in place to keep her safe, for leading everyone on a wild goose chase, and for lying . . . to her, to Patrice, to everyone.

As Davies left the post office, she phoned Dr. Hughes and cancelled their second meeting. After Davies had successfully accessed Kelli's safe, Marsh felt that Davies had enough information to sort through. He ordered Davies to return to D.C. Besides, if the need arose, Davies could always fly back to Boston to pay Hughes another visit. In that, Davies was slightly disappointed. Hughes could offer more insight into Kelli's motivations so, naturally, Davies wanted to investigate that avenue further. Unfortunately, Marsh had made it abundantly clear that the priority was *finding* Kelli Freeman. Marsh assumed that if there was a paper trail that linked Kelli to Ferry's murder in any way, the trail would end with the contents of the safe. Marsh's mission was to find the person who killed his friend; end of story.

Davies' cell phone chimed in her jacket. She retrieved it from her pocket and opened the line. "This is Davies," she announced.

"Agent Davies." A.D. Marsh sounded relieved to hear her voice. "Have you heard from Agent West?"

"No, sir. Not since I gave you the information about the firearm and the cash."

Marsh released a frustrated sigh.

"Is everything all right, sir?"

"No," Marsh responded. "When I spoke to West, he said he was about to make contact with our target and that he would call in with a sit-rep shortly thereafter. That was hours ago."

"That's atypical of him," Davies responded. "I'm sure he's all right. What could have gone wrong?"

"I'm not sure, but I've got a bad feeling."

Davies' brow furled as she realized the true nature of Marsh's call. She shook her head slightly before saying, "You want me to go to New York." It was a confirmation, not a question.

"Asap," Marsh replied.

Davies rubbed her eyes. "I'll be on the next available flight."

"Keep me informed."

"Of course, sir."

The call ended. Within minutes, Davies had gathered her bag and was in search of the next flight to La Guardia.

෩෧

BRONX, NEW YORK

With their guns drawn and leveled at everyone in the back section of the medical building except each other, Peppers and Kincaid ushered the gathering into an exam room at the far end of the corridor. Everyone in the room was on edge. Suri helped Iris up onto the exam table. Kincaid, who was unfamiliar with Kelli or how she factored into any of this, kept his gun trained on her as he led her to the stool in the corner of the room. Kelli sat and immediately bent forward, placing her head into her hands. Once behind the closed door, Suri spoke up.

"You must give me time to perform the transplant," the doctor pleaded.

"No can do, Doc," Kincaid responded. "Our orders were to apprehended you and bring you back unharmed."

"Good," Iris said. "Then you can't leave without my mother. Maybe you can help us get her back-"

"Sorry," Peppers interrupted. "We were sent here for you and Dr. Suri. Agent Molina is on her own."

Iris became incensed. "What do you mean *on her own*?"

"He means to say that *we* are the mission at hand," Suri explained. "They want you and me. Apparently, Agent Molina has become . . . expendable."

"What?" Iris screamed. "No. We can't leave her there. I won't leave without her."

"It's not up to you," Kincaid remarked. "I think you know that."

"Anyone care to explain why an FBI agent was there in the first place?" Peppers asked. All eyes, including Kelli's, landed on him. He could almost hear the question that was begging to be asked.

Iris obliged everyone. "How did you know an FBI agent was there? How do you even know where *there* is?"

"We were there," Peppers admitted.

"Watched the whole thing go down," Kincaid added.

"You bastards! Why didn't you help?" Iris' anger level increased. She jumped off of the exam table and landed squarely in front of Agent Peppers. She looked up at the taller man, who easily stood at least a foot taller than she, with fire in her eyes. The volume of her voice was at a constant scream. "You could have helped her. If you had, she wouldn't be in the custody of the FBI."

Peppers demeanor remained calm and seemingly unaffected. "Like the doctor said, you two are the mission."

Kincaid released a small boyish giggle. "That was pretty ballsy though, you know, kidnapping someone out in the open like that." Kincaid did a quick count of the people in the room. "Where is the girl you abducted anyway?"

"She's in the other room," Suri stated as he turned to Peppers. "Listen, Agent . . .?"

"Peppers."

"Agent Peppers. If you must take us back, can you at least allow me time to perform the surgery first? Iris will die without a healthy kidney. We've come so close. Please give me a few hours."

"A kidney?" Kelli asked softly, her tone laced with bitterness. Her eyes were suddenly locked on Iris'. "You kidnapped Zenaida to steal her kidney?"

"Who is this?" Kincaid asked.

"She's the one with the answer to your question about the FBI agent," Iris replied. "In fact, she may be the answer to all of our problems."

"Iris?" Suri's voice was heavy with caution.

"You have to call this in, right?" Iris asked Peppers.

"That is protocol, yes."

"Good. Do it." She pointed at Kincaid. "You, take a picture of her with your cell phone," she ordered, gesturing to Kelli.

Kincaid dismissed Iris with a raise of his eyebrow. "We don't take orders from teenagers."

Iris turned back to Peppers. "There's a situation room down the hall, through the doors to the left. Let's go."

"Iris?" Suri called to her again. "What are you doing?"

Iris turned to the doctor. "Saving us all."

Peppers had heard enough. "No one is going anywhere. Agent Kincaid here will keep an eye on you while I go to the sit-room and make the call."

Peppers moved to the door. Kincaid called out after him, "Tell Mr. Five I said hello," he said.

"Screw, Mr. Five," Iris responded. "We're going to go into that room and call Mr. One. When he finds out who that girl is, I'm certain that your orders will definitely change."

Kelli grimaced at the reference to Mr. One. *No, not now. Not like this.* Kelli began to panic. For months she had been secretly taking photos of Mr. One, working on her plan to get her life back once and for all. The beauty of her plan lies in the fact that Mr. One thinks she is dead. How many times during her surveillance at the D.C. cafe had she sauntered in as Kyle and taken a seat just a few booths behind him? How many times had she listened in on his conversations as he laughed and made plans with his daughter? How meticulously had she gone over just how she was going to play her hand? But now, once Iris revealed to Mr. One that she was alive, and in their custody, Kelli knew that all of her planning, all of her surveillance, and all of her footwork was about to go up in smoke with all of her hopes.

Peppers sat at the table in the situation room. He was alone. Despite Iris' persistence to join him in the conversation, Peppers knew Iris would relent once Kincaid pulled Suri across the room and placed the barrel of his weapon at the base of the doctor's neck. Peppers did not really care for the use of weapons when children were involved; however, Peppers surmised that Iris was no ordinary child, and that extreme measures were necessary to gain her compliance. Within minutes, Peppers had entered the situation room and activated the white phone that sat in the center of the table. He had opened the speaker, and listened as the phone rang only twice.

"We have an unusual situation," Peppers said to Mr. Five after the phone was answered.

"Oh?"

"Yes, two actually," Peppers said as he relaxed slightly. As per Agency policy regarding communication, Peppers knew he could divulge names and situations more freely now that he was finally on a secure Agency line. "Agent Molina has been apprehended by the FBI."

"The FBI?" Five's voice questioned. "We've received no reports. Are you certain?"

Peppers nodded. "Quite certain. I apologize that I can't explain why it hasn't been called in yet."

"Not to worry, Agent Peppers." Five sounded forgiving, then added, "We'll look into it. Do you know the name of the agent who took Molina into custody?"

"No, sir," Peppers admitted reluctantly. "The girl that we have in custody claimed to not know his name."

"Which girl? Iris?"

"No, sir." Peppers paused. Though he was following his orders to the letter, he still did not like being the bearer of bad news, especially when he was reporting that news to Mr. Five. Peppers swallowed, and then continued, "That's the other situation. While Agent Molina was being apprehended, her daughter abducted a young woman and brought her back to this medical facility."

"Yes, Agent Peppers. We are aware of her intentions with Miss Rodriguez and her kidney."

"You misunderstand, sir," Peppers said. "They did take Miss Rodriguez, however, they also abducted another young woman."

"Which woman? Who?" The tone in Five's voice had changed.

"Iris seems to think that her identity will be especially important to Mr. One," Peppers added.

"Who is this woman?" Mr. Five urged impatiently.

"A woman named Kelli Freeman."

"Impossible," Mr. Five snapped back at him.

"Iris said that you might say that," Peppers responded. "So I'm sending you a picture." Peppers retrieved Kincaid's cell phone from his pocket. A photo of a battered Kelli Freeman graced the screen. Peppers typed in the numerical destination of the photo and pressed send.

There was an extended silence on the other end. After a moment, Peppers heard a small click that indicated that he'd just been put on hold. Peppers could not imagine that Iris, a mere teenager, would have any information or any person of interest that Mr. One would alter the course of a mission over. Peppers was aware that he was only privy to information that he needed to know, regardless of the mission. Still, he couldn't fathom that Iris knew something so important that Mr. One would involve himself beyond his normal role of delegation and supervision. In fact, Peppers had never spoken directly to Mr. One. When he and Kincaid were on assignment overseas, their point of contact was Mr. Twelve. Since they'd been given orders to report to D.C., they had only spoken to Mr. Five. Why on Earth would Mr. One show up now?

The phone line clicked. Peppers could hear that he was no longer on hold. He expected to hear Mr. Five's voice any second. However, his heart jumped unexpectedly when an unfamiliar voice bellowed through the line.

"Agent Peppers. This is Mr. One. When was that photo taken?"

Peppers was in shock. What was going on? "Just a few minutes ago, sir. I witnessed it myself."

Another extended pause. When Mr. One spoke again, his voice was stern and direct. "Go get Iris Molina. I want to talk to her."

WASHINGTON, D.C.

Mr. One disconnected the call. It would take a few minutes for Peppers to retrieve Iris Molina and secure their hostage. Mr. One instructed Peppers to call back as soon as the younger Molina was in the situation room.

Mr. One looked at the photo that had been sent to Mr. Five's burner cell. It was unmistakably Kelli Freeman. Apparently, the FBI report concerning the incidents at Rocketdyne almost seven years ago had been falsified. That report documented the death of Kelli Freeman, claiming she perished in an explosion at the site in Simi Valley. But how? That report was supplied by FBI Director Eisen himself. Unless . . . A.D. Marsh. Perhaps Marsh turned in the report that he had been given by Agent West. Since Director Eisen was an old friend and had assured Mr. One that the report was accurate, One never questioned its authenticity. But now, it appears that may have been a mistake. If this photo from Peppers was, in fact, real, perhaps Mr. One could correct a mistake that he'd made almost seven years ago. In any event, Mr. One decided that he needed to take a closer look at Assistant Director Steven Marsh, and Special Agent Donald West, as well.

Mr. Two approached the table. While Mr. One spoke to Agent Peppers, Two had made a phone call of his own. He slipped his mobile device into his pocket and signaled to Mr. One with a nod. Though it had yet to be confirmed, he and Mr. One already had an idea as to the identity of the FBI agent who apprehended Agent Molina.

"I've initiated contact with our man in the D.C. field office," Two said. "If Agent West has Agent Molina, we'll know soon enough."

Special Agent Bonner had been stuck in the office most of the day. His report on the Navarro case had been completed and submitted for review, and he waited anxiously for A.D. Marsh to give him another assignment. He needed something, anything to take his mind off the fact that his partner, Agent West, was currently off the grid.

He closed his laptop screen and reached into his desk drawer. He pulled out his car keys, which he shoved into the pocket of his slacks, and his sunglasses, which he deposited into the small pocket on his shirt. It had been a long day, and he decided that there was nothing else going on at this late hour for which his presence in the office was required. As he stood, the soft vibration from his silenced cell phone caused the device to rattle on his desk. Bonner scooped it up. It was a text message sent from the same number as before. Bonner pressed the button and read the message: *Time for that Hail Mary. Contact me for further information.*

Bonner typed an immediate response: *I'm leaving the office now. It's safe to call my cell phone in five minutes.*

Bonner gathered his suit jacket, placed his cell phone in his pocket and exited the office. Five minutes later, Marsh marched through the room before arriving at Bonner's empty desk. He looked at his watch and regarded the late hour. He glanced around the office and caught a glimpse of Agent Lacee approaching him.

Lacee carried a case file in his left hand. He issued a salute as he handed the file to Marsh. "The Larkin case, signed, sealed and delivered as promised," Lacee said to him.

Marsh took the file, but ignored Lacee's words. "Have you seen Agent Bonner?" Marsh asked.

"I think I just saw him leave," Lacee answered. "I can go chase him down if you like."

Marsh shook his head. "Don't worry about it, Garrett. I'll call him on his cell."

Lacee smiled. "No problem. I'm going to head out, as well. That is, if you don't need me."

"No," Marsh said with a sigh. "Have a good night."

Lacee nodded and headed back to his desk to gather his things. Marsh turned and made a bee-line for his own office. He was looking for Bonner in hopes that he might have heard from Agent West. Marsh and West had agreed that it was in Bonner's best interest to keep Bonner in the dark regarding their investigation into the Agency. Despite that agreement, Marsh had hoped that West might have checked in with his partner, which was a tactic West employed from time to time to keep Bonner from suspecting that West was working on any serious assignments. Marsh's call to Bonner's cell phone went unanswered. He left instructions for Bonner to return the call, but until then, Marsh had nothing.

❦

BRONX, NEW YORK

Peppers returned Kincaid's cell phone to him as he entered the exam room, then he turned and gestured to Iris, "Mr. One wants to talk to you."

"I knew it," Iris said smugly.

A cold chill crept up Kelli's spine. Mr. One had been alerted to the fact that she was alive. The cell phone picture for which she was forced to pose confirmed it. Kelli knew it was only a matter of time before the two agency operatives came to take her to D.C. and deliver her to Mr. One. She could not let that happen. Not today. Not ever. Kelli had to escape. Her first attempt did not go as planned. Fortunately, Kelli had another idea.

"What about her?" Kincaid asked, dropping his cell phone into the hidden depths of his inside jacket pocket.

"Tie her up somewhere," Peppers suggested.

"No," Iris protested. "She's too strong. She'll escape."

"That's right," Kelli said, and then shot Iris an evil gaze.

"I could stand guard," Kincaid suggested. "I think I can handle her."

Iris and Kelli exchanged a look. They both knew how strong Kelli was, how strong they both were. Iris shook her head.

"No, you can't," Iris declared.

"That's right," Kelli said again, planting the bait.

"I can sedate her," Suri suggested.

"No!" Kelli shouted. *Yes!* Kelli had learned in Pasadena, during her first ordeal with the Agency, that the effects of sedatives and tranquilizers could be neutralized by her system if she shifted genders shortly after the injection. It was Kelli's hope that after the sedative was administered, she would be left alone, at which time she could shift, and then escape without further confrontation.

"Do it," Peppers ordered.

"Right away." Suri exited the exam room in a hurry.

Peppers eyed Kelli carefully. He asked aloud, "Why is she so important?"

Iris smiled. "You don't need to know." It gave her guilty pleasure to say that to Agent Peppers. Up until now they had been treating her like a child, but Iris suspected that was all about to change.

The two men stood guard with Iris, watching over Kelli until Suri returned with a needle in his hand. As soon as he entered, Kelli knew it was time to give the performance of her life.

"No," she shouted again, as Suri approached her. Kelli stood and took a step backwards, seemingly retreating into the corner. "Stay away from me."

"Everything will be alright," Suri said assuring her.

Kelli screamed louder. "No. Don't put me to sleep. Please." She looked at Iris. "Iris, don't do this."

Iris looked at Peppers, then at Kincaid. She breathed a sigh of frustration. "Guns, please."

Peppers and Kincaid exchanged a brief look before raising their weapons in Kelli's direction. Kelli went silent. Slowly, cautiously, Kelli returned to the stool and took a seat.

"Give her the injection, Doctor," Iris commanded.

Suri stepped closer to Kelli. He had witnessed her combat capabilities earlier when she fought Iris, so Suri was understandably apprehensive about being anywhere near her. "I need you to roll up your sleeve," he said to her.

Kelli did not want to appear too eager to receive the sedative, so she kept her eyes on Suri while she rolled up her sleeve slowly to mid-bicep level.

Suri swabbed the area of injection with an antiseptic wipe before inserting the needle into Kelli's vein and forcing the drug into her body.

It did not take long for Kelli to start feeling the effects of the sedative. She had to shift genders before she fell asleep in order to neutralize the drug and stay awake. Kelli knew she had to move things along. With a single thrust of her arm, she pushed Suri away from her. She stood immediately and lunged towards the door. "You happy now?" she screamed.

Peppers and Kincaid stepped into Kelli's path. Kelli, in response, stopped short. The effects of the sedative were coming on much stronger now, and Kelli knew she only had a short window in which to shift into her male form. She allowed herself to stumble backwards towards the exam table. Her eyes rolled back into her head and she fell towards the floor. Kincaid reached her first. He holstered his weapon and then grabbed Kelli as she fell into him. The smell of Kincaid's cologne filled her nostrils. Her hands groped at him clumsily in a simultaneous effort to push him away and grab hold of him for balance. Kincaid attempted to hoist her onto the bed. Peppers grabbed hold of Kelli's legs and helped Kincaid lay her body flat on the table.

Kelli struggled to stay awake as she lay stretched out on the table. She managed to yell a dreary sounding, "Get out," before she allowed her body to go limp. She began to slip into sleep. She tried to concentrate on shifting, but nothing happened. Her eyes closed as the dark of slumber enveloped her senses.

Iris chuckled. "Sorry, Kelli, but I'm giving the orders around here now," she said as she raised an eyebrow at Kincaid. With that, she turned and exited the exam room with Suri in tow.

Kincaid looked at Peppers. "I don't think I like her very much."

"I'm sure we haven't seen anything yet."

The two men looked back at Kelli's still form lying on the table. Convinced that the young woman was no longer a threat, the two men exited, leaving their unconscious prisoner behind.

14

WASHINGTON, D.C.

Outside of his personal and family life, Mr. One had very few occasions to laugh in his lifetime. It was safe to say that Mr. One was a stoic man, someone who took his responsibilities as the head of Department 12 very seriously. So it was surprising to those in the room, Mr. Two and Mr. Five, when One emitted a small chortle after hearing the proposal put forth by young Iris Molina.

"I beg your pardon, young lady," Mr. One began. "What makes you think you are in any position to make demands?"

"It's not a demand," a slight pause, then, "sir." The three men heard Iris release a nervous breath through the phone line before she spoke again. "Please hear me out. I believe that my solution is in both of our best interests."

One glanced over at Mr. Two who was shaking his head in disbelief. The silent question of *who does this girl think she is?* passed between them. Still, Mr. One was interested in the young girl's train of thought. She was a genetically enhanced human with an abnormally high IQ, after all. "Elaborate," he responded.

"You wish for Dr. Suri and me to return to D.C., but I need to free my moth- . . . Agent Molina. If you would *allow* Agent Peppers and Kincaid to assist me, then I would be more than willing to hand over Kelli Freeman as soon as we're done."

"That sounds an awful lot like an ultimatum," One said. "I don't take too kindly to those. Because you're so young and new to field work, I'm going to give you a pass and not have Agent Peppers take *you* into custody."

"Please," Iris pleaded. "It's not an ultimatum, more of a cry of desperation. I know that we should not have run off without Agency authorization, but Dr. Suri and Agent Molina felt that this transplant was my only hope for survival. I urged them to come." A lie. "We will return to face the consequences. Unfortunately, we didn't foresee Agent Molina getting apprehended by the FBI."

Mr. Two stepped behind Mr. One and whispered into his ear, "Don't forget we still need to question her about the phone call before the explosion." Though One nodded in response, he had no intention of letting the young girl on the phone know that he needed more from her than her mere return to D.C. Instead, Mr. One had another idea.

One leaned forward. "What makes you think you can pull off such an operation and secure the safe rescue of your mother?" He placed slightly more emphasis on the word mother.

Iris' response came without a missing beat. "Because that's what I've been trained to do, sir."

One glanced at the two men in the room. Mr. Five shrugged slightly. Mr. Two, however, regarded Mr. One with a knowing gaze. Of all the twelve men who made up Department 12 and convened on Agency decisions, Mr. Two had known Mr. One the longest, and because of that, he knew Mr. One the best. Mr. One was up to something, and Two knew it.

"Very well, Miss Molina," One said finally. "You have Agent Peppers and Agent Kincaid to guide you. They have years of experience with recon and recovery missions. Use their knowledge. But make no mistake, you are not in charge. Am I clear?"

A brief silence followed as Iris swallowed her pride on the other end of the line. "Yes, sir."

"Oh, and Agent Kincaid?" Mr. One called out.

"Yes, sir," Kincaid's voice returned.

"Delete the photo you took of Miss Freeman from your phone. That's documentation you no longer need to be in possession of."

"Right away, sir."

"Good. Report once you have completed your mission." With that, One cut the connection. One was pleased with his decision. Though absolute verification of Kelli Freeman's identity couldn't be confirmed until she was transported to D.C., Mr. One knew that the idea that she was, indeed, alive could possibly present Mr. One with the one thing he needed right now. A miracle. Despite the necessity to maintain an air of business, the issue regarding Kelli Freeman had suddenly become very personal.

"She's quite tenacious," Five said, referring to Iris.

"Of course, she is. We made her." One said, with a hint of pride.

"What's your plan?" Two asked.

"I'm going to wait a few minutes before I contact Agent Peppers. I've decided to tweak his mission parameters."

Two and Five were all ears.

"Once they arrive at the site where Agent Molina is being held, I'll have Agents Peppers and Kincaid sterilize the scene."

"What of our two *products*?" asked Five.

"Iris and Miss Freeman will be returned to us alive. Everyone else, Suri, Agent Molina, and anyone else who has the misfortune of being there, will be eliminated."

BRONX, NEW YORK

The air in the situation room in the back of the medical clinic had grown slightly cold. Iris rubbed her arms as she stood and looked at the two agents who were in the room. Suri was not among those present during the call-in to Mr. One. In the interest of time, Suri had thought it best to begin the cross-matching and blood work necessary to perform the transplant in the unlikely event that Iris was granted permission to pursue her plan to rescue her mother. Iris had been confident that Mr. One would agree. She had read the Harmony Project file, so she knew how important Kelli Freeman was to the project. What she did not know, however, was the same thing that had her curiosity piqued. If Kelli Freeman was so important, a successful product of the Harmony Project, why did the Agency try to have her terminated? Iris did not understand, but she had a few hours to kill before they moved on with their rescue mission, and she intended to use that time to find out.

Peppers turned to Kincaid. Kincaid was sifting casually through the inside pockets of his jacket in search of his cell phone. First the left pocket, then the right. A look of distress formed on his face as he reached into his pant pockets, much more frantically now, as he groped for his mobile device. He pulled his hands from his pants. Both of them were empty.

"You gave me my phone, right?" Kincaid asked Peppers.

"Yeah. Back in the exam room."

"Strange," Kincaid said, confused. "I must have dropped it. Be back in a sec." The young agent exited the room.

Peppers stepped closer to Iris. Her conversation with Mr. One had surprised him. Peppers was impressed with how the young girl handled herself, how she seemed undaunted despite the fact that she was addressing one of the most mysterious, and quite possibly, one of the most powerful men in the world. Ten minutes prior, Peppers assumed she was just some bratty kid, but Iris' mention of being trained, and Mr. One's subsequent turn around, made him realize that young Iris was so much more. "Hey," he said. "Good job."

Iris turned to Peppers, a look of surprise was on her face. She had not expected a compliment. Her demeanor softened. "Thank you." She wanted to tell Peppers just how nervous she had been during her discourse with Mr. One, but she didn't want to give him the impression that she was inexperienced, even though she knew it to be true.

"You ready for this?" he asked her.

Iris nodded. "I have to be. They've got my mother."

Peppers could understand Iris' determination and motivation. He couldn't imagine being in her shoes, having such a deep, familial connection with someone tied to your mission. How could he? Peppers had no one. No mother, no father, no siblings. Not a soul. That was a prerequisite for recruitment into the Agency. He wondered how this young girl and her mother managed to circumnavigate that. What made Iris Molina so special? Peppers was tempted to ask her, but then reminded himself that if the Agency wanted him privy to that information, then he already would be. Peppers refocused on the mission at hand. "This would be a lot easier if we had a layout of the building where she's being held."

"I know," Iris said, realizing she hadn't even thought of that. It was in that instant that the full realization of the situation hit her. *I'm out of my league.* Though Iris wished to appear strong and experienced, she was far too intelligent to attempt to pull off this mission without help. She looked up at Peppers. "Where do we start?"

"We start by contacting the FBI agent who has her in custody."

Iris grinned smugly. "I know just the person to help us do that."

BRONX, NEW YORK

The alley behind the urgent care clinic was extremely narrow, leaving just enough space for two vehicles to move past one another in opposite directions. The evening sky was beginning to grow darker. Agent Swann would have preferred to wait unit night fell before exploring the back of the building where she followed the white van through the streets of the Bronx.

As Swann stepped into the alley, she decided to forego the stealth and walk casually. That way, if anyone happened to be in the alley, particularly the driver of the van, she would appear to be one of the locals who was simply using the narrow strip as a means to go wherever. Luckily, there was no need for the ruse. Swann was alone. Her gaze fell upon the white van that was parked closely against the building. There were two other vehicles parked next to the van. Swann's attention was drawn to the blue one.

I knew it, she thought. Earlier, as Swann was trailing the van through the streets, she noticed that the blue sedan that had pulled out in front of her seemed to be following the same route. She had been on the job long enough to recognize the driving pattern, but decided not to bet the house on it. She kept the van in her sights as best she could, while trying not to alert either vehicle of her presence. Once the two vehicles pulled into the small plaza that housed the urgent care, Swann parked her car in the front parking lot, waited until she suspected that the coast was clear, and then came back to the alley to investigate. The question was, what was she hoping to find?

She moved quickly to the rear of the van. One last glance in both directions assured Swann that she was still alone. She reached out and pulled on the handle to the rear door. To Swann's surprise, it opened. Unfortunately, there wasn't much to see. The back of the van was sparse, with no aesthetic modifications whatsoever; not even a carpet. Further, there was no evidence that would give

Swann any indication of what was happening inside the clinic. *And why did they take Kyle? Based on what I witnessed, she didn't seem to be the target. Still, could she just be collateral damage, or, as I suspected earlier, is something else going on?* Swann decided it was the latter.

She closed the door to the van, and then turned her attention to the sedan. *Definitely government issue.* Swann froze in place as she contemplated another realization. *Did I just stumble onto someone else's investigation? And the girl that was grabbed, who is she? And what does Kyle have to do with it, if anything?* Swann's first inclination was to call her superiors and ask those very questions. However, Swann knew that she was only privy to the information she *needed* to know. She dismissed the flurry of questions that began forming in her head. *Stick to your assignment, Noami. Don't get distracted.*

Swann stepped to the driver's side of the blue sedan. She pulled on the driver's door handle. As she expected, the door was locked. She peered into the car through the windows and found just what she expected to find. Nothing. She took a step back and gazed at the back of the clinic. *My assignment is to surveille Kyle Cuffee, and I can't do that if I don't know what's going on in there.* She continued to stare at the building. As she did, she reviewed her mission parameters. *Keep your distance. Observe and Report. Don't intervene.* She recited the rules silently to herself several times. After a few deep breaths, she decided to go back to her car. Perhaps this would be a good time to report the situation and ask for guidance. *Good idea.*

She exited the alley quickly. As she moved around the side of the building, she continued to review the protocols in her head. Finally, she arrived in the parking lot that served the urgent care clinic, and headed straight for her Honda. Halfway to her vehicle, she stopped dead in her tracks. She turned to her left. Her gaze rested on the front door to the clinic. *Don't do it, Naomi.* She considered her own words. She took a deep breath before taking another step towards her car. She stopped once more. One more deep breath. She imagined what the response would be once she reported to her superiors that she may potentially lose the target. She decided that the response would not be favorable. *Screw it!* Swann turned abruptly to her left and headed for the clinic door. *I don't lose people. I'm the best. And I didn't come this far to lose track of Kyle. I'm going in.*

WASHINGTON, D.C.

One looked at his reflection in the restroom mirror as he washed his hands. It wasn't difficult to see the fatigue, both physical and mental, that was taking its toll on him. Mr. One had been the head of Department 12 for more than half his life and, considering the events of the last few days, he was wondering if it might be better to pass the torch sooner than later. *That is why I'm grooming Mr. Five,* he thought to himself. *Once I step down and Mr. Two takes the helm, Five will need to assume a more administrative role.* And, of course, there was the cancer issue. It pained him to have such power and influence, and yet, still have no recourse against the disease. But now, there may be hope. Could it really be possible that Kelli Freeman was, in fact, alive?

The door to the restroom opened and Mr. Two strolled in.

"There you are," Two said with a hint of relief.

"I'm an old man," One replied. "If I disappear suddenly, it's a safe bet I'm in the *head*."

Two did not respond. Instead, he raised an index finger, and then pointed it towards the bathroom stalls to his left.

One shook his head. "We're alone." He pulled a paper towel from the dispenser that hung below the mirror and began to dry his hands.

Two stepped forward, closing the distance between them. "It seems that you may have your miracle."

One nodded. "Indeed."

"If the girl in the photo is, in fact, Kelli Freeman, we may need Dr. Suri alive to perform the necessary procedure to extract the cure."

"No," One said immediately. "Too many loose ends; Dr. Chen can perform the procedure, whatever that entails. And don't forget we still have Dr. Simons at our disposal. Besides, Suri has already demonstrated where his true loyalties lie. We will proceed as planned."

"Very well," Two responded. "What about after?"

"After what?"

"After Miss Freeman has served her purpose, what do we do with her then? We expended numerous resources trying to kill her seven years ago."

"That was reactionary."

"Oh? Meaning?"

"Meaning we have time to consider our options this time. Studying Miss Freeman's genetics could catapult the Harmony Project to heights we haven't begun to imagine.

Think about it. We might finally unlock all of the secrets that Dr. Connelly and Dr. June took to their graves. We could achieve the ultimate goal of the Harmony Project, maybe even go beyond its current directive."

"The thought of that *is* fascinating. However, I can't imagine that Kelli Freeman is going to be cooperative."

One tossed the damp paper towel into the trash can by the door. "Once she's in our custody, her cooperation won't be required."

※

BRONX, NEW YORK

"You are Kyle. Kyle is you. Learn to embrace all the facets of who you are," Dr. Hughes said to her. Though Kelli could sense that she was in Dr. Hughes' office, there was still a darkness that clouded the space between them.

"I don't want to lose who I am," Kelli responded. "By Friday afternoon, after being Kyle around the clock, I don't feel like myself, I feel incomplete. Kyle and I have very different likes and dislikes, and his traits become more and more prevalent the longer I am him. How can I accept that I am Kyle, when I feel like two different people?"

"You can start by listening to yourself," Hughes replied. "You said that *you feel* like two different people. You stopped saying *we are* two different people."

"Is there a difference?"

Hughes smiled. "You tell *me*."

"I. . .I don't know how to answer that. I don't know how to embrace all of who I am, who Kyle is."

"You do it by figuring out why you hate Kyle."

"Because he represents why I'm separated from my family."

"Is that all?"

"Yes."

"Are you sure, Kelli?" Hughes leaned closer to her. "Are you absolutely sure?"

The peaceful darkness of slumber was snatched back abruptly. Her body jerked and she sat up, quickly exhaling the knot of air that had gotten trapped in her throat. She looked around the small exam room, and everything came rushing back.

Kelli looked at the clock that hung behind her on the wall. Only a few minutes had passed since the sedative had caused her to fall asleep. *How is that possible? How am I awake?* She hopped off of the exam table and gazed into the mirror. Instantly, her questions were answered. Looking back at her was Kyle Cuffee. In spite of herself, Kelli smiled.

Oh my God. It worked. Somehow, even as I fell asleep, I shifted. Strange. Kelli had trained herself over the last few years to resist shifting in her sleep, and for the most part, except at those times when she was extremely fatigued, she was successful. Still, she had trained herself not to revert into her female form if she happened to fall asleep as Kyle. Only once, when her shifting ability first manifested itself, had she shifted into Kyle during sleep. How then did she manage to do it now? Was it possible that she had control of this all along? Unfortunately for Kelli, she did not have the luxury of time to contemplate it. Her plan had worked. She was awake. She was alone. And now it was time to escape.

A last look at her reflection revealed that her wounds had already begun to heal. By this time tomorrow, there would be no evidence that she'd been in a fight at all.

Kelli stepped away from the mirror. As she moved, an object fell from inside her sweatshirt and landed on her foot. Kelli looked down. She bent quickly and retrieved the cell phone she had pick-pocketed from Agent Kincaid's jacket pocket as he struggled to control her flailing, drug induced slide into slumber. She pushed the door slowly, moving it only an inch at a time, until she could see into the hallway. *All clear in that direction.* She pushed the door further, stopped, and then listened. No footsteps of any kind; none walking casually, none charging at the door. Kelli peaked around the door and found the hallway to be absent of personnel in that direction, as well. Kelli exited the exam room and moved quickly up the hallway. She kept her back to the wall as she passed the closed doors of other exam rooms. With Kincaid's cell in her right hand, she dialed the phone number of someone whom she had not called in over two years. Agent West.

Kelli placed the phone against her ear as she rounded the corridor to the left and continued to move stealthily through the hallway. The line connected and the phone began to ring. "Come on, come on," she said under her breath. Instinctively, she began counting the rings. Two, three, four. "Come on, pick up!" she ordered quietly into the phone. The fifth ring sounded into her ear as she reached the end of the corridor. The ringing stopped suddenly and the line snapped open. A second later, Kelli heard a familiar voice.

"Agent West," he announced through the phone.

Kelli's heart jumped as she rounded the corner. In her excitement and relief to hear West's voice, Kelli realized a second too late that she'd heard footsteps approaching from around the bend. The collision startled her, causing her to drop the cell phone at Agent Kincaid's feet.

"Hello?" West's voice could be heard coming from the phone.

The sound of the cell phone hitting the floor drew Kincaid's eyes. He focused on the phone only long enough to realize that it belonged to him before lifting his gaze towards Kelli. Unfortunately for Kincaid, Kelli was already in motion.

Kelli was still in male form. Though Kincaid lingered on his cell phone, Kelli knew she had a mere split second before he looked up at her; at Kyle. Kelli launched a left jab that landed neatly on Kincaid's chin. The unexpected blow startled him and caused him to stumble backwards. Kelli knew she had to be careful. In her male form, she was exponentially stronger than Kincaid, and the slightest miscalculation of strength could cause severe harm, or worse, death. Despite all of her confrontations with Agency operatives, Kelli had managed to avoid actually killing any of them, or anyone else for that matter. And though she had taken up marksmanship training, she wasn't certain that she was ready to take another person's life.

Kelli pressed forward and attempted to land another left jab. Kincaid, more alert now, sidestepped the jab and launched an offensive left hook of his own. Kelli ducked the hook, shifting back into her female form as she moved under and past him to position herself to Kincaid's rear left. Kincaid kept his left arm in motion, reversing his momentum in an attempt to catch Kelli off guard with a left elbow strike. Kelli was ready for it.

Kelli caught Kincaid's elbow with her right hand. As she stepped into Kincaid's body, she moved her right hand up the length of his arm to his wrist, and applied pressure until his arm was completely extended. With her left hand, she reached out and pressed her hand against the back of Kincaid's shoulder, completing the shoulder lock, rendering Kincaid helpless. The agent jerked his body in attempt to free himself, but Kelli was too strong. He jerked once more, causing his foot to kick the cell phone inadvertently, sending it sliding up the hallway.

Kelli applied more pressure to Kincaid's arm, causing him to fall to his knees in submission. He released a loud agonizing groan. Kelli knew that if Kincaid continued to scream, it would only be a matter of time before the others arrived. Kelli moved her left hand from behind Kincaid's shoulder, and then applied a quick back-fist blow to the nape of his neck. Kincaid blacked out, his body going limp in Kelli's grasp. She lowered him to the ground. Kelli turned up the hallway towards freedom, but then halted. *I don't know where I am. How will I get from wherever I am back to Agent West and my dad? I need cash.* Kelli looked down at Kincaid's unconscious form in front of her. She knelt down and began searching his body. The first item she came across was his weapon. Kelli had done enough research before purchasing her Glock to recognize the make of the .40 caliber Ruger that rested in Kincaid's holster. Kelli freed the weapon and placed it on the floor by her knee. She groped his jacket pockets until she came across something that felt like a wallet, or a billfold. She reached inside and retrieved the item. *Bingo.* Kelli opened up the wallet, and without bothering to count any of it, grabbed every bill inside. She stuffed the money into her pocket. Her keen hearing picked up a scuffling sound in the distance at the end of hallway in the direction of the exam room. She turned. Iris stood at the end of the corridor, her mouth hung slightly ajar in surprise. Before Iris could take one step, Kelli scooped up the Ruger and pointed it directly at Iris. Iris froze.

Due to her training on the numerous gun ranges over the last six months, Kelli had become quite the marksman. Her enhanced hand-eye coordination made hitting paper targets and soup cans remarkably easy from rather long distances. However, this was the first time since taking up the sport that she'd actually pointed a weapon at another human being. At this distance, Kelli knew she was more than capable of putting a bullet in the exact center of Iris' forehead. Still, Kelli wasn't certain that she had the heart to pull the trigger. To compound the issue, shooting Iris would be like shooting Francine. She had already seen Francine get shot, and though she knew the two girls were not one and the same, the image would be no different.

Iris' heart pounded in her chest. During her upbringing, she had been through countless combat and artillery training scenarios. Each and every training session had safeguards in place to ensure that neither Iris nor any of her fellow classmates were in danger of being shot accidentally. In spite of the years of training, Iris realized that nothing prepared her for the surge of paralyzing horror of having an actual live weapon being leveled at her. Iris was aware that Kelli possessed heightened senses just as she did. She knew how easy it would be for Kelli to kill her right then and there. However, Iris noticed Kelli's hesitation. As their eyes burrowed into one another from opposite ends of the hallway, Iris saw the barrel of the weapon waver ever so slightly. Then again. And again. *She's shaking.* Iris locked her gaze back onto Kelli. And instantly she knew. A smug grin touched the corner of her mouth.

Kelli saw Iris' smile. *Dammit.* Iris was on to her. She knew that, for whatever reason, Kelli was not going to shoot her. Kelli's eyes dropped and focused on the cell phone that lay in the hallway mid-way between their positions. Her ears told her that the line was no longer open. West must've hung up after receiving no response. Kelli shifted her gaze back to Iris. Iris, too, had noticed the cell phone. Suddenly, the phone began to ring. *West must be calling back.*

Iris took a step forward. Kelli lowered the weapon slightly and fired a shot that landed an inch in front of Iris' left foot. Iris halted as her heart threatened to jump through her chest. The phone continued to ring. The two young women locked eyes again.

"If you want that phone, you're going to have to shoot me," Iris yelled through gritted teeth.

Kelli weighed her options quickly. She had fired the weapon. Everyone in the building had now been alerted to the fact that something was wrong. It would be mere seconds before someone came to investigate. If she retrieved the phone, she risked wasting the precious few seconds she would need to escape, and even that was not guaranteed. However, if she decided to leave the phone, and with it, a possible chance to connect with Agent West, she might actually succeed and escape her captors.

Kelli decided there was no real choice to be made. She cursed under her breath. She sent another glare at Iris, and then turned and ran up the corridor in hopes of finding freedom, leaving the phone, and Agent West behind.

Kelli was not certain if she was, in fact, heading for any of the exits. She did, however, know that the direction in which she was moving brought her farther away from the exam room where she had been held. She listened for any rapid footsteps that would indicate someone was in pursuit. Thankfully, she heard none. She turned another corner and eyed a set of double doors at the far end. She accelerated her pace and covered the distance within seconds. She burst through the doors and found herself in a large room. Sections of the room were broken up into small exam areas separated by yellow curtains. Kelli could hear voices coming from behind some the curtains as she moved past them in the center aisle towards the door on the far side of the room. From the bits and pieces she heard, Kelli could tell that patients were being tended to by their nurses or physicians. Kelli quickened her pace. She reached the door, and without hesitation, turned the knob, pulled the door open and stepped through.

Kelli found herself in another short hallway that ran perpendicular to another hallway directly ahead. Kelli traversed the distance and found herself facing a decision. Left, or right? To the right was a long hallway with a door at the end. To the left was another door. Above the left door was a sign that read: Waiting Area. Kelli chose the left. She raced to the door, grabbed the knob and pulled the door open. She stepped into the waiting area. A woman sitting in the corner looked up at Kelli. A look of terror crossed her face as she jumped up in attempt to get as far away from Kelli as she could. Kelli turned to the right. An African-American female nurse stood behind a long, raised desk that separated the waiting room from the nurses' area, and was protected by a sheet of glass that extended from the ceiling down to within a half a foot of the desk. The nurse, who was writing on a medical form of some kind, took in the sight of Kelli and stepped back in fear. It dawned on Kelli that she was still in possession of Kincaid's weapon, and it was locked tight within the grasp of her right hand. Kelli stuffed the weapon into the waistband of her sweats. She eyed the metallic sign with red lights that displayed the word exit. Kelli dashed for the double doors. Two seconds later, the double doors were spreading apart as she approached. Another second later, Kelli crossed the threshold into the moonlit night and ran full speed towards freedom.

❧❦

Moments earlier, Agent Swann had entered the waiting area lobby of the Bronx Netherland Clinic. She took note of her surroundings; patients waiting for medical attention, nurses milling about, some sitting at the desk behind the protective glass, and one walking around the lobby tending to a man in a wheelchair. Nothing out of the ordinary. She surveyed the two doors on the opposite sides of the waiting area, surmising that either one could grant her deeper access into the building. *Okay, where do I start?*

Before Swann could take another step forward, a faint bang emanated from somewhere deep within the building. *Was that a gunshot?* As if in answer to her question, several of the patients rose from their seats, suddenly afraid.

"Was that a gunshot?" an elderly man repeated Swann's question aloud.

"Of course not," The female nurse in the lobby replied, raising her hands in any effort to maintain order. "Everyone calm down."

Another elderly patient stood up. "I know a gunshot when I hear one."

The female nurse did not relent. "Please calm down. Remain seated. I assure you, there are no guns in the building." She turned to the two nurses sitting at the desk behind the glass. "Can you find out what that was?"

"Uh, sure," the male nurse replied. Hesitantly, the male nurse rose from his seat and disappeared deeper into the nurses' area.

Swann watched as the nurse in the lobby moved from patient to patient, calming them down. "Please sit. Everything's going to be okay," she heard the nurse say.

The patients began to comply. Several of the patients were mumbling amongst themselves as they sat down. Suddenly, one of the doors that led to the back of the clinic was pulled open. Kelli rushed through the doorway into the waiting area.

Swann's eyes widened. It was Kyle. Instinctively, Swann began to walk towards her but stopped when she saw the weapon in Kyle's right hand.

A swell of voices arose as everyone in the lobby caught sight of the weapon, as well. Swann watched as Kyle stuffed the weapon into her waistband, then made a beeline for the exit door. Within seconds, Kyle rushed through the door.

Oh no, Swann thought. *I can't lose her.* Swann darted out of the door. As she stepped into the parking lot, she caught a glimpse of Kyle sprinting onto the sidewalk. *Oh crap. How'd she get through the lot so fast?* Swann knew that she'd never be able to keep up with Kyle on foot, not with the head start Kyle had, so she turned and ran at full speed to her Honda. She fiddled with her keys as she approached the vehicle. She unlocked the door remotely, pulled the door open and slid behind the wheel. Within seconds, the cherry-colored Honda was maneuvering its way onto the street in hot pursuit.

Swann had driven several blocks, looking from side to side, in an attempt to locate Kyle. No luck. Swann squinted further up the block. Nothing. No sign of her. *Did she duck down a side street?* Swann pressed the accelerator and sped down the block. It was only after she had traveled ten or so blocks before she had to admit the undeniable truth. Kyle Cuffee was gone.

"Goddammit," she cursed at the top of her lungs. She slapped her fists against the steering wheel repeatedly. "God…dammit." *I lost her.*

Bling stood in the small room that Arthur had set up as a temporary office. Arthur thought it was best to clear the area of anyone who did not need to be there, so he gave his three remaining employees the night off and sent them home. Not long after, Arthur, with Cassius and Wilma in tow, left as well. Though West protested, Arthur promised to return.

"Stay home with your wife and kids where it's safe," West had urged him.

Arthur shook his head. "I can't. Not until *all* my kids are safe." Before Arthur took his leave, he gave West a set of keys to another building that was under reconstruction at the end of the block. "That building is part of our watch, too. Move Agent Molina down there. That way we only have to keep an eye on one direction."

"Good idea," West agreed.

"I'll be back as soon as I can." With that, Arthur took his two youngest children, and headed home.

West entered the office and began to pace across the floor. His mind was preoccupied with trying to decipher all of the information that Agent Molina had just divulged. Bling turned to him.

"She say anything else to you?" Bling asked, regarding Agent Molina.

"I'm not sure if she has anything else *to* say," West responded.

"You don't believe that."

West stopped and looked at Bling. "You're right. I don't."

"But what about what she *did* say? You really think they came here for a kidney?"

"Her story tracks. Iris is Francine's clone. Who better to give Iris a kidney than a sibling?"

"Zenaida is not Iris' sibling," Bling scoffed in protest.

"Her genetics say differently," said West flatly.

Bling cursed to himself. He did not want to accept that Zenaida had been kidnapped so one of her kidneys could be harvested. Despite Molina's assurances that Zenaida would be returned unharmed post-operation, Bling feared the worst for his girlfriend.

"What do we do next?" Bling asked.

"We're going to move Molina to the building at the end of the block and set up camp there. Then we wait."

"For the phone call?"

West nodded. "Molina seems to think they will call with terms for her release."

Bling threw his arm up in disgust. "Come on, West. What the fuck? They've got Zenaida *and* Kelli. Why on Earth would they come back for one agent?"

"Because Molina knows her daughter. She believes Iris will try to get her back."

"Dude, even Molina thinks that's a bad move on Iris' part. She said it herself."

West snapped. "Yes, Bling. I know. But right now, I'm dealing with what I've got. Okay?" West took a deep breath in an attempt to calm himself. He was unsuccessful. Bling's continued tirade only served to make it worse.

"What you've got is a woman with fingerprints. Screw the bargain, man. Run her damn prints."

West's temper flared. "Why? So the Agency can get wind of this and send in their cleaners before we can get another step closer to exposing them? No! We are one step ahead of them this time and I'm not about to let that advantage slip away." West caught his breath as his own words echoed in his ears. *Is that what this means to me now? Winning? After so many years of pursuing leads on the Agency, has it come down to me simply wanting to win? To beat them at their own game?* He turned away from Bling and paced to other side of the small room. A few deep breaths allowed him to calm himself and clear his mind. Without turning to

Bling, he said, "I'm not exactly sure what I should do. It seems as if we're the ones in a no-win situation. None of our options look good."

"How are they supposed to contact us? Molina wasn't carrying a cell phone."

"Like you said," West answered, turning to face Bling. "They've got Kelli."

"You mentioned calling someone for help," Bling said.

"Already en route," West said, tapping the cell phone in his back pocket. "I just hope the flight gets in on time." Then, as if on cue, his cell phone rang. West yanked the phone from his back pocket. It rang twice before he looked at the number that appeared on the screen. A strange looked crossed his face.

"What's wrong? Is that our help?" Bling asked curiously.

Third ring.

West shook his head. He did not recognize the phone number. "It might be Iris," the phone rang a fourth time. West pressed the button as the fifth ring began to sound. "Agent West."

To his surprise, a sound resembling a blunt impact greeted West on the phone. He listened for a moment, hoping whoever it was that was calling, would respond to him. Nothing.

"Hello?" West called again into his phone. He pressed his ear closer to the phone. He thought he heard some movement, but it was too indistinct to recognize. A moment passed, then another sound that was similar to impact, followed by, what? West couldn't decipher it.

"Who is it?" Bling inquired.

West shrugged. He pulled the phone away from his ear and disconnected the call. "Possibly a wrong number, but . . ." his voice trailed off.

"What?"

West shook his head again. A feeling of dread grew in his gut that he couldn't shake. He tapped the phone icon on the bottom of the phone screen and brought up the 'recent calls' menu. The phone number of the last incoming call was at the top of the list of several other numbers. West swiped his finger across the top number to the right. Instantly, his phone connected to the wireless network, and placed a return call to that number.

The phone rang six times before a voice mail system answered the call and repeated the following automated message. "The party you are trying to reach is not available at this time. At the tone, please leave your name, the number you are calling from, and a brief message. Thank you." West heard a short tone, and then the line clicked open. West did not leave a message. Instead, he ended the call.

"No answer," West reported.

"But you have the number, right?"

West nodded.

"Correct me if I'm wrong," Bling began, "but just because you agreed not to check this woman's prints, doesn't mean you can't run a check on that phone number. I mean, it could be nothing."

West smiled. "Or it could be the one thing that leads us to Kelli and Zenaida." He nodded at Bling. "Brilliant."

"Well, you know, a brotha does what he can," Bling responded playfully.

West accessed his phone list once more. After a brief search, he swiped a number, and then brought the phone back up to his ear. The phone opened after the third ring. The voice that came through the line was that of A.D. Marsh. He was not happy.

"It's about time, Agent West! Where the hell have you been?"

"I'm still in New York, sir. And I think I may have a lead on our Agency investigation."

❧❧

"Agent West, did you say?" Peppers asked.

"Yes, Special Agent Donald West," Five responded.

Peppers stood alone in the situation room, though his current conversation with Mr. Five was being transmitted via Peppers' cell phone, not the sit-room phone. Whatever it was that Mr. Five called about, Peppers gathered that it was for his ears only.

Five continued. "By tracking the usage of West's bureau credit card, our man in the D.C. field office confirmed that West is currently in New York. Given his past history with Kelli Freeman, and his constant snooping into Agency affairs, we are confident that he's the FBI agent who apprehended Agent Molina. He matches the description given by young Iris."

"Thank you, sir."

"Our man procured West's personal cell number, as well. We'll text it to you right away."

"Thank you, sir," Peppers repeated. "I'm sure that will come in handy."

"Now, Agent Peppers. I trust that you and your partner will have no problems carrying out these new orders."

"No problem at all, sir. Once we arrive at the site, we will tie up all the loose ends."

"Excellent. I await your report." Without another word, Five ended the call.

Peppers stood alone with his thoughts, contemplating the best strategy for locating Agent Molina and then carrying out the task of eliminating everyone there. And what of Dr. Suri? Peppers couldn't eliminate Suri until after they returned from the pending mission. To do so beforehand would alert Iris to their true intentions. No, Suri would live. For now.

Peppers looked around the room and took note of the silence. He decided to sit down and enjoy the solitude that so often eluded him when out on a mission. He closed his eyes, took several deep breaths and allowed himself to relax, and take in the quiet. To his dismay, the quiet was shattered by the unmistakable sound of a gunshot.

Peppers jumped from his seat and pulled his weapon from its holster all in one fluid motion. He exited the room and moved carefully through the hallways, his weapon out in front of him at eye level the entire time.

As he rounded the corner and moved up the adjacent corridor, he heard a loud voice calling out in fear. Peppers quickened his steps in pursuit of the voice. It called out again. This time, Peppers recognized the voice as Dr. Suri's.

"Iris!" Suri called out again. "Where are you?"

Peppers surmised that Suri had heard the gunshot, as well. He turned left at the bend and followed Suri's voice until he found him standing alone in the corridor. Peppers stepped beside him and gazed up the hallway in front of them. There, standing in the center of the corridor, holding a cell phone, was Iris.

"What happened? I heard a gunshot," Peppers asked. His gaze travelled past Iris and rested upon Kincaid who was on the floor, struggling to pull himself into a seated position against the wall. Peppers refocused his attention on Iris. "Iris!" he shouted at her. "What the hell happened?"

"She's gone," Iris answered calmly, turning to Peppers. "Kelli Freeman escaped."

15

This was not good. Peppers arrived in the corridor only to learn that one of the girls they were holding hostage had gotten away. Personally, this eventuality meant nothing to Peppers. However, to Iris, losing Kelli Freeman meant losing any leverage she might have had in her deal with Mr. One.

"Who fired the shot?" Peppers questioned as he approached Iris.

"She did. Kelli."

"Where did she get a gun?"

"I believe she has mine," Kincaid said from his seated position against the wall, his hand groping his empty holster.

"Splendid," Peppers responded sarcastically. "I thought she was sedated." He looked at Suri. "Did you wake her?"

"No," Suri spoke up hurriedly in defense. "Why would I?"

Peppers turned to Iris. Iris looked at both men blankly. "Don't look at me. I didn't wake her either."

"But you left the situation room so you could have Dr. Suri wake her. We needed to question her about who to call to set up the exchange for Agent Molina." Peppers made no attempt to hide his frustration.

"The Freeman girl claimed that she didn't know who the FBI agent was," Suri reminded them.

"She knew," Peppers assured him. It was a fact Peppers was certain of since Mr. Five had confirmed it only a few minutes prior.

"I never made it to Dr. Suri," Iris explained. "I walked by the exam room where Kelli was sleeping and I saw that the door was opened slightly. I just assumed your partner was looking for his phone. But when I looked in, she was gone."

"Why didn't you come and get me?" Peppers asked.

"Because I have a better chance of subduing her," Iris said. She gestured to Kincaid who was still sitting on the floor. "Need I say more? Besides, I thought I heard him scream or something so I came as fast as I could."

"Not fast enough apparently," Kincaid joked.

Peppers moved up the corridor and knelt down next to his partner. "You okay? How'd she manage to disarm you?"

Kincaid looked up at Peppers. He was almost too embarrassed to say, "She was . . . strong."

Peppers stared at him, confused. "Well this is just great. Not only did we lose Mr. One's prize, but now she's running around New York with a gun."

"Don't worry," Iris said. "She's not going to shoot anybody. Trust me."

Peppers stood and faced Iris. "I'm done trusting you, little lady. Because that girl escaped, this location is now compromised."

"She's not going to go to the cops," Iris said confidently. "Kelli Freeman is supposed to be dead. In case you hadn't noticed, it was a secret. Not even Mr. One knew she was alive."

"That doesn't stop Miss Freeman from reporting the whereabouts of Miss Rodriguez in there," Kincaid chimed in. "Pepp is right. We have to assume that this location is toast."

"Everybody pack your things," Peppers ordered. "It's time to evacuate."

Iris began to protest. "We can't leave yet. The doctor is still running tests."

"On the contrary," Suri corrected her. "I've completed the blood work. As I suspected, the cross-match is negative. You and your *sister* are compatible."

"What about the HLA typing? I thought that took more time."

Suri placed his hands on Iris' shoulders. "My dear, Iris. I am a bio-geneticist. I helped engineer your enhancements, believe me when I say, we are ready to proceed."

"You may have to hold off on that, Doctor," Peppers warned.

"Yes, I know. We must relocate. Not to worry, I know of another medical facility where we can go."

"Get ready to move." Peppers turned and walked away. "I'm going to the sit-room. I've got to report this."

"Wait." Iris ran past Peppers and planted herself in his path. He stopped and looked down at her as a father would before scolding a disobedient child.

"What are you doing, Iris? We lost Kelli Freeman, and we've lost this location. I have to call it in."

Iris began to worry. If Mr. One learned that Kelli Freeman has escaped, he may pull out of their bargain. If so, Iris would lose the opportunity to rescue her mother. "What about our plan? My mother?"

"We'll see what the big shots have to say." Peppers attempted to walk around Iris. She stepped into his path once more. Peppers glared down at her. "Move."

"Why do they need to know?" she asked desperately. "Why can't we just proceed as planned?"

"We had no plan, Iris," Peppers reminded her. "We hadn't even called Agent West yet."

"Agent West?"

Peppers nodded. "Yeah. Mr. Five called and gave me the name and number of the FBI agent who has your mother."

"The number? Wait." Iris was still holding Kincaid's cell phone. She remembered how preoccupied Kelli seemed with it during their last meeting in the hallway. It occurred to her that Kincaid's weapon wasn't the only thing that Kelli Freeman had managed to take from him. Iris tapped a button and brought up the call menu. She turned and showed the number on the screen to Peppers. Peppers' eyes widened. He retrieved his cell phone from his jacket pocket, and after tapping the proper buttons, stared at the number that Mr. Five had texted to him. The number was the same.

"Where did you get that?" Peppers asked.

"Kelli must have been trying to contact Agent West when Kincaid found her," Iris surmised.

Kincaid, finally back on his feet, approached Peppers from the rear. "She's right," Kincaid confirmed. "Somehow she'd gotten hold of my cell. She was calling someone when I ran into her."

"Did they speak to one another?" Peppers asked.

Kincaid shook his head. "I can't be sure."

Peppers focused his gaze on Iris once again. "All the more reason to assume this place is compromised, and for me to report in. Now, Iris. Get out of my way."

Iris exhaled heavily. She contemplated fighting Peppers to keep him from going to the situation room. She had no doubt that she could overpower him, but she decided that cunning and guile were her best options for getting what she wanted. Without a word, she stepped aside.

Peppers nodded and proceeded down the hallway. As he reached the bend, he heard Iris' voice behind him.

"Agent West. This is Iris Molina."

Peppers spun around on a dime. Iris had not moved from her previous spot, but she was holding Kincaid's phone up to her ear. Peppers could hardly believe what he was seeing. Iris had dialed Agent West.

"I'd like to discuss arrangements for a prisoner exchange. Zenaida Rodriguez for my mother."

Most of the lights were turned off, dressing everything in the house in darkness. Were it not for the familiarity one gains from living in the same space for more than twenty years, Diane Freeman would have certainly tripped over a piece of furniture as she moved silently through the hallway in her home.

Diane had just checked in on her two youngest children, Cassius and Wilma. Thankfully, both of them had managed to fall asleep. When they arrived home with her husband, Arthur, more than one hour ago, both of them were clearly shaken up by the turn of events that left their older sister, Kelli, missing.

Diane made her descent down the stairs into the family room, and then crossed the room without making a sound. As she approached the family's home office, she noticed a sliver of light sneaking out from under the door. Diane stepped in front of the door quietly and placed her ear against it. There was a slight rustling sound coming from inside. Diane pushed the door open to reveal Arthur stuffing his personal Smith & Wesson into a body holster.

"I thought we decided you were going to stay home." Diane whispered, startling him.

"Woman!" he said, after catching his breath. "You scared the devil out of me."

"You're going back, aren't you?" she asked.

He gestured for her to come into the office. "Close the door." Diane complied.

"We discussed this, Arthur. You said you were staying home." It was true. Though Arthur had informed West that he would return to the security site, a quick conversation with his wife changed his mind. Or so she thought.

"I'm sorry, Diane. I can't. Not while Kelli is out there somewhere." He stepped forward and took Diane's hands into his. "You've got to understand."

"I do understand. But you're not a cop anymore."

"Maybe I should be," he retorted.

"Hey, nobody forced you to retire. That was your decision."

"I know," conceded Arthur quickly. "But what am I supposed to do, Baby? This is our girl."

"You still have friends on the force. Call somebody."

Arthur lifted his coat from where it hung on the back of the office chair. He slipped it on as he spoke to his wife. "I wouldn't know who to call. We're dealing with the Agency. They've had officers in their pockets long before we were even aware that the Agency existed."

"What about your ex-partner? You trust him, right?"

"Andrews? Of course. But he's also retired, and on vacation in the Bahamas right now."

Diane became pensive, her brain searching for another alternative. As if he could read her mind, Arthur responded to her unspoken thoughts.

"I have to do this. I wouldn't be able to sleep knowing Kelli's being held out there. I've got to go help West get her back."

Diane began to weep. "What if they've hurt her already?"

Arthur pulled her close and wrapped his arms around her. "They haven't. According to Agent Molina, this is about Zenaida. Kelli was just in the wrong place at the wrong time."

"The story of her life," Diane managed to say through her tears.

"We're going to get through this, Baby." He squeezed her tighter. "Everything's going to be okay. You'll see."

"You call me every hour." It was not a request.

"You got it," Arthur promised. "Come here." Arthur dropped to his knees. He pulled Diane down with him until they were both kneeling on the floor in the center of the office. Together, as they often did whenever their lives seemed to spin out of control, they prayed.

When his cell phone rang, West assumed it was A.D. Marsh calling him back with information about the cell phone number he had supplied to him. Saying that A.D. Marsh was upset with West would have been a gross understatement. Marsh was livid.

"I'm sitting on my hands waiting for an update hours after you claimed you were about to make contact with our target. Then, nothing. What the hell is going on?"

West was aware that he should have contacted Marsh long before he did. But with everything that was going on, and the promise he'd made to Agent Molina not to run her prints, West needed time to think. It had taken West a few moments to calm Marsh enough to catch him up on the entire investigation. The contact with Kelli, the kidnapping of Zenaida Rodriguez, the capture of Agent Molina. Everything. Once Marsh was back in the loop, he was more willing to listen to West's lead about the phone number, and offer assistance.

"I'll get someone on it," Marsh had said. "It's hard to know who to trust with this Agency business. Normally, I'd have Bonner do it, but he seems to have disappeared for the night."

"He'll turn up," West said dismissively. "I need whatever info there is, sir."

"It may take some time, but as long as the cell phone remains powered on, we'll track it," Marsh declared. With that, Marsh was gone. Now, the phone rang in West's hand. His eyes widened as he looked at the number of the incoming call.

"It's from the same number," he announced to Bling.

Bling's eyes met West's gaze. He shrugged. "Answer it."

West pressed the phone icon and opened the line. "Agent West," he said, identifying himself. Though West expected a phone call from Iris, he was, nonetheless, taken aback by the youthful voice that came back through the line.

"Agent West. This is Iris Molina. "I'd like to discuss arrangements for a prisoner exchange. Zenaida Rodrigucz for my mother."

"Fine. We can discuss that," West replied cordially. "What about the other young lady you happened to leave here with?"

"Oh, you mean Kelli Freeman?"

West's heart jumped. He had not expected Iris to know Kelli's name. Did Kelli tell them? What else did Kelli say?

"You'll be happy to know that Kelli escaped," Iris announced.

"How can I be sure of that?" West asked.

"I'm pretty sure she'll contact you once she finds herself a phone to use. She tried to call you from this number earlier, but she was interrupted."

"Interrupted? Is she hurt? How long ago did she escape?" West questioned

"Escape?" Bling interjected. "Who escaped?" West waved at him dismissively in order to silence him.

"I didn't call to talk about Kelli Freeman. I called to discuss terms for a swap. Are you prepared to do that or not?"

West weighed his options. He did not know much about Iris. What he did know of her, he didn't like.

Though she had the voice of a young girl, West knew her to be the same person who murdered three men just two days prior. Until he saw or heard from Kelli Freeman, he was not willing to believe anything that Iris had to say to him. Agent Molina, however, was the exception to that rule. West knew that Iris wanted to recover her mother and might stoop to any level to make it happen. After all, she was a killer. Right now, that was the only thing he trusted concerning Iris. "Yes. I am," he said finally. "It's my understanding that you need Miss Rodriguez's kidney."

Dead air came through the phone line. Then, "That's right."

"I find it hard to believe that you've come all this way to swap Miss Rodriguez before you get what you came for."

"You're right," came Iris' immediate response. "The surgery is about to begin, after which, we will call to inform you where you can find Miss Rodriguez and release my mother."

"Hold on a minute," West protested. "We're supposed to sit here quietly and let you steal that woman's kidney, and then turn Agent Molina over with no questions asked?"

Bling shook his head in frantic protest.

Again, Iris' reply was immediate. "Yes."

"That doesn't sound like a deal at all," West said, growing more irritated with each second. *Who does this little brat think she is?* "How about you return Miss Rodriguez completely unharmed, we give you your mother, and everybody goes their separate ways?"

"You said it yourself, Agent West. I didn't come all this way to leave without what I need. That's my deal, take it or leave it."

West hated Iris' cavalier attitude. The last thing he wanted to do was to give in to such an unfair, completely lopsided trade. He had one more hand to play, and the time had come to play it. "And what if I leave it?"

"What?" The young girl sounded surprised.

"You heard me. What if I say no deal?"

"Then, after the surgery, you don't get Zenaida back alive. You can bring my mother in for questioning, but the Agency will come for her, and you will be left with nothing, if you're left alive at all." She was on the verge of screaming at him.

"Fine," West said, not budging. *I'm not letting this little wench have things her way.* "But we both know that the Agency won't be welcoming Agent Molina back with open arms. She ran off with you and attempted to kidnap a young woman to harvest one of her kidneys, all without any type of authorization from Mr. One." West paused to let the sound of Mr. One's name sink in. Iris did not respond. West pressed on. "And if you're telling the truth about Kelli, you've already let one hostage escape. No, I can't imagine that the Agency is too happy with either one of you right now. So go ahead, have it your way."

There was silence on the line. West surmised that Iris was weighing her options. He couldn't believe he was negotiating a prison exchange with a teenager. He looked over at Bling who had been making frantic, silent gestures the entire time.

"What is she saying?" he whispered at a barely audible volume. "What's going on?"

West raised a finger to silence Bling, but Bling was far beyond the point of patience and maintaining composure.

"No," he said at a slightly higher decibel. "West, talk to me. What the f . . . West!"

Iris' voice came back through the phone. "Looks like we have ourselves a stalemate."

"Looks like," West agreed, unwavering.

"You know I can't give you Zenaida until after the surgery. But I can guarantee her safe return afterwards. I'll even have the doctor call you with updates during the procedure."

"That's not good eno-"

"It's going to have to be," Iris interrupted. West couldn't be certain, but he detected a sense of urgency in Iris' voice. Was she being rushed? Coerced? "There are a lot of lives at stake here, Agent West. Think about which ones are important to you," she said sternly. "I'll call back in an hour for your decision." The call was cut off.

West lowered the cell phone from his ear and cursed aloud. Bling stood in front of him, arms outstretched, waiting for the report.

"Well?" Bling said in frustration.

West shook his head in despair. "We may not get Zenaida back before she loses a kidney."

"No!" Bling shouted. "Unacceptable." He turned and headed for the door. "I'm going to talk to this bitch," he said, referring to Agent Molina. "She's going to tell us where Zenaida is even if I have to beat it out of her."

West grabbed Bling's arm. "Bling, no-"

"Why not? That woman in there is responsible for two people I care about being driven off in a van," Bling continued to shout. "And what are we doing about it? Nothing, man. We're just sitting here." He yanked his arm free of West's grasp. "I thought you were the FBI, man. You're supposed to know what the hell to do."

"I'm doing it, Bling. I'm keeping Molina complacent until the lead about the phone number pans out. When it does, we'll track it, and then we'll get Zenaida back."

West's cell phone rang again. Both West's and Bling's eyes were drawn to the screen.

"Another unfamiliar number," West announced as he answered the call. "Agent West!"

"Agent West! Thank God. It's Kelli."

❧

Iris' heart raced as she stared at Kincaid's cell phone in her hand. Her body was trembling and she took several deep breaths in order to calm her nerves. She couldn't believe it. She had just negotiated her mother's release. Iris knew that if Agent West wanted Zenaida's safe return, he had to agree to her terms. All things considered, she was proud of herself. Unfortunately, Agent Peppers did not feel the same.

"What's with you?" Peppers asked, pointing a condescending finger at her. "Don't you get it? We have to leave. Now. We don't have time for a surgery."

"I know that," Iris retorted. "But Agent West doesn't. And by the time he figures it out, it'll be too late."

Kincaid stepped to Iris' side and snatched his cell phone from her grasp. He stuffed it into his jacket pocket and turned to Peppers. "What do we do?"

"Nothing has changed," Peppers stated. "We report in. This has gotten way out of hand."

Iris nodded her head. "Fine. Let's go." She stepped around Kincaid. Peppers, in response, put his hand out and halted her.

"No way. I'm making this call *alone*. You three are going to pack up, take Miss Rodriguez, and get out of here right now."

"But-" Iris tried to object.

"Now!" Peppers said firmly. "Remember. Mr. One put *us* in charge."

Iris bit her bottom lip. She looked at Dr. Suri. The look on his face represented a silent plea for Iris to comply with Agent Peppers' orders.

Reluctantly, she agreed with a noticeable pout. "Whatever." Iris stormed off with Suri in tow.

"Keep an eye on her," Peppers said to Kincaid before marching off towards the situation room.

Kincaid nodded as he proceeded down the hallway to catch up with Iris and the doctor. Over the ten minutes that followed, Kincaid supervised as Iris, Suri and the three nurses loaded supplies into the back of the white van. Suri double-checked the van's inventory before he signaled that the van was fully stocked and ready to go.

"All that remains is to put Miss Rodriguez into the van, as well," Suri announced. The three nurses responded and each of them left to retrieve Zenaida who was still sedated in one of the back exam rooms.

Iris climbed into the passenger seat of the van. She reached under the seat and withdrew a small, plastic carry case that resembled a miniature suitcase. Iris opened it and examined the contents within. The Glock 23 that she had used to dispatch Dr. Patel and the two Agency operatives was nestled snugly into the padding of one of the pistol-shaped slots. The other pistol-shaped slot, the one where Iris' mother kept her weapon, was empty. Iris' cell phone rested within a small zippered compartment on the underside of the lid. Iris stuffed the phone in her pocket. She closed the case quickly and shouted towards the back of the van. "I have to go get my weapon."

The back door to the van was still open. Kincaid stepped into view. "Which weapon?"

"My Glock," she said. "It's still in the exam room where we stashed Zenaida." Iris hopped out of her seat and circled the van. Kincaid met her on the other side.

"I'll get it," he said.

"What? You don't trust me?"

"Let me see," Kincaid said, pretending to consider her query. Then, he issued his blunt reply. "Hell no. You stay here."

"Fine," Iris said. "It's the exam room with the broken door."

Kincaid waved at her dismissively and disappeared into the building. Suri was securing the gurney upon which Zenaida would be transported. Iris rushed to his side.

"Give me the keys to the airport rental," she said in a hushed tone.

"What? Why?"

"Just give them to me. Hurry." Iris maneuvered back to the passenger side of the van. She opened the door and snatched the small gun case from the seat. She returned to Suri's side as he pulled the keys to their airport rental from his pocket. Iris snatched them from his grasp. "Listen. I'm going to text you Agent West's phone number. In exactly one hour, I need you to call him and tell him the surgery is going well with no complications whatsoever."

Suri was confused. As far he knew, Iris would be accompanying him to another Agency medical outpost to undergo the kidney transplant. That was the plan she had suggested to Agent West, after all. "Where are you going?"

"I'm going to get my mother."

"What? Now?"

"Just do it!" she snapped as she moved towards the rental sedan they acquired from the airport. "One hour. Got it?"

"And what do I tell *them*?" Suri asked nervously, gesturing towards the door, indicating Peppers and Kincaid.

Iris shrugged and offered a smug smile. "Tell them where I went." With that, Iris opened the door to the sedan and slid into the driver's seat. Within seconds, the engine was turning over. The car rolled backwards into the alley. Once it was clear of other cars, the sedan sprang forward and raced towards the far end of the road. Just then, Kincaid burst through the door to the building.

"I didn't see any gun," he said, before pausing to look around for Iris. A quick survey of the van turned up negative results. He looked at Suri, who pointed at the blazing red tail lights of the sedan that was turning the corner at the opposite end of the alley.

Kincaid raised his arms in disbelief. "Where is she go . . ." his voice trailed off as he, silently, answered his own unfinished question. Kincaid stood silent for a moment, dumbfounded. Finally, he turned to Suri. "I *really* don't like her."

❧❧

Peppers cringed as he reported the latest turn of events to Mr. Five. The knot in his stomach became tighter as Mr. One took over the conversation, making certain that Peppers knew just how displeased he was.

"How did she escape?" Mr. One asked.

"Uncertain, sir. The doctor sedated her. She should have been out for hours. I don't know how-"

"I know how," Mr. One interrupted him with an irritated tone. "Can you get her back?"

"Possibly. Iris seems to think the Freeman girl is returning to the place where Agent Molina was apprehended."

"That's a good bet, especially if Agent West is still there."

"What are your orders now, sir?" Peppers asked.

"They haven't changed. Do what you have to do."

"Yes, sir."

The line clicked and the call ended. The door to the situation room opened and Agent Kincaid rushed in. He wasted no words. "We've got a problem."

❧❧

Kelli passed two twenty-dollars bills to the cab driver. He took the fare and turned to count out Kelli's change. "Keep it," Kelli said. She didn't care about the six and a half bucks that he owed her. If she had more money, she would have gladly given him a larger tip in gratitude for getting her to her destination on Overlook Terrace so quickly.

Kelli stepped out of the cab and took a deep gulp of the chilly March air. She looked towards the buildings that were under the 24-hour guard of her father's security company, and she couldn't help but smile. Kelli had made it back safely. Her only regret was that she had to leave Zenaida behind.

Almost an hour had passed since she burst through the doors of the medical clinic and made a dash for her freedom. As she sprinted at full speed, it took only a second for her to get her bearings. After all, Kelli had spent most of her life in the Bronx, so it came as a comfort to her to see familiar surroundings as she ran through the parking lot on Riverdale Avenue. She turned quickly and took note of the name of the business that was displayed above the clinic door. After that, she did not look back again. It was a mere six minutes and three miles later before Kelli turned down a side-street, and then another. Two minutes later, she found herself in a residential neighborhood. It was there that she took a moment to catch her breath and confirm that she was not being pursued. She peered from behind a large tree on the sidewalk and kept an eye out for anything that she might deem suspicious; a slowing car, flashlights, even Iris herself who is the only other person who would have had a chance of keeping pace with Kelli on foot. Ten more minutes had passed before Kelli was convinced that she had made a clean break and had evaded any pursuers. She allowed herself to relax. Unfortunately, with relaxation came a cascade of overwhelming emotions that flooded her senses, causing her to fall to her knees in submission. She began to cry uncontrollably as images of Iris filled her mind's eye. Kelli fought against the image, forcing herself to remember the times she had spent with Francine many years ago. "They are not the same," she reminded herself. *Iris has your face, Francine. But she is not you.*

A pair of distant voices caused Kelli to stiffen. She heard accompanying footfalls that indicated two people were approaching. Kelli listened more closely and determined that the voices were male. Based on their conversation, Kelli surmised the males were young, high-school aged boys. Kelli's first instinct was to remain quiet behind the tree and allow the boys to stroll by her unaware. Then, another idea came to mind.

Kelli stood and wiped her tears away quickly. She stepped out in front of the boys as they reached her, startling them both. "Excuse me," she said quickly.

"Yo," the first boy said, his hand on his chest as if he was manually controlling his racing heartbeat. "What the hell? You almost caught it, shorty!"

"Word," the other boy agreed quickly. "You can't be jumping out at people in the dark. You crazy?"

Kelli looked the two young boys over rapidly. Both of them were African-American. The boy on the left was the same height as Kelli. He wore a fleece-lined, hooded sweatshirt that displayed a large New York Giants logo on the front. He wore a matching knitted cap, and a pair of jeans that hung loosely on his narrow frame. The other young boy was dressed in a black, hoodless sweatshirt and a pair of equally loose black jeans. A black Brooklyn Nets cap sat on his head. Even under the dark, moonlit sky, Kelli's keen eyesight allowed her to decipher a cell-phone-shaped bulge in the front pocket of the boy in the blue jeans.

"I'm sorry," Kelli apologized. She pointed at the bulge in the boy's pocket. "Can I use your phone?"

The boys exchanged a look that conveyed the message, *This girl is crazy.*' Kelli reached into her pocket and retrieved the money she'd stolen from Kincaid's wallet. She stripped off a twenty and brandished it in the moonlight.

"I need to make a phone call. It'll only take a minute."

The two young men surveyed the area quickly, trying to make certain that this was not some type of set-up or scam to steal their phones. After both young men had confirmed to one another that Kelli was alone, the first boy reached for his phone. It was an action that was not without a further act of circumspection. "You're alone, right? Nobody's gonna jump out and jack my cell?"

Kelli could appreciate the boy's wariness. She was a complete stranger after all. Kelli did her best to put the young boy at ease. "No. I promise. I just need to make one phone call. I swear."

The boy put out his hand. Kelli handed him the twenty in exchange for his cell phone. Ten seconds later, the phone was ringing. Kelli held her breath. The line clicked and a familiar voice came through the line loud and clear.

"Agent West."

Kelli exhaled. Her heart raced as she spoke into the phone. "Agent West. Thank God. It's Kelli."

"Kelli!" West responded excitedly. "Where are you?"

"I think I'm in Yonkers, somewhere near Highland-"

"Are you okay?" West asked quickly. "Are you safe?"

"Yes, I'm okay, I guess. I mean, I escaped, but Zenaida . . . West, they still have Zenaida." Kelli choked back tears. The two young boys exchanged a worried glance.

"I know," West said.

Kelli could hear Bling questioning West impatiently in the background, "Is she okay?"

"I'll come and get you," West offered.

"Don't worry about it," Kelli said. "I'll come there. I'm not far off the avenue so I'll just catch a cab."

"Are you sure?"

"Yes," she said, then added. "I know where she is."

"Zenaida? Where?"

Kelli rattled off the name of the medical clinic along with the address. West promised to contact the local PD and have them send a unit to investigate.

"Since you escaped, they probably won't be there when the cops arrive," West told her. "They have a way of disappearing into thin air."

"It's worth a shot," Kelli said. She looked at the two young boys and realized they had overheard more than they should have. Kelli decided to end the call. "I have to go. I'll be there soon."

"Are you sure? I can come get you," West repeated his offer.

"I'm sure. See you soon."

"Okay. Be safe."

Kelli ended the call and handed the phone to its owner. He looked at her, this time more closely. It was then that he noticed the bruising on her face. "Are you okay?" he asked sincerely.

"Do you want us to call you a cab?" the other boy asked.

Kelli smiled. She was touched by their concern. Still, she knew that they had heard and seen too much already.

The only way to keep them safe was to leave right then and there. "No," she said. "Thank you."

Kelli stepped around the boys and then accelerated into a sprint. Within sixty seconds, the boys were several blocks behind her. Kelli found her way to South Broadway and hailed a cab. She said, "Overlook Terrace, Manhattan," as she slid into the back seat, and then added, "As fast as you can," before closing the cab door. The cab driver nodded and sped away from the curb.

During the journey back to Overlook Terrace, the cabbie attempted to engage Kelli in conversation, but Kelli was too preoccupied with looking out of the rear window in search of pursuers to reciprocate his friendly banter.

True to his word, the cab driver traversed the distance in fifteen minutes. Kelli emerged from the back of the cab, happy to see the familiar landscape that included her father's job site. Kelli jogged across the street to where she had parked her Audi. She opened the door and pulled her backpack from the back seat. A rapidly approaching set of footfalls caught Kelli's attention. *Oh, God! They're here*, she thought fearfully. She reached around her back and pulled the Ruger from the waistband in her sweats. She turned and leveled the weapon at her would-be attacker.

"Kelli, it's me! It's me!" Monica Davies raised her arms. Her skin became instantly pale as terror caused the blood in her face to drain away. "Jesus Christ!"

Kelli lowered the weapon. A chill ran up her spine as she realized how close she had just come to shooting another human being at point blank range. "Agent Davies? What are you doing here?"

Davies lowered her arms. Her heart was still beating at an accelerated pace. "I could ask you the same thing." She took a step forward and gestured towards the pistol in Kelli's grasp. "Give me that before you kill someone."

Kelli did not hesitate. She handed the weapon over to Davies without a second thought. Davies inspected the weapon quickly. She was surprised to discover that it was not a Glock 23. She looked up at Kelli, confused. "Is this yours?"

"No," Kelli protested immediately.

Given the number of deceptions that she had recently uncovered about Kelli, Davies was not convinced. "No?"

"No, I swear."

"Where's your Glock?" Davies asked.

The question caught Kelli off guard. She opened her mouth to feign ignorance but her mind was too preoccupied with the question of how Davies knew she owned a weapon at all. Despite her urge to deny it, Kelli couldn't resist asking, "How did you know I-"

Davies was not in the mood for a Q and A. "Your Glock 23? Where is it?" Davies noticed the backpack that sat on the ground at Kelli's feet. "Is it in there?"

Kelli blinked. She realized that Davies' demeanor had transformed from her initial state of fear, to one of anger. It occurred to Kelli that Davies, like West, had, in fact, been looking for her. Kelli took a small step forward. "Is this about me not checking in with you? Is that why you and West suddenly showed up here?"

"Partially," Davies replied, annoyed that Kelli still had not answered her query about the Glock. "But we were primarily interested in proving that you aren't a murderer."

"What?" Kelli was confused. Though she had spent a major part of the night with Iris, Kelli was still unaware of Iris' connection to West and Davies' unexpected arrivals in New York. As far as Kelli knew, the two FBI agents were tracking her for breaking protocol.

"West didn't tell you?"

"Tell me what?"

Davies released a frustrated sigh. She was puzzled as to why West hadn't informed Kelli about the Agency-involved shooting, the investigation, and the perpetrator who fit her description. She looked at the tall, vacant buildings in the distance. "Take me to Agent West. It's time we all got on the same page."

16

Bling hugged Kelli tightly. He was genuinely happy to see her and was relieved that she had managed to escape. However, he could not shake the feeling of despair he felt when he thought about Zenaida and the violation she was about to endure. Kelli shared his anguish.

Agent West took the next few moments to explain how the investigation began; the explosion, the murder of Paul Ferry, and Iris. As West spoke, Kelli realized that, if not for Iris' description being so close to her own, no one would have ever come looking for her. No one would have noticed that she had broken protocol. Once Kelli had been brought up to speed on the investigation, she gave an account of what happened during her brief time in Iris' custody. Sadly, Kelli clarified that she had no choice but to leave Zenaida behind.

"The last time I saw Zenaida," Kelli explained, "she had just been sedated."

"So they can steal her kidney," Bling stated with disgust.

"Any word from the local police?" Kelli asked West.

The expression on West's face changed to one of hopelessness. "Yeah. PD went to the address you gave but found nothing out of the ordinary. All of the medical staff had the proper credentials and it didn't appear as if the back section of the facility was in use. I'm sorry, Kelli. They cleared out and left without a trace."

"Which means Iris still has Zenaida," Bling added.

Kelli nodded. "I don't think the doctor intends to harm her, I mean, beyond removing her kidney."

"That's harm enough," West said. "But I don't think the doctor is calling the shots. It's all Iris."

"No, it's not," Kelli corrected him. "It's the other two guys."

West turned to her. "What other two guys?"

"There were two agents that showed up the first time I tried to escape. Agent Kincaid and . . . Peppers, I think I heard them say. They stopped me. They're running the show."

West began to pace across the floor. "That changes things. Iris made it sound as if it was just her and the doctor." He paused and turned back to Kelli. "And they know where we are?"

"They do," Kelli confirmed.

"We need to get out of here," Davies suggested.

"Agreed," West said.

"What? It wasn't a good idea when *I* said it?" Bling complained.

"Why *are* you still here?" asked Davies.

"Quite honestly," West began, "there was nowhere else to go. I couldn't go to the New York field office or the local PD without fear of the Agency getting wind of us. Besides, Iris kidnapped Zenaida. Iris is the one in hiding, not us."

"Still, even if Iris *is* undergoing a kidney transplant, those other two agents could be on their way right now," Davies explained.

"Where are we going to go?" Bling questioned. "It's the middle of the night."

"We'll figure it out," West said. "In the meantime, let's stick to our plan. Davies, I need you to move Agent Molina to the far building at the end of the block. Bling, Kelli, this is where you two get off. There's no reason for you to stay. It's too dangerous."

"No way," Kelli objected. "The Agency cloned my best friend. They need to pay for that."

"Not to mention, they still have Zenaida," Bling chimed in. "You can't really expect us to sit on the sidelines."

West stood by his word. "Yes, I do. Kelli, I called your dad after you phoned me earlier. He's on his way to pick you up. Bling, you go with them."

Bling folded his arms and did not move. "I'm not going. I don't care what you say."

"We don't have time to argue about this, Bling."

"Then let's not argue," Bling said. "Let's grab Agent Molina so we can all get the hell out of here."

West took a moment to contemplate the current situation. He knew that he wanted to keep Bling and Kelli safe, especially now that Kelli had escaped capture. It didn't take him long to come to the conclusion that the best way to keep everyone safe, was for everyone to leave together. West swallowed his pride. "Okay. Let's make it happen. Bling, go help Davies move Agent Molina-"

"Actually," Davies interrupted. "Why don't *you* take Bling to move Molina. I'd like a moment with Kelli."

"Uh, sure," West agreed. "There's a set of two-way walkie-talkies just outside in the hallway. Grab as many as you can and meet us in the far building when you're done."

Davies agreed. West and Bling exited the office and headed for the room where Molina sat, tied to a chair. Davies and Kelli began gathering the radio equipment. As they did, Davies spoke.

"I know I seemed upset with you earlier," Davies began. "I guess I am, in a way. I wish you would have come to me, talked to me . . . I don't know . . . trusted me more."

"I'm sorry about ditching my scheduled check-ins, Agent Davies. But I felt as if nothing was being done to fix the problem. I was stuck in Boston, away from my family, while Mr. One and the Agency got to do as they pleased. I had to do something."

"You should have come to me," Davies repeated.

Kelli shook her head. "You would've tried to talk me out of it."

Davies pulled one of the two-way radios from its charging cradle and hooked it to her belt. She extended the cord that held the microphone behind her back, over her left shoulder, and then clipped the microphone to her jacket. "You're right. I definitely would have advised against owning that weapon in your bag."

"How do you even know about that?"

Davies handed a radio to Kelli. "I know a few things that I didn't know yesterday. For instance, I know that you drive a new car, you're renting a new apartment, and you have one hundred thousand dollars invested in a company called Quinlan Pharmaceuticals."

Kelli's jaw dropped. The quizzical expression on her face begged the unspoken question, *how did you know?* Davies was happy to oblige her.

"I broke into your apartment, your new apartment. Patrice Bass told me where you lived."

Kelli was speechless. She was stunned by the amount of information that Davies had uncovered. Kelli figured the information regarding her new address and new car would be easy enough to come by once Davies knew to look for them. Furthermore, she wasn't surprised that Davies had made contact with Patrice. However, Kelli was caught off guard by Davies' mention of Quinlan and the large sum of money she had invested there. Still, the most astonishing revelation was that Davies had broken into her apartment. Kelli's initial inclination was to respond angrily; to chastise Davies for violating her privacy and her trust. Unfortunately, Kelli realized that she did not have a right to make that argument, not when it was she who violated Davies' trust as well as the protocols that were in place to ensure her safety.

Davies continued. "You should have known I'd come looking for you sooner or later, Kelli. This investigation only accelerated the inevitable."

Kelli strapped the two-way radio on to her body in the same manner as Davies. She remained silent as she processed everything that Davies was telling her.

Davies could see Kelli's wheels turning. She thought back to her conversation with Dr. Hughes and now, for the first time, could actually see the turmoil that boiled just beneath the surface of Kelli's skin. In that moment, Davies' heart went out to her. She placed a hand on Kelli's shoulder, and then asked softly, "You want to tell me what's going on?"

Kelli took a deep breath. She hadn't planned on telling anyone what she had been up to, at least not yet. She had imagined relaying this story after the fact, once her plan had worked and she had her life as Kelli Freeman back. But now, for whatever reason, the moment just seemed right. Slowly, Kelli began to talk.

"I wanted to find a way to get back to my old life. I hate living in Boston and I had grown impatient. I decided to take matters into my own hands but I knew I wouldn't get very far if I was still tethered to the FBI; to you. So, I started avoiding you; cancelling our face-to-face meetings. I returned your calls in order to quell any suspicions you might have had that I was up to something. Initially, it was just a game I was playing to see if I could do it. It was a little easier once I moved out of the Farmers' house and got my first apartment. But after I won the money, I saw no reason to delay my plans."

"The money. Where'd you get it?"

Kelli tried to stifle a grin. She failed. "While I was living with the Farmers, I discovered that I could count cards. I practiced and honed the ability for two years before I was old enough to get into the casinos in Atlantic City. I spent a couple weeks going from one casino to the next."

"You could have been caught."

"I was careful. I allowed myself to lose plenty of money before I won it all back."

"What about Quinlan Pharmaceuticals?" Davies asked. "Why invest so much money with them?"

Kelli grabbed two more radios. She strapped each one to her waistband and clipped the microphones to their bases. She turned to Davies. "Do you remember Jeremy Platt?"

Davies thought for a moment. "The journalist? Weren't you captured by the Agency at Platt's house seven years ago? The night Platt was killed."

Kelli nodded. "About fifteen years ago, Jeremy Platt ran an exposé about Congresswoman Betty Royce."

Davies' eyes widened. "I found pictures of her and her father on your camera."

Kelli raised an eyebrow. *What else did she find while she was snooping around in my apartment?* Kelli continued. "Well, according to the papers at the time, Platt had accused Betty Royce of gaining her position in politics by sleeping her way to the top. Supposedly, it was a huge scandal."

"I think I remember something like that," Davies said.

"You were supposed to," Kelli responded. "I have a friend, a hacker, who's incredibly talented. He uncovered Platt's original news story. The 'sleeping around' scandal was fabricated. It was a false story circulated by the media to cover up what Platt had really discovered."

"Which was?"

"Betty Royce's entire political platform is grounded in healthcare reform. Platt discovered that Royce accepted sizeable campaign contributions from Quinlan Pharmaceuticals in exchange for pushing an agenda that would be beneficial to Quinlan. When Platt released the story, he was advised to let it go."

A light bulb came on in Davies' head. "Wait a minute. Jeremy Platt is the guy to whom Dr. Connelly gave the original Harmony Project papers. Platt knew about the super-soldier program, and Harmony June."

"Yes, and when Platt began investigating Dr. Connelly's claims, he discovered which pharmaceutical company was supplying the Agency with the unapproved experimental drugs and equipment for the super-soldier program."

"Quinlan."

"Bingo," Kelli confirmed. "Platt's discovery of Quinlan is what led him to Betty Royce. Platt ran the story. Two days later, the story disappeared along with Platt's career."

"And you believe the Agency is behind it all?" Davies scratched her head. "I don't get it. Why invest your money there?"

"Becoming a shareholder was the only way I could track Quinlan's earnings. My hacker found out that Quinlan sold public stocks through a private auction; only the super-wealthy were privy to it. Granted, I only had enough money to buy a few shares, but it was enough to get me quarterly reports."

"To what end?"

Kelli's eyes narrowed and her tone was serious. "The key to destroying any business is destroying their income stream. I don't know how I'm going to do it yet, but I'm going to take down the Agency, and Quinlan Pharmaceuticals is the key."

❧❦

To say that her heart was racing would have been a gross understatement. Never before had dialing a phone number caused such stress to the point where her hand was shaking. In truth, some of the stress that Swann was feeling was self-induced. She couldn't believe that she had lost track of her target. That had never happened before, so Swann was having difficulty accepting her failure. Still, the stress of losing Kyle paled in comparison to the duty of having to report that failure.

Her hand continued to shake as she punched the final number into her phone and pressed send. The phone only rang twice before it was answered and Swann reported the latest occurrence.

"You lost her?" the unhappy voice on the phone asked. "Explain."

Swann recapped the events of the last few hours. She began with tracking Kyle to a set of buildings on. . . a quick look at her notes. . . Overlook Terrace. Swann recounted the unexpected abduction of Kyle, along with another woman, and then explained the events that transpired at the medical clinic.

There was an awkward silence on the other end of the phone, and then, "Report back to D.C. immediately. Your work is done."

"But I can pick up her trail again. If not on Overlook Terrace, then perhaps at her hotel or-"

"The close-up photo you sent earlier was satisfactory," the voice interrupted. "Report back to D.C."

Swann opened her mouth to protest further. She wanted to finish the job. As she searched for the proper words to say, the voice on the other end of the phone filled the void.

"Immediately." With that, the phone line clicked, and the call ended.

Swann sat in her car in silence for several moments. After losing Kyle, she had turned onto a side street and deliberated with herself over her next move. *Do I call it in, or do I just say screw it and go look for her?* She reminded herself that saying '*screw it*' at the clinic is what led to Kyle running right past her. Perhaps if Swann was already in her car when Kyle burst through the doors, then maybe, just maybe, she could have caught up with her before she disappeared into the adjacent neighborhood. But no, it didn't happen that way, and Swann didn't want to risk anything else going wrong by not following protocol a second time. Instead, she made the call. And now, she'd been ordered back to D.C. Though she felt the compulsion to go rogue once again, Swann wouldn't want to face the consequences if she mishandled this case any further.

Feeling resigned and defeated, Swann started the engine to her dark, cherry-colored rental and drove away. As she maneuvered through the Bronx towards the expressway, her mind kept returning to one regret. *I didn't find out what's really going on. Goddammit.*

⚜

West and Bling guided Agent Molina through the door and out into the night. The light fixtures and the moonlight offered just enough light for Molina to see the tarred pathway beneath her feet. Her hands were still bound behind her back, and she could tell that something more than just changing locations was going on.

"Why are you moving me?" Molina asked.

"As if you don't know," Bling snapped.

They walked slowly along the path en route to the building at the far end of the block. West spoke to Molina without turning to look at her.

"It seems as if you lied to us, Agent Molina," West said.

"What are you talking about? I told you everything you asked."

"You left out the part about two Agency operatives being part of your team," West replied.

Molina's heart began to pound slightly harder. "What operatives? What are you talking about?"

"Don't bother denying it," Bling advised her with a hard tug on her right arm. "Our girl escaped. She told us about the other two agents."

"Iris failed to mention it, as well," West added.

"Iris? You spoke to her?" Molina asked.

"I did," West answered. "But she didn't mention anything about Agent Peppers or Kincaid."

Molina was confused. *Those two clowns back in D.C.? What are they doing here?* "I have no idea what you're talking about. I swear. There were no other agents with us."

"Well, they're there now." Bling said bluntly.

"No," Molina said. Her voice was laden with fear. "If there are Agency men here, that means they found us."

Bling refused to buy her story. "Give it a rest."

"It's too soon," Molina said. Tears welled up in her eyes as she proceeded to ramble under her breath. "If you spoke to her, then there's no way the transplant could have been completed before the two agents arrived; there wasn't enough time. And if they arrived after you spoke to her, then they could have stopped the transplant and taken her back to the Agency."

"Shut the hell up," Bling ordered her.

They approached the door to the far building. West pulled Arthur's key from his pocket and slid it into the lock.

"Agent West, call her again," Molina pleaded. "I need to know if Iris is okay. I need to know-"

West reached behind Molina's back and tugged hard on the ropes that bound her wrists. The unexpected jerk caused Molina to lose her balance. West stopped her fall, and then brought his face close to Molina's.

"Know this," West said through gritted teeth. "The only reason I've gone along with your play for this long is so I can keep Zenaida Rodriguez alive. I don't care about Iris. As far as I'm concerned, your daughter is a murderer, and if I find out you're lying to me, and your daughter and those agents pull something, I will greet them as I do all murderers, with lethal force."

∽∾

Peppers and Kincaid parked several blocks from the buildings on Overlook Terrace where, earlier, they had witnessed the capture of Agent Molina and the kidnapping of Zenaida Rodriguez. They double-checked their weapons as they moved slowly down the sidewalk towards the intersection that led to the buildings.

Kincaid spoke to Peppers. The volume of his voice was just above a whisper. "You think it was safe to let Suri run off like that?"

"Yeah," Peppers answered. "The doctor's main concern is Iris. He won't leave until she's had her transplant. He'll be at the rendezvous point as planned."

The two Agency operatives reached the intersection. The four large buildings were nestled towards the end of the next block, not far from residential housing on both sides of the street.

A rustling in the bushes behind Kincaid startled him. He whirled around. His hand went to his holster. There, standing inconspicuously amidst the trees and tall grass, was Iris.

Iris smiled smugly. "Relax. It's only me."

Peppers took a step towards her. Despite his attempt to remain calm, Peppers was visibly angry and frustrated. "You are going to get yourself killed, young lady. This isn't a game."

"I never said it was," Iris replied, her smile gone. "But you might want to step in here for cover. Someone might see you."

"I'm not climbing into the bushes," Kincaid protested, his annoyance with Iris was clear, as well. "If you weren't a kid, I swear I would strangle you right here."

"You're endangering this whole op," Peppers said. Iris shook her head quickly. "Actually, I was just conducting a little surveillance while I waited for you to show up."

Peppers and Kincaid exchanged a glance.

"What?" Iris asked innocently. "Dr. Suri told you I was here, right?"

"Yes," Peppers snapped, "but that still doesn't give you the right to run off without us." The older agent took a deep breath. He had allowed himself to become emotional, and to Peppers, emotionality invited recklessness. He forced out a heavy sigh. "What have you found out?"

Iris resisted smiling. "As far as I can tell, they are operating out of this first building directly in front of us and that far building down there. I saw two men escorting my mother to that far building about five minutes ago. It sounded as if they were discussing something, maybe even arguing."

"And you didn't try to rescue her?" Kincaid asked.

"I thought about it," Iris confessed. "But I haven't gauged their numbers yet. I didn't want to charge in and find myself suddenly outnumbered."

"You mean like you and your mother did when you kidnapped the girl earlier?" Kincaid said, taunting her.

Iris glared at Kincaid. She wanted to curse at him and tell him *where to go*. Unfortunately, she could not. Kincaid was right. Despite the many years of training that Agent Molina and Iris had between them, they underestimated the situation when they kidnapped Zenaida Rodriguez. In their desperation to abduct Zenaida, they overlooked their inadequate assessment and, as a result, Agent Molina was captured. Iris was in no rush to repeat that mistake. Instead of spouting a nasty pejorative at Kincaid, Iris offered a reluctant, "Yeah."

"Smart," Peppers admitted. "So you don't know how many people are in this first building?"

"No," Iris said. "I was hoping to have an idea before you . . ." Iris' voice trailed off. In the distance, she saw movement along the path that circled around to the side of the first building. "Take cover," she whispered to the two adult agents.

Peppers and Kincaid stepped into the bushes and crouched down. A moment later, two bodies emerged onto the path across the street.

"I can't tell who it is," Kincaid whispered. "Once they pass that light post-"

"It's Kelli Freeman," Iris whispered back. "She's with a white woman I've never seen before."

"How can you possibly see that far in this light?" Peppers asked, unaware of Iris' enhanced vision.

"It's them," she assured him. "It looks like they are headed for the far building."

"Could be where they're setting up shop," Kincaid suggested to Peppers, who nodded in agreement.

"We'll remain staked out here for a few minutes. If there aren't any more of them roaming around, we'll assume it's just the four of them and your mother."

"Then we'll make our move?" Iris asked eagerly.

Peppers nodded in the darkness. "Then we'll make our move."

WASHINGTON, D.C.

Mr. Two entered the conference room. He reached for the wall and flicked the light switch into the *on* position. The light illuminated the room. Mr. Two was not surprised to find that the room was already occupied by a sole individual. Mr One.

Mr. One did not react to the lights coming on around him. In fact, Mr. One was deeper in thought than he imagined he ever could be. This week had not been kind to him. No. Not kind at all. First, he received word that Dr. Patel had run off with the latest super-soldier subject, Iris Molina. Soon after the Patel situation was resolved, his family oncologist called with his daughter's terminal diagnosis. Within hours, Agent Molina, too, had run off with young Iris, only this time, Dr. Suri accompanied them. Within a day, the news that Kelli Freeman was, in fact, alive reached his ear. Though Mr. One did not show it, he was hopeful. Perhaps he had found his miracle; a cure for cancer. Then, like a dangling carrot that falls from the string into a pool of mud, Kelli Freeman escaped. No, Mr. One did not react to the light in the room. For Mr. One, it was difficult to see light anywhere right now.

Two crossed the room. "I wasn't sure if you'd gone home," he said to One.

Mr. One stared at the wall blankly. "No point. I'm not sleeping well right now anyway."

"I just wanted to inform you that A.D. Marsh just requested a phone trace from Langley."

"Interesting," One responded stoically. "Marsh must have a friend there."

"Should I kill it?"

One pondered for a moment. "Let it go through. No need to arouse suspicion."

"Also," Two continued. "We broke the encryption on Patel's phone. We traced the call to a geneticist named Raj Naran in South Carolina."

"A geneticist. Hmm. Send a few agents to pay Dr. Naran a visit."

"And if he has a family?"

"Make him understand that his silence is their salvation."

"And if he's single?" Two asked. "Should we eliminate him?"

One considered the options. Then, "No. Bring him in. If he's talented, we could use him."

"Very well." A brief pause. "Are you going to be alright, Roger?" Two asked.

One turned his head and gazed at his longtime friend and colleague. "I don't know. I need to go make a phone call. Ask me again in an hour."

MANHATTAN, NEW YORK

"Everything locked up over there?" West asked Kelli and Davies as they entered the large room on the first floor of the back building. Though the room was practically vacant, save a few computer desks and an equal amount of soft computer chairs, it was easy to tell that this room was being renovated to serve as a lobby or reception area. Davies handed a radio to West. Agent Molina sat on a computer chair in the corner. The light in the room had been adjusted to a low level of illumination.

"All locked up," Davies replied.

"Good." West turned to Kelli. "Your father should be here any minute. I want you and Bling to go."

"We already discussed this, man," Bling reminded him. "We're staying."

West's eyes narrowed in Bling's direction, but he decided not to respond. Instead, West pointed to the stairs. "Take Agent Molina upstairs, fourth floor will do."

Though Bling did not respond, he did, however, stroll across the room to retrieve Agent Molina. West's phone rang and he answered the call on the second ring.

"Agent West," he announced.

It was A.D. Marsh. "West. I've got a colleague on the line who works over at Langley. He's ready to complete the trace on that number you gave me."

"Great. Let's do it."

"West, be advised that as soon as he runs the trace, it is likely that the Agency will know you're tracking one of their operatives. This might bring more heat to your doorstep that you can handle."

Marsh was right. Still, West was not shaken by Marsh's warning in the slightest. "The person in possession of that phone could lead us right to Zenaida Rodriguez. I have to risk it."

"Very well," Marsh said. "Stand by."

The mention of Zenaida's name caused Bling to pause at the doorway as he was leaving to escort Molina to higher ground. Molina was glad Bling stopped. She, like Bling, was very interested in West's conversation.

Marsh's voice came back on the line. This time, however, he seemed confused. "Agent West? Didn't you say your location was on Overlook Terrace in Manhattan?"

"Yes, sir, it is."

"According to the phone trace, that phone is at the same location."

West's brow furled at the news. He looked at Kelli. "Kelli. Did you bring that phone back with you somehow?"

"No," Kelli said, shaking her head. "I left it at the medical clinic."

"Then how come Marsh is telling me . . .?" It took a fraction of a second for the answer to West's unfinished question to flash across his mind. "Holy crap," West spoke rapidly into the phone. "Sir, send a team. They're here."

"What?" Davies questioned as she reached for her weapon instinctively.

West disconnected the call and began barking orders to the others in the room. "Bling, take Molina upstairs. Don't take your eyes off of her. Kelli, find someplace to hide. Davies, find cover." West moved quickly to the wall and turned off the lights.

Everyone scattered as they followed West's commands. Bling hurried Molina down the hall to the stair well. He pushed open the door at the end of the hall and began ascending the stairs, pulling Molina alongside him.

Kelli grabbed her backpack and moved into the corridor located on the far side of the room. She turned and ducked into the first room on her left and crouched down. She reached into her backpack and felt around for a moment. Her hand moved past her track phone, which began to vibrate. Seconds later, she pulled her Glock 23 from the bag. Kelli groped inside the bag again, found an inside zipper, and then pulled it aside. She reached into the small pocket and retrieved the clip for her firearm. She shoved the clip into the magazine well and racked the weapon, chambering the first round. Kelli could feel the blood coursing through her veins as her heart rate kicked into overdrive. An eerie silence fell over the area as if all of the air had been sucked out of the room. Though she tried to focus on any sound whatsoever, Kelli heard nothing. One minute later, she heard Agent West yell, "Freeze! Drop your weapon," followed by a single gunshot.

17

Arthur pushed the gear shift into the park position and then turned the key, silencing the engine. He had advised West to move Agent Molina to the far building, so Arthur parked his car around the bend on 184th Street. He was eager to get inside so he could bring Kelli home. He had already phoned Diane and told her of Kelli's escape. Diane broke down into tears of joy when she heard the news and urged Arthur to hurry and bring their girl home.

Arthur tapped the button on the key fob in his hand, locking the car doors remotely. As he approached the building, he could see dim light emanating through the windows on the first floor and surmised that West and the others must already be inside. Arthur quickened his pace. As he stepped onto the pathway that led to the building's front entrance, the lights inside went out suddenly. Arthur stopped in his tracks. The instincts he had developed after twenty-five years on the force told him that something wasn't right. He considered dialing West's cell phone to find out what was happening inside. Instead, he decided to call Kelli.

Arthur pulled his trac-phone from his back pocket and pressed speed dial number 9. The screen flashed and displayed the message: Calling KC. The phone rang four times before Arthur ended the call, put away his phone, and pulled out his firearm. He crossed the distance to the front entrance. Gently and slowly, he grabbed the knob and gave it a soft turn. The door was locked. He reached into his coat pocket where he kept the master key for all of the entrance doors. Carefully, he inserted the key and rotated it to the left. He pulled the key from the lock and stuffed it back into his jacket pocket. He gripped the knob once again. This time, the knob turned. Slowly, Arthur pulled the door open. With his weapon at eye level, Arthur inched into the corridor. He moved to the far wall and placed his back against it. He crouched down, and then began making his way through the corridor to the future reception area that opened up ahead.

Arthur could see stray beams of moonlight entering through the elevated windows of the reception area. As he reached the end of the hallway, Arthur's weapon reflected a stream of moonlight. Suddenly, a voice screamed at him from the darkness.

"Freeze! Drop your weapon!"

Instinctively, Arthur dropped to the floor and rolled into a pocket of darkness on the other side of the hall. A gunshot sounded. Arthur crouched against the wall. He pointed his weapon towards the reception area. *Wait,* he thought. *I know that voice.*

"Agent West?" Arthur called out hopefully.

A few seconds ticked by before West responded, "Arthur?"

Arthur relaxed, but only slightly. "It's me," he said. "You okay?" Arthur squinted into the darkness. Finally, Agent West stepped into a stream of moonlight. There was a look of worry on his face.

"I should be asking you," West said as he moved towards Arthur. "Please tell me I missed."

"We're good. You didn't shoot me."

"Thank God."

"Where's Kelli?" Arthur asked.

Kelli stepped into the reception area. "I'm here."

Arthur turned towards the sound of his daughter's voice. Though there was very little illumination in the room, he had no problem navigating the space in order to reach her. They embraced and held each other tightly. "Oh my God, you had me so worried."

"I'm okay, Daddy," Kelli said through a rush of unexpected tears.

West and Davies approached them from behind. "I hate to break this up, but we can't stay here," West announced.

"What's going on?" Arthur asked.

"Let's get upstairs," West said. "I'll explain on the way."

⁂

Bling escorted Agent Molina up two flights of stairs. He pushed her ahead of him while keeping a tight grip on each of her arms. Molina misjudged a step and stumbled near the top of the stairs, mere inches shy of the third-floor landing. She regained her balance before her knees slammed against the stairs.

"Slow down," Molina sneered at Bling.

Bling ignored her. "Keep moving." He gave Molina a hard shove.

Suddenly, the sound of a gunshot rang out from the first floor. Startled, Bling turned slightly. "What the-"

Molina turned as well. She noticed Bling's attention had been diverted by the unmistakable sound of a firearm discharge. Without a second thought, Molina took advantage of the distraction. She extended her right leg and launched a back-snap kick into Bling's stomach. The unexpected blow caused Bling to relinquish his grasp on Molina, and sent him flailing uncontrollably down the stairs.

Bling landed hard on his back. The momentum of the fall, coupled with gravity, caused Bling to tumble helplessly, end over end, down the steep steps. He groaned in pain as he landed on his left arm, then his knees, then the back of his head. He slammed into the wall. He reached out aimlessly and managed to grab hold of the handrail. He stopped his rapid descent at the expense of pulling a muscle in his right shoulder. He howled in pain. The sound of footfalls landing on the stairs above him told him that Agent Molina was on the move. Still, he looked up. Just as he expected, Agent Molina was gone.

Agent Davies kept her weapon at eye-level as she moved into the large room located halfway down the hall on the fourth floor. The dim beams of light outlined a waiting area that sat in front of a counter that separated another area of the room. Off to the right, there was another door. From the layout, Davies surmised that this space was once used as a private doctor's office of some kind. Her eyes darted around the room looking for any signs of movement. Davies saw none. Unfortunately, this was not what she expected.

"Where's Bling?" Davies asked as West, Arthur and Kelli filed into the room behind her.

West looked around. "I don't know. He was supposed to meet us in here."

"Are you sure?" Arthur asked.

West nodded. "Yeah. He chose this room because there's another exit through that door there."

"Makes sense," Arthur said. "We've been guarding these buildings for months. He knows the layout well."

"All the more reason that he should have been here by now," West added.

"Should I call him?" Kelli asked, gesturing towards the two-way radio that hung from her waistband.

"No," West responded quickly. "If something is wrong and he's hiding somewhere, calling him could alert someone to his location."

A lump of fear lodged in Kelli's chest. The thought of Bling being alone right now terrified her. "But what if he needs us?" Kelli questioned.

West and Davies exchanged a worried look. Arthur saw their visual exchange and voiced their unspoken concern. "It's too risky, Kel."

"But, Daddy-"

"I'm sorry," Arthur said. "Until we know where these people are, we can't risk it."

Kelli turned to the other door in the room. "Maybe he's in there." Kelli maneuvered around her father and stepped towards the side door. She reached for the door, but then stopped cold. *What is that?* Kelli turned her head to the side slightly and sniffed the air. A familiar scent tapped faintly at her senses. *Oh, God. I know that cologne.*

Kelli turned to the group and pointed at the door through which they had just entered. "They're outside."

West barked an order. "Everybody get down."

As everyone dove for the floor, bullets splintered the wooden door that led to the hallway. Almost simultaneously, the door was violently forced open. Standing on either side of the door were Agents Peppers and Kincaid. The barrels of their weapons peeked just beyond the door frames, each one firing rounds into the room in rapid succession.

Davies rolled to her right. Bullets slammed into the wall above her. She raised her weapon and returned fire. Arthur, who had rolled into a position in front of Kelli, returned fire as well. West had fallen to the floor, rolled onto his back, and began shooting at the main door in concert with the others.

In the hallway, Peppers and Kincaid took refuge on either side of the doorway. Kincaid made a hand gesture to Peppers in the shape of a gun. Peppers responded by raising three fingers. Kincaid nodded.

Inside the room, Arthur reached up from his position on the floor and pulled the side door open wide enough for a person to slip through the doorway. Davies crawled on all fours and managed to scramble behind the counter.

West saw a flash of movement in the doorway. He squeezed the trigger of his Sig repeatedly, laying down suppression fire to keep their attackers from drawing a bead on anyone in the room. "Go," he yelled to Arthur.

Arthur sprang to his hands and knees, pulling Kelli into a kneeling position next to him. Davies joined West in firing rounds at the doorway, giving Arthur and Kelli the cover, they needed to slip into the adjacent room.

Davies kept firing as West rolled towards the side door. He aimed his weapon towards the main door, and fired two more rounds. West had kept count of the number of bullets he had fired. He knew there was only one more bullet left in his weapon. With his left hand, he tapped the magazine release button. As the clip fell from his weapon, West pulled a fully loaded clip from his belt and slammed it into the magazine well. Without missing a beat, West continued firing.

Davies, also a Quantico graduate, was very familiar with how to 'combat load'. As soon as West commenced firing again, Davies followed the same procedure for reloading her weapon in a combat situation. Within seconds, Davies was locked and loaded once again.

Outside the door, Peppers pulled a small, thin flashlight from his shirt pocket. He held it up and looked at his younger partner. Kincaid, who was aware of their orders, knew the time had come. For an instant, his mind wandered back to the conversation he and Peppers had the previous morning. *We're supposed to be the good guys*, he told himself again. *These guys are FBI. Aren't these the good guys, too? Aren't we all on the same team?* Kincaid knew this wasn't the time to debate the morality of his mission. Even if he did have a moment to discuss it with Peppers, Kincaid knew already what Peppers would say: *We get an assignment, we carry it out. We don't ask why.* Kincaid swallowed hard as he forced himself to accept the situation, and his orders. Besides, Peppers hadn't steered him wrong yet. With that, Kincaid responded with two quick nods.

Peppers raised the flashlight above his head, extending his arm. He pressed the button, and with one quick motion, moved the tip of the flashlight into the room, illuminating it briefly.

Reflexively, West and Davies aimed their weapons at the sudden flash of light. As they squeezed their triggers, Kincaid took a step back, and glanced quickly into the room. From the angle at which he stood, Kincaid caught only a small glimpse of Davies behind the counter. West and Davies fired at the flashlight. Peppers dropped it. As he did, Kincaid peered into the room once again, this time, however, he demonstrated why he was recruited by the Agency in the first place. From his hip, he pointed his weapon into the room and fired once. Then, as quickly as he had fired, he took refuge on the left side of the doorway once again.

West, from his position in the room, heard the single gunshot that was fired into the room. What he failed to hear now, however, was the discharge of Davies' weapon. An ice-cold wave swept through West's torso as he realized that Davies had just been killed or seriously injured. Sweat beaded from his forehead as another realization set in. He was a sitting duck.

Peppers looked at Kincaid inquisitively. Kincaid responded with a quick 'thumbs up'. As Peppers' flashlight fell, Kincaid saw his bullet land squarely in the center of Davies' forehead, followed by the splatter of blood on the wall behind her which resulted from the projectile exiting the back of her skull. Again, Kincaid repeated the gun shaped hand gesture. This time, Peppers raised only one finger, signifying that only one shooter remained. With that same finger, Peppers pointed into the room. It was time to move in and end the gunfight.

Arthur and Kelli crawled into the adjacent space that sat beyond the side door. Instantly, Arthur sprang to his feet, pulling Kelli away from the door where the gunfight between West, Davies and the two Agency operatives continued to blaze. The room was wide and stretched for several feet. There was a door frame on the opposite wall but no door in place. A second room was visible beyond the door frame. Arthur led Kelli into the second room. As he crossed the threshold, he saw another exit door that, undoubtedly, led back into the hallway.

Kelli shook uncontrollably. The sound of weapons discharge from the other room brought back frightening memories of seven years ago when West, Bling and she found themselves in a similar fight for their lives in James Connelly's Pasadena home. *Oh, God. How can this be happening to me again?*

Arthur pulled her into the far corner of the room and pushed her to the floor. "Stay down," he whispered, and began to turn away. Kelli reached out and grabbed his arm.

"Where are you going?" Kelli asked fearfully.

"I can't leave them in there alone," Arthur said quickly.

"But Daddy-"

"Stay down," he repeated. Arthur pulled his arm away. He turned and moved towards the exit door. He glanced back at Kelli. "I'll be right back," he said. Arthur pulled the door open, stepped through the doorway, and disappeared into the hall.

West considered making a desperate leap through the side door. Unfortunately, with no cover fire from Davies, there was no way to defend himself while he made his move. Instead, West dove for the front wall. He landed against the wall with a very audible thud. He crouched against the wall with his weapon trained on the main door. From his current position, anyone standing in the hallway would have to look into the room in order to see him. When they did, West was prepared to squeeze the trigger.

In the hallway, Peppers nodded at his partner. Simultaneously, he and Kincaid moved towards the door. Just as they were about to cross into the room, Peppers caught a glimpse of a shadowed figure moving towards them from behind Kincaid's position. His heart jumped.

"Get down," he yelled at Kincaid. Unfortunately, his warning came too late.

Arthur fired two shots that landed squarely in Kincaid's back. Kincaid stumbled forward towards Peppers, who, out of sheer reflex, tried to break his partner's fall. He was unsuccessful as Peppers was forced backwards. He lost his footing and fell to the ground, bringing Kincaid down on top of him.

Arthur continued to advance on Peppers' and Kincaid's position on the floor. He squinted to distinguish their shapes from the darkness. As he moved closer, he managed to see one of the bodies being pushed aside. The man on the bottom raised his weapon. Arthur dove backwards and to the side of the hallway for cover as the man fired blindly in his direction. Two bullets sailed over

Arthur while one other embedded itself into the wall just inches from his head. Arthur pushed off from the wall and rolled onto his back. He aimed his weapon in his assailant's direction and fired four shots in rapid succession. He paused for a moment, and listened. He heard frantic scuffling down the hall, away from his position. Arthur looked up and could barely make out the shape of the man retreating towards the back stairwell. Arthur leveled his weapon to take aim, but then West appeared in the doorway, startling him.

"Arthur?" West questioned.

"Yeah," he answered. "You guys all right?"

West shook his head. His attention was drawn to the man's body on the floor. Then, his thoughts went to Davies. "I don't think so. Where's Kelli?"

Arthur pulled himself to a standing position. "She's safe," he answered. "She's in the other room."

"Take your daughter and get out of here, Arthur."

"What about you guys?" Arthur asked. He stared directly into West's eyes. It was then that he knew. He glanced into the room behind West but saw no one standing there. He attempted, unsuccessfully, to ignore the blood splatter on the back wall. His heart grew heavy in his chest.

West thought about Davies, who was either dead or injured in the room behind him. There was an icy feeling still chilling him from the inside. "Let the FBI handle this from here," he said stoically. "Your job is to get your daughter to safety."

The veteran cop in Arthur wanted to assist West in handling the situation, especially now that West was alone. However, the father in him agreed with West. Kelli's safety was paramount, and it was his duty as her father to protect her. Arthur nodded. "Okay. The other guy ran down the hall. There's a back stairwell so he could be headed anywhere in the building."

"Got it," West said.

"What about Bling?" Arthur questioned.

"I'll find him," West answered quickly. "Go."

Arthur turned and headed back to the room where he had left Kelli crouched in the corner. Within seconds, he and Kelli were moving quickly down the corridor towards the front stairwell.

West, in the meantime, walked back into the room. He took a deep breath before circling the counter. Though the blood splatter on the back wall had already confirmed his suspicion, West walked behind the counter anyway. There, lying on the floor with a single bullet hole in her forehead was Special Agent Monica Davies. Immediately, uncontrollably, West burst into tears. He cursed under his breath as a mixture of sadness and rage erupted inside of him. The anger was so consuming, so overwhelming, that West felt as though it was burning his internal organs. Images of his past relationship with Davies flashed before his eyes. His knees gave out and he fell hard upon them. *Dear God, why? How can this. . . wasn't it just two days ago that we were on an op in Indiana?* Crying and motionless, West rested on his knees for several moments before he became aware of his situation once again. Though he didn't want to abandon Davies' body, West knew that he had a job to finish. One of the Agency operatives was still loose in the building, and Bling and Agent Molina were both unaccounted for. He would have to save his mourning for later.

West could hear the faint wail of distant sirens coming from the darkness outside. It wouldn't be long before the building would be a surrounded by NYPD's finest. West knelt down and retrieved Davies' firearm. He shoved it into his shoulder holster. He knelt again, this time, over Davies' corpse, and felt around her waist area. Strapped to the front of her belt, off to the left, was her remaining clip. It was fully stocked. West pulled the clip from her belt, stood and then exited into the room.

West stepped into the hallway. His heart skipped a beat at the unexpected sight of a man standing in the corridor. The man's back was turned to West, and there was a pistol in his left hand. West looked to the floor and realized that the fallen Agency operative was no longer there. Instead, the man was standing right in front of him. Suddenly, the man, Kincaid, turned around.

Bling raced up the stairs towards the sixth floor. If his ears had not betrayed him, he was certain that Agent Molina had only run up three flights before she managed to pull open the door and make her way out of the stairwell.

He pulled the door open and stepped into the wide hallway of the sixth floor. He reached to the rear of his tactical belt and yanked his flashlight from its holder. He flicked the switch and illuminated the long corridor that stretched out before him. There were several rooms on both sides of the hallway, most of which had no door. Still, there were quite a few that did have doors, and Agent Molina could be hiding behind any one of them. Bling knew he had to find her before she found a way to get out of her bonds. He had already tangled with Molina in the street earlier, so he was well aware of just how dangerous she could be.

Bling moved down the corridor slowly, pausing every three or four steps to stop and listen for any sounds that would lead him to Molina. He stopped at the first door on the right and twisted the knob gently. The door was unlocked. Bling knew that, with the exception of a few, most of the doors would not have the locks engaged. He surmised that Molina would choose a room with an unlocked door over a room with no door at all. Considering that Molina's hands were still bound behind her back, Bling figured her best chance of freeing herself would be to secure herself in a room by locking the door, and then working on the rope that held her wrists together. *How difficult would it be for her to lock a door behind her while her hands are tied?* he wondered to himself. Bling was unsure of the answer, so in the interest of being thorough, he opened the door. A quick check of the room revealed it to be empty. Bling turned and continued down the hallway, checking each door he came upon. Bling stepped in front of the fifth door in the hallway. He turned the knob. The door opened and Bling shined his light inside the room. Except for a small desk, this room was empty as well. Bling took a step into the room when, suddenly, the sound of gunfire began emanating from somewhere on the floors beneath him. Bling knew it was the fourth floor. That's where he was supposed to meet Kelli and the others, before he was kicked down a flight of stairs and lost his captive.

"Dammit," he cursed aloud. The thought of his friends being ambushed frightened him, but Bling couldn't just stand there while Kelli and the others were in danger of being killed. He considered turning back and running towards the main stairwell. Instead, he continued down the hallway at full speed in the direction of the stairwell in the rear of the building. Bling wasn't armed, and he figured the darkness of the long hallways would conceal his movements once he made it to the fourth floor. He knew that running towards a firefight was a dangerous move, but if he hoped to see Kelli and, ultimately, Zenaida again, he had to do whatever he could.

As Bling disappeared down the hallway, Molina emerged from behind the small desk. She tried to find solace in the fact that Bling had not found her, however, Molina could hear the gun battle. Her thoughts went instantly to her daughter. *Where's Iris?* Molina hoped with all of her heart that Iris was not on the premises. Despite Iris' training, Molina felt things had gotten out of control and it was far too dangerous for her daughter to be involved. Molina had to find out.

She ran to the entrance of the room and examined the door frame as best as she could. The amount of light that managed to find its way through the windows was minimal. Still, Molina managed to see the grooves in the frame. She turned around and pressed the rope against the grooves. She began moving the rope up and down, increasing the speed in hopes of severing the rope and freeing her hands. The unmistakable sound of a footfall behind her caused her to turn suddenly. There, standing before her, was Iris.

"Mija," Molina said excitedly.

"Mom." Iris ran to her mother and embraced her. "I'm so glad I found you. Are you alright?"

"I'm fine, baby," Molina managed to say through a burst of joyful tears. She stepped back and looked at Iris. "What are you doing here?"

"I'm here to get *you*," Iris said, confused by the question. *Why else would I be here?*

The gunfire below ceased. Then, almost as abruptly as it stopped, the shooting started once again.

"It's too dangerous, Mija," Molina said. "We've got to get out of here."

"Let me untie your hands," Iris said.

"Do it on the way," Molina said. "We have to get as far away as we can."

"This way." Iris pointed towards the front stairwell. Just moments prior, Iris had entered the hallway from the stairwell in the rear of the building. In fact, Peppers and Kincaid had forced a door open in the rear of the building which allowed them all to enter undetected. Peppers and Kincaid had been shadowing the movements of Kelli's group from the moment they moved up to the fourth floor. It was there that they discovered Agent Molina and one other were missing from their numbers. Once Peppers was certain that everyone else in Kelli's group was in the same room, he and Kincaid moved in. Iris, on the other hand, went in search of her mother.

She had moved through the fifth floor quite rapidly, but it was the sound of running footsteps that alerted her to the fact that someone was on the floor above her. Iris made her way to the front stairs and ascended one flight. As she stepped onto the sixth floor, she noticed a young man holding a flashlight, looking into a room not far down the hallway. With her keen eyesight, Iris could tell it was the same man who was fighting in the street when

Zenaida was apprehended earlier. Further inspection revealed to Iris that the young man was searching for someone. *Mom.*

Iris raised the Glock in her hand to eye level and took aim. Suddenly, gunfire erupted from the floor below. Out of sheer reflex, due to her training, Iris backed up against the wall and took refuge in the small shadow in the corner. She looked up as the young man turned and bolted in the opposite direction. Iris stepped into the center of hallway. She raised her weapon once more. Given her superior visual acuity coupled with equally superior hand-eye coordination, hitting the young man at this distance would be child's play. Iris began to squeeze the trigger when something caught her eye. Movement at the door where the man had been standing just seconds before. Her heart pounded with joy as she realized the figure in the dark was her mother.

Now, with her mother by her side, Iris moved back towards the front stairs. She breathed a small sigh of relief. It would only be a few more minutes before she and her mother exited the building and left this place behind.

Peppers sat to catch his breath on the first-floor landing of the rear stairwell. He winced in pain as he touched the spot where he'd been shot in the last volley on the fourth floor. Whoever had come out of the other room had managed to catch him on the hip, directly below his Kevlar vest. He wiped blood on his trousers before proceeding to reload his weapon. Above, the sound of a door opening grabbed his attention. Someone was moving through the stairwell. *Are they coming up or going down?* After listening briefly, Peppers determined that whoever was in the stairwell with him was descending quite rapidly. It would be mere minutes before the person was upon him. He continued to listen. The footsteps descended four flights before Peppers heard a door open. The footsteps moved into the corridor and disappeared behind the closed door. Peppers had no idea who it was. Maybe it was Kincaid. Though Kincaid had been shot in the back, Peppers knew that Kincaid was wearing Kevlar, as well. He was certain that Kincaid was alive when he had to retreat down the hallway. Unfortunately, Peppers was unsure of what had transpired after he was gone. For all he knew, his young partner was dead.

Peppers shook off the thought. Regardless of Kincaid's fate, there was still a mission to complete. Peppers was determined to complete it, or die trying.

West rushed the man in front of him without hesitation. He tackled Kincaid, slamming his body into the wall. Kincaid's left wrist twisted against the wall as his full weight, and the weight of his attacker pressed against it, forcing him to drop his weapon. Kincaid bellowed in pain.

West took a quick step back. With his left hand pressed against Kincaid's shoulder, West punched violently with his right. His fist impacted Kincaid's right cheek three times in rapid succession. Kincaid, who was already in pain from the two gunshots that had hit his bullet-proof vest, fell to his knees. However, much to

West's surprise, Kincaid reached back and grabbed hold of West's right ankle. From his position on the floor, Kincaid lunged forward. West's ankle was dragged out from under him. He lost his balance and landed hard on his back. Kincaid pulled himself to his feet. The light from Peppers' flashlight cast enough light for both men to see each other amongst the strange shadows of the dark hallway.

Kincaid launched himself at West, knocking the FBI agent back to the floor as he attempted to stand. Kincaid stood. He turned and scanned the floor quickly for his weapon. He eyed it resting against the baseboard of the wall to his left. West saw Kincaid turn away from him. He knew that his adversary was going for the weapon. West looked to his right. He must have dropped his own weapon when he first engaged Kincaid. There was no way to reach it in time. Then, he remembered that Davies' weapon was in his shoulder holster. West reached for it, but it was too late. Kincaid had retrieved his weapon from the floor and was turning to level it at West. Then, suddenly, Kincaid froze in his tracks as he focused on something behind West.

Agent West twisted slightly and watched as a man with a gun in his hand stepped out of the shadows. West recognized the man as his partner, Special Agent Quentin Bonner.

Bonner grinned. "Hey, Buddy."

West released a deep breath, and then smiled. "It's about time."

"I could say the same," Bonner retorted, referring to the text messages West had been sending him, and then the subsequent phone call when he asked Bonner for a

'*Hail Mary*'. It was then that West had come clean. He told Bonner about the Agency, his on-going investigation, everything. Finally.

Bonner trained his weapon on Kincaid and signaled for him to drop his weapon and assume the position. Reluctantly, Kincaid complied. Bonner extended a hand and helped West to his feet. Three seconds later, West had a pair of handcuffs in his grasp.

West locked his handcuffs onto Kincaid's wrists. Once Kincaid was secured, West pulled Kincaid up in a seated position up against the wall. West grabbed the young Agency operative by the face and squeezed hard.

"Which one of you did it?" West demanded.

Kincaid said nothing.

West placed the barrel of his weapon against Kincaid's face. Bonner stepped forward.

"Whoa, Buddy, slow down," Bonner suggested.

West shook his head. "Can't do that, Q. One of these scumbags killed Agent Davies."

Bonner's jaw dropped open. "What?"

"That's right," West said. He pushed harder on the barrel. "That woman had a family, people who loved her; parents, sisters and a brother. She didn't deserve to die." West was practically snarling, his face only inches from Kincaid's. "So you're going to tell me which one of you killed her or so help me, I'm gonna blow your face off right here, right now."

Kincaid's eyes blazed with fear. He believed that Agent West was capable of killing him in cold blood on the spot. And why wouldn't he? Why shouldn't he? After all, Kincaid did the same to Davies. Despite the overwhelming terror of having the barrel of a loaded weapon pressed against his cheekbone, Kincaid was able to think logically. Perhaps this was his atonement for following orders and ignoring his conscience. Maybe this was how it's supposed to end for the man the Agency dubbed Brandon Kincaid.

Bonner placed a hand over the weapon that West held against Kincaid's face. He knelt down beside his partner and spoke with a concerned tone. "Donnie. Buddy. Don't do this. Not like this. If you kill him, you'll never know who killed Davies."

"Ballistics will tell me," West countered.

"Maybe so, but, if you do it like this, if you kill this man in cold blood, it's going to haunt you forever."

West continued to glare at Kincaid. Never before had West felt such rage. Still, his conscience began to emerge and get the better of him.

"Come on, Buddy," Bonner urged him again. "Let's do this right. For Davies."

A single gunshot rang out from a lower floor. Kincaid jerked, certain that West was going to follow suit and shoot him as well. West, however, withdrew the weapon from Kincaid's cheek. Slowly, West stood. He turned to Bonner and gave him a quick nod.

"We need to find the others," West said.

"What about him?" Bonner asked, gesturing to Kincaid.

"We can lock him in one of these rooms for now."

"Sounds good," Bonner said.

The two men dragged Kincaid by his legs into the room where Davies' was killed. As they turned to leave, Kincaid mumbled softly, "I did it."

West stopped and turned back. "What did you say?"

"I did it," Kincaid confessed. "I killed the woman."

Without thinking, West raised his weapon and leveled at it Kincaid's head. As he squeezed the trigger, Bonner slapped his arm to the right causing the bullet to miss Kincaid's head by mere centimeters.

Bonner grabbed hold of West's wrist. Softly, he said, "Donnie."

West stood motionless. He wanted nothing more than to end this man's life right then and there. West knew it would be wrong, but considering how angry he was, he knew it would also be easy. West turned his gun around and grabbed it by the barrel. Without saying a word, he struck Kincaid with the butt of the weapon as hard as he possibly could. Once, twice, three times. Kincaid fell unconscious.

West turned to Bonner.

Bonner nodded. "Yeah. He deserved that."

Kelli and Arthur hit the third-floor landing. Arthur, with his gun leveled in front of him, led the way. They began their speedy descent towards the second floor when Arthur halted. He raised his finger to his lips, signaling Kelli to remain silent. Arthur peered over the handrail onto the stairs below. In the dim light, Arthur could discern one thing. There was an unfamiliar man moving up the stairs towards them, and he was armed.

Kelli glanced over the handrail quickly. She recognized Agent Peppers. He looked up at her. Their eyes locked.

Arthur signaled to Kelli to retreat up one flight of stairs. Kelli, still standing by the handrail, was already looking up. Her attention had been drawn by the sound of someone rushing down the stairs from above. Her brow furled as she saw Iris looking down at her from the landing above.

"You," Iris said with a snarl, and then began running down the stairs towards her.

Arthur and Kelli raced back up to the third-floor landing. They had to get to the door first or Iris would cut off their only escape route. Iris rounded the corner and hit the platform between the third and fourth floor. Kelli leapt from the stairs. The strength in her legs propelled her to the door. She pulled it open, and then turned to reach for Arthur. As she did, Iris dove off the stairs towards Kelli. Their bodies collided, forcing them both through the door and into the third-floor hallway. The door closed behind them.

Arthur rushed onto the third-floor landing. He turned and raised his weapon as Agent Molina came down the stairs from the fourth floor.

"Freeze!" he ordered. Molina complied instantly.

Arthur did a quick visual inspection of Molina. He saw that her hands were still securely bound. He moved to the edge of the landing and peered over the side. Peppers continued to make his ascent. Arthur aimed his weapon and fired two shots. Each one landed center mass, impacting Peppers' torso merely inches from one another. Peppers dropped his weapon, fell backwards and tumbled down the stairs. Arthur began to release a heavy sigh until a thought occurred to him. *Wait. I tied Molina's hands behind her back. But now they're tied in front.* By the time Arthur reacted to this thought, Molina was already on him.

Molina delivered a blow to the nape of Arthur's neck. She grabbed him by the shoulder and used the leverage gained from his body to throw her knee into his ribcage. Arthur swung his left arm blindly. Molina easily ducked his assault. She leapt in the air and launched a forward snap-kick, attacking his ribcage once more. Arthur fell backwards against the wall at the top of stairs. The force of the impact caused him to drop his weapon. The firearm bounced down the stairs, out of reach. Molina charged at Arthur. In defense, Arthur threw a right cross. Instinctively, Molina dropped to the floor, evading the punch while simultaneously sweeping Arthur's left ankle. Arthur stumbled to his left and fell to his knees. Molina pushed herself from the floor and threw her right knee into Arthur's forehead. The back of Arthur's head bounced off the wall, dazing him. Molina stood, grabbed Arthur by the shirt and, with all of her remaining strength, pulled Arthur towards her, stepped back, and then pushed him down the stairs. This time, Molina didn't run away as she had with Bling. Instead, she stood and watched as Arthur tumbled down the entire flight and landed at the bottom. She stared at him for several seconds. He did not move. Then, Molina heard a single gunshot ring out from the third floor. A short breath got trapped in her throat. *Iris.* Molina dashed for the door. She pulled the door open and stepped onto the third floor.

18

The emptiness of the third-floor hallway caused Iris and Kelli to impact the floor with a resounding thud. The two women separated as momentum from Iris' leaping tackle sent them, and their respective weapons, sprawling into the corridor. Kelli rolled to her knees and turned toward Iris. The two-way radio clipped to Kelli's waistband was dangling from her pants, the microphone swinging loosely by her feet. Iris found her footing and stood as well. Increasingly loud sirens from the outside indicated that the NYPD were close to arriving on scene. It wouldn't be long before blue and red flashing lights would be bouncing off the walls, bathing the ensuing battleground between Kelli and Iris as if they were in a disco.

The two women charged at each other. They met in the center of the hallway and grabbed hold of one another. Iris delivered a front snap-kick to Kelli's abdomen. Kelli fell back several steps before regaining her balance and pressing forward once again.

Iris threw a left jab towards Kelli's jaw. Kelli side-stepped and grabbed Iris' wrist with her left arm. Kelli rotated her body and applied pressure to Iris' left elbow. Before Kelli could secure the wrist lock, Iris reached across her own body and jabbed Kelli in the left eye with her index and middle fingers. Kelli stumbled back and cursed aloud. Iris leapt into a spinning back kick, contacting Kelli on the side of her face, dropping her to the floor. Kelli landed hard on all fours. Despite being dazed by Iris' last attack, Kelli could still feel Iris close the distance between them. Iris grabbed the microphone cord that dangled from the two-way radio on Kelli's waist. She wrapped the cord around Kelli's neck, pulled it tight, and began to squeeze.

Instinctively, Kelli reached for the cord and attempted to pull it free. Iris pulled harder in response. Kelli leaned forward on her knees, forcing Iris to bend over her to retain her grip on the cord. With Iris now standing behind her, Kelli reached back and wrapped each of her arms around the back of Iris's knees. In one motion, Kelli brought her arms to together in front of her. Iris, now unbalanced, fell backwards but held tight to the cord. Kelli pressed the advantage. She spun her body around, throwing Iris, head first, into the wall in front of her. Iris relinquished her grasp on the cord and fell to the floor. Finding herself free of the microphone cord, Kelli crawled across the floor, gasping for air. She spied a pistol on the floor mere feet from her position in the hallway. Kelli lunged for it. As she did, Iris tackled her from behind.

Kelli was forced into a prone position. She reached for the weapon which lay only inches beyond her grasp. Iris began punching Kelli in the back of the head.

"Go to sleep now, Kelli," she said as she pummeled her from behind. "I need to bring you back to Mr. One."

Kelli tried to buck Iris from her back, but each blow to the back of her head disoriented her more and more. Suddenly, Iris was gone as if she'd been forced away. As Kelli regained her bearings, she felt someone pulling her to a standing position. As she rose, she grabbed the Glock and wrapped her hand tightly around the handgrip. When she stood, she was staring directly into Bling's eyes.

Bling had come up the hallway from the rear stairwell. He witnessed the deadly brawl as he advanced on their position. When the opportunity presented itself, Bling stepped in and pushed Iris off of his friend. Kelli was relieved, but she knew the battle was far from over. Kelli turned around and leveled her weapon at Iris.

Iris stood slowly. She watched as Kelli pointed the gun at her. For a moment, fear blazed up Iris' spine but then vanished as quickly as it had arrived. Iris smiled smugly and began walking slowly towards Kelli.

"You're not going to shoot me," Iris said boldly.

Kelli did not respond. Instead, she gripped the weapon tighter.

"What are you doing?" Bling asked Kelli. "Shoot her."

"I don't think so," Iris predicted as she took another careful step towards them.

The gun in Kelli's hand grew heavy suddenly. Kelli had to concentrate to keep the pistol upright. Every fiber in her being screamed at her to pull the trigger. Her brain told that she had to, but her heart wouldn't let her cross the line. Was it because, despite all of her preparation and self-training, Kelli had yet to shoot another human being, or was it that shooting Iris would be like shooting Francine and causing her death all over again? Kelli couldn't decide.

Iris took another step.

"Shoot her," Bling screamed at her, but it was too late.

Iris took one more step before lunging at Kelli and grabbing hold of the weapon. Bling latched on to the weapon, as well. The three of them struggled for control of the firearm, twisting it one way, then the other. Iris placed her hand under the barrel of the weapon and pushed it backwards towards Kelli. Kelli released a cry of pain as her thumb was forced back and open. Iris continued to push the weapon, then she twisted it downward. She shoved her finger into the trigger well and squeezed. The weapon discharged a single bullet. Bling screamed aloud, and then fell to the floor.

Kelli threw all caution to the wind and forfeited the weapon to Iris. She turned to Bling as he writhed in agony from the bullet wound in his thigh. Kelli fell to the floor, placing herself between Iris and Bling.

"Oh my God. Bling. Bryan."

Bling cursed aloud several times.

Iris leveled the pistol at Kelli. Oh, how she wanted to put a bullet in Kelli's back and end her; but Iris knew that she couldn't. She still had hope that bringing Kelli to Mr. One would be enough of a bargaining chip to ensure her and her mother's salvation. Iris cursed under her breath. She needed Kelli alive. Reluctantly, she slid her finger out of the trigger well.

Kelli began to cry as she spoke comforting words to Bling to calm him. "You're going to be okay. Bling. Baby." Kelli caressed his face as she kneeled down close to him.

Iris took notice of Kelli's level of affection towards the wounded young man. She realized that Kelli's interest in Bling went far beyond mere friendship.

"Get up," Iris ordered her.

The door at the end of the hallway opened Agent Molina rushed in. She paused as she took in the sight of Iris standing over Kelli and Bling, holding them at gunpoint. Slowly, she began to move towards her daughter.

Iris kicked Kelli in the shin. "Get up now or I'll kill him."

Kelli looked up and glared at Iris. She turned back to Bling and touched his cheek lightly. "It's going to be okay," she whispered to him.

"No," Bling protested. "Don't do it."

As Kelli began to stand, she noticed the other weapon on the floor behind Bling. She paused for an instant as she debated her next move.

"Let's go!" Iris screamed.

Kelli brought her leg forward slowly until she was kneeling on one knee. In a sudden burst, she pushed off of her foot and sprang upward. She connected with a left hook to Iris' face. Caught off guard, Iris spun around violently. The Glock fell from her grasp and landed at Agent Molina's feet.

Kelli dove for the pistol that rested behind Bling. Molina knelt quickly and retrieved the gun in front of her. Molina dropped to one knee as Kelli picked up the other weapon. Unfortunately, years of training had given Molina the edge. She raised her weapon.

The door to the third-floor landing sprang open. Arthur burst through the door. His heart jumped as he saw his daughter caught in Agent Molina's cross-hairs.

"No!" Arthur screamed. He swung his firearm in Molina's direction.

Instinctively, Molina turned her weapon towards Arthur. Without a second thought, she fired two shots into his chest. Blood squirted in the air as Arthur's body fell backwards and landed lifelessly on the floor.

"Daddy!" Kelli screamed in horror as her father lay on the floor, not moving. Tears spilled down her cheeks as rage overwhelmed her senses and burned at the back of her eyes. Kelli looked at Molina, leveled her firearm, and squeezed off a shot. Molina fell to the floor. Blood poured from the hole in her chest, just below her right clavicle. Her hand covered the wound as she struggled to breath.

"No!" Iris shouted. She ran to her mother's side.

Kelli sprang from the floor and crossed the distance to her father in a single tick of the clock. She fell to her knees and knelt over him. "Daddy?" she called to him softly, fearing that he would not answer. Though she tried, Kelli could not avoid looking at the blood that continued to soak through Arthur's sweater and jacket. Kelli grabbed her father by the shoulders and shook him. His body flailed lifelessly in her grasp. A glimpse into his absent eyes confirmed the truth that Kelli did not want to face. A hollow chasm opened up in the pit of Kelli's stomach as tears rained uncontrollably from her eyes. A knot formed in her throat, cutting off her air and negating the scream of horror that sat trapped beneath the weight of sudden, overwhelming loss and despair. Kelli's head fell onto Arthur's shoulder as the air escaped her lungs, allowing her to cry inconsolably.

Across the hall, Iris placed her hand over Molina's wound in a futile attempt to cease the blood flow that poured from her mother's body.

"You're going to be okay, Mom," Iris assured her mother as she cried by her side. "We're going to get out of here. You'll see."

Molina looked into her daughter's eyes. Images of the past flashed through her mind. Images of when she first laid eyes on Iris as a baby, images of Iris's first birthday, and the memory of the day when Iris first called her *Mom*. Though Molina wasn't sure if she was actually dying, she was certain that the pain of watching her daughter cry was far worse than the physical pain she was experiencing as a result of her gunshot wound. Inside, Molina's heart was breaking. She reached up and gripped the silver necklace that hung around her neck. At the end of the necklace was a small silver key.

"Iris," Molina managed to say. "Take this."

Iris looked at the key. Though she had never seen it before, Iris knew that her mother was giving it to her because Molina feared the worst. Iris would not accept it. "What? Mom, no. Give it to me later. We have to go. We have to go."

Further down the hall, hidden by the shadows, Bling sat against the wall. He watched as Kelli and Iris wept uncontrollably next to their respective parent. Bling could hear Molina's voice coming through the darkness, but his heart sank as he realized that all he could hear from Kelli's direction was the sound of Kelli weeping. Though he could hear Kelli call out for her father between sobs, Bling knew that Arthur was not going to reply.

Molina's hands were dripping with blood. She pulled the necklace from her neck, snapping the chain. She pushed it at Iris. "Mija, please. We don't have much time."

"No," Iris refused. She tried to pull Molina towards her. Molina winced in pain. Iris loosened her grasp.

Molina looked into Iris' eyes once again. "Mija, listen. The safe behind the Tres Reyes painting in the office at home; everything you need to know is there."

"Mom, no. Why are you talking like this?"

Molina reached up and grabbed her daughter's face, marking Iris' cheeks with blood. Iris was shocked into silence. "Promise me you will get home and get to the safe," Molina said. "Promise me."

Iris began to cry harder. Her eyes locked on to her mother's eyes. A silent communication passed between them; an understanding that Iris, from this point on, might have to go it alone. Reluctantly, she accepted the necklace from her mother.

"Good," Molina said. She coughed up a stream of blood. She turned to Iris. "Now go, Mija-"

"No," Iris protested.

"Mija, you must g . . ." Molina's words trailed off as her eyes widened and focused on something, no, rather someone, behind Iris. Before Iris could turn, Kelli grabbed her by the hair and pulled her from Molina's side.

Kelli hit Iris squarely between the eyes with the butt of her Glock, and then cast the dazed girl aside. The whole time, her eyes were focused on Molina.

Anger scorched Kelli from the inside out. She pointed her weapon at Molina. Her hand shook nervously. "You killed my father," Kelli screamed at her, and then fired a shot into Molina's stomach. Molina released a bloodcurdling scream.

Iris had regained her composure. She leapt at Kelli but her assault came a fraction of a second too late.

Kelli squeezed the trigger again. Iris collided with her body, causing Kelli's shot to go off course and strike the floor to Molina's left.

The two girls fell to the floor. The Glock bounced and slid across the floor and disappeared into the darkness. Iris continued to roll and landed on all fours. Kelli's head slammed into the floor, causing a flash of light to inundate her senses. She rolled onto her knees. As she did, Iris kicked her in the ribs. Kelli grunted in response. The pain was overwhelming and Kelli was certain that some of her ribs were now broken. Unfortunately, Iris did not relent.

Iris followed up with another kick to Kelli's ribs. Kelli screamed in pain and fell onto her back. Iris jumped on Kelli and began punching her in the face with unceasing fury. Though Kelli tried to defend herself, she became weaker with each blow that she received. Amidst the onslaught, Kelli tried to concentrate. If she could shift into her male form, perhaps she could overpower Iris. Alas, Iris' anger burned just as hot as Kelli's rage. Iris continued to pummel her, striking her face repeatedly, preventing Kelli from focusing enough to make the shift. Eventually, Kelli was beaten into unconsciousness. Still, Iris continued her assault.

She struck Kelli again and again. Three, four, five times. It was only the sound of a male voice screaming her name that caused Iris to halt her attack and look towards the door. Agent Peppers crossed the threshold into the corridor, his weapon pointed at Iris. The two bullet holes in his shirt revealed a Kevlar vest underneath.

"Mr. One wants her alive," Peppers said to her.

"Who cares what he wants?" Iris screamed back at him through gritted teeth. She turned and punched her unconscious opponent in the face once more.

"We do," Peppers reminded her. "We follow orders. That's all we do."

"She shot my mother. Twice." Iris gestured to Molina who was sitting in a small pool of her own blood, writhing in pain against the wall.

Peppers glanced over at Molina. He could tell that her wounds were severe. It would only be a matter of time before she died. However, the hallway was now filled with flashes of red and blue from the police lights that had arrived on scene outside. Peppers knew that time was not a luxury that he had. Besides, he still had a mission to complete. He took a deep breath, exhaled, and then shifted his weapon from Iris to Agent Molina.

Iris took a step forward. "What are you doing?" she shouted.

"Following orders."

With Peppers' weapon leveled at her, Molina accepted her fate. She turned her head and looked at Iris. She extended her arm in Iris' direction and managed to utter, "I love you."

Peppers discharged his firearm. The bullet found its mark in Molina's chest and sliced through her heart, ending her pain. Agent Maribel Molina was dead.

"No!" Iris screamed, and then charged at Peppers. Peppers turned his weapon on Iris and screamed at her in response.

"Stop!" he ordered her. Iris kept coming. "Stop now or, orders or not, I *will* kill you."

Iris froze in her tracks. "Orders?" Iris questioned; the word drenched in disgust. "You had orders to kill my mother?" she yelled at him.

"And everyone else," Peppers confirmed. "All except you and the Freeman girl. I understand that you're angry, but you're going to have to settle that score with Mr. One yourself. You can't do that if you're dead. Stand down."

Iris looked over at her mother's body. She spied her own Glock just inches away from where her mother fell.

Peppers saw the Glock, too. He knew exactly what Iris was thinking. "Don't even think about it."

Obscured by the shadows, Bling crawled into one of the rooms without a door. As he pulled himself through the door, he caught a glimpse of the two-way radio that had fallen from Kelli's waist during her melee with Iris. Bling grabbed the radio before moving into the safety of the room.

Iris glared at Peppers. The hatred that ignited within her was so intense that it caused her body to tremble visibly. "I'm going to kill you."

Peppers did not flinch. "Perhaps." He gestured to Kelli's unconscious form on the floor. "Wake her up."

Iris did not move.

"Do it." Peppers ordered more sternly.

Iris held her gaze. The last thing she wanted to do was take orders from the man who just killed the only person in the world she cared about. She did, however, want to charge at Peppers and kill him with her bare hands. With her strength, it would be easy. Still, Iris knew that she had more than one score to settle. Mr. One had ordered her mother's murder, and if Iris was going to make him pay, she had to get out of this situation alive. Reluctantly, she turned and took a step back towards Kelli. She kicked the unconscious girl in the thigh as hard as she could. The pain jarred Kelli back to consciousness.

Kelli looked up. Her face was badly bruised, and bathed in a grotesque mixture of blood and tears. The sight of Iris standing over her startled her. She peered beyond Iris and saw Peppers with his gun leveled in her direction.

"Get up," Peppers ordered her.

Kelli glanced over at her father's body. Instantly, she began to cry. Tears streamed down her face once again. Iris grabbed Kelli by the arm and yanked her up, pulling Kelli to her feet. Iris stepped in front of her and stared into her eyes. Kelli returned her gaze unflinchingly. The hatred that burned between them could sear a stone wall. If looks could kill, both girls would have surely dropped dead on the spot.

"Move," Peppers ordered as he pointed towards the opposite end of the hallway. "That way."

The two girls turned and walked down the corridor in silence. Both girls stole one last glance at the fallen parent they were leaving behind; both girls filled with rage and loathing towards the other. Peppers followed them at a safe distance, keeping his weapon trained on their backs.

Bling watched from the shadows as the trio marched past the door of the room in which he had taken refuge. With all that had transpired, he was confident that both Kelli and Iris had forgotten all about him. Even if they hadn't, neither of them said a word as they walked by the room. Bling waited a few moments. He wanted to make sure they had travelled far enough down the hall before he turned off the two-way radio he had picked up from the floor. He reached for the microphone that was connected to his own radio. He squeezed the lever and spoke softly into the mic. "West, I hope you can hear me. Kelli's in trouble."

Moments earlier, the sound of approaching sirens penetrated Kincaid's senses, waking him from his state of forced unconsciousness. His head throbbed from the impact of West's weapon, and his wrists, which were handcuffed behind his back, ached from being secured much too tightly. Despite his current predicament, Kincaid did not panic. In fact, once Kincaid realized that he had been left alone, he was quite relieved.

He rolled onto his back. He cursed as the handcuffs cut into his skin. He brought his knees up towards his chest and rocked back. His long, flexible arms allowed him to extend the cuffs past his buttocks. He slipped his legs through the space created by his handcuffed wrists and brought his arms comfortably in front of his body. Kincaid pulled himself to his feet and stepped into the hallway. Aside from the approaching red and blue police lights that began to bounce off the walls throughout the hallway, Kincaid noticed that Peppers' small flashlight was still illuminated on the floor. He bent and retrieved it.

Kincaid unscrewed the head of the flashlight. Though the light went out, the flashing lights from outside provided enough illumination for Kincaid to work. He tipped the flashlight over. The batteries slipped out and fell to the floor. Kincaid turned the flashlight head over. He smiled as he eyed the metal spring underneath. After a few tugs, the spring came free of the flashlight. Kincaid pulled on the spring from opposite ends until the metal piece had almost straightened out completely. He angled his wrists and shoved one end of the metal wire into the handcuff keyhole. He wiggled it gently from right to left until the spring slipped under the locking lever. He shifted the spring slightly. He smiled as the handcuff clicked and then slipped off his wrist. He grabbed the other end of the straightened spring and repeated the process on the other cuff. Within seconds, Kincaid was free of his bonds. He wondered where his partner had gone. A few gunshots alerted him to the fact that Peppers was probably still alive somewhere in the building. However, the sirens outside had ceased and Kincaid could tell that the NYPD had finally arrived. Kincaid knew that the building would soon be surrounded. Though he felt compelled to search for Peppers, Kincaid's common sense, and protocol told him to get out while he still could. With the decision made, Kincaid turned towards the rear stairwell and ran down the hallway at full speed.

๑๏๛

Kelli and Iris rounded the corner at the end of the hallway. The rear stairwell was directly ahead at the end of the corridor. Peppers still maintained a safe distance behind his two captives. His finger rested only an inch away from the trigger. Though the two young women had been marching in complete silence up until this point, Iris decided she needed to make a few things abundantly clear.

"Just so you know," Iris said to Kelli without turning to look at her. "I'm going to kill you. But before I do, I'm going to make you watch as I kill every member of your family."

Kelli's jaw tightened. "Not if I kill you first."

"Quiet," Peppers ordered. "And speed it up."

The trio approached the door at the end of the corridor. Kelli and Iris stopped in front of it.

"Iris, open the door," Peppers commanded.

Iris grunted her discontent regarding Peppers and his orders. She stepped forward and pushed the door open. The barrel of a weapon greeted her from the other side. Iris looked up and took in the sight of a black man whom she had never seen before. Iris stepped backwards into the hallway. Agent Bonner followed her in, stepping into the doorway. Peppers' eyes widened. As he shifted his weapon towards Bonner, West appeared from inside the opened door on the left. He pressed his weapon against Peppers' left temple.

"Give me a reason," West said flatly, his voice full of rage.

Peppers, with his many years of experience, both in the military and in service of the Agency, was smart enough to know when it was time to surrender. The time was now. Peppers dropped his weapon.

Iris glanced into the room to her right which, like many of the rooms in the hallway, was missing a door. From where she stood, Iris could see the window against the far wall. As West bent to retrieve Peppers' gun, Iris turned and bolted to her right. She accelerated into the room and leapt into the air. Her body shattered the glass as she sailed through the window, and then dropped out of sight.

"Whoa," Bonner exclaimed in surprise.

West stood quickly and returned his gun to the side of Peppers' head. He nodded at Bonner. In response, Bonner ran to the window and looked to the ground three stories below. He expected to see Iris' body, or at the very least, a very injured young girl. Instead, all he saw was broken glass. Iris was nowhere in sight.

અન્ડ

West and Bonner maneuvered through the lobby area on the first floor. Bling leaned on Bonner for support. West had one arm wrapped around Kelli, the other arm was extended forward, his gun trained on the back of Peppers' head. Peppers' wrists were firmly secured behind his back with Bonner's cuffs.

Kelli continued to weep. West's heart had taken a nosedive at the news of Arthur's death. It was even harder to look at his body when they walked past him as they exited the third floor. West refrained from telling Kelli that Agent Davies was dead, as well. Kelli had been through enough. Besides, West was sure that Kelli would notice Davies' absence eventually. For now, he knew that Kelli was still focused on the man she admired most. The man she had just lost. Her father, Arthur Freeman.

West paused and turned to Kelli. "Don't go out there," he said to her. "It'll just raise more questions."

Despite the fact that Kelli was tired of hiding, tired of being separated from her family and her life, she knew that West was right. If she were to go outside, it wouldn't be long before the question of her identity would come into play, and then she would have to explain how a woman who was believed to be dead had surfaced suddenly after seven years.

As the group approached the door, it was pulled open from the outside. An army of NYPD officers rushed in with their guns at the ready. They swarmed the group and forced each of them to the floor. After much screaming, Agents West and Bonner managed to identify themselves as federal agents. Bling verified his identity, as well. West released Peppers into the custody of the NYPD. As for Kelli, she had disappeared up the front stairwell once again. As far as the police knew, Kelli Freeman was never there.

Iris had injured her right leg in the fall from the third story window. However, it wasn't enough to stop her. She jumped to her feet and limped rapidly around the back of the building and into the trees that surrounded the property. She waited until the police had been occupied with West and the others before she crept stealthily to the car she had parked around the bend on 184th Street. She opened the door and slipped behind the wheel. She retrieved her keys from under the driver's seat and slid them into the ignition. Suddenly, there was a thud on the passenger side window. Iris turned. Kincaid was staring at her.

"Open up. Quick."

Although Iris wanted to drive off and leave him there, she realized that his presence might be useful. She tapped a button and unlocked the door. Kincaid opened the door and slid into the passenger seat.

"Drive," he ordered her.

Without uttering a sound, Iris started the car, slipped the gear into drive, and drove away.

It wasn't long before the FBI team that A.D. Marsh dispatched arrived and took over the crime scene. The FBI and local PD engaged in a heated argument about jurisdiction before an order came from the precinct to give the FBI their full cooperation.

It was almost two hours before Kelli found a way to slip out of the building and make her way to her car. While she hid in the building, she thought of her father lying dead on the third floor. Though she wanted to go up there, she couldn't bring herself to do it. Instead, she avoided the police and the FBI as they combed the building, and followed up on the verbal account given by West and Bonner. Kelli cried as she sat alone in her car. She lowered herself behind the wheel as she watched the dead bodies being carried out of the building, each one covered with a white sheet. Luckily, Kelli had remembered to grab her backpack while she waited for the right moment to slip into the moonlight and creep to her car. After another hour of sitting in her car crying, it wasn't hard for her hearing to pick up the vibrations of her cell phone in her backpack. Kelli unzipped her pack and reached in. She pulled out the phone and looked at the screen. There were several missed calls and four text messages. All were from her mother. There was no doubt that Diane had been notified of Arthur's death by now. Kelli tapped the message icon and read the latest incoming text which was comprised of three words. 'Where are you?'

With that, Kelli knew it was time to go. Her family needed her, and she needed them. Kelli started her car and drove into the approaching dawn towards home.

WASHINGTON, D.C.

Mr. One slipped in the backseat of the black SUV that had once again pulled up and parked on the corner of First Street NE and Maryland Ave. As usual, he fiddled with his cane before closing the door and turning to face Rebecca Thorn. Without her uttering a sound, One could tell that Rebecca was not happy. The tone of her voice confirmed it.

"I hear there's quite a party going on in New York right now, and unfortunately, everyone was invited; NYPD, FBI, a few civilians, and a number of our operatives."

"Yeah, it'll be quite the mess to clean up," One said, avoiding eye contact.

"You think?" she asked sarcastically. "We've got a dead FBI agent on our hands. The Bureau is launching an internal investigation. It makes the clean up a little more complicated."

"Yes, I get it. It's a clusterfuck."

Rebecca raised her voice. "I don't think you get it at all. If you screw up, I look bad. I'm the one who v-"

"Yes, I know. You vouched for me; for forty years you've never let me forget it." *As if I'm supposed to be grateful to you.* "But that's not why I called."

"You should have called three hours ago," she said condescendingly. "Instead, I had to get this news from one of my contacts at the Bureau." She leaned towards him. "I'd hate to think that you've forgotten how this works."

One looked Rebecca in the eyes. "No, I haven't. But if you'll give me a minute, I've got some news that changes everything."

Still fuming, Rebecca sat back in her seat and waited.

"It turns out that Kelli Freeman is alive."

"I know."

One blinked in surprise. "You know? How? I just found out tonight."

"Which is another epic failure on your part. Get comfortable, Roger. We have much to talk about."

19

Iris and Kincaid drove for over an hour down Interstate 95 to the New Jersey Turnpike before transitioning to Route 38 towards Mount Laurel, New Jersey. They made their way to another medical outpost facility where Doctor Suri met them at the rear entrance and ushered them into the hidden medical corridors of a closed Urgent Care. Suri had spoken to Iris on the phone earlier when she called for directions to his location. It was then that Iris informed the doctor of her mother's fate. When Suri asked for details, Iris choked up and replied, "I can't discuss it right now." Suri had dropped the subject.

Kincaid stumbled into an exam room and sat with a hard thud. He moaned heavily as he tried to stretch the kinks out of his back.

"Are you injured?" Suri asked the agent.

"He took two bullets in the back at close range," Iris explained. "He was wearing a vest."

"Still hurts like you wouldn't believe," Kincaid complained. "Knocked the wind right out of me."

"And your face?" asked Suri, referring to the blood, multiple bruises and swelling.

"Got pistol whipped. For a minute there, I didn't think I was going to make it through the night."

Suri stepped in Kincaid's direction. "I can tend to you, if you'd like."

Kincaid stood and waved Suri away. "I'm alright. I need to report in." Kincaid pulled his cell phone from his jacket pocket as he stepped into the hallway in search of a quiet corner in which to contact Mr. Five. Kincaid had not dared to make contact while Iris drove them along the interstate. He didn't want to risk Iris hearing anything that would make her suspicious about his orders. Now that they had found a temporary haven, Kincaid could call in his situation report in privacy. As Kincaid disappeared around the corner, Iris turned to Suri.

"Get me a sedative. Something strong," she ordered him.

"Are you feeling ill?" Suri asked, always concerned for Iris' well-being.

"It's not for me," she whispered. "Hurry. Before Kincaid comes back."

Confused, Suri scampered off. Iris turned and crept in the opposite direction.

She kept her keen hearing peeled as she listened for Kincaid's voice. It wasn't long before she came upon the closed exam room door that muffled the sound of Kincaid's conversation. Iris stepped to the door and placed her ear against it softly. Though she couldn't hear the voice of Mr. Five, Iris' augmented auditory senses picked up Kincaid's every word.

"That's correct, sir. Agent Peppers was taken into custody." A slight pause. "Agent Molina is dead. Yes, sir. Her daughter confirmed it." More silence as Kincaid listened to the voice on the phone. Then, he said, "The doctor is here." Another pause. "It's as good as done."

Iris turned and darted back up the hallway. The door to the exam room opened as Iris rounded the corner safely, leaving Kincaid unaware of the fact that she was there at all.

Kincaid took his time walking through the corridor. He was no longer in possession of a firearm, but he was certain he could find something he could use to dispatch Doctor Suri quickly. He made his way back towards the first exam room where the doctor was checking the vital signs of the still-sedated Zenaida Rodriguez. Suri turned as Kincaid entered.

"There you are," Suri said to him, as if to convey that he had been searching for him.

Kincaid looked at the Rodriguez girl, then back at Suri. He glanced around the room before asking, "Where's Iris?" The answer to his question presented itself in the form of a needle jabbed, unexpectedly, into his neck.

Kincaid tried to pull away. Iris grabbed him by the collar with her left hand and pulled him back towards her. With the thumb on her right hand, she pushed the plunger down into the syringe, sending a concentrated dose of Propofol into his system. Without pulling the needle from his neck, Iris kicked Kincaid in the back and sent him careening into the wall in front of him.

"Iris, what are you doing?" Suri begged to know.

Kincaid fell to the floor. He rolled over and looked up at Iris, who was now towering over him. He reached clumsily for the needle and extracted it from his neck. "What did you stick me with?" he asked. He repeated the question, but this time he was yelling at the top his lungs. "What did you stick me with?" Kincaid tried to stand, but the sedative had already begun to affect his system. He fell back against the wall and sank to the floor.

"He was going to kill you," Iris said to Suri.

"What?" Suri said in disbelief.

"Tell him," Iris said to Kincaid. "Tell him about the orders you and Peppers had to kill my mother, and to kill him."

Kincaid fought to stay conscious, but it was a battle he knew he was losing.

"They killed my mother!" Iris exclaimed. "Peppers, Mr. One, Mr. Five, Dr. Chen, Kelli Freeman; they are all to blame. And they're all going to pay." She knelt down in front of Kincaid and brought her face close to his. "Starting with you." Iris wrapped her hands around Kincaid's neck, and with all of the strength she could muster, she squeezed.

Kincaid attempted to pull Iris' hands away from his throat. Little did he know, that even if hadn't been drugged, he still wouldn't have been able to pry Iris' vice grip from around his neck. His eyes began to bulge and his skin began to transform from a bright red to a faint blue. His feet kicked violently and his body convulsed. Iris stared into Kincaid's eyes to make certain that the last thing he saw as she squeezed the very life from his body, was her face. Five full minutes had passed before Suri placed his hand on Iris' shoulder. Tears of hate streamed from Iris' eyes. She relinquished her grip on Kincaid, and then stood back to gaze at his lifeless corpse. Her eyes remained on Kincaid's dead body for a moment before she glanced at the needle on the floor. Iris knew that she had no real need to drug Kincaid. With her strength, she could have killed him easily with little to no struggle at all. Still, Iris drugged Kincaid so that he would feel exactly what she felt in the moment that her mother was murdered before her eyes; complete and utter helplessness.

As Iris stood there, a strange sensation overwhelmed her. Her mind drifted back to Monday and the events that had led her to kill three people, including Dr. Patel. In truth, the whole ordeal had felt wrong to her, malicious, especially the unfortunate execution of her doctor. However, Kincaid's death brought with it an unexpected feeling. Satisfaction. Unlike her actions that ended the lives of three people in the safe house, this murder felt right.

Suri stood in shock next to the young girl. Iris turned and looked over at Zenaida Rodriquez. Suri gazed at Zenaida, as well.

"I need to do one more thing before we get started," Iris said.

"Don't you think we've waited long enough?" Suri asked. "Everything is prepped and ready for the surgery."

"Can it wait three more hours?"

"I don't understand-"

"Can it wait?" she shouted.

Suri swallowed hard. Though he felt confident that Iris had no intention of harming him, Suri reconsidered debating a mere three hours with a young woman who had just killed a grown man with her bare hands. He nodded slowly. "It can wait."

"Good. Load Zenaida and whatever equipment you'll need into the van. We're going for a ride."

Three hours passed. Agent Bonner had escorted Bling to a nearby hospital to tend to the gunshot wound in his leg. The bureau notified the Rodriguez family of Zenaida's abduction, though, many of the details were left *'under*

investigation'. Agent Peppers was transferred into the custody of the FBI, and all of the bodies discovered at the Overlook Terrace crime scene were transported to the coroner's office.

Kelli sat on the bed in her old bedroom. Despite the fact that she had not lived under her parents' roof for close to seven years, the room had not been changed much at all. She stared blankly out the window as the early morning sun settled on the Bronx and offered a hint of warm relief from the crisp air. So many times, Kelli had dreamed of the day when she could watch the sunrise from her old bedroom window again, but she never imagined that her fantasy would turn out to be a bittersweet nightmare.

There was a soft knock at the door. After a moment, the door opened slowly and Agent West entered the room. He closed the door after he stepped beyond the threshold and walked to the edge of Kelli's bed. He watched Kelli as she stared out over her yard, and he could tell that in that moment, Kelli was lost. Her face still had considerable swelling from the brutal beating she had endured at Iris' hands, but signs of her accelerated healing ability were already evident. West took a seat on the bed behind Kelli.

"Your mother finally went to lie down. She's in the other room with Wilma."

Kelli did not turn in West's direction. She remained still. West began to question whether Kelli heard his voice at all, until Kelli responded with, "No one's going to be sleeping for a while."

"I know," West replied for lack of something better to say.

"I should have stayed in Boston," Kelli said.

"Hey" West responded soothingly, "Don't-"

"Don't what? Don't tell the truth? If I had stayed in Boston, if I had just followed protocol . . . Davies wouldn't have come looking for me, and my dad . . ." Kelli's eyes welled up once more. "None of us would have been there last night." Tears poured down her cheeks. "What was I thinking?"

West wanted to tell Kelli that she had it all wrong. He wanted to hug her and assure her that the deaths of Davies and her father were not on her. But he couldn't. As cruel as it was to admit it, Kelli was right. West shook his head. How do you console someone who is the architect of their own misery? How do you explain, and get them to understand, that an elevated IQ is no substitute for life experience? West did not have the answers. All he had was his presence and his desire to be there for her, finally, after two years. West prayed that it was enough. He placed a hand on her shoulder. "We can figure this out later."

"That's the problem," Kelli said as she turned to him. "There's no need."

"You want to tell me about it?"

Kelli wiped the tears from her cheeks and eyes to no avail. The cascade continued to flow down her face. Still, Kelli took a breath and began to relay the events that led her to where she was today. She recounted the discovery of her card-counting ability, her escapade through the casinos of Atlantic City, and her investments into Quinlan Pharmaceuticals. She divulged the truth about hiring Joseph Woods to hack into government systems and fish out whatever information she needed to pursue her cause.

Kelli discussed her obsession with photography, martial arts and marksmanship. She went as far as to disclose her motives for evading Davies' calls, and why she decided to shut West out, as well. Kelli talked for quite some time. West sat and listened.

"I thought, because of my abilities, I could do this by myself. I wanted to take on the Agency and get my life back, and I didn't want anyone getting in the way, or telling me what to do. The problem was, I was too blinded by my desire to appear grown up that I didn't recognize that I was behaving like an impulsive child."

"What about the surveillance you conducted while you were in D.C.?" West asked. "Davies found a ton of photos of Chief Justice Roger Tolin. Most of them were taken at some coffee shop."

"I wasn't following Tolin. I was following his daughter."

"Betty Royce? Why?"

"Because Betty Royce was the leverage. It wasn't that hard, really. They meet every Monday morning for coffee, nine a.m. sharp."

"Wait. Leverage for what?"

"For getting out of Boston, getting my life back, and ending this once and for all."

West took a moment to consider Kelli's words. Finally, he asked the question that begged to be asked. "Tolin is Mr. One, isn't he?"

Kelli did not utter a sound. Instead, she nodded one time.

"How does his daughter figure into it? How does she get you out of Boston?"

"I had an interview at her law firm last week, right in D.C."

"What?"

"Yeah," Kelli said with air of pride. "Betty's husband, Jacob Royce, interviewed me himself. Needless to say, he was quite impressed with Kyle Cuffee."

West couldn't believe what he was hearing. "Why would you do that? I know you hate Boston, but do you know how dangerous that would be? What if the Agency found you?"

"Actually, I was thinking that, if I left Boston, the safest place would be in the last place Mr. One would think to look; his own backyard, working at his daughter's firm. It's not like he even knows about Kyle Cuffee."

As crazy as it sounded on the surface, West had to admit to himself that Kelli was probably right. Often times, the best hiding place was the one that was in plain sight. "I guess you could still do it," West said finally.

Kelli scoffed. "God, no. I never wanted to be a lawyer."

"What?" West questioned, confused. "Then why you'd go to law school?"

"The same reason you did."

West's eyes widened. "You can't join the FBI, Kelli. You're in witness protection."

"If I take down Mr. One, I wouldn't have to be."

"You're forgetting that Kyle Cuffee is the one who went to law school," West reminded her.

"If we get rid of Mr. One, none of that will matter."

"I don't get it," West confessed. "Why would you want to join the FBI, especially after all you've been through?"

Kelli lowered her gaze and stared at the space on the bed between them. She knew the answer to West's question, but considering all that had happened over the last twenty-four hours, how could she tell him that she was doing it all to follow in the footsteps of the one man she loved and admired most in the world? How could she find the words to express that all she'd ever wanted was to be like her father? It wasn't that she was embarrassed to tell West how she felt, but rather, it was the pain of saying the words out loud, and then facing the bitter truth that her father would never know of her plan to honor him. Somehow, though it tore at her very soul, Kelli forced the words from her mouth.

As Kelli spoke about her father, tears fell from West's eyes. He was touched by her aspiration to follow her father's path and pursue a field of law enforcement. West wished he'd had such a noble motivation for joining the Bureau. In truth, he did not. His mother was a lawyer, and she did not hide her low opinion of police officers and other law enforcement agencies. West didn't become an FBI agent to make his mother proud. After he graduated law school, he became an FBI agent to spite her. West glanced at Kelli. A part of him was glad that she had no desire to become a lawyer. He would hate for her to become the type of woman who had tunnel vision and saved no time for her family; a woman like his mother. Still, West wasn't crazy about Kelli's dream of joining the bureau either.

"I'm still a little confused," West said. "You said your leverage with Betty Royce would help you get your life back. How?"

"It doesn't matter now," Kelli said. "Now I have to use that leverage to protect my family, or have you forgotten what I told you? Iris promised to kill them."

"And I told you that A.D. Marsh assigned a protective detail; one for each member of your family."

"For how long?" Kelli asked. "We both know that Marsh can only keep those men assigned for so long before he'd have to explain it to his boss. And then what?"

"I don't know. We figure something else out."

"No," Kelli replied. "I have to use the leverage I've got to keep my family safe."

"What leverage?"

Kelli leaned closer to West. It only took a few moments to disclose what she had planned. After hearing her intentions, West was not pleased.

"It's too dangerous, Kelli."

"I have to try. This is my mother and siblings we're talking about."

"There has to be another way," said West.

"There isn't another way," Kelli responded, raising her voice slightly. She stood and fought to choke back another flood of tears. "I've already proven that I can't do this by myself, but I know I need to do something. Iris is out there. I need to protect . . ." Kelli's emotions overwhelmed her and she began to cry once more. West stood and took her in his arms.

"Okay," West said finally. "I'll help you."

Kelli stepped back and looked up at him. "You will?"

"Yeah. But this time, we're going to do things my way."

֍

McLEAN, VIRGINIA

Doctor Chen stepped into the garage of his home in a Virginia suburb. He held a thermos of warm coffee in his right hand. As per his daily routine, Chen straightened his tie as he looked at his reflection in his driver's side window. Then, once he was satisfied with what he saw, he opened the door and lowered himself into the driver's seat. He placed his thermos in the cup holder, and then started the engine of his white BMW X6. He reached up and tapped the button on his rear-view mirror. The garage door began to lift. Chen shifted the car into reverse. A quick glance in his side mirror caused him to step on the brake suddenly. The sight of someone standing in his driveway had caught his eye.

Chen shifted the car back into park. He opened the door. As he did, Iris strode into the garage. She pulled a gun from her jacket and leveled it in Chen's direction.

Chen's heart jumped. "Iris. What are you doing?" Though his heart was beating uncontrollably, Chen could see that Iris looked run down. He knew that it had been a few days since her last peritoneal dialysis treatment, and it was clear that she had not yet undergone the transplant procedure. Whatever Iris had been through during her escape to New York, it was evident to Chen that it had begun to take its toll. He opened his mouth to ask her about the kidney transplant, anything to distract and deter her from pulling the trigger, but Iris spoke first.

"You knew for months that I could've received a transplant, but instead, you let them use me."

Chen raised his hands in the air. Iris took another step closer to him. He could see that a silencer was screwed into the barrel of her weapon. She raised the weapon and pointed it at Chen's head.

"Iris, wait. You don't understand. I wanted to help you, I really did. I was just following or-"

"Ugh!" Iris exclaimed loudly as she squeezed the trigger once and put a bullet in Chen's forehead. Iris watched him fall backwards into a lifeless heap onto the floor. "I'm so tired of hearing that." With that, she turned and exited the garage.

❧❦

PHILADELPHIA, PENNSYLVANIA

Two full days had passed and the FBI had yet to turn up any leads in the kidnapping of Zenaida Rodriguez. Then, out of the blue, Zenaida Rodriguez turned up on the doorstep of a hospital north of Philadelphia. Taped to her jacket was a typed letter that explained what procedure had been done to her, and outlined the steps that needed to be taken to ensure her proper care and survival. Once she was safely in a hospital bed, the doctors questioned her about what, if anything, she could recall. Zenaida claimed to remember nothing. However, once the FBI arrived, Zenaida did make one request. An hour later, Agent West called Kelli to inform her that Zenaida had turned up safe and sound, and she wanted to see her and Bling as soon as possible. Kelli was relieved. *The doctor had kept his word.* Within ninety minutes, West, Kyle Cuffee, and Bling, who was walking with the help of a pair of crutches, boarded a flight to Philadelphia. An hour later, Kelli and Bling stood at Zenaida's bedside.

Zenaida demanded to know the story about the girl who looked like her late sister, Francine, and the truth behind Kelli's not-so-sudden resurrection. Kelli had grown tired of the secrets and the lies. Like her, Zenaida had paid a heavy price because of the Agency, and Kelli felt that Zenaida deserved to hear the truth. Zenaida listened in silence.

Kelli began with the day she discovered her gender-shifting ability. She told Zenaida about Francine's initial reaction to it and how it led to Francine and herself being out on the street when the Agency operatives appeared. She revealed that Francine died because she took a bullet meant for Kelli. She recounted the subsequent chase across the country, and then followed up with bits and pieces of her life in Boston. Then, she did what she could to explain Iris; who she was, and how she was created. After Kelli finished, Zenaida broke her silence. She asked Kelli to shift, and though it made them both uncomfortable, Kelli complied.

Zenaida took in the familiar sight of *Kyle* standing before her. She stared at Kelli's male form for a mere moment. To Kelli, it felt like an eternity. Then, Zenaida had seen enough.

"Okay. Stop. Please."

Kelli reverted back to her female form. Zenaida, for the first time, turned and addressed Bling.

"You knew about this the whole time," she said to Bling. It wasn't a question.

"Yeah," Bling replied softly.

Zenaida glared at her boyfriend. "How could you date me and not tell me the truth about how Francine died? We were led to believe it was a random drive-by shooting, a case of mistaken identity, not some government cover-up."

"You wouldn't have believed me," Bling said in his defense.

"Maybe not," Zenaida conceded. "But you should have trusted me enough to try."

"Oh, come on!" Bling exclaimed. "It would have sounded crazy and you would've dumped me on the spot."

"At least your conscience would have been clear." Zenaida glanced over at Kelli. "All those times Bryan went to Boston to visit Kyle, he was actually visiting you, for days at a time. Every time you came to New York, smiling in my face, pretending to be Kyle. What else have you two been keeping from me?"

Bling stepped forward. "Nothing, Zee. It isn't like that. Kelli and I are just friends. That's it."

"Really?" Zenaida asked in response. Her eyes lingered on Kelli.

Kelli's eyes dropped to the floor. Though Bling spoke the truth about the nature of their relationship, Kelli did not want to give away the truth that she harbored romantic feelings for him. "There's nothing going on between us," Kelli managed to say. Despite her best efforts, Kelli's body language betrayed her.

"Zee," Bling reached out and touched Zenaida's shoulder. "You gotta believe me."

Though it pained her physically to move, Zenaida pushed Bling's hand away. "I don't have to do any such thing. Now, I'd like you both to leave. My family will be here soon."

"Are you going to tell them the truth?" Kelli asked.

"Which truth is that, Kelli? The one where you can become a guy, or the one where I was kidnapped by my dead sister's clone? Let's not forget that the clone stole one of my kidneys. Hell, maybe I'll toss in the part about the secret government agency for good measure. Don't worry. I won't tell them any of that, but not because I don't trust them enough to be honest. It's because I don't want them to have to deal with the fact that Francine's memory has been desecrated by some scientific abomination."

Kelli began to cry. "Zenaida, I'm so sorry."

"Just get out!" Zenaida yelled. "And when you're gone, I never want to see either of you again."

"What?" Bling asked.

"You heard me," said Zenaida. "I should be back in my apartment in a week or two. Don't be there." With that, Zenaida turned her head and did not utter another sound.

Kelli turned and walked out of Zenaida's hospital room. Bling stared at Zenaida for a moment, devastated. Reluctantly, Bling followed Kelli into the hall.

Zenaida watched as the door closed behind Bling. Once she was confident that he was gone, she reached under her bed sheet and pulled out a small, crumpled piece of paper. Earlier, after Zenaida had regained consciousness in the hospital, one of the nurses had handed the wrinkled piece of paper to her.

"We found this in your hand," the nurse had told her. Zenaida had looked at the paper, but up until now, she had not fully understood the message that read: *She loves him*. It was signed with one name. *Iris*.

Beyond the hospital room door, Kelli walked up the corridor to where West was waiting patiently. She looked to her side and noticed that Bling was not there. Kelli turned around. Bling was hobbling on his crutches in the opposite direction.

"Bling. Bryan. Where are you going?"

Bling turned and faced Kelli. Tears filled his eyes. His lip tightened. When he spoke, his voice was stern. "You've destroyed enough lives this week. Stay out of mine."

Kelli felt her heart fall into her stomach. She burst into tears. "What? You don't mean that."

"Like hell I don't," he snapped. Bling looked at West. "Can you find me a different flight back to New York?"

West was at a loss for words. As if losing her father wasn't hard enough on Kelli, now she had lost her best friend. West did not know what to say except, "Yeah. Sure."

With that, Bling turned and walked away.

Kelli began to move in Bling's direction. He couldn't have meant what he said to her. Kelli could not just let him go. "Bling."

West grabbed Kelli's arm and pulled her back. "Let him go," West advised.

"I just need to talk to him."

"Kelli, no," West said. "We've got things to do, remember. The fewer people in your life right now, the better. Understand?"

Kelli watched as Bling disappeared around the corner. She hated to see him go, but she knew West had a point.

If Kelli was going to proceed with West's plan, it was best that there was distance between her and anyone she cared about, including Bling. She turned to West. "I understand."

"Good. Let's go. We've got a busy day tomorrow."

20

WASHINGTON, D.C.

Mr. One took a sip of his coffee as he sat in a booth at his favorite coffee shop. He looked across the table at the cup of chamomile tea that he had ordered for his daughter. He looked at his watch. It read 9:05 a.m. Betty was late. Her tea was growing cold.

"Sorry I'm late," a female voice said to him from behind.

Mr. One looked up from the table as Kelli Freeman slipped into the booth and sat across from him.

"Excuse me, young lady," Mr. One began, not recognizing her. "I believe you have the wrong table . . ." And then, realization set in. Kelli Freeman, the young girl whose death he'd ordered seven years ago, and who had slipped through his fingers just three days prior, was sitting in front of him. Mr. One was instantly mesmerized by her presence; her beauty, her posture, not to mention her boldness.

Kelli stared directly into Mr. One's eyes. She could tell that he knew who she was. Kelli did not smile. In fact, Kelli's skin was crawling under her clothes. Over the last six months, Kelli had watched Mr. One and his daughter from afar as they met in this very coffee shop. The images that she captured on film had crept unwelcomed into her dreams and had taken on a variety of different scenarios, the majority of which ended with Mr. One's demise. But now that Kelli was actually here, inside the coffee shop, and sitting across from the man whom she blamed for her exile from her family, all she wanted to do was run away. Only, she couldn't. Kelli was on a mission, and she was determined to hold her ground until her mission was accomplished.

"Good morning to you, too, Mr. Tolin," Kelli forced herself to say. Mr. One glanced over his shoulder quickly. Kelli leaned forward. "Don't worry, you sent an email to your daughter asking to meet at 9:30 instead."

"I sent an email?"

"Actually, I sent it from your email account about twenty minutes ago." *Thank you, Joseph.*

Mr. One couldn't help but to be impressed. "Clever. What can I do for you, Miss Freeman?"

"At the risk of sounding cliché, I'm more interested in what we can do for each other, Mr. One."

Mr. One's brow furled slightly. Still, he couldn't deny that he was interested. "Do tell."

"I'm going to go out on a limb here and assume you have some influence within the FBI," she said with an air of sarcasm.

"Cut to the chase, Miss Freeman."

"I need you to call whoever you need to at the bureau and have a protective detail assigned to my family indefinitely."

"That's quite a tall order."

"I wouldn't have to do it if you hadn't unleashed a teenage psychopath named Iris Molina who threatened to kill my family."

"Your facts are a little inaccurate, I'm afraid," One said to her. "We didn't unleash Iris. In fact, we were trying to reel her in."

"Potato po-tah-to," Kelli retorted.

"And what, might I ask, are you going to do for me?"

Kelli's eyes narrowed. "You already know," she said confidently. "I know that your daughter Betty is dying of cancer, and we both know that I have the ability to cure it."

Mr. One felt a pang in his heart. "You have no idea what you're talking about," One said defensively.

"Let me tell what I know," Kelli began. "I know that Betty was born Elizabeth Anne Tolin. I know that you call her Lizanne. I also know that when she decided to pursue a career in politics, she started going by the name Betty to shake the shadow of her Supreme Court Justice father. Marrying Jacob Royce helped her to put distance between her and the Tolin name; she didn't want her success to be attributed to nepotism."

"You've done your research," One conceded. "Most of that is public knowledge."

"The cancer isn't, though. Not yet."

The hair on the back of Mr. One's neck stood on end. "Are you threatening to expose my daughter's health issue, Miss Freeman?"

"Not at all," Kelli replied. "I couldn't care less about your daughter's health. But to protect *my* family from Iris, I'm willing to cure a member of *yours*. Do we have a deal?"

Mr. One sat back. He admired Kelli's audacity and her willingness to do everything in her power to protect the ones she loved. That was a quality to which Mr. One could most definitely relate. "We do, Miss Freeman."

Kelli decided to push the envelope. "And I want my life back."

"Pardon me," One said.

"I want to live my life without having to look over my shoulder. I want to go back to my family and live a normal life."

Mr. One contemplated silently for a moment before he said, "I'm a reasonable man, so as a token of gratitude, I'm willing to call off the dogs. After you help my daughter, you can disappear. I won't come looking. However, in regards to going back to your family," he shook his head, "I'm sorry, Miss Freeman. I can't give you that."

"Why not?" she asked through gritted teeth.

"Because the world thinks you're dead, young lady. How are you going to explain your miraculous resurrection? Your disappearance? You can't exactly start spreading rumors about the existence of my organization. It would raise too many questions, ones that could lead someone to discover who and what you are. That would not be good. Not for the country. Not for you. Not for your family."

Kelli leaned forward and lowered her voice to an audible level that only Mr. One could hear. "I wouldn't have to do it if you didn't try to kill me seven years ago."

"And yet, here we are, in need of one another."

"But you could make it happen," she snapped.

"I can't, and I won't even try, Miss Freeman. You misunderstand how this works. You brought checkers to a chess match. This is quid pro quo. You help me, and then I help you. If you want something else, you have to give something else. So, grow up and be happy with what you're getting."

"You're willing to let your daughter die over this?" Kelli asked.

"Miss Freeman, I'm an old man who's been making life and death decisions in service of this country for a long time. And when it's been necessary, I've let hundreds of thousands of people die over the years. So, I pose the same question to you. Are you willing to let *your* family die over this?"

Kelli's heartbeat raced furiously inside her chest. Mr. One had mentioned chess, but to Kelli, it felt more like a game of Blackjack or Poker, only she couldn't tell if he was bluffing, and there were no cards to count. Finally, knowing she was not willing to risk the lives of her remaining family members, Kelli gave the only response that she could. "No. I'm not."

"Then it's settled," Mr. One said.

Kelli sat back in the booth. Reluctantly, she nodded her agreement.

"How can I reach you to make arrangements?" Mr. One asked.

"Don't worry," Kelli told him. "I'll reach you. And the arrangements have already been made."

"Unacceptable."

"Too bad. I'm the one with the cure." Kelli leaned closer and sneered, "Be happy with what you're getting."

Mr. One's bottom lip tightened. He did not like the fact that Kelli was in control of the arrangements that would save Betty's life. Mr. One was accustomed to having control of everything in his world, and he knew that relinquishing that control would not be easy. However, for the sake of Betty's survival, Mr. One agreed. "Fine."

Kelli made a motion to stand, but then she addressed Mr. One again. "I would like to know one thing. How did you get Francine's DNA?"

"You are one tenacious young lady," One commented.

"She was my best friend," Kelli said before she stopped and swallowed a wave of sadness. "Now, someone is running around with her face. I need to know." She paused, and then added. "Please."

One took a slow, deep breath. "We acquired it the night Francine was killed. Agent Towers of the FBI extracted a blood sample from Francine when her body arrived at the morgue."

"But why? Why her?"

"It's not good policy to clone people who are still alive," One replied calmly.

Kelli stared at Mr. One blankly. She was barely able to conceal the fact that she was disgusted by what she had just heard. If it wasn't for the fact that she needed his help, Kelli would kill him on the spot. *Just like in my dreams.* She choked back her emotions. "I don't get it. If you created Iris, why didn't you just give her the transplant?"

"Because the HP-47 vaccine was running low. Once we got word that Lizanne was sick again, I needed every drop of the vaccine to slow her decline."

"HP-47?"

"A vaccine that was engineered using your blood as the base."

"My blood?" Kelli asked, surprised.

"Yes. When you were held captive at Rocketdyne seven years ago, Dr. Simons extracted a few vials of your blood-"

"Wait a second," Kelli interrupted. "If you had my blood, why didn't you just clone me? After all, you thought that I was dead."

"We tried, several times, in fact," One confessed. "But we failed every time. It had something to do with the June Gene that Dr. Marcus June isolated when he created the very first super-soldier."

"Harmony June," Kelli said softly.

One nodded. "Keep in mind, we discovered the problem with the June Gene a number of years before you showed up on our radar seven years ago. Unfortunately, despite our best efforts, we couldn't regulate the gene. Whenever we thought we had a viable embryo, it would suddenly die. I believe Dr. Simons called it *premature apoptosis*. After a few failures, we decided to take the easy route by cloning those who didn't have a functioning June Gene in their DNA."

"Which is why Iris can't change her sex," Kelli surmised aloud.

"Precisely. We cloned Francine, and we used your blood to manufacture the HP-47. Eventually, we used it to strengthen Iris' weakened renal system; and it worked. But after Lizanne's terminal diagnosis, I didn't hesitate to take the vaccine from Iris." He looked into Kelli's eyes. "It seems as if we're alike, Miss Freeman. Like you, I do what is necessary for my family."

A cold wave chilled Kelli's spine. Slowly, without saying a word, she stood. As she walked past Mr. One towards the exit, she said, "I'll be in touch."

"By the way," he called to her without turning around. "That job at my daughter's law firm is yours if you still want it."

Kelli stopped in her tracks, but did not turn to face him.

"It appears I know a few things, too," said One smugly.

Oh, God. He knows I'm Kyle. How? Kelli's upper lip tightened. As much as she wanted to turn and ask One how he knew about her alter ego, she resisted the urge. The last thing she wanted him to see was how much more frightened she had suddenly become. Instead, she drew in a deep breath, and proceeded to the door. Two seconds later, Kelli disappeared amongst the pedestrians on the street.

Back at the table, Mr. One had already sat back and relaxed in the booth. He dropped his gaze slightly and stared at the miniscule wireless microphone that was adhered to the back of the pepper shaker. A look of calm washed over his face, and he allowed a small smile to creep across his lips.

※

Several moments earlier, A dark SUV with tinted windows parked across the street from the café in which Kelli and Mr. One sat. Inside, from the rear driver-side seat, Rebecca Thorn watched them from the distance. A small wireless earbud was nestled in her left ear.

"You were correct," Rebecca said, and then turned to the woman who sat to her right. "She's here."

Agent Swann nodded slightly. "She came here almost every day, watching *him*, taking his photos. It was just a hunch really."

"Don't undersell your abilities, Naomi. You're good. That's why I keep using you." Rebecca returned her gaze to the café. "Any chance you want to go back to being a field agent?"

"No, thank you," Swann replied, "I'm not very fond of getting shot at." A brief silence hung in the air before Swann continued. "Ma'am, you know that I don't usually ask too many questions, but the circumstances of this case turned out to be a bit unusual. If you would, can you tell me what put Kyle Cuffee on your radar?"

Rebecca turned to Swann once again. She considered telling Swann that it was none of her business as it was standard protocol to supply information on a need-to-know-basis. However, Rebecca figured she could satisfy Swann's curiosity without divulging any highly classified information while, at the same time, dangle a carrot in front of her. "Kyle Cuffee's name showed up on a list of shareholders for one of our pharmaceutical companies. Normally, we like to vet our shareholders before allowing them to invest, but somehow, Cuffee circumvented that. Red flag number one. A background check revealed Cuffee to be a 21-year-old law student, one who had recently experienced quite the financial windfall."

"Red flag number two," Swann surmised.

"Yes, but only because the background report also revealed Cuffee's past to be perfect; too perfect, in fact. I've been in this business long enough to know a fabrication when I see one. That's when I called you."

"Were you surprised when I reported that Kyle Cuffee was a female?"

Rebecca nodded. "For about a second. But then I realized you had found something that I thought we'd lost."

A bit cryptic, Swann thought. Her curiosity had been piqued even further.

Rebecca could see Swann's interest. She decided to dangle another carrot. "Do you remember your assignment at Camp Pendleton a few years back, when you were training the cadets?"

"Of course," Swann answered, a hint of confusion in her voice. *Where did that question come from?*

"I read your status reports. There was one particular student that you raved about. What was her name again?"

Swann smiled as memories of her time at Camp Pendleton slipped to the forefront of her mind. "Iris. She was small for her age, but she was strong, determined. She reminded me a lot of myself. I often wonder what happened to her after I left."

"A field agent with a special security clearance could be privy to that information, under certain circumstances, of course."

Swann shook her head. She knew when she was being baited, but she failed to understand why. Several questions filled her head. *Why did she bring up my post at Camp Pendleton? And what does that have to do with anything? I was still enlisted at the time; we hadn't even met yet. What's going on? And what does this lady want?* Swann didn't have the answers to any of those questions, but she wasn't willing to be manipulated in order to get them. Instead, she decided to stand her ground and reaffirm her position. "As I said earlier, I'm not interested in being a field agent again."

Rebecca didn't appear fazed. "Suit yourself."

"Ma'am, may I ask why-"

"No," Rebecca said, interrupting Swann. "I'll be in touch, Agent Swann." Without speaking another word, Rebecca turned her attention back to the café. The silence that followed told Swann that her access to any additional information had just been cut off.

"Yes, Ma'am," Swann said, annoyed. With that, the conversation was over. Swann opened the door and slipped out of the SUV. Thorn didn't bother to turn to watch her leave. Within seconds, Swann was on the street heading towards her own vehicle. She had hoped, after receiving Thorn's call this morning, that she'd finally have some answers regarding her surveillance of Kyle Cuffee. And though Rebecca Thorn offered some information, Swann was left with more questions than she had before, the most important one being, *Why does she want me to be a field agent, again? And is that something I want?* Swann cursed to herself. Despite her adamance about not regaining her field agent status, she began to realize that, before getting answers to her questions about Thorn, she may have to answer a few personal questions of her own.

❧❦

Kelli walked north on the sidewalk. A large knot had formed in her stomach as a result of Mr. One's revelations about the circumstances regarding the cloning of Francine, not to mention the revelation that her life as Kyle Cuffee had been exposed. *How the hell did he find out?* Kelli kept her jaw clenched tight so she would refrain from screaming at the top of her lungs.

As Kelli approached the corner, she noticed a woman in the crosswalk coming in her direction. Kelli recognized the woman as Betty Royce. Betty brushed by Kelli as she made her way to the coffee shop. Little did she know that Kelli, a complete stranger, knew intricate details about her life, her family, and her illness. Kelli wondered if Betty Royce had any idea that her father, Roger Tolin, was the head of a secret government agency that wielded unspeakable power, and that he went by the name of Mr. One. And if Betty Royce was, in fact, privy to this information, did she care? Did she hate her father for what he was, or was Betty his biggest supporter? A thousand questions ran through Kelli's mind, but for now, every one of them would have to remain unanswered.

Kelli turned right at the corner and headed for a large, black SUV that was parked by the curb. Kelli climbed into the passenger seat before releasing a long, emotion-laden sigh. Despite the small accomplishment of securing a protective detail for her family, a heavy sadness still hovered over her. It was a sadness that Kelli felt would never go away.

As she settled in, Kelli reached behind her ear and removed the earpiece that had been easily concealed by her dreadlocks. She turned to West who sat in the driver's seat.

"Did you get that?" she asked him.

"Loud and clear," West assured her. "You did good."

"He knows about Kyle Cuffee."

"I heard," said West. "It makes no difference. You don't like being Kyle anyway, right?"

Kelli paused. After all that she'd gone through to reclaim her life as Kelli Freeman and put Kyle Cuffee in her past, why was she bothered by the fact that there was suddenly no reason to hide behind Kyle again? "Um, right." Kelli pushed the thought from her mind. She needed to focus on the plan. "What's next?"

"You need to lie low for a few days. I have friend in Indiana, Agent Redding, who's offered to help us out."

"What about my dad's funeral?"

"Don't worry. We'll get you there."

"And then?"

"Preparation," West answered.

"For what?"

"For Iris. You said it yourself. She's out there. Agent Bonner and I are going to take you under our wing."

Kelli tilted her head curiously. "How?"

"We're going to train you the right way. Next time Iris shows up, you're going to be ready."

❧❧

"That went better than expected," Rebecca said to One as she approached his table inside the coffee shop.

One looked up at her. A look of surprise was on his face. "What are you doing in here? Didn't you hear everything through the microphone?"

Rebecca nodded. "I did. But I thought I would come in and follow up right now; save us the trouble of doing it later."

One scoffed. "For someone who's an expert at telling lies, you're doing an awful job of it."

"You have no idea what you're talking about."

The coffee shop door opened. Betty Royce entered the small café. She removed the gray scarf around her neck as she moved towards the usual table at which she and her father sat on a regular basis. She stopped short of the table as she took sight of Rebecca Thorn.

Rebecca turned and made eye contact with Betty. A silent tension thickened the air between them.

"I guess I'll be going," Rebecca said to One with a hint of bitterness in her voice. Her gaze still fixed on Betty. "Hello, Lizanne. How are you? I heard about the diagnosis."

Betty responded without affectation. "I'm fine, Rebecca. Are you leaving or should I come back later?"

"No," Rebecca replied firmly. "I'll go." Her eyes lingered on Betty for a brief moment longer before she said, "We'll talk later, Roger."

Betty slid into the booth opposite her father as she watched Rebecca exit the café. Once the coffee shop door closed, Betty wasted no time asking, "What was she doing here?"

"You know the nature of my business with Rebecca," One answered calmly.

"Is she your regular liaison again?"

"Yes. Listen. Don't you dare interrogate me. Rebecca was just concerned-"

"Bullshit. She's only ever been concerned about herself," Betty proclaimed. "And I don't want her here. This is our space. If I want to see her, I'll go to her."

"As if you'd ever do that."

"No. I wouldn't." Betty admitted. "You know how I feel about her. That woman is dangerous, and she can't be trusted. The fact that she gave birth to me doesn't change a damn thing."

It was close to noon. Constitution Park was full of the usual tourists, joggers and everyday citizens who used the park as a place to take a much-needed break during the day.

Mr. Five sat comfortably on the far end of a bench that rested along one of the many paths within the meadows that occupied the beautiful, green landscape. Another man sat at the far end of the adjacent bench, an open newspaper was spread out in front of him. To the untrained eye, it appeared as if these two men had barely taken notice of one another. In truth, the two men were deep in conversation.

"We wanted to thank you for being our eyes and ears in the D.C. field office over the past week," Mr. Five said. "The intel you provided on Agent West and his whereabouts was of great value to the Agency."

"Thank you, sir."

"About your partner," Mr. Five began. "Did you know of her involvement in this case?"

"No, sir. I did not."

"For what it's worth, I'm sorry."

A slight pause. Then, "It couldn't be helped."

"I'm glad you feel that way," Five said. "With the way things turned out in New York, we were hoping that you would continue to keep us apprised of any pertinent and relevant information that comes through A.D. Marsh's office."

Agent Garrett Lacee turned his head slightly and nodded. "Of course, sir. I want to help in any way that I can."

❧❧

BRICK, NEW JERSEY

Doctor Suri reached the top step within the old-style two-story home. He moved steadily, being careful not to spill a drop of the hot tea he was carrying to the room at the end of the hall. As he entered, he shook his head as he took in the sight of Iris lying in bed, reading through the documents she had acquired from the safe in the home she had shared with her mother. Iris made a point of stopping at her former home and retrieving the items from the safe before she drove to the home of Doctor Chen and killed him. Iris was glad she did. Among the envelopes that were filled with paperwork and a large amount of cash, Iris found a gun. It was the gun she used to end Chen's life.

Within hours of killing Chen, Iris and Suri arrived at a private medical facility north of Philadelphia. It was there that Suri performed the transplant surgery in hopes of saving Iris' life. Suri kept a close watch on both Iris and Zenaida for two days before he felt confident that Zenaida could be safely transported to a hospital where she would receive further care. Afterwards, Suri brought Iris to a secluded home in Brick, New Jersey where the young girl could complete her recovery, as well. Since then, three days had passed.

"You know you should be resting," Suri said as he entered the room. He placed the tea on the nightstand next to her bed. He eyed the bottles of Cellcept and Prograf, two immunosuppressant drugs designed to prevent Iris' immune system from rejecting her newly implanted kidney. Suri tapped the lid of one of the bottles with his finger. "Did you take your medication yet?"

"Yes, I did."

"Good," Suri said approvingly. "It's very important that you don't miss a dosage. Ever."

"I understand, Doctor."

Suri looked at the documents that Iris had spread all over the bed. "Learn anything new?"

"Everything I'm learning is new," Iris replied. "My mother lived a completely different life before she joined the Agency. It's like I'm reading the biography of someone I'd never met."

"Apparently Agent Molina wanted you to know about her life before you came along. Why else would she have compiled it all?"

"I guess you're right," Iris said. "And this house. Who knew?" The deed to the home in which Iris now resided, along with a single key, was one of several deeds with keys that was among the paperwork that had been stored in the safe behind the painting. Five days ago, Iris had no idea the house even existed. And yet, the house had everything. All indicators pointed to the fact that Molina had planned on living here with Iris someday, after all the experiments were done and the Agency had been left in the past. Unfortunately, it was a plan that would never come to fruition.

Iris pulled a sheet of paper from one of the piles and held it up. She read the words that were printed across the top of the paper. "Major Juana Salgado, United States Marine Corp." Iris looked at Suri. A single tear rolled down her cheek. "Juana Salgado. That was her name. That was her life."

Suri reached out and wiped away Iris' tear. "And then you became her life. Although her identity as Maribel Molina was fabricated, her love for you was undeniably real."

Iris allowed herself a small smile. "I know."

"Let me take these things from you for a while," Suri said as he began to clear the documents from her bed before she could protest. "You need to rest."

Iris nodded. "Okay."

Suri gathered several small piles of paper from the bed and placed them in a stack on the nightstand. He turned to collect more when he brushed against the Harmony Project file that he had brought to Molina on the day they left for New York in search of Zenaida Rodriguez. Suri picked up the file and stared at it for a moment. He couldn't help but notice that Iris had scribbled two words on the file's cover. Project Rebirth. His upper lip tightened. *That could be a problem.*

"Are you going to miss working for the Agency?" Iris asked.

"I'm going to miss the work. Nothing more."

"Don't worry," Iris said. "When I'm back on my feet, we're going to fix everything."

"You don't have to do anything if you don't want to," Suri reminded her. "You *can* walk away."

"No, I can't," replied Iris. "My mother is dead, and everyone who was involved is going to end up dead, too. Mr. One, Mr. Five, Agent Peppers, and Kelli Freeman."

"And how do you propose you're going to find them? We don't even know who Mr. One and Mr. Five really are."

"I'll figure it out," Iris said confidently. "As for Kelli Freeman, I'll lure her to me."

"Lure her?"

"That's right . . ." Iris' memory flashed back to the third floor of the building on Overlook Terrace. She recalled how Kelli touched Bling and looked at him after he'd been shot; so tenderly, so lovingly. The mental image caused Iris to grin. ". . . and I know the perfect bait."

GET FREE EXCLUSIVE
HARMONY PROJECT MATERIAL

Thank you for coming on this writing journey with me. My hope is to build a fun and adventurous relationship with my readers. I will be sending out occasional newsletters with details about new and upcoming releases, any special offers, and other bits of news relating to the Harmony Project Series and future upcoming series.

Sign up to my mailing list and you will receive:

1. An exclusive, **FREE** copy of the introductory, companion Harmony Project Classified Document file.

Find the mailing list here at
http://randyvdanielsauthor.com/

DID YOU ENJOY THIS BOOK?

Thank you for reading The Enemy Clone. I hope you enjoyed the story. If so, I would be grateful if you would spend just 5 minutes and leave a rating and review on the site where you purchased the book.

Reviews can make a huge and impactful difference in the quest to reach new readers.

Thank you.

ALSO BY RANDY V. DANIELS

The Harmony Project

Kelli Freeman is a high school senior who leads a normal life. When she discovers the ability to morph into a boy, life becomes everything but normal. A clandestine government organization begins pursuing her, and Kelli, realizing that she's in danger, runs for her life. With the help of two unlikely allies, Kelli embarks on a mission to find out the truth behind her new sex-morphing ability, and why her own government wants her dead.

Books page at randyvdanielsauthor.com
http://randyvdanielsauthor.com/books-2/

Universal Book Link (UBL)
https://books2read.com/u/b5BZpO

About Randy V. Daniels

A passionate fan of science fiction, Randy V. Daniels began writing at a young age. His other interests include martial arts, fitness and travel. He is currently working on the follow up to "The Enemy Clone", as well as several other literary projects. Daniels has three children and lives with his wife in Simi Valley, California.

Daniels' online home can be found at www.randyvdanielsauthor.com

https://www.facebook.com/MenascusBooks/
https://twitter.com/RandyVDaniels
instagram@randyvdanielsauthor

www.ingramcontent.com/pod-product-compliance
Lightning Source LLC
Chambersburg PA
CBHW050103120726
47904CB00004B/1199